GOGOR

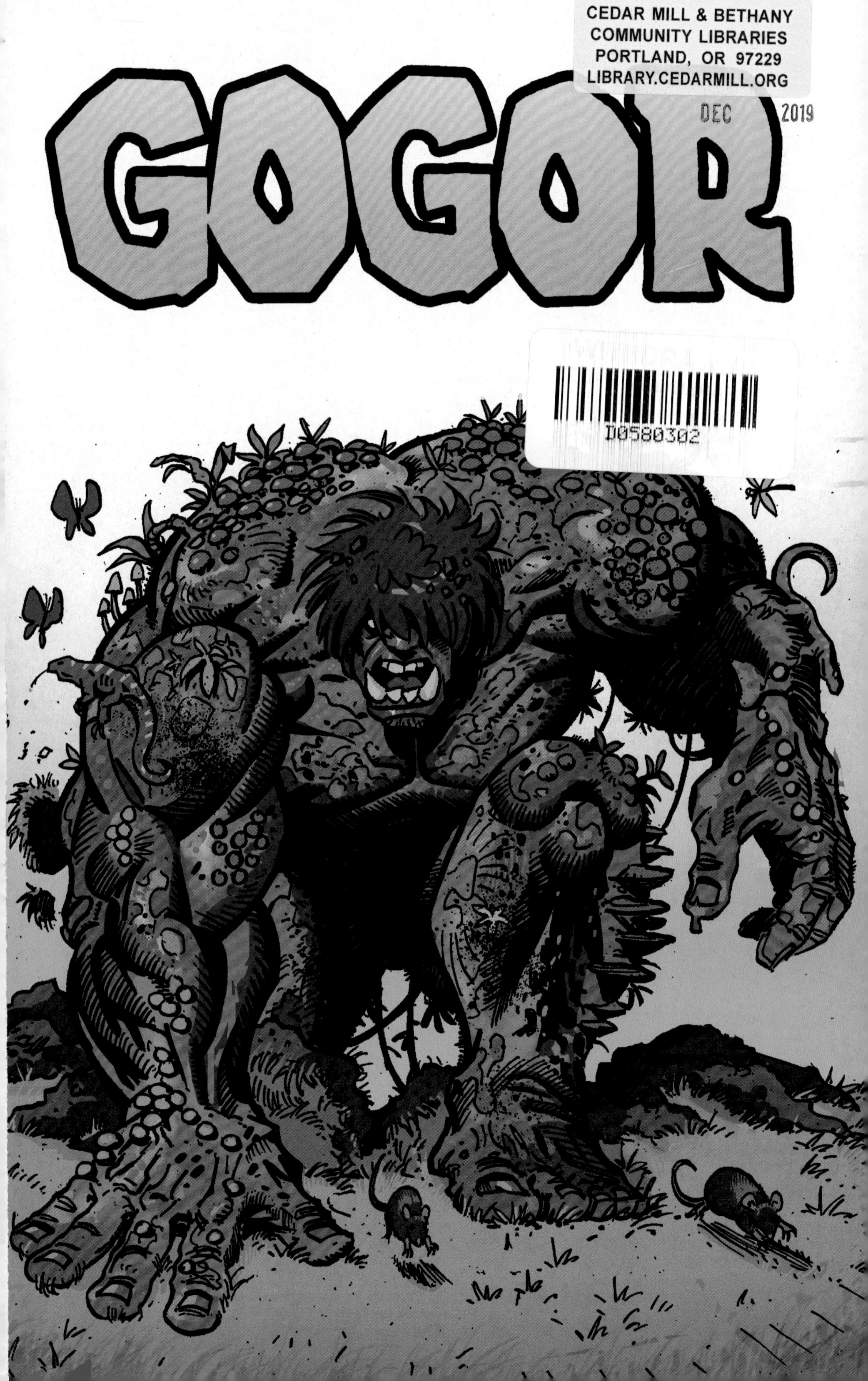

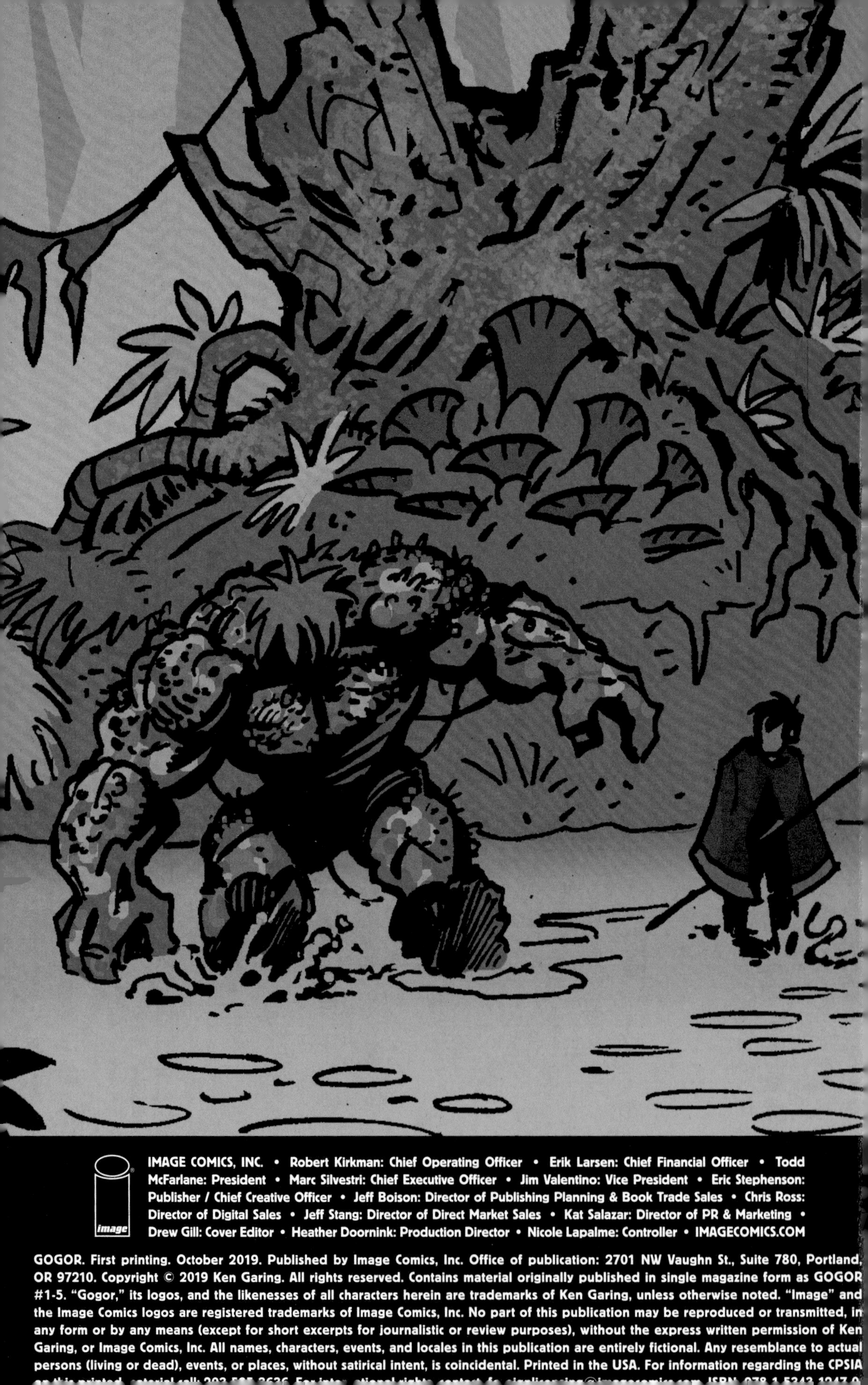

GOGOR. First printing. October 2019. Published by Image Comics, Inc. Office of publication: 2701 NW Vaughn St., Suite 780, Portland, OR 97210.

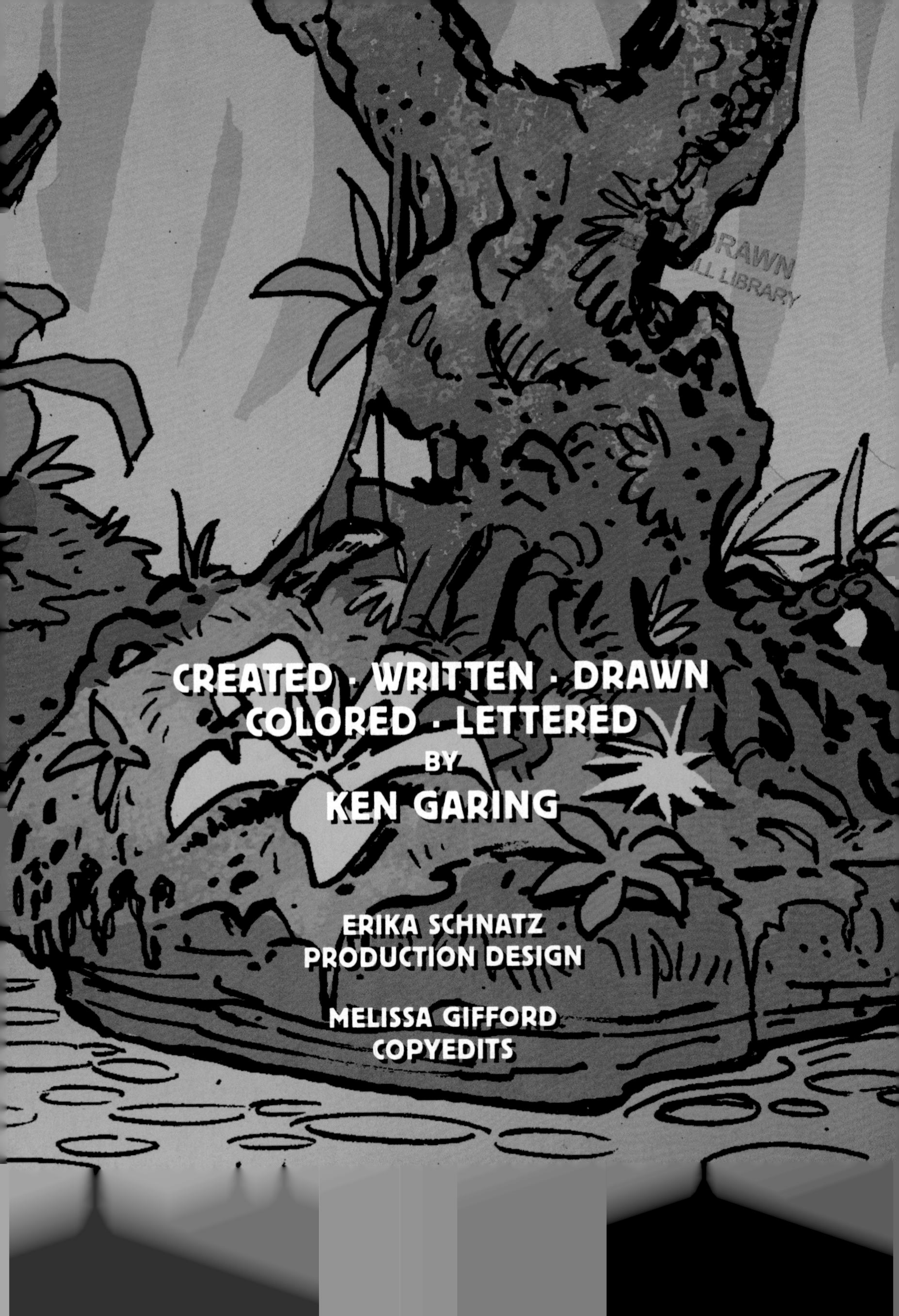

CREATED · WRITTEN · DRAWN
COLORED · LETTERED
BY
KEN GARING

ERIKA SCHNATZ
PRODUCTION DESIGN

MELISSA GIFFORD
COPYEDITS

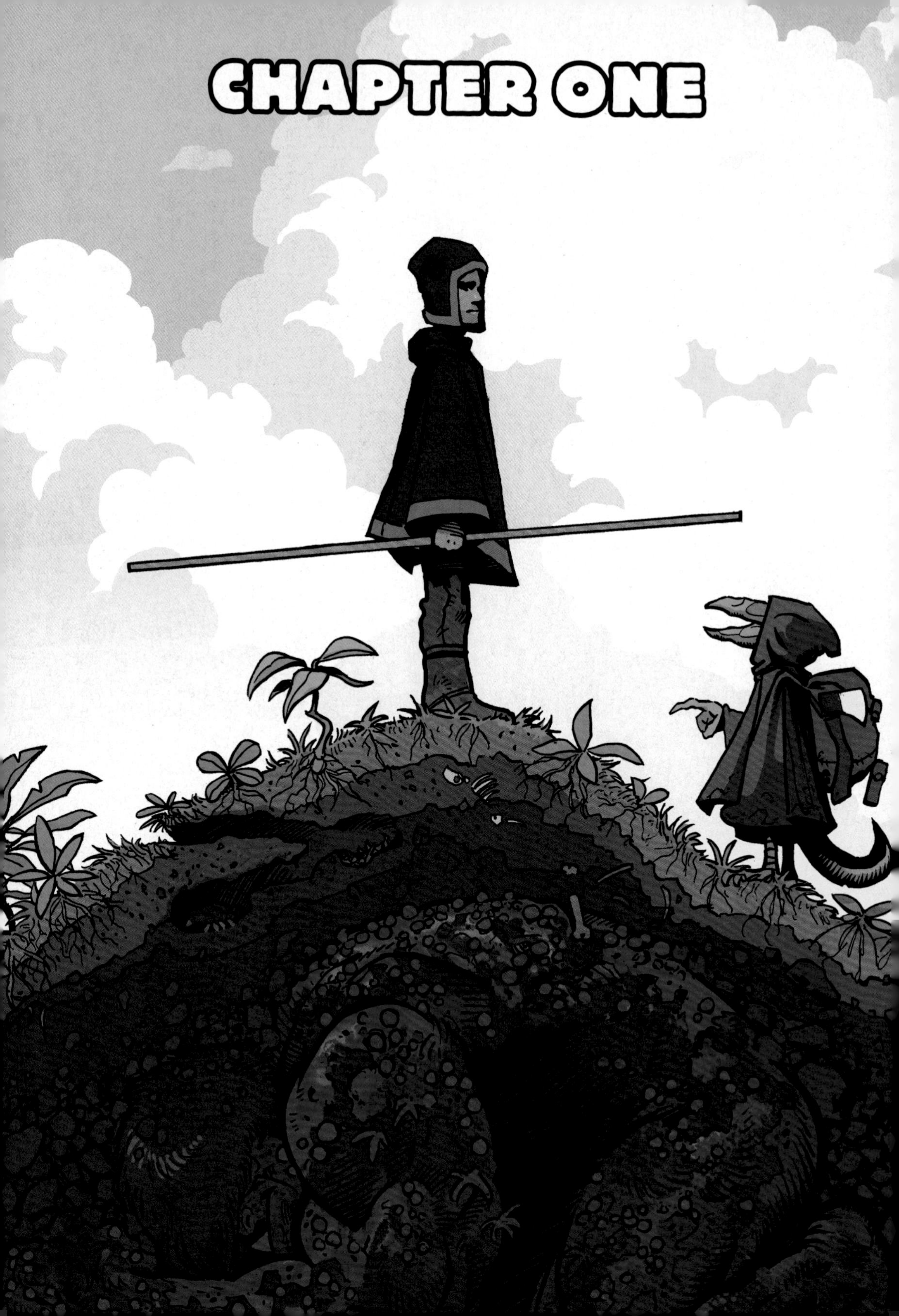
CHAPTER ONE

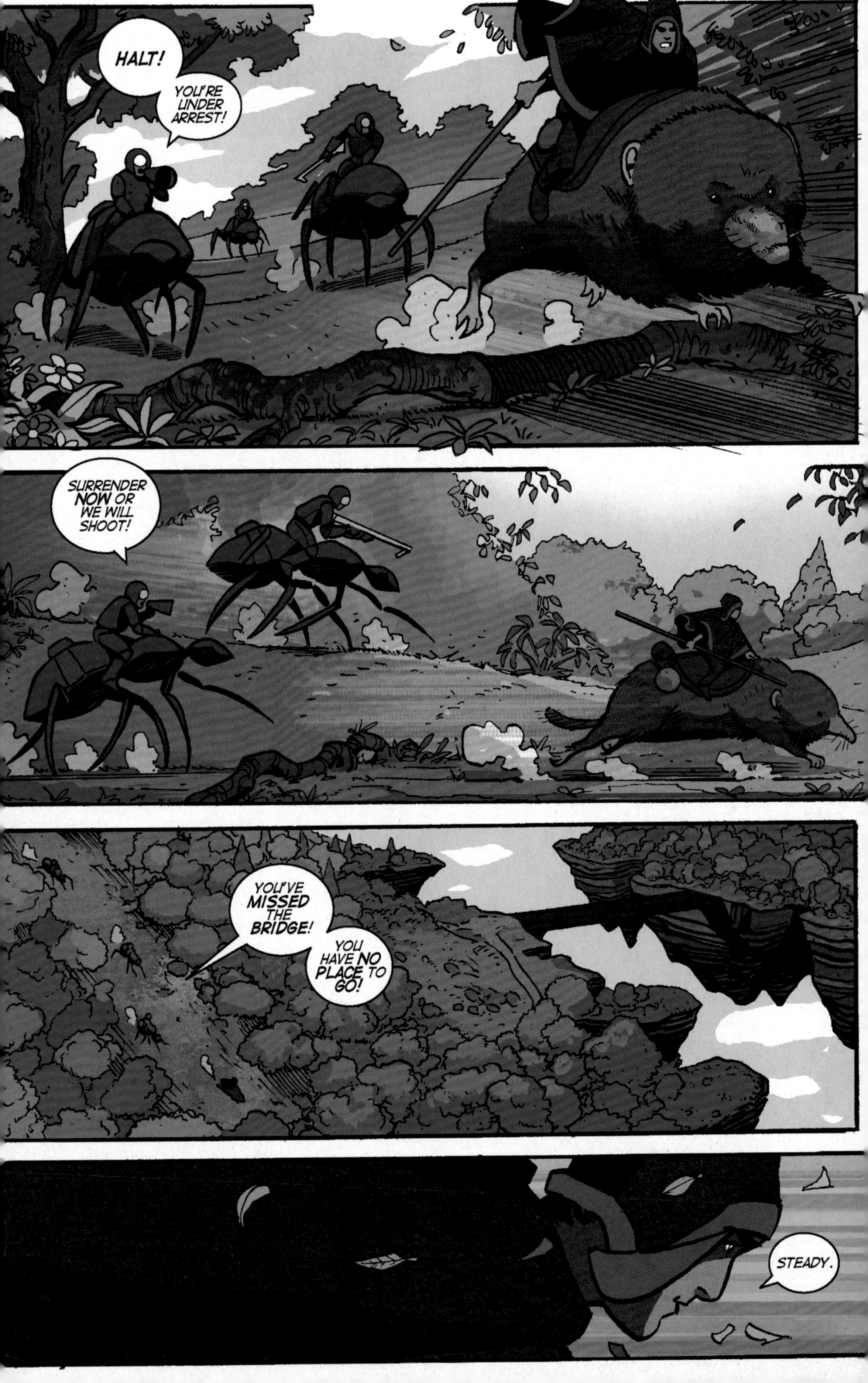
HALT!
YOU'RE UNDER ARREST!
SURRENDER NOW OR WE WILL SHOOT!
YOU'VE MISSED THE BRIDGE!
YOU HAVE NO PLACE TO GO!
STEADY.

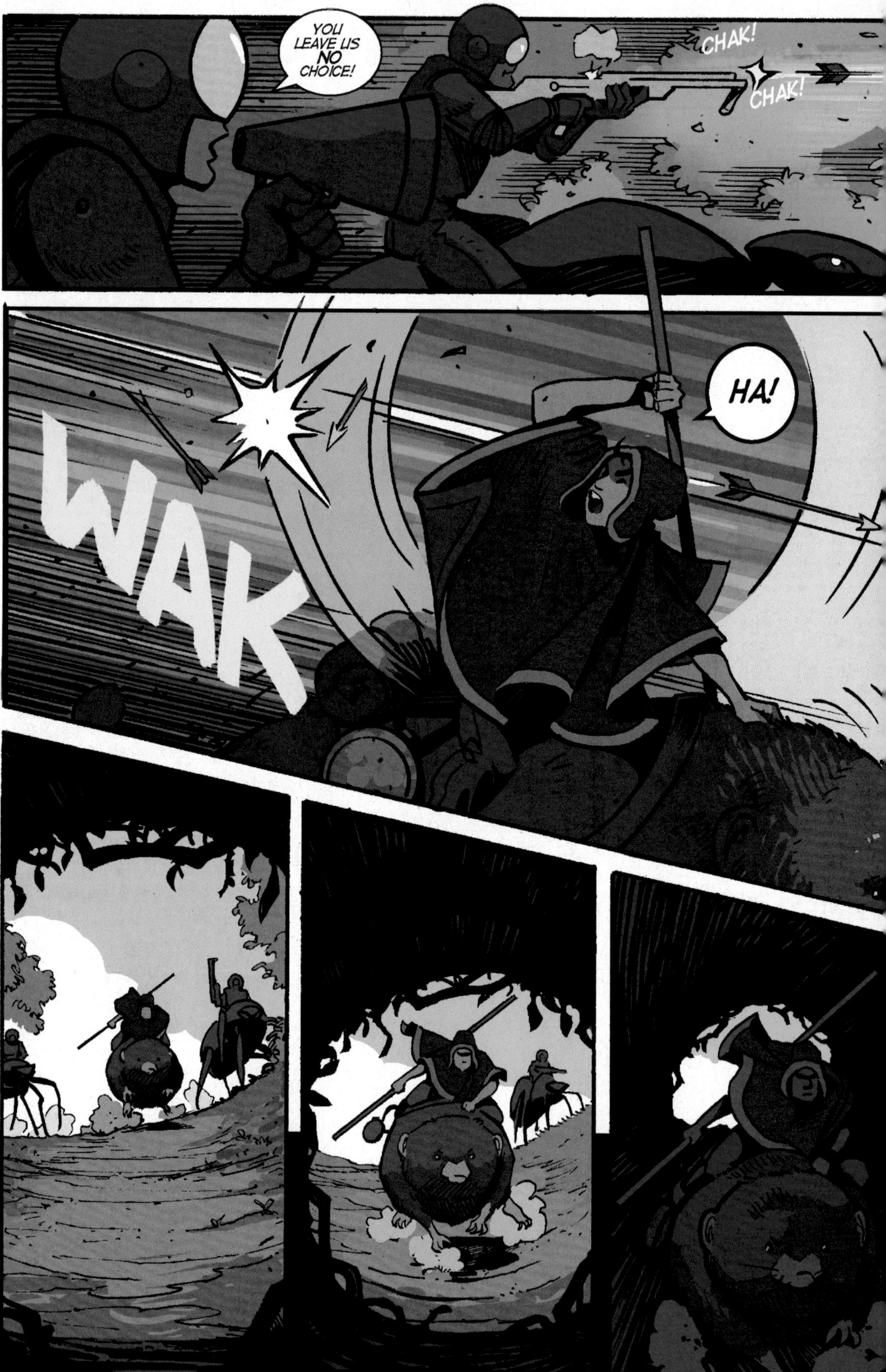
YOU LEAVE US NO CHOICE!
CHAK!
CHAK!
WAK
HA!

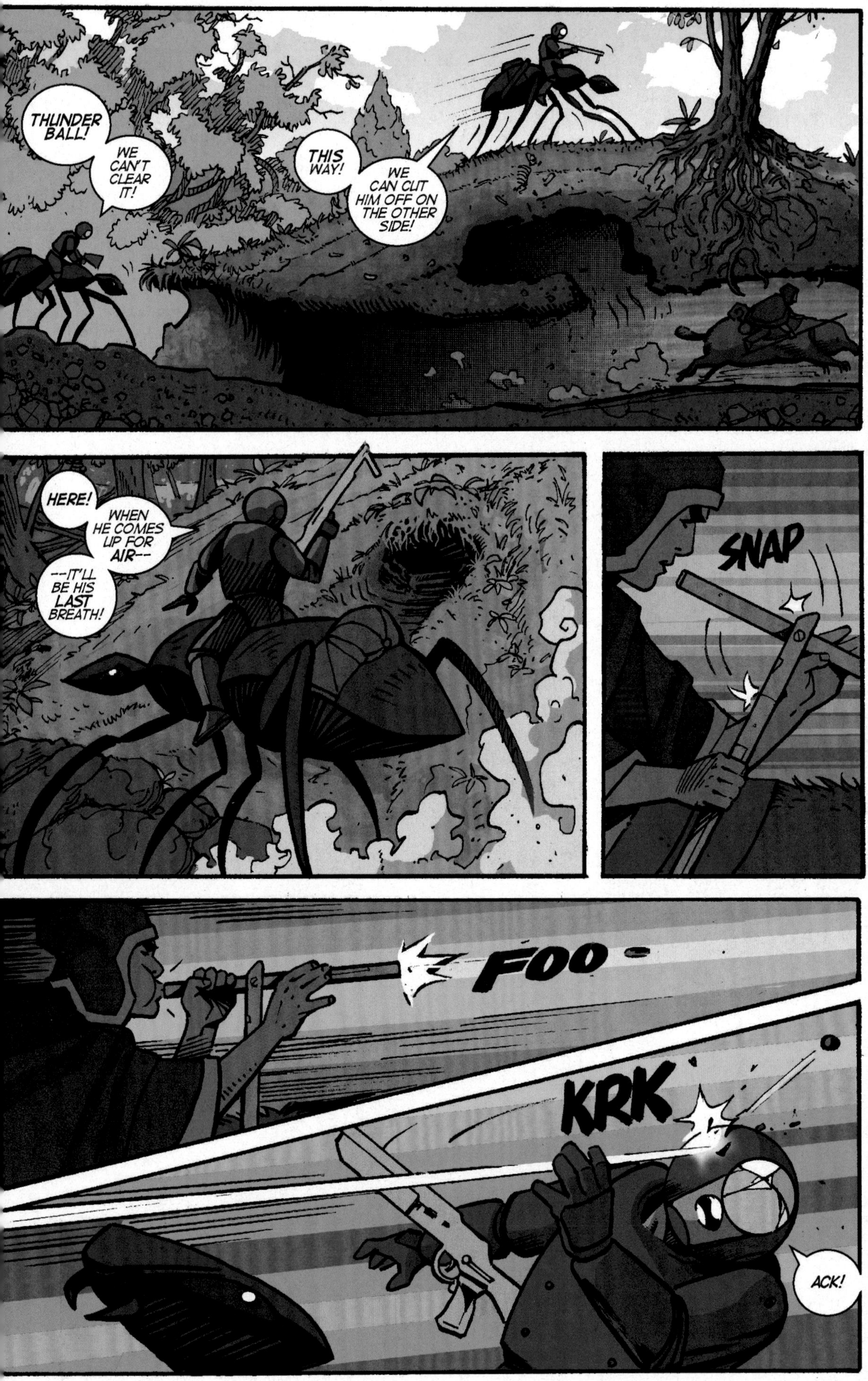
THUNDER BALL!
WE CAN'T CLEAR IT!
THIS WAY!
WE CAN CUT HIM OFF ON THE OTHER SIDE!
HERE!
WHEN HE COMES UP FOR AIR--
--IT'LL BE HIS LAST BREATH!
SNAP
FOO
KRK
ACK!

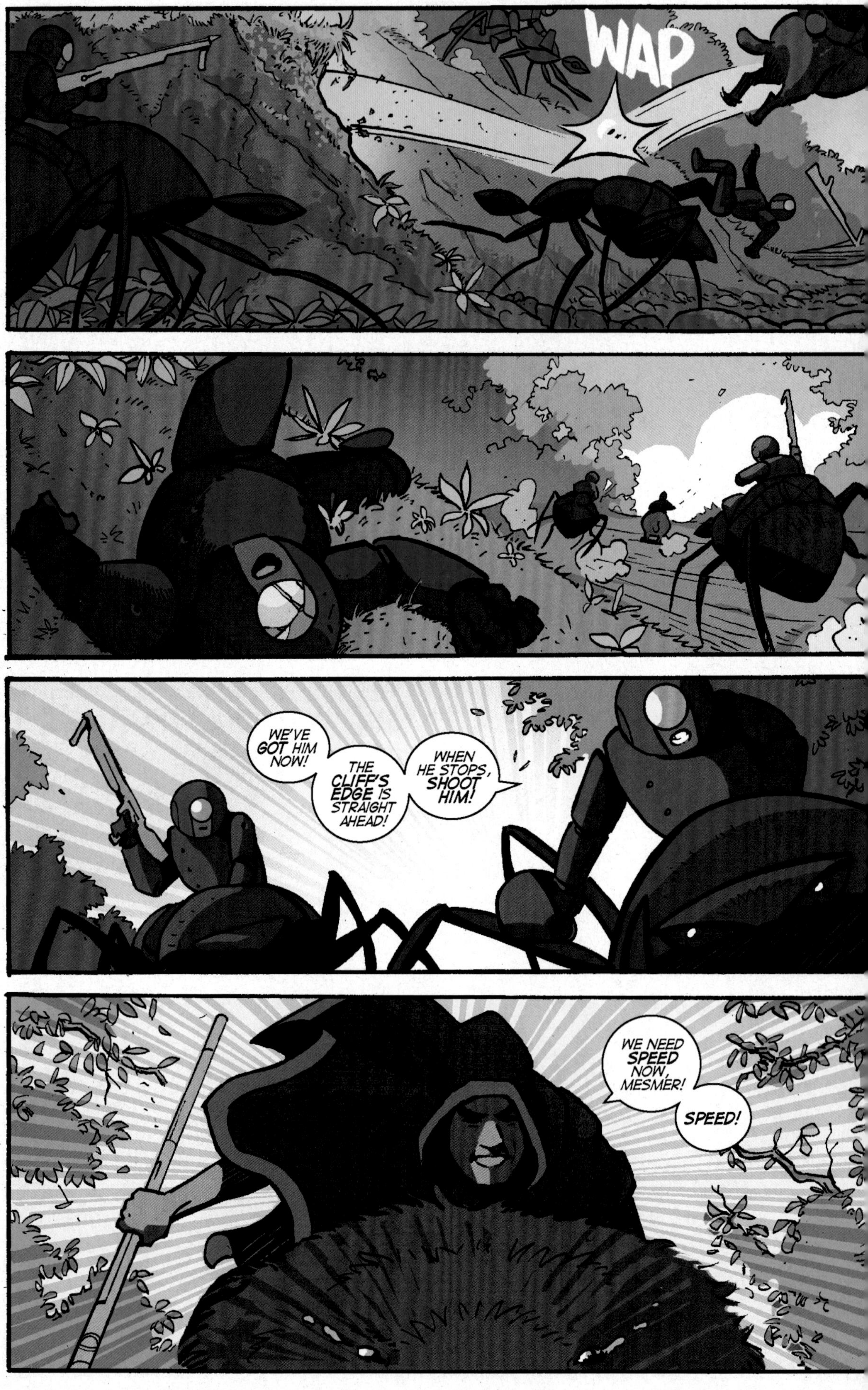
WAP
WE'VE GOT HIM NOW!
THE CLIFF'S EDGE IS STRAIGHT AHEAD!
WHEN HE STOPS, SHOOT HIM!
WE NEED SPEED NOW, MESMER!
SPEED!

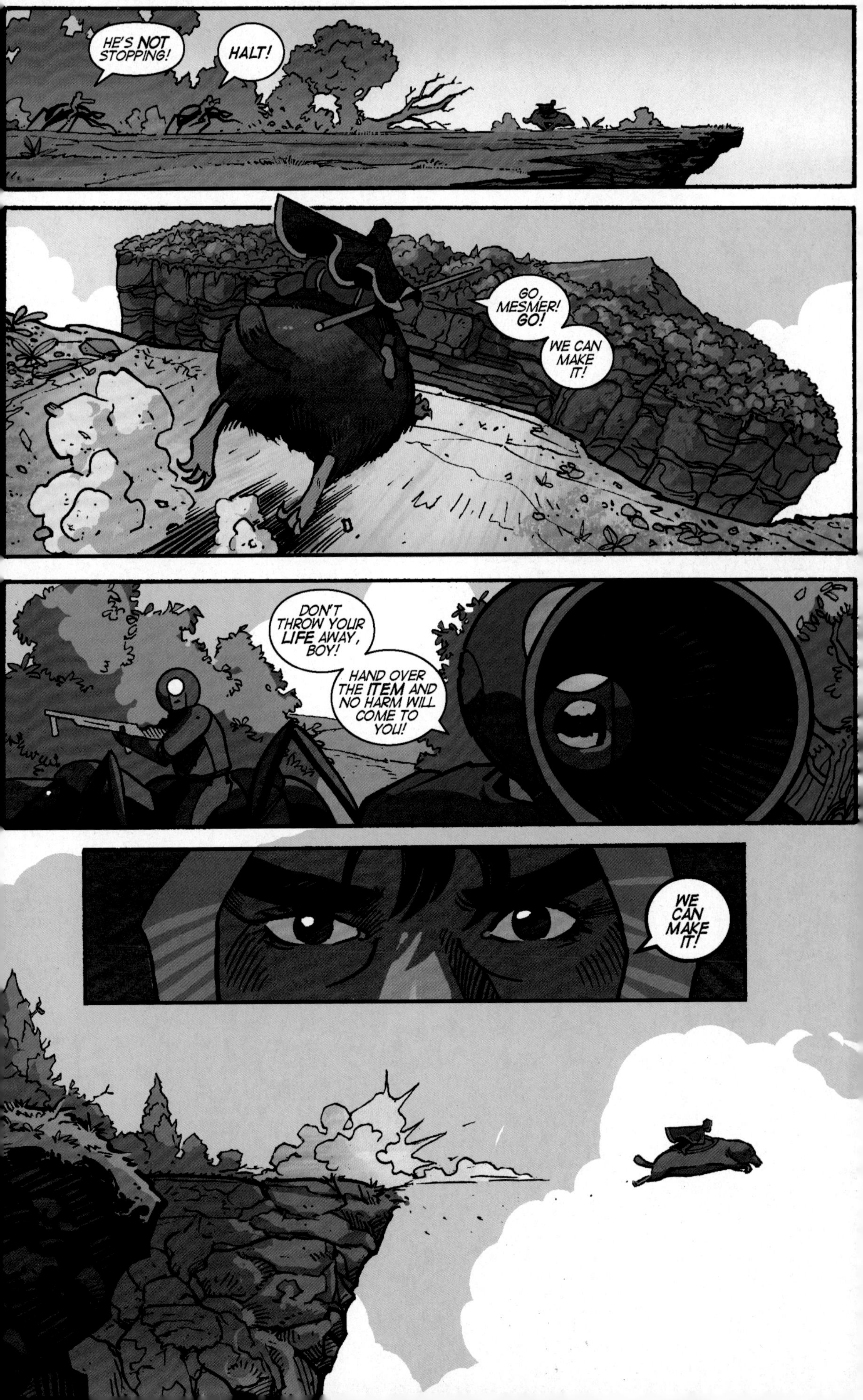
HE'S NOT STOPPING!
HALT!
GO, MESMER! GO!
WE CAN MAKE IT!
DON'T THROW YOUR LIFE AWAY, BOY!
HAND OVER THE ITEM AND NO HARM WILL COME TO YOU!
WE CAN MAKE IT!

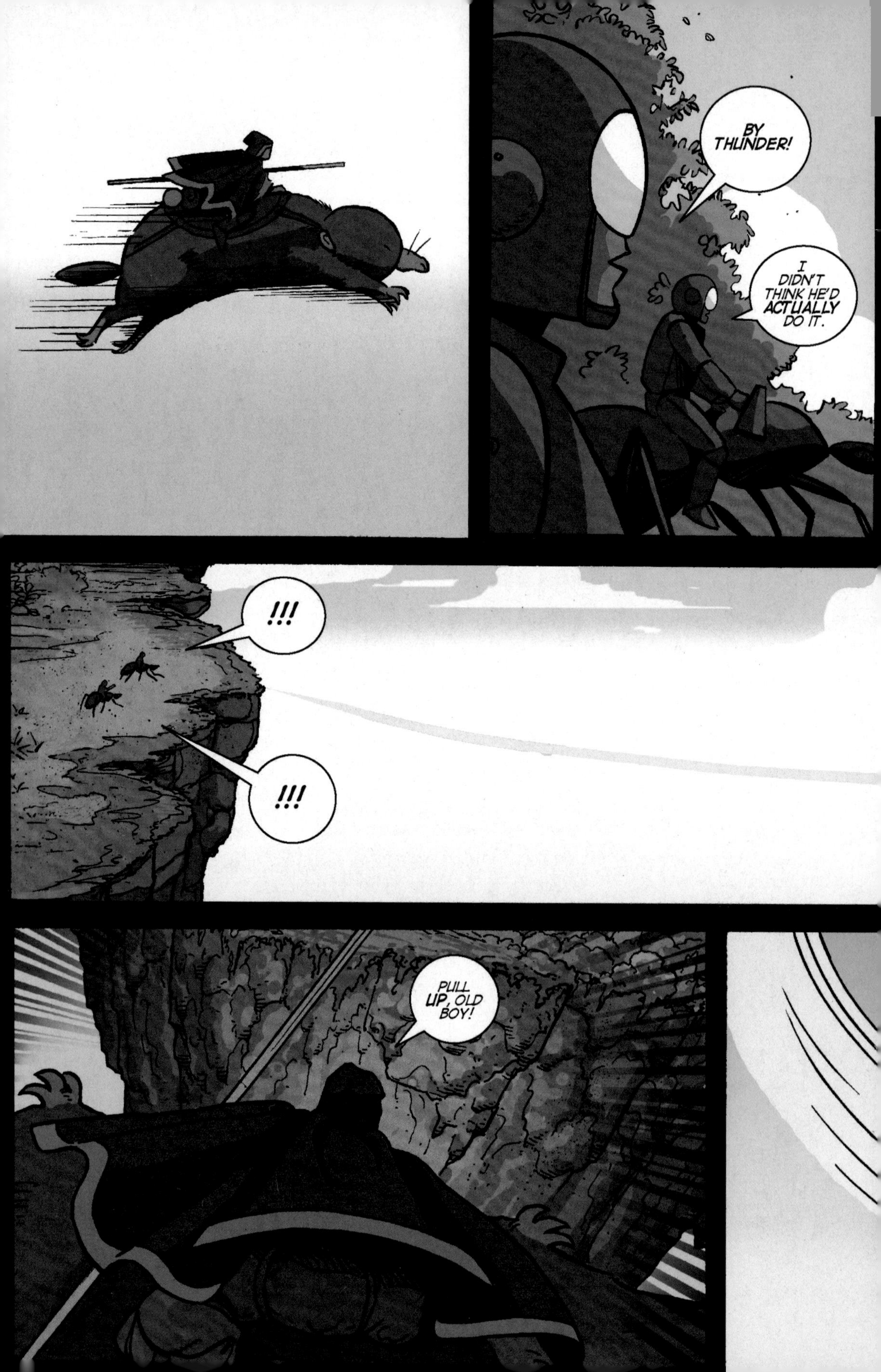
BY THUNDER!
I DIDN'T THINK HE'D ACTUALLY DO IT.
!!!
!!!
PULL UP, OLD BOY!

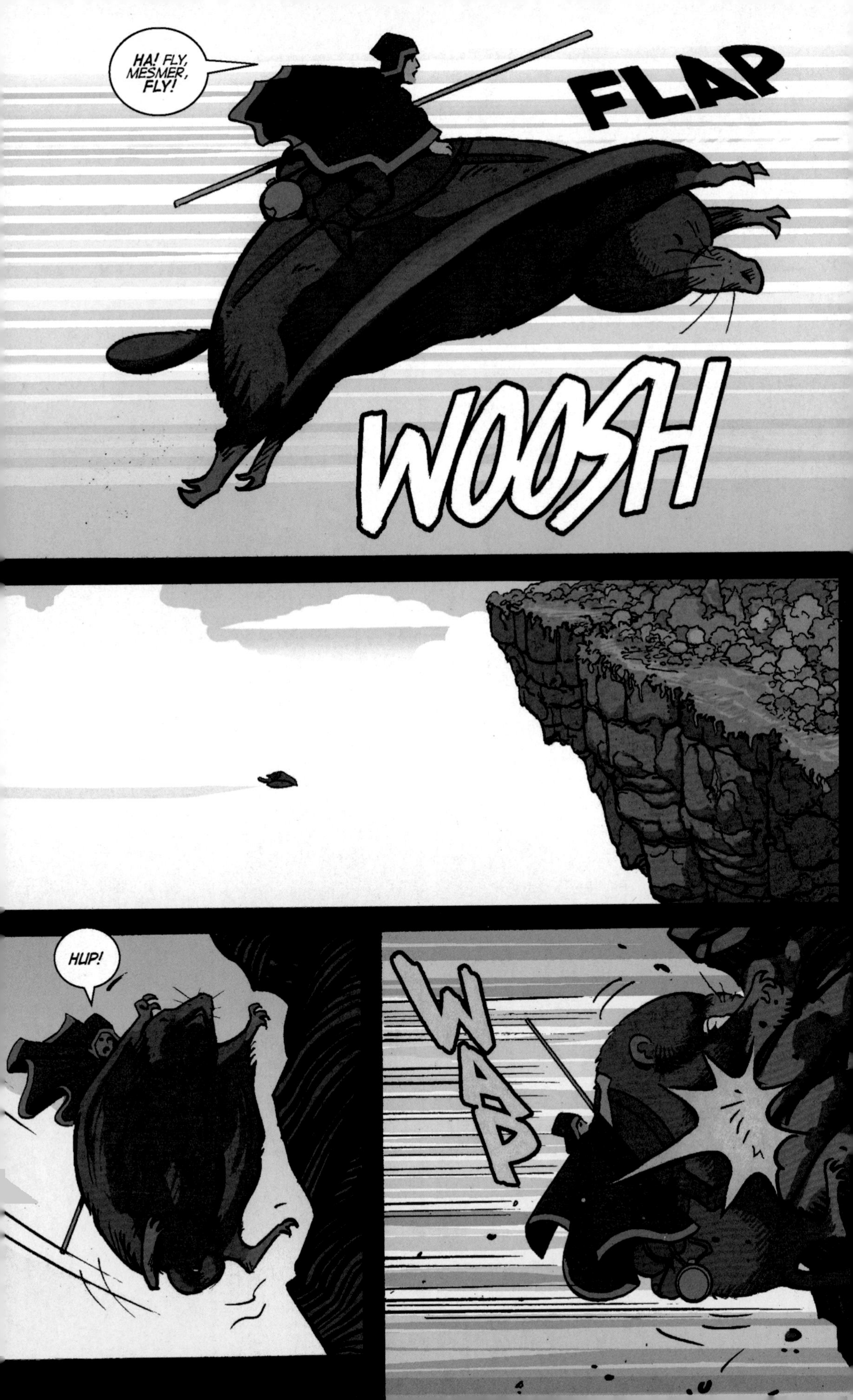
HA! FLY, MESMER, FLY!
FLAP
WOOSH
HUP!
WAP

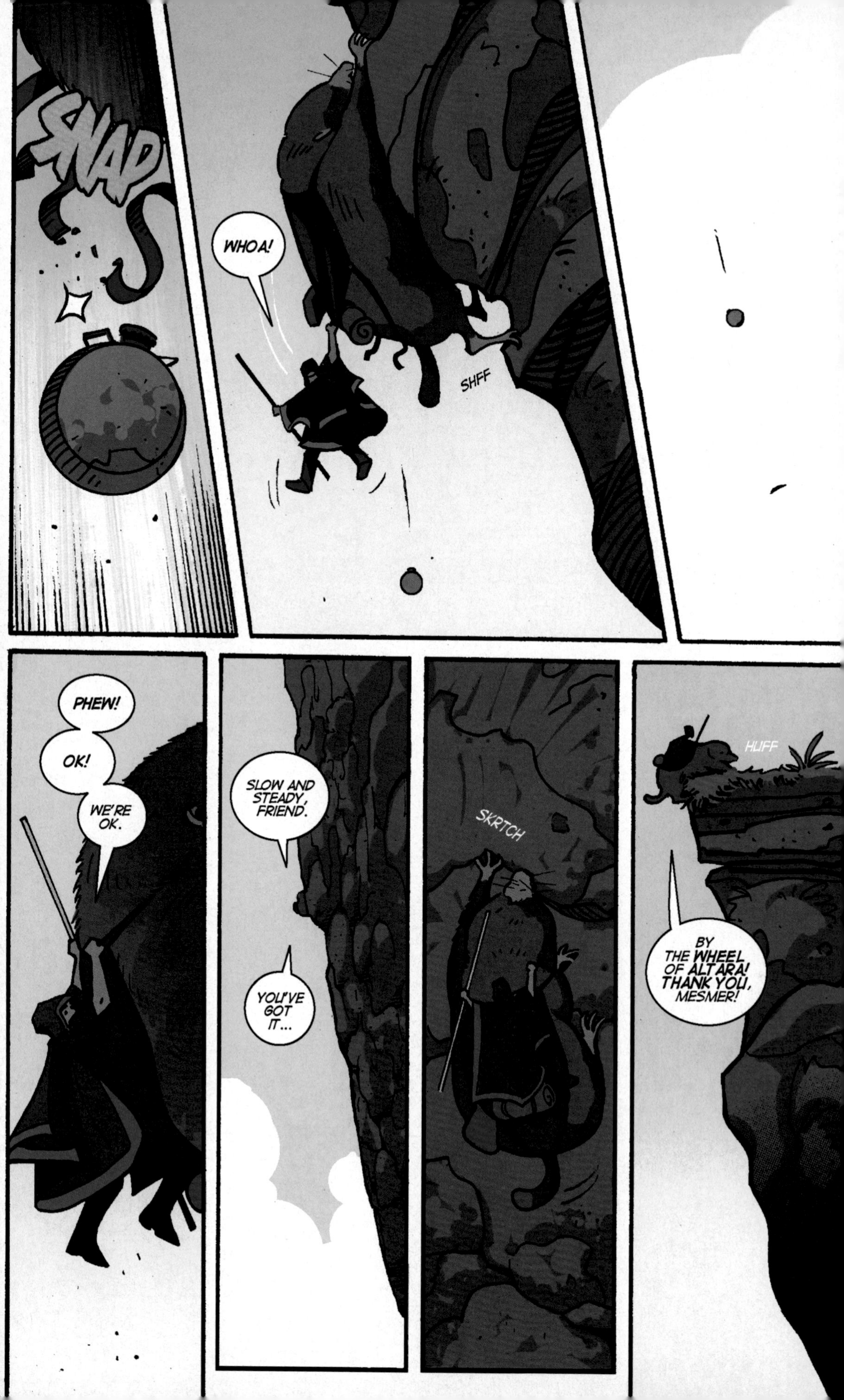
SNAP
WHOA!
SHFF
PHEW!
OK!
WE'RE OK.
SLOW AND STEADY, FRIEND.
YOU'VE GOT IT...
SKRTCH
HUFF
BY THE WHEEL OF ALTARA! THANK YOU, MESMER!

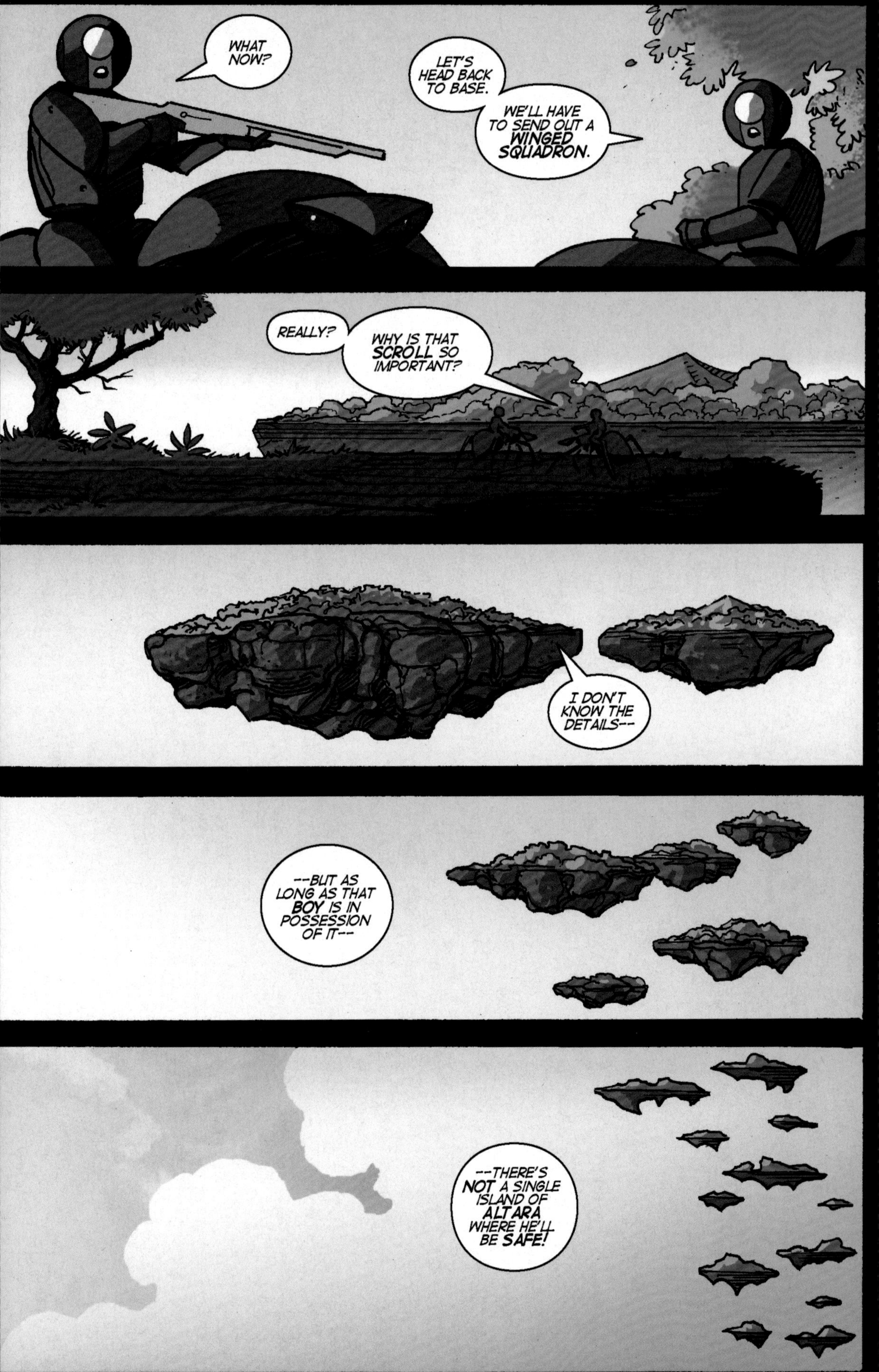
WHAT NOW?
LET'S HEAD BACK TO BASE.
WE'LL HAVE TO SEND OUT A WINGED SQUADRON.
REALLY?
WHY IS THAT SCROLL SO IMPORTANT?
I DON'T KNOW THE DETAILS--
--BUT AS LONG AS THAT BOY IS IN POSSESSION OF IT--
--THERE'S NOT A SINGLE ISLAND OF ALTARA WHERE HE'LL BE SAFE!

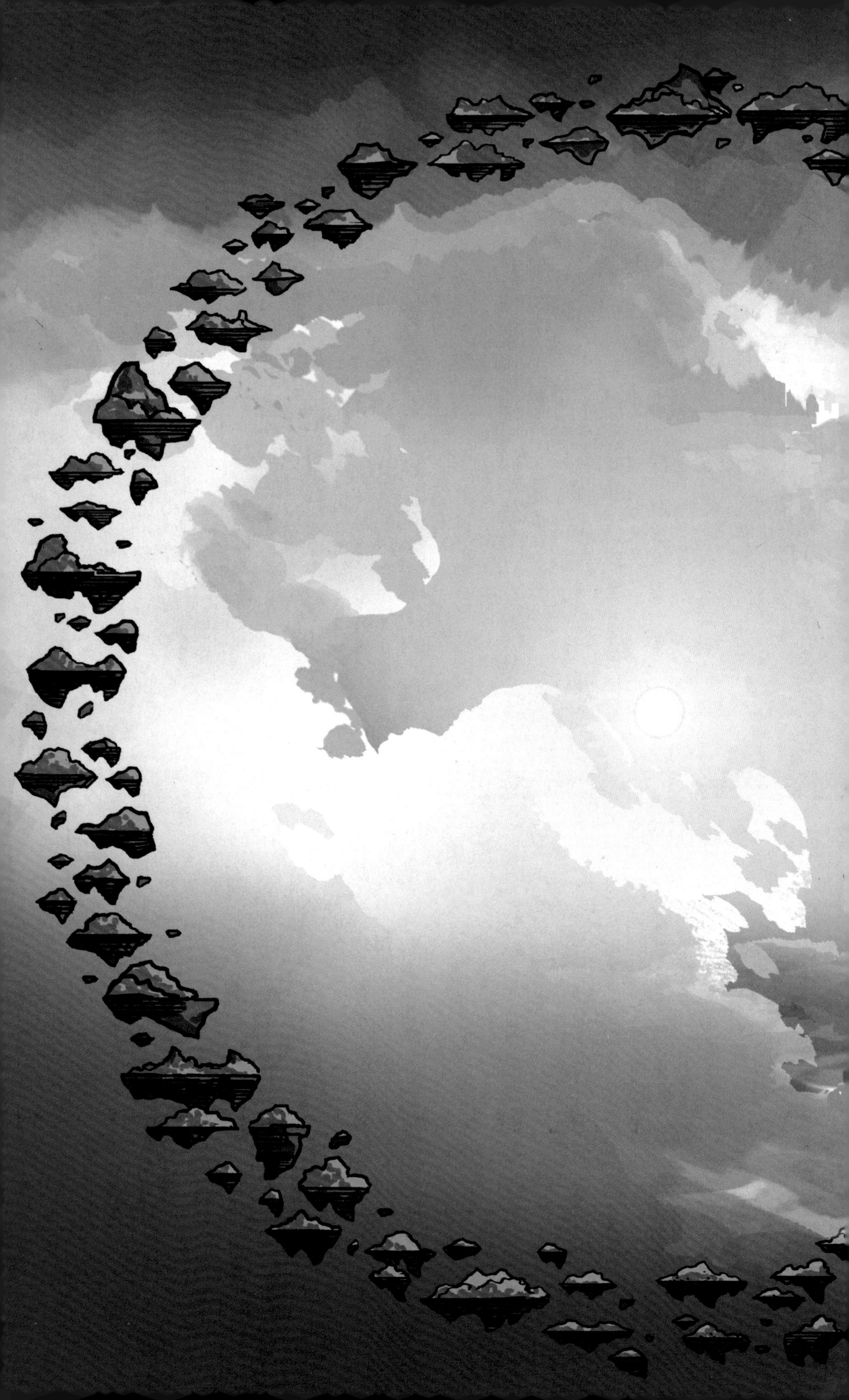

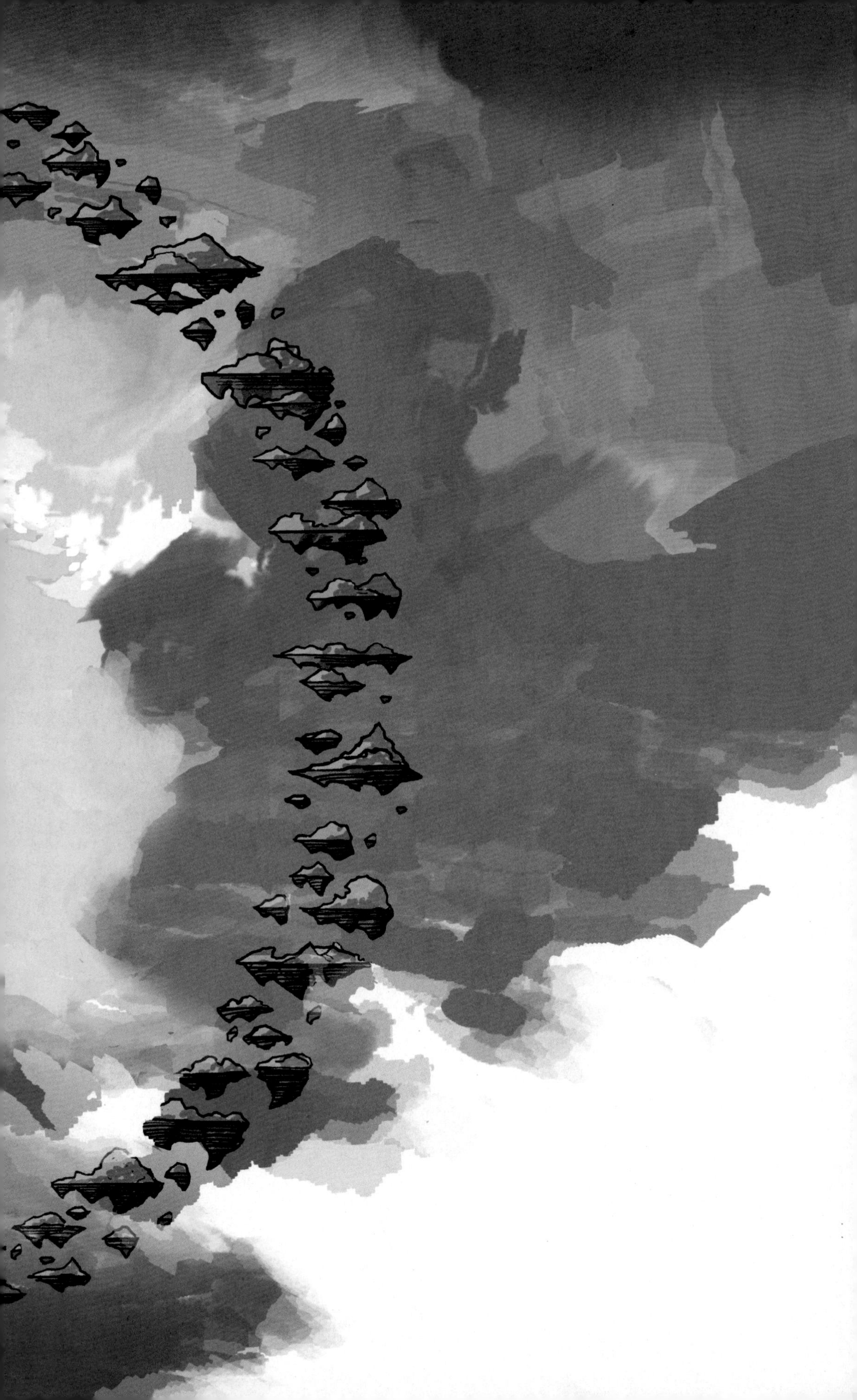

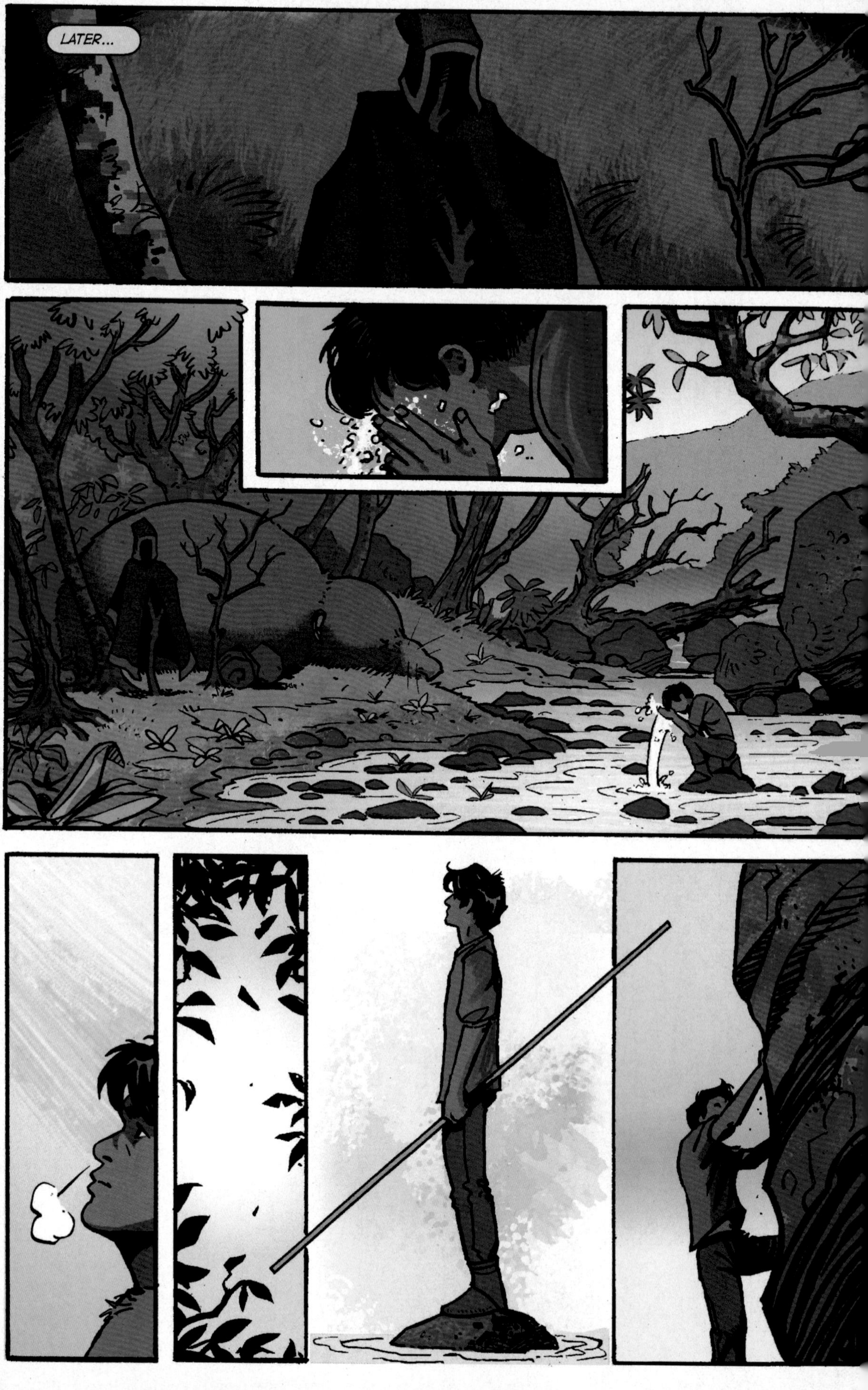
LATER...

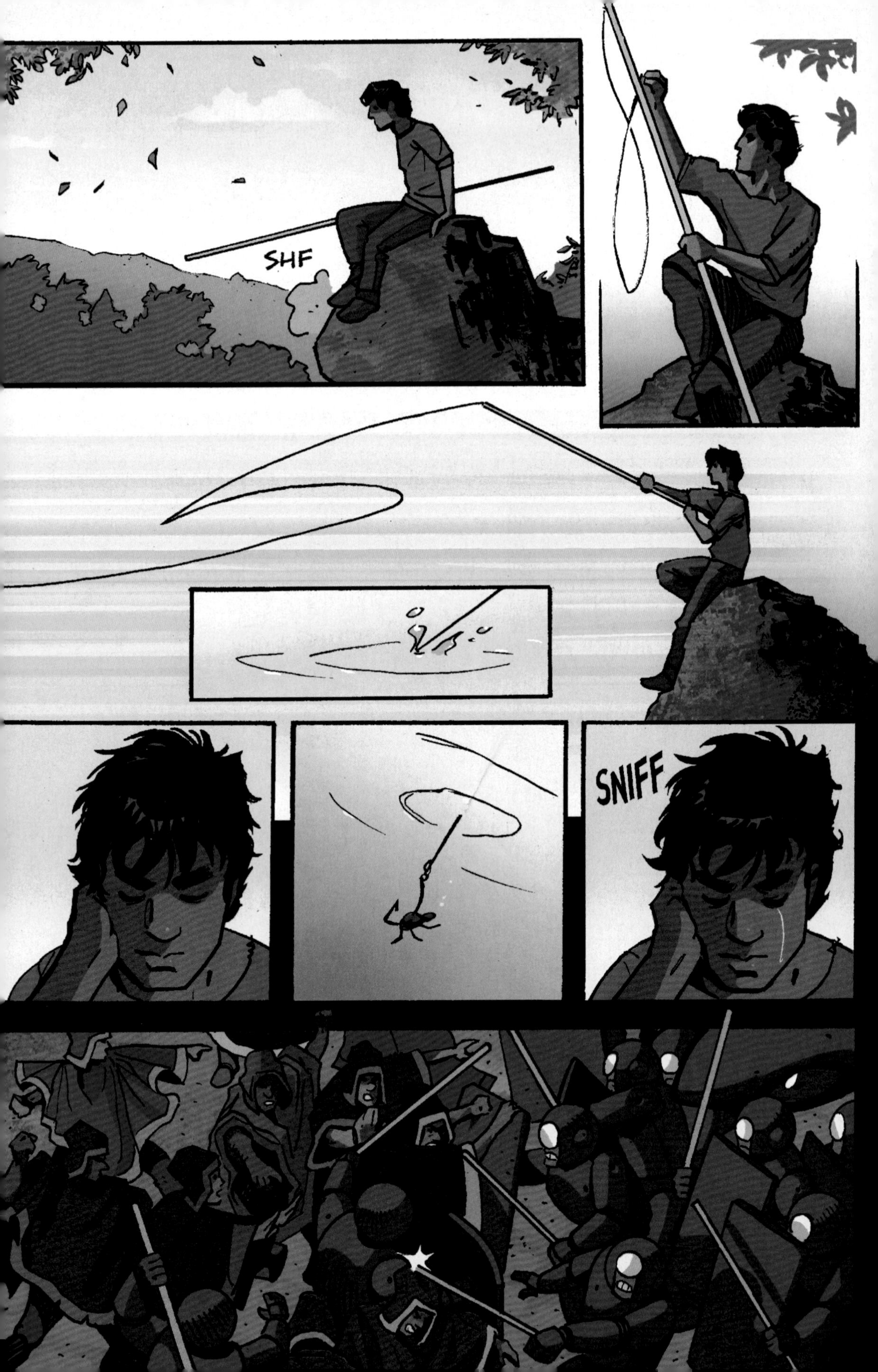
SHF
SNIFF

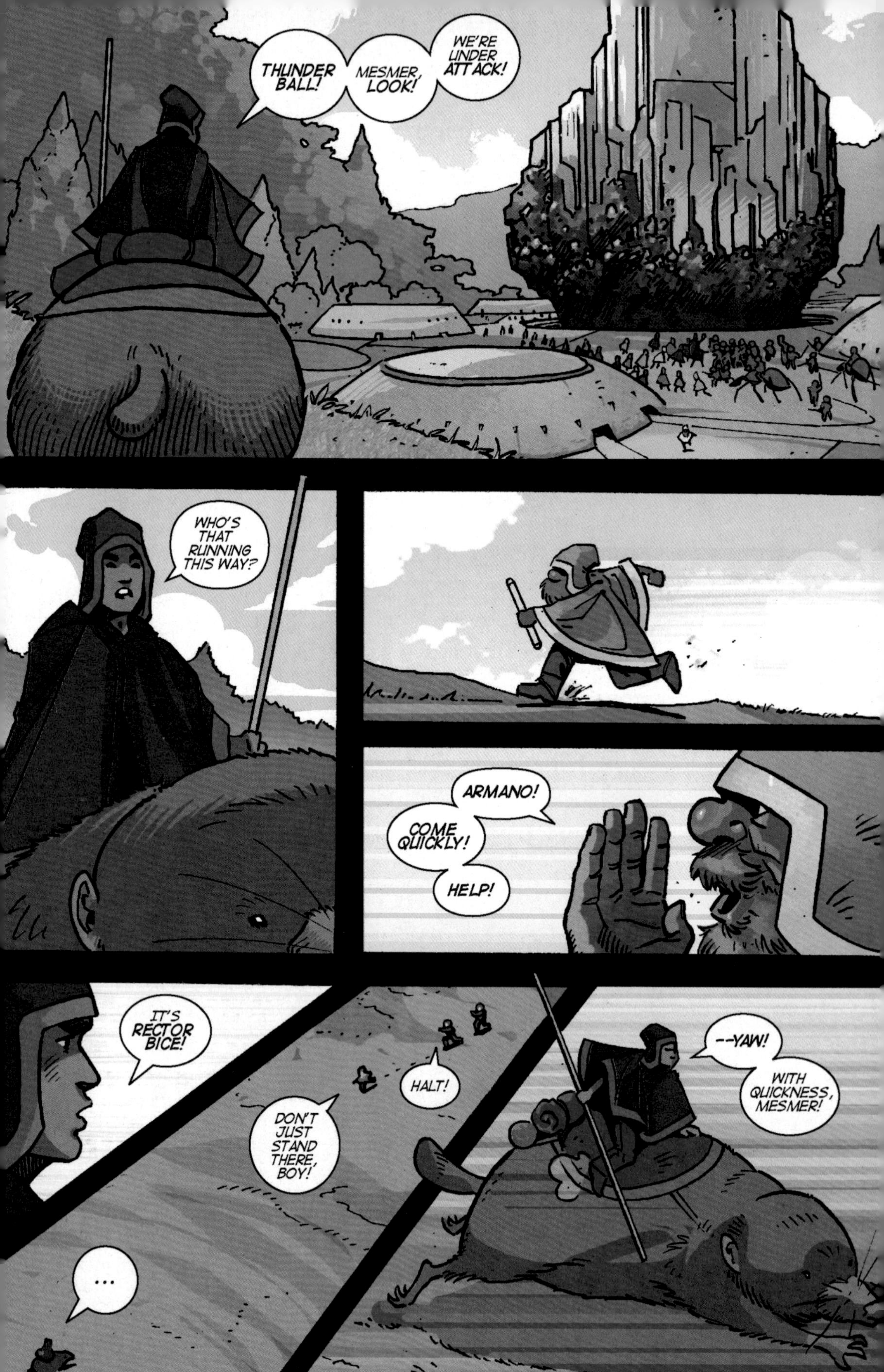
THUNDER BALL!
MESMER, LOOK!
WE'RE UNDER ATTACK!
WHO'S THAT RUNNING THIS WAY?
ARMANO!
COME QUICKLY!
HELP!
IT'S RECTOR BICE!
HALT!
DON'T JUST STAND THERE, BOY!
...
--YAW!
WITH QUICKNESS, MESMER!

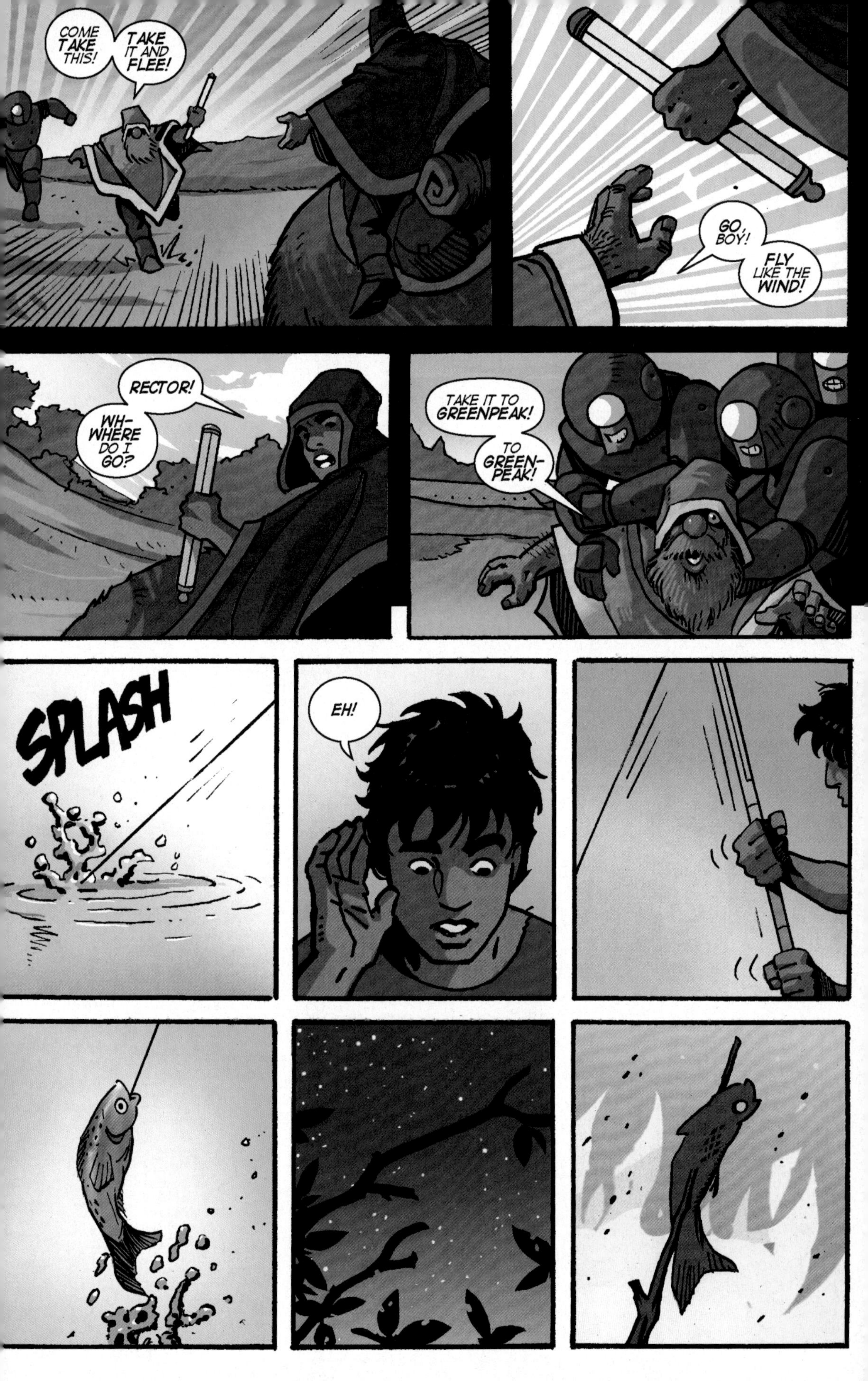
COME TAKE THIS!
TAKE IT AND FLEE!
GO, BOY!
FLY LIKE THE WIND!
RECTOR!
WH-WHERE DO I GO?
TAKE IT TO GREENPEAK!
TO GREEN-PEAK!
SPLASH
EH!

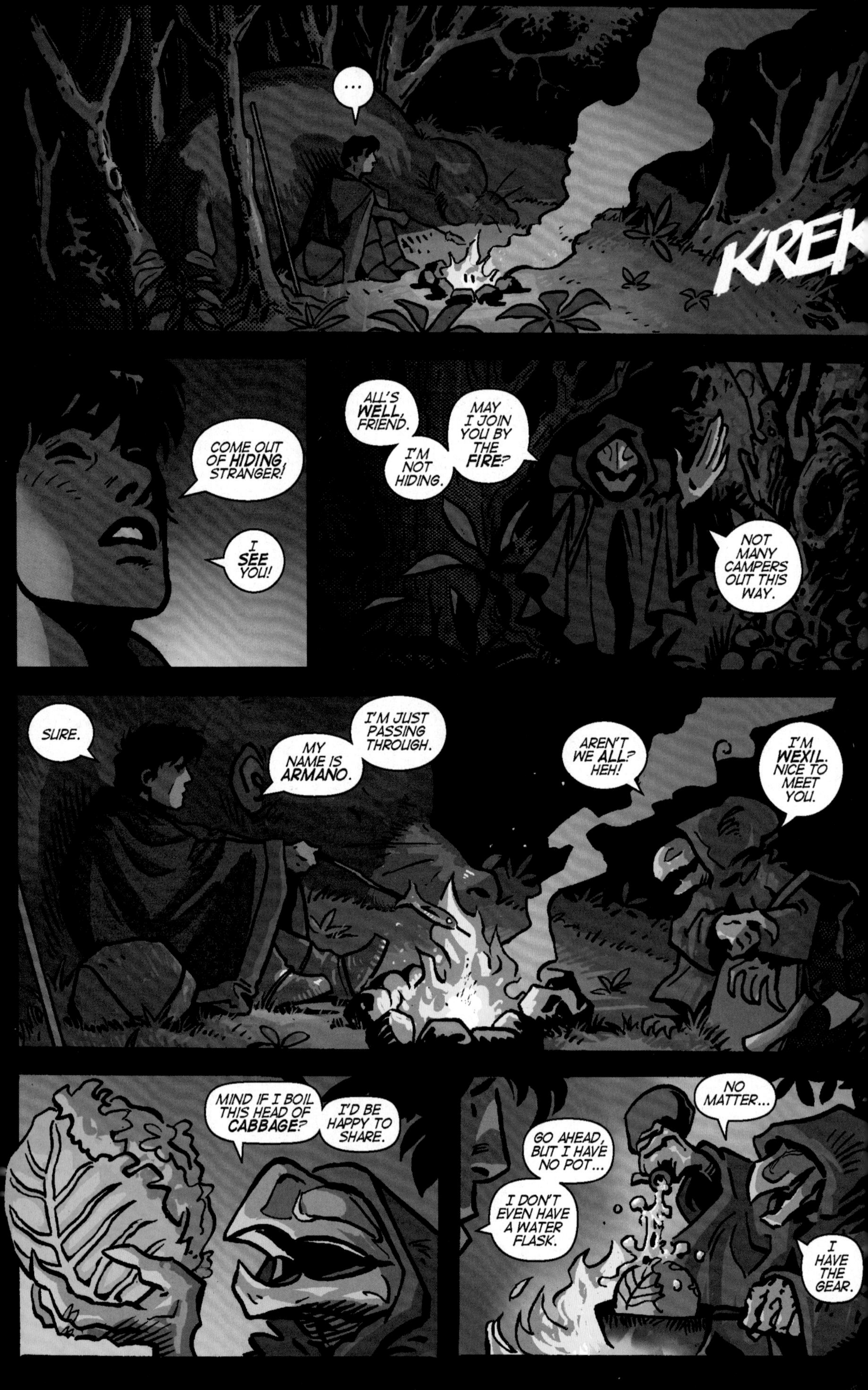
...
KREK
COME OUT OF HIDING, STRANGER!
I SEE YOU!
ALL'S WELL, FRIEND.
I'M NOT HIDING.
MAY I JOIN YOU BY THE FIRE?
NOT MANY CAMPERS OUT THIS WAY.
SURE.
MY NAME IS ARMANO.
I'M JUST PASSING THROUGH.
AREN'T WE ALL? HEH!
I'M WEXIL. NICE TO MEET YOU.
MIND IF I BOIL THIS HEAD OF CABBAGE?
I'D BE HAPPY TO SHARE.
GO AHEAD, BUT I HAVE NO POT...
I DON'T EVEN HAVE A WATER FLASK.
NO MATTER...
I HAVE THE GEAR.

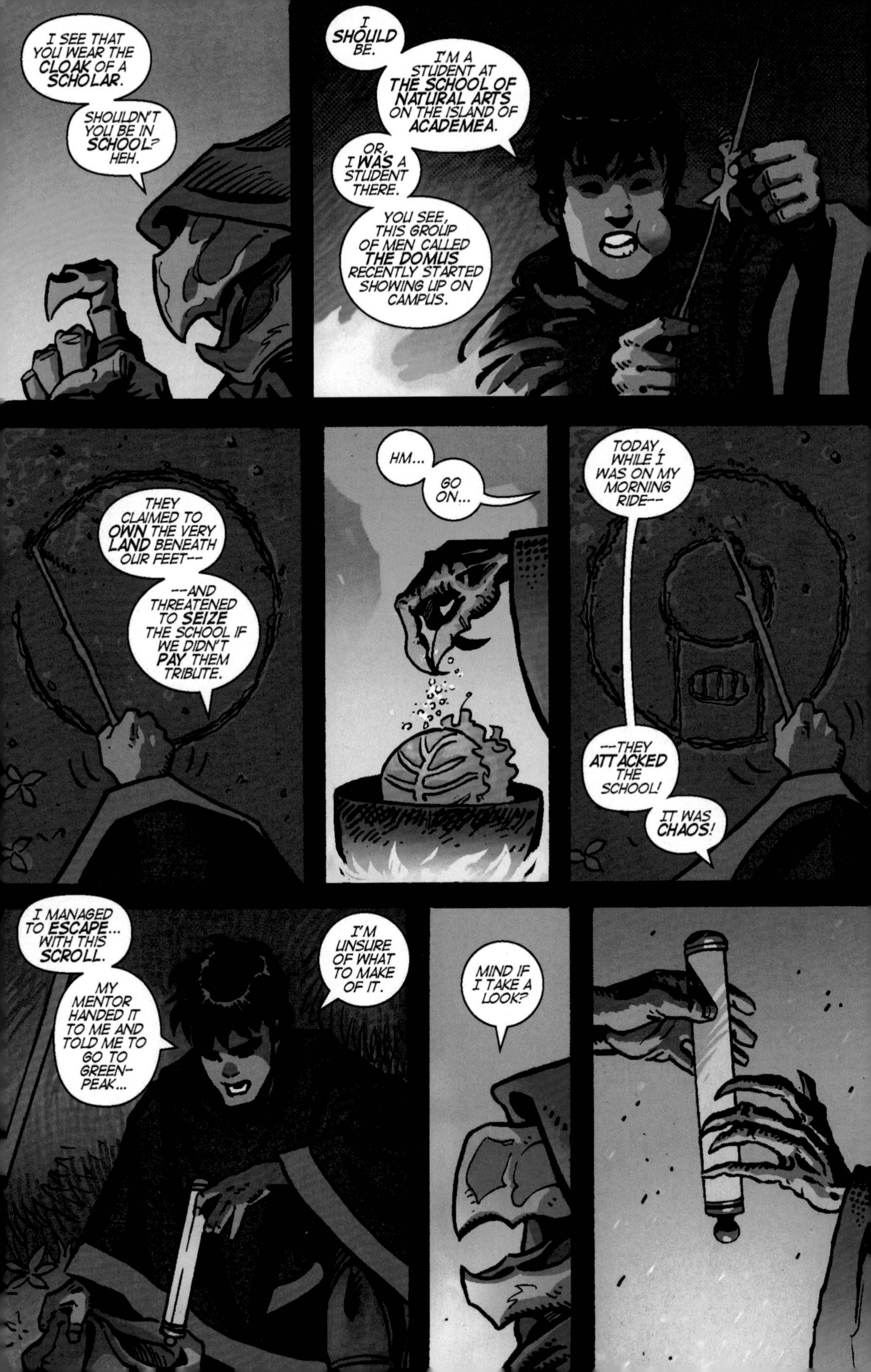
I SEE THAT YOU WEAR THE CLOAK OF A SCHOLAR.
SHOULDN'T YOU BE IN SCHOOL? HEH.
I SHOULD BE.
I'M A STUDENT AT THE SCHOOL OF NATURAL ARTS ON THE ISLAND OF ACADEMEA.
OR, I WAS A STUDENT THERE.
YOU SEE, THIS GROUP OF MEN CALLED THE DOMUS RECENTLY STARTED SHOWING UP ON CAMPUS.
THEY CLAIMED TO OWN THE VERY LAND BENEATH OUR FEET--
--AND THREATENED TO SEIZE THE SCHOOL IF WE DIDN'T PAY THEM TRIBUTE.
HM...
GO ON...
TODAY, WHILE I WAS ON MY MORNING RIDE--
--THEY ATTACKED THE SCHOOL!
IT WAS CHAOS!
I MANAGED TO ESCAPE... WITH THIS SCROLL.
MY MENTOR HANDED IT TO ME AND TOLD ME TO GO TO GREEN-PEAK...
I'M UNSURE OF WHAT TO MAKE OF IT.
MIND IF I TAKE A LOOK?

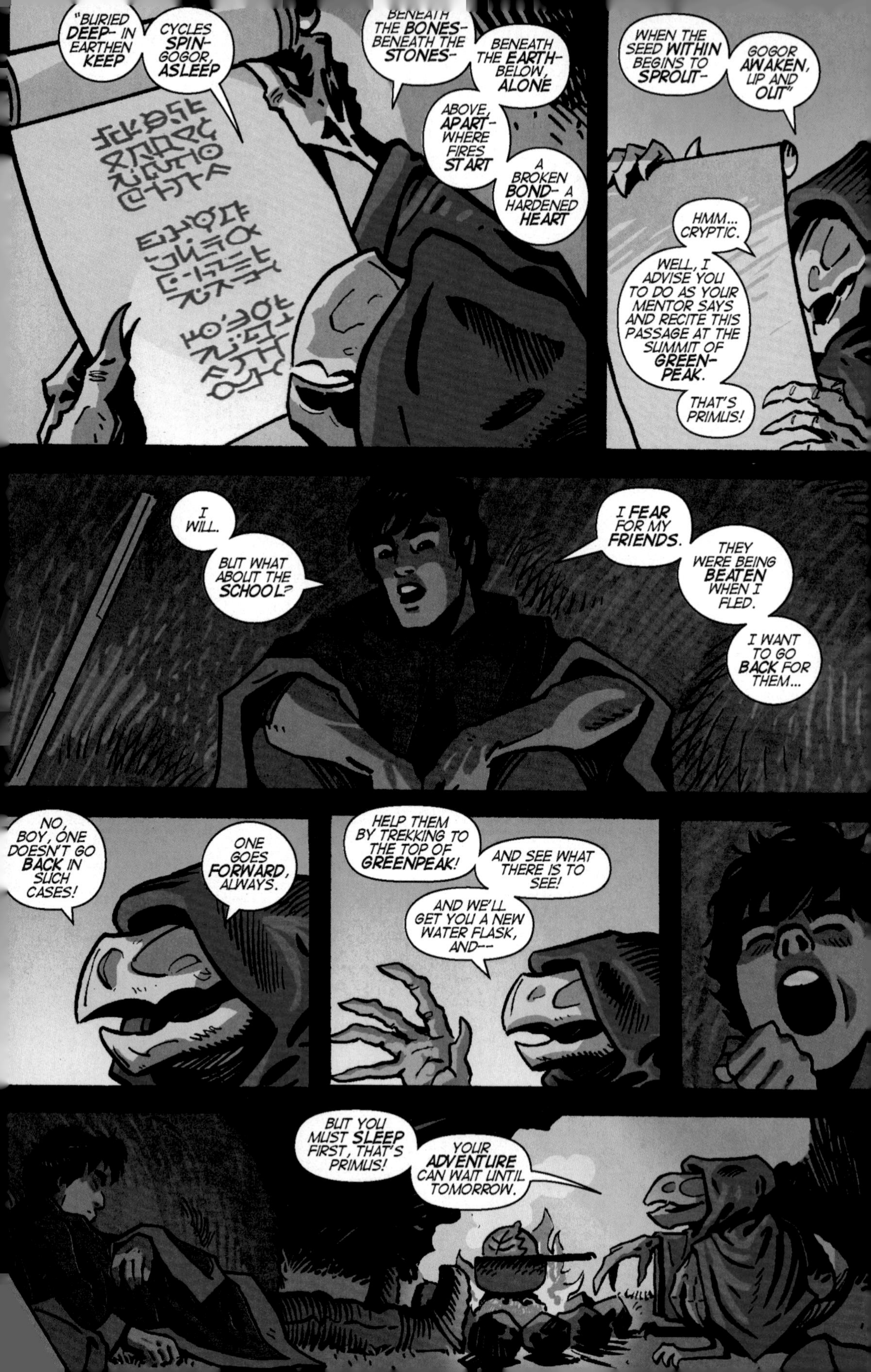
"BURIED DEEP- IN EARTHEN KEEP
CYCLES SPIN- GOGOR, ASLEEP
BENEATH THE BONES- BENEATH THE STONES-
BENEATH THE EARTH- BELOW, ALONE
ABOVE, APART- WHERE FIRES START
A BROKEN BOND- A HARDENED HEART
WHEN THE SEED WITHIN BEGINS TO SPROUT-
GOGOR AWAKEN, UP AND OUT"
HMM... CRYPTIC.
WELL, I ADVISE YOU TO DO AS YOUR MENTOR SAYS AND RECITE THIS PASSAGE AT THE SUMMIT OF GREEN-PEAK.
THAT'S PRIMUS!
I WILL.
BUT WHAT ABOUT THE SCHOOL?
I FEAR FOR MY FRIENDS.
THEY WERE BEING BEATEN WHEN I FLED.
I WANT TO GO BACK FOR THEM...
NO, BOY, ONE DOESN'T GO BACK IN SUCH CASES!
ONE GOES FORWARD, ALWAYS.
HELP THEM BY TREKKING TO THE TOP OF GREENPEAK!
AND SEE WHAT THERE IS TO SEE!
AND WE'LL GET YOU A NEW WATER FLASK, AND--
BUT YOU MUST SLEEP FIRST, THAT'S PRIMUS!
YOUR ADVENTURE CAN WAIT UNTIL TOMORROW.

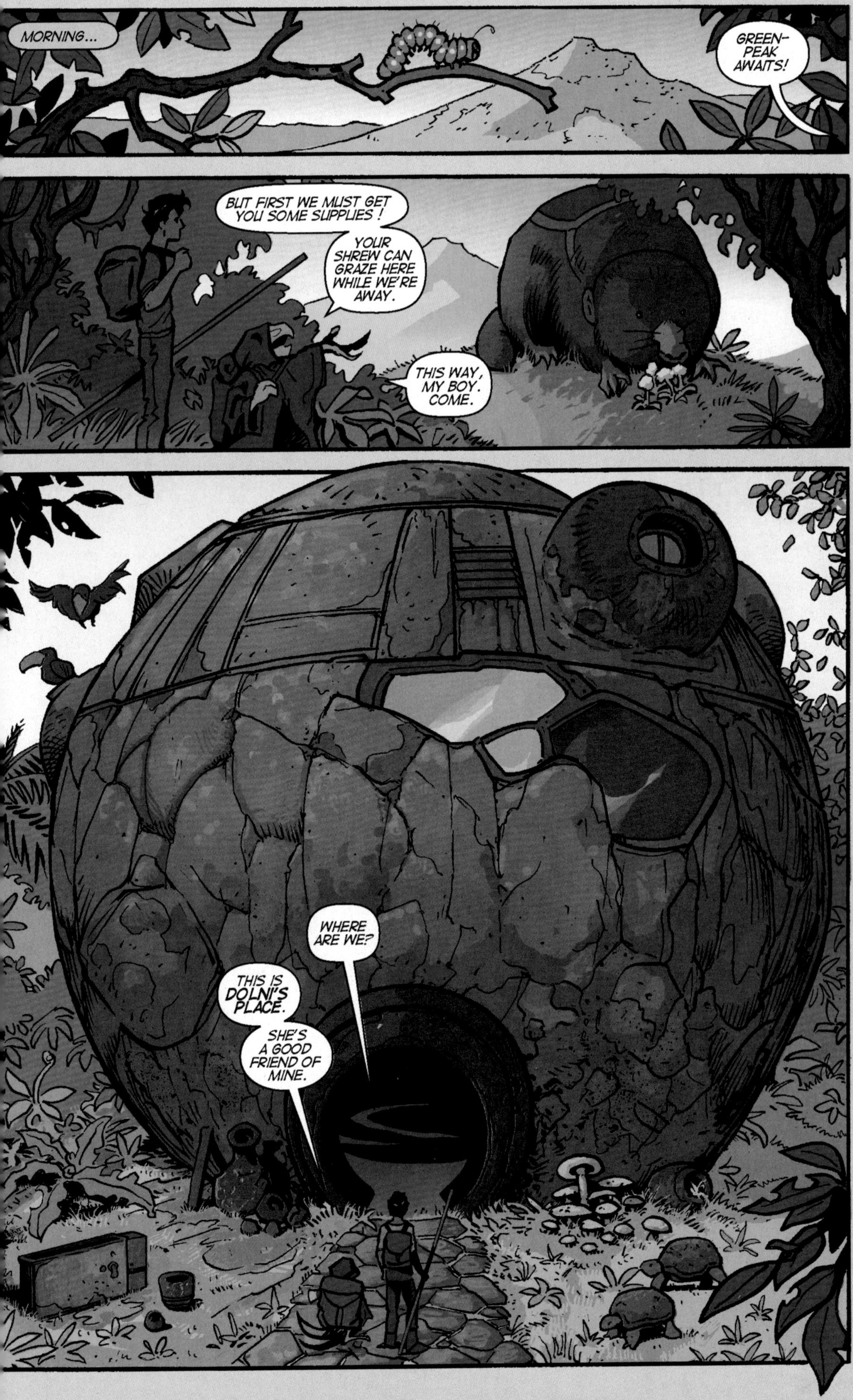
MORNING...
GREEN-PEAK AWAITS!
BUT FIRST WE MUST GET YOU SOME SUPPLIES!
YOUR SHREW CAN GRAZE HERE WHILE WE'RE AWAY.
THIS WAY, MY BOY. COME.
WHERE ARE WE?
THIS IS DOLNI'S PLACE.
SHE'S A GOOD FRIEND OF MINE.

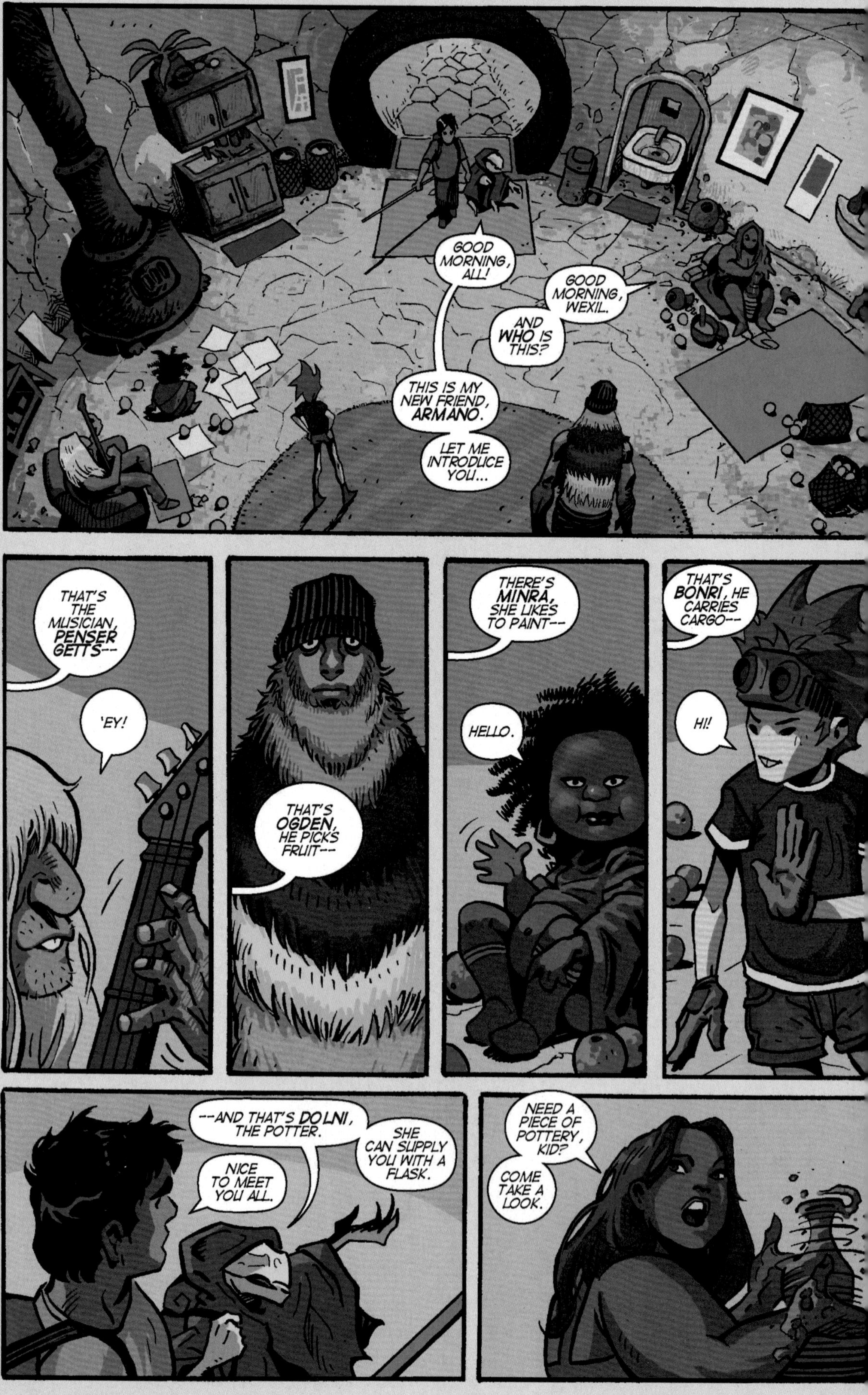
GOOD MORNING, ALL!
GOOD MORNING, WEXIL.
AND WHO IS THIS?
THIS IS MY NEW FRIEND, ARMANO.
LET ME INTRODUCE YOU...
THAT'S THE MUSICIAN, PENSER GETTS--
'EY!
THAT'S OGDEN, HE PICKS FRUIT--
THERE'S MINRA, SHE LIKES TO PAINT--
HELLO.
THAT'S BONRI, HE CARRIES CARGO--
HI!
--AND THAT'S DOLNI, THE POTTER.
NICE TO MEET YOU ALL.
SHE CAN SUPPLY YOU WITH A FLASK.
NEED A PIECE OF POTTERY, KID?
COME TAKE A LOOK.

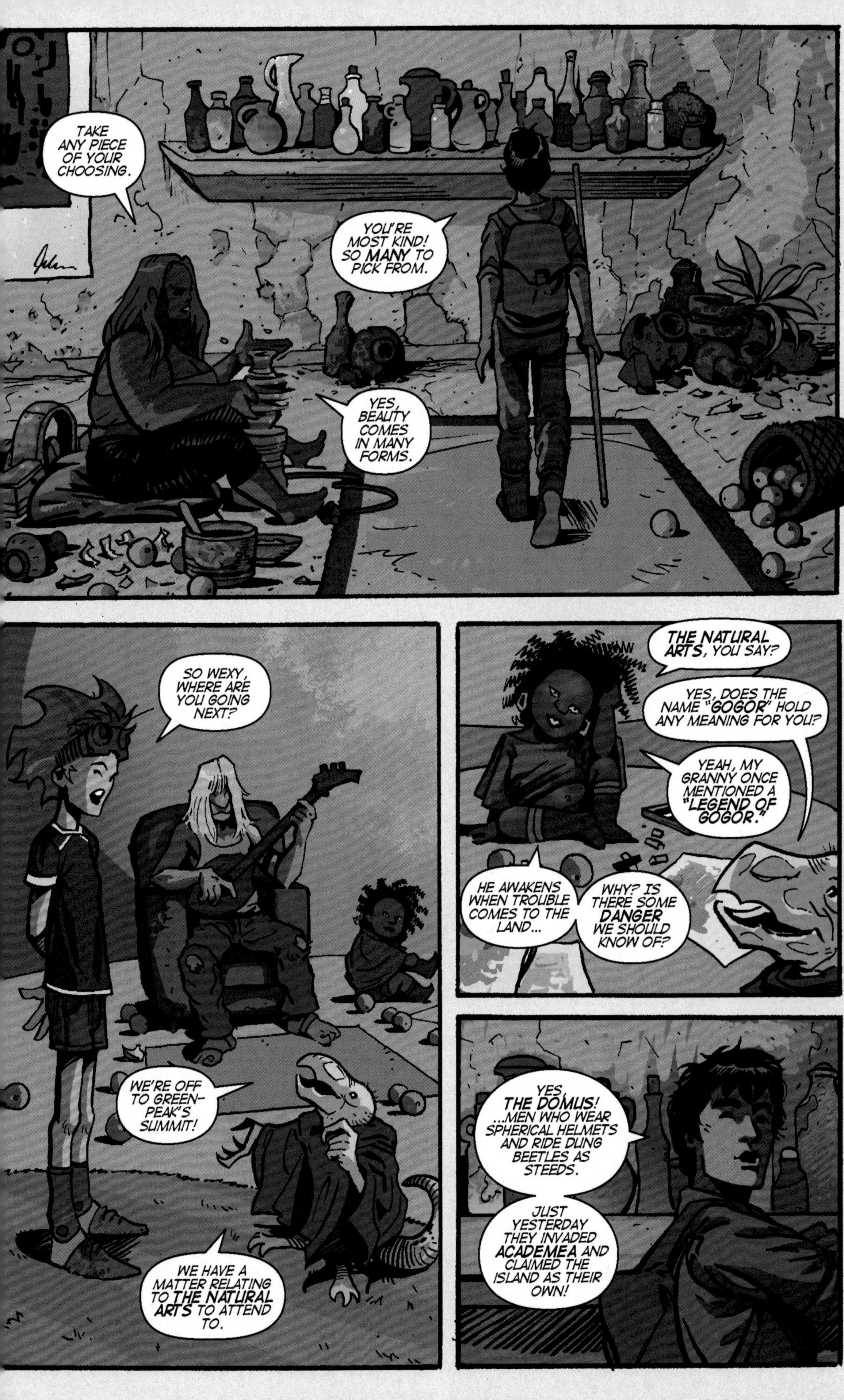
TAKE ANY PIECE OF YOUR CHOOSING.
YOU'RE MOST KIND! SO MANY TO PICK FROM.
YES, BEAUTY COMES IN MANY FORMS.
SO WEXY, WHERE ARE YOU GOING NEXT?
WE'RE OFF TO GREEN-PEAK'S SUMMIT!
WE HAVE A MATTER RELATING TO THE NATURAL ARTS TO ATTEND TO.
THE NATURAL ARTS, YOU SAY?
YES, DOES THE NAME "GOGOR" HOLD ANY MEANING FOR YOU?
YEAH, MY GRANNY ONCE MENTIONED A "LEGEND OF GOGOR."
HE AWAKENS WHEN TROUBLE COMES TO THE LAND...
WHY? IS THERE SOME DANGER WE SHOULD KNOW OF?
YES, THE DOMUS! ...MEN WHO WEAR SPHERICAL HELMETS AND RIDE DUNG BEETLES AS STEEDS.
JUST YESTERDAY THEY INVADED ACADEMEA AND CLAIMED THE ISLAND AS THEIR OWN!

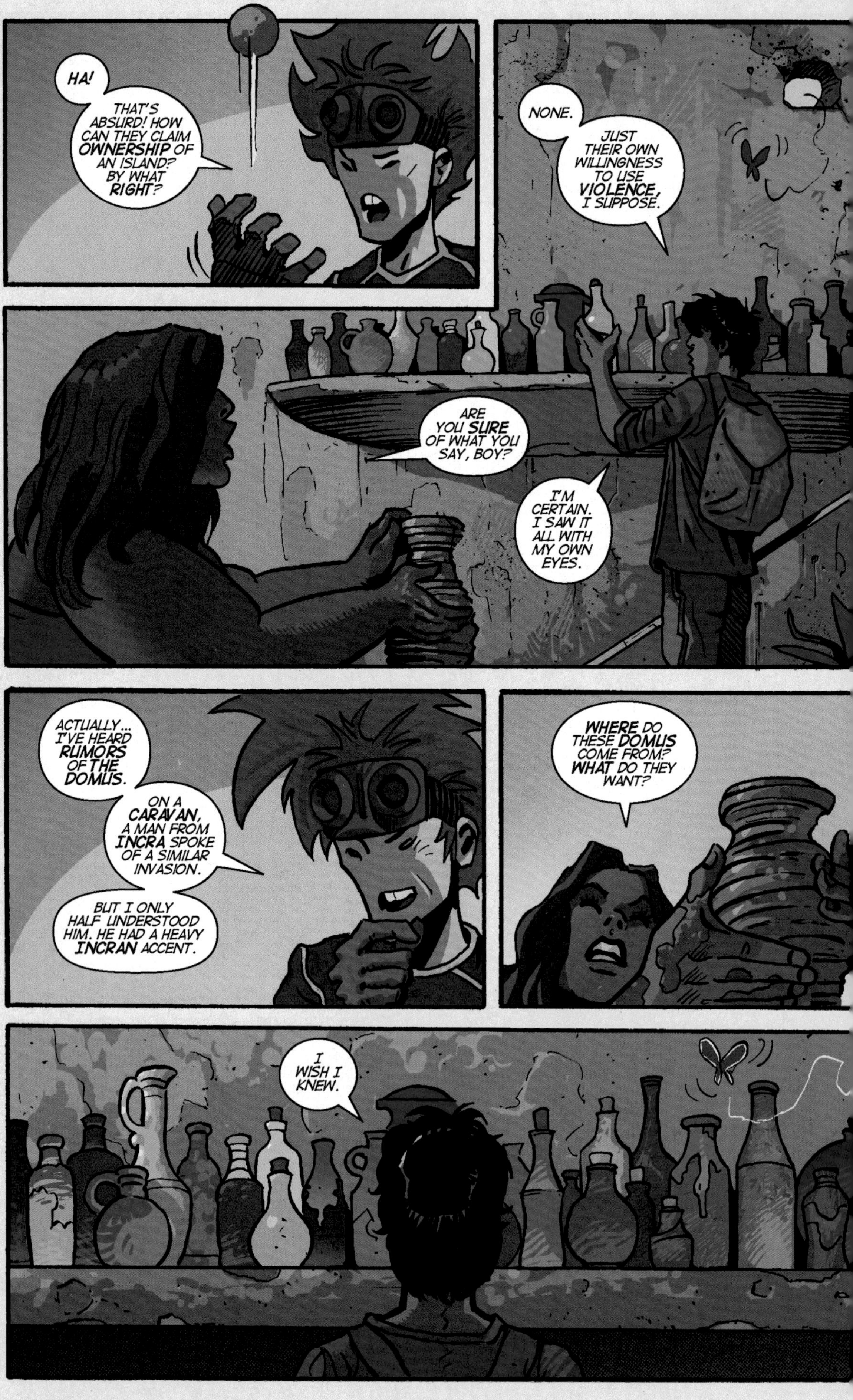
HA!
THAT'S ABSURD! HOW CAN THEY CLAIM OWNERSHIP OF AN ISLAND? BY WHAT RIGHT?
NONE.
JUST THEIR OWN WILLINGNESS TO USE VIOLENCE, I SUPPOSE.
ARE YOU SURE OF WHAT YOU SAY, BOY?
I'M CERTAIN. I SAW IT ALL WITH MY OWN EYES.
ACTUALLY... I'VE HEARD RUMORS OF THE DOMUS.
ON A CARAVAN, A MAN FROM INCRA SPOKE OF A SIMILAR INVASION.
BUT I ONLY HALF UNDERSTOOD HIM. HE HAD A HEAVY INCRAN ACCENT.
WHERE DO THESE DOMUS COME FROM? WHAT DO THEY WANT?
I WISH I KNEW.

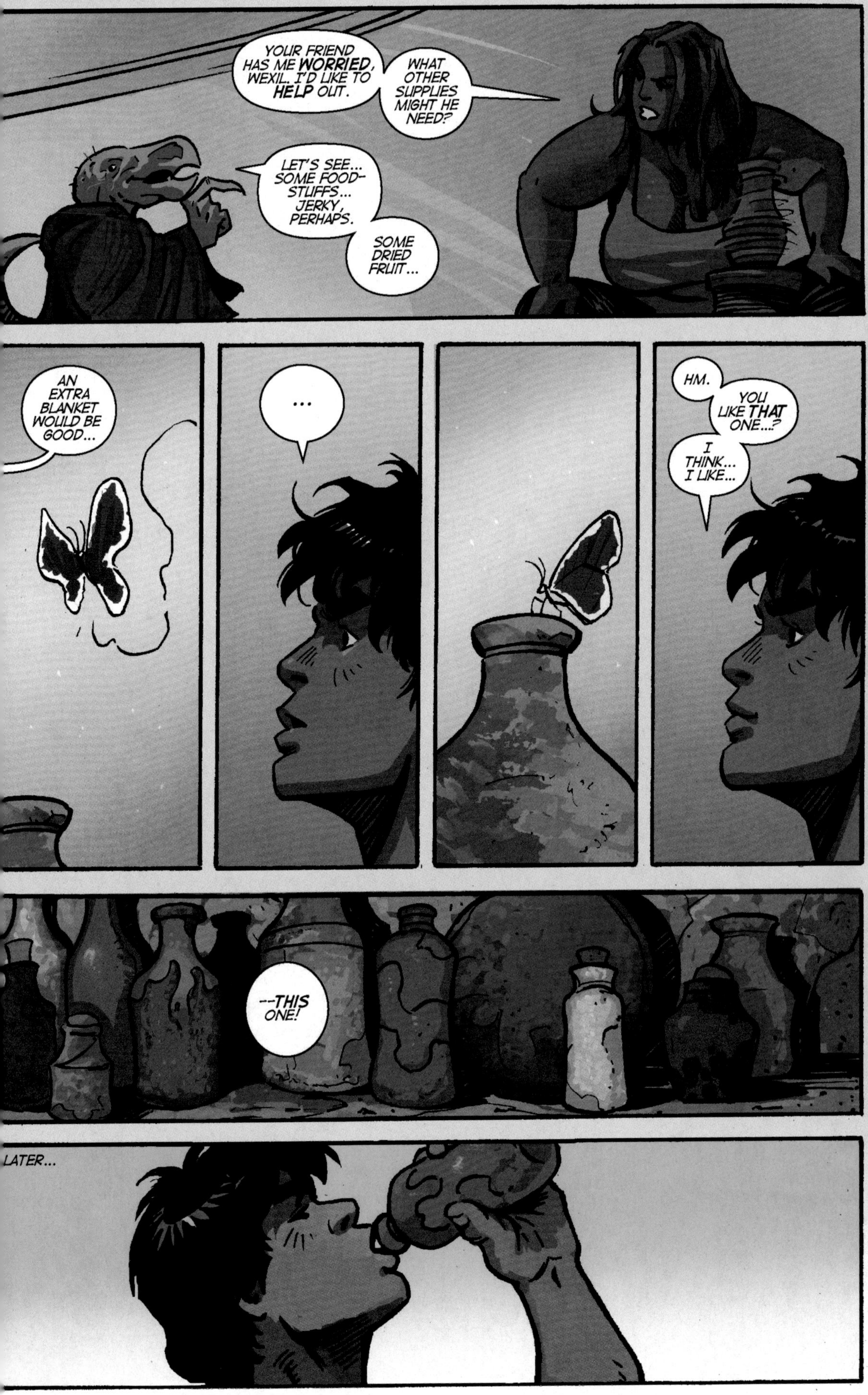
YOUR FRIEND HAS ME WORRIED, WEXIL. I'D LIKE TO HELP OUT.
WHAT OTHER SUPPLIES MIGHT HE NEED?
LET'S SEE... SOME FOOD-STUFFS... JERKY, PERHAPS.
SOME DRIED FRUIT...
AN EXTRA BLANKET WOULD BE GOOD...
...
HM.
YOU LIKE THAT ONE...?
I THINK... I LIKE...
--THIS ONE!
LATER...

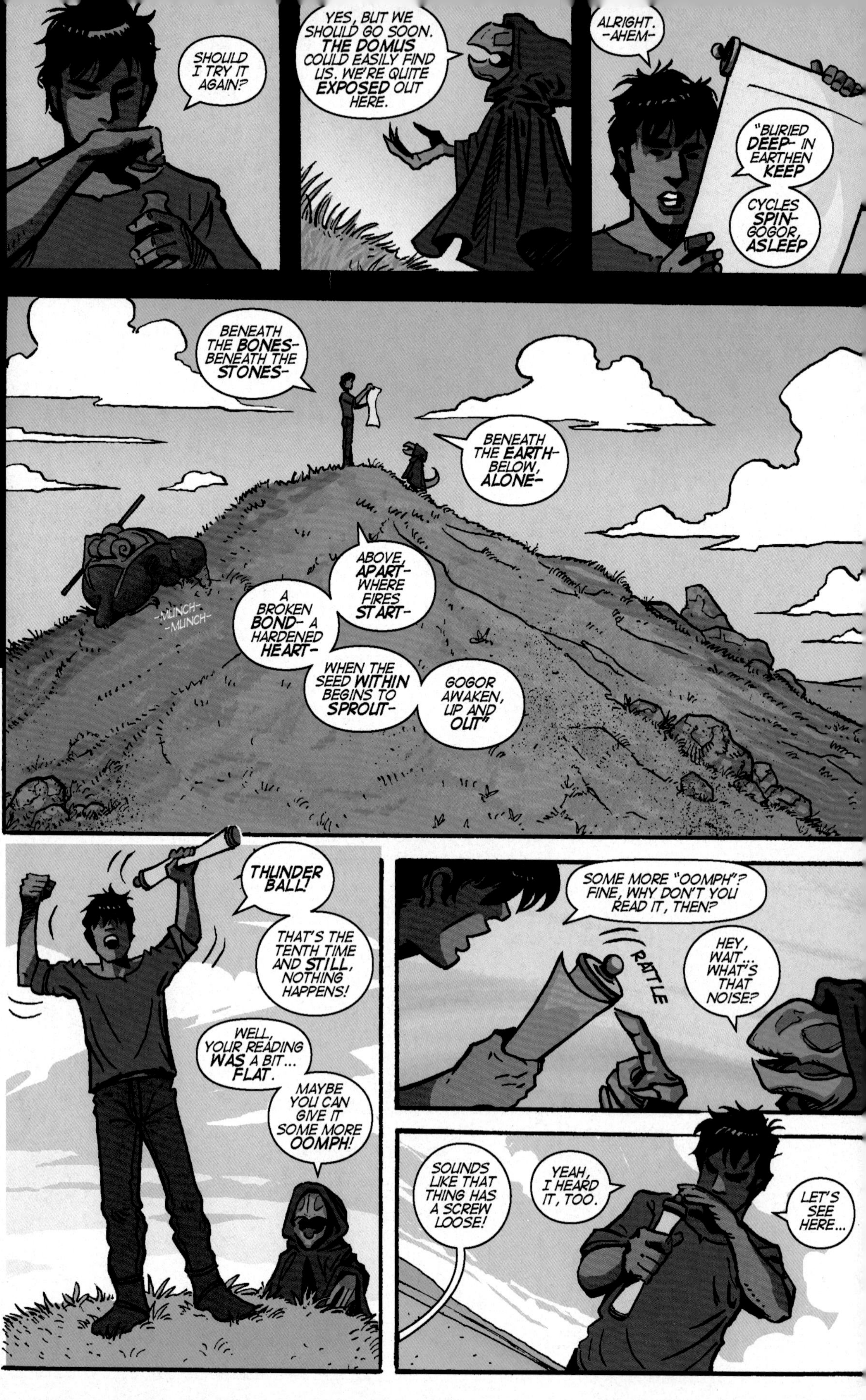
SHOULD I TRY IT AGAIN?
YES, BUT WE SHOULD GO SOON. THE DOMUS COULD EASILY FIND US. WE'RE QUITE EXPOSED OUT HERE.
ALRIGHT. -AHEM-
"BURIED DEEP- IN EARTHEN KEEP
CYCLES SPIN- GOGOR, ASLEEP
BENEATH THE BONES- BENEATH THE STONES-
BENEATH THE EARTH- BELOW, ALONE-
-MUNCH-
-MUNCH-
ABOVE, APART- WHERE FIRES START-
A BROKEN BOND- A HARDENED HEART-
WHEN THE SEED WITHIN BEGINS TO SPROUT-
GOGOR AWAKEN, UP AND OUT"
THUNDER BALL!
THAT'S THE TENTH TIME AND STILL, NOTHING HAPPENS!
WELL, YOUR READING WAS A BIT... FLAT.
MAYBE YOU CAN GIVE IT SOME MORE OOMPH!
SOME MORE "OOMPH"? FINE, WHY DON'T YOU READ IT, THEN?
RATTLE
HEY, WAIT... WHAT'S THAT NOISE?
SOUNDS LIKE THAT THING HAS A SCREW LOOSE!
YEAH, I HEARD IT, TOO.
LET'S SEE HERE...

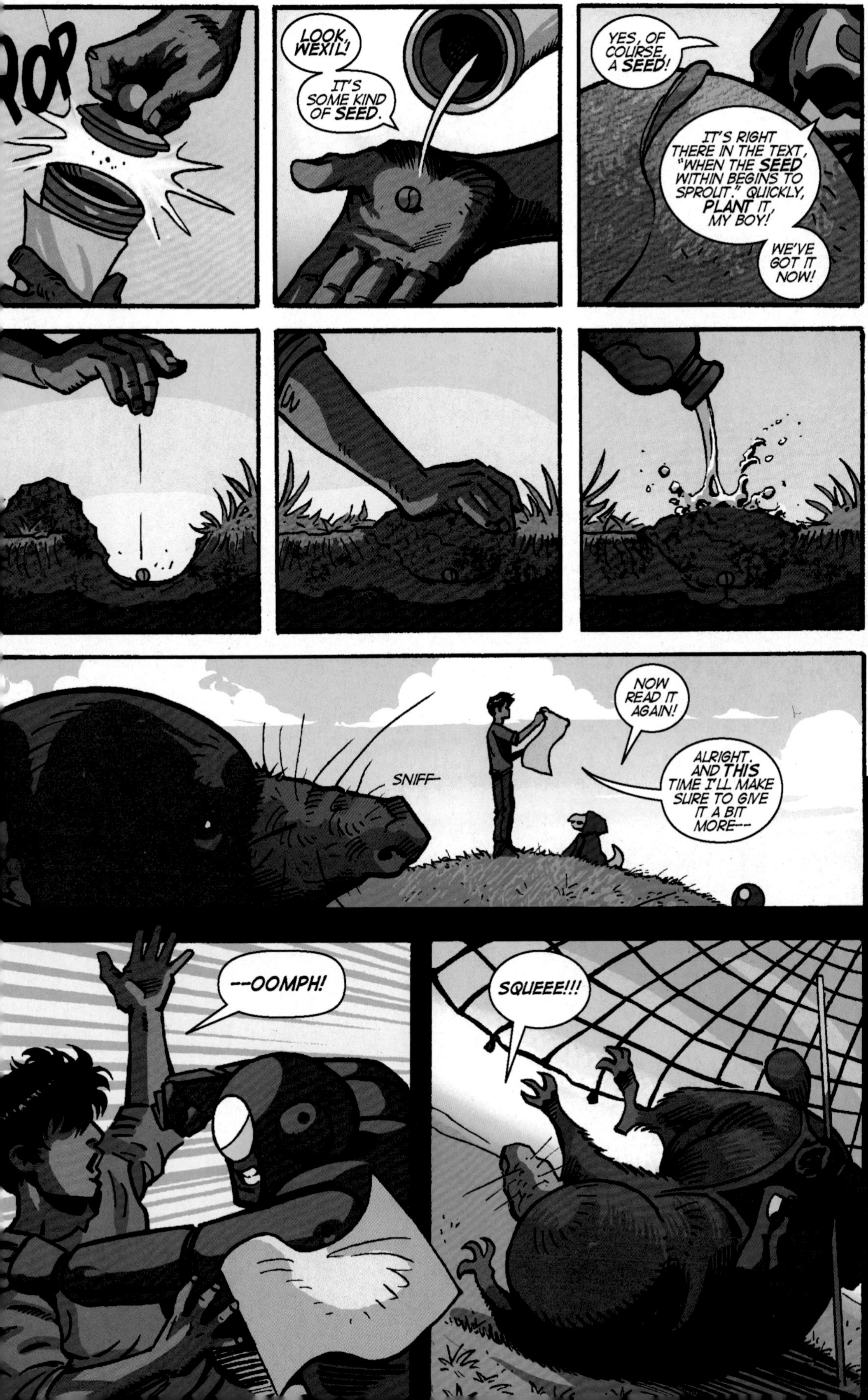
POP
LOOK, WEXIL!
IT'S SOME KIND OF SEED.
YES, OF COURSE, A SEED!
IT'S RIGHT THERE IN THE TEXT, "WHEN THE SEED WITHIN BEGINS TO SPROUT." QUICKLY, PLANT IT, MY BOY!
WE'VE GOT IT NOW!
SNIFF--
NOW READ IT AGAIN!
ALRIGHT. AND THIS TIME I'LL MAKE SURE TO GIVE IT A BIT MORE--
--OOMPH!
SQUEEE!!!

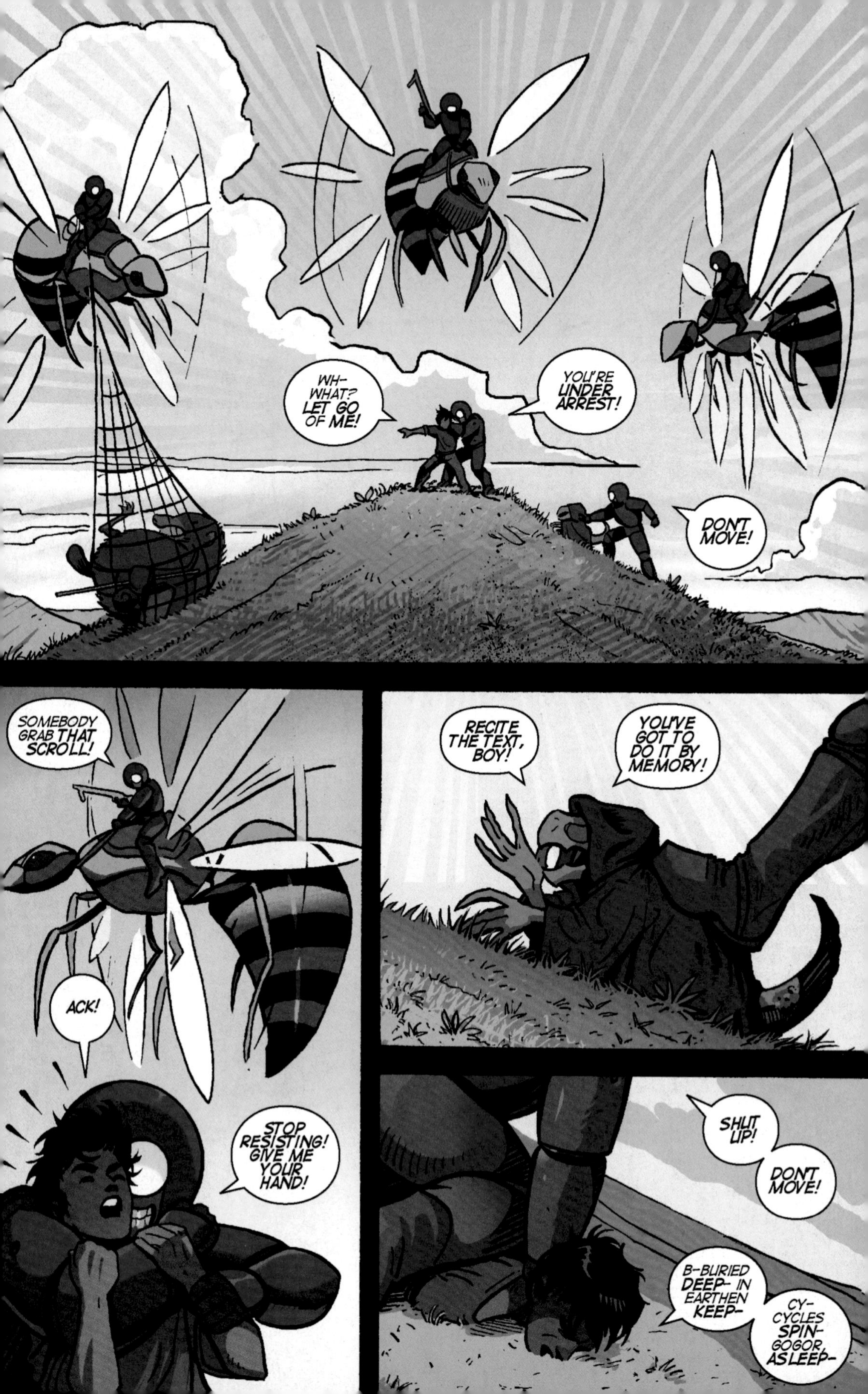
WH-WHAT? LET GO OF ME!
YOU'RE UNDER ARREST!
DONT MOVE!
SOMEBODY GRAB THAT SCROLL!
ACK!
STOP RESISTING! GIVE ME YOUR HAND!
RECITE THE TEXT, BOY!
YOU'VE GOT TO DO IT BY MEMORY!
SHUT UP!
DONT MOVE!
B-BURIED DEEP- IN EARTHEN KEEP-
CY-CYCLES SPIN-GOGOR, ASLEEP-

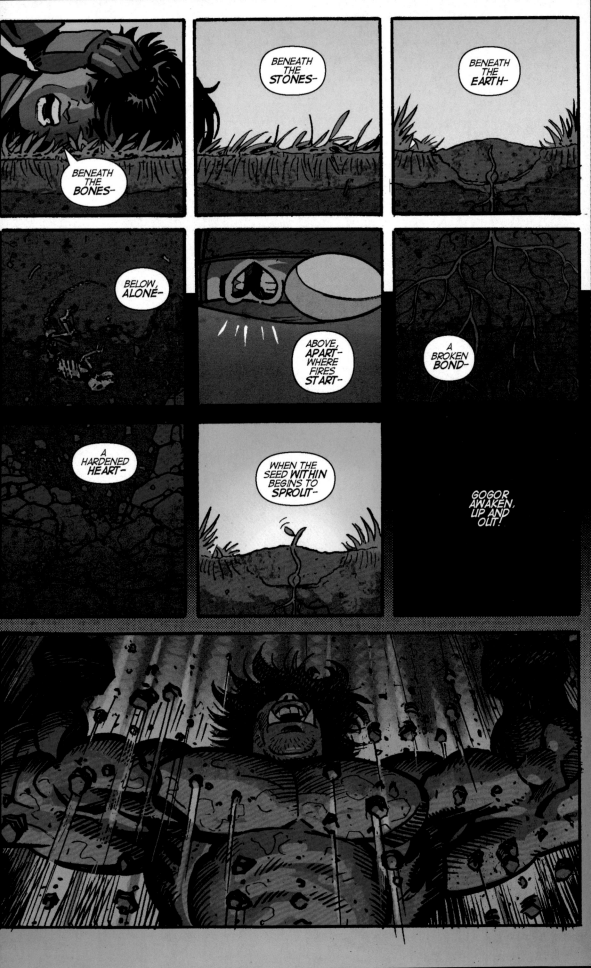

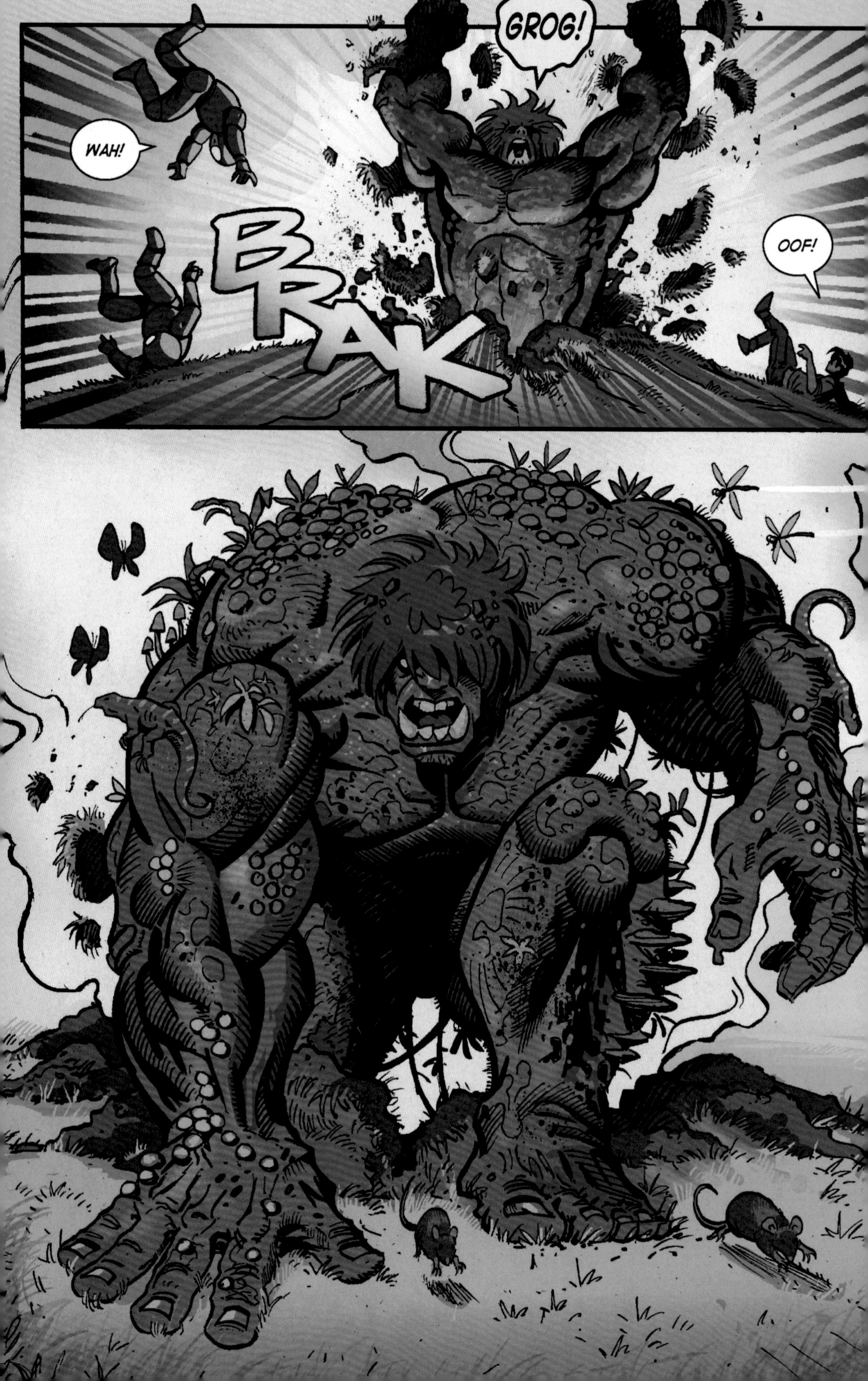
GROG!
WAH!
BRAK
OOF!

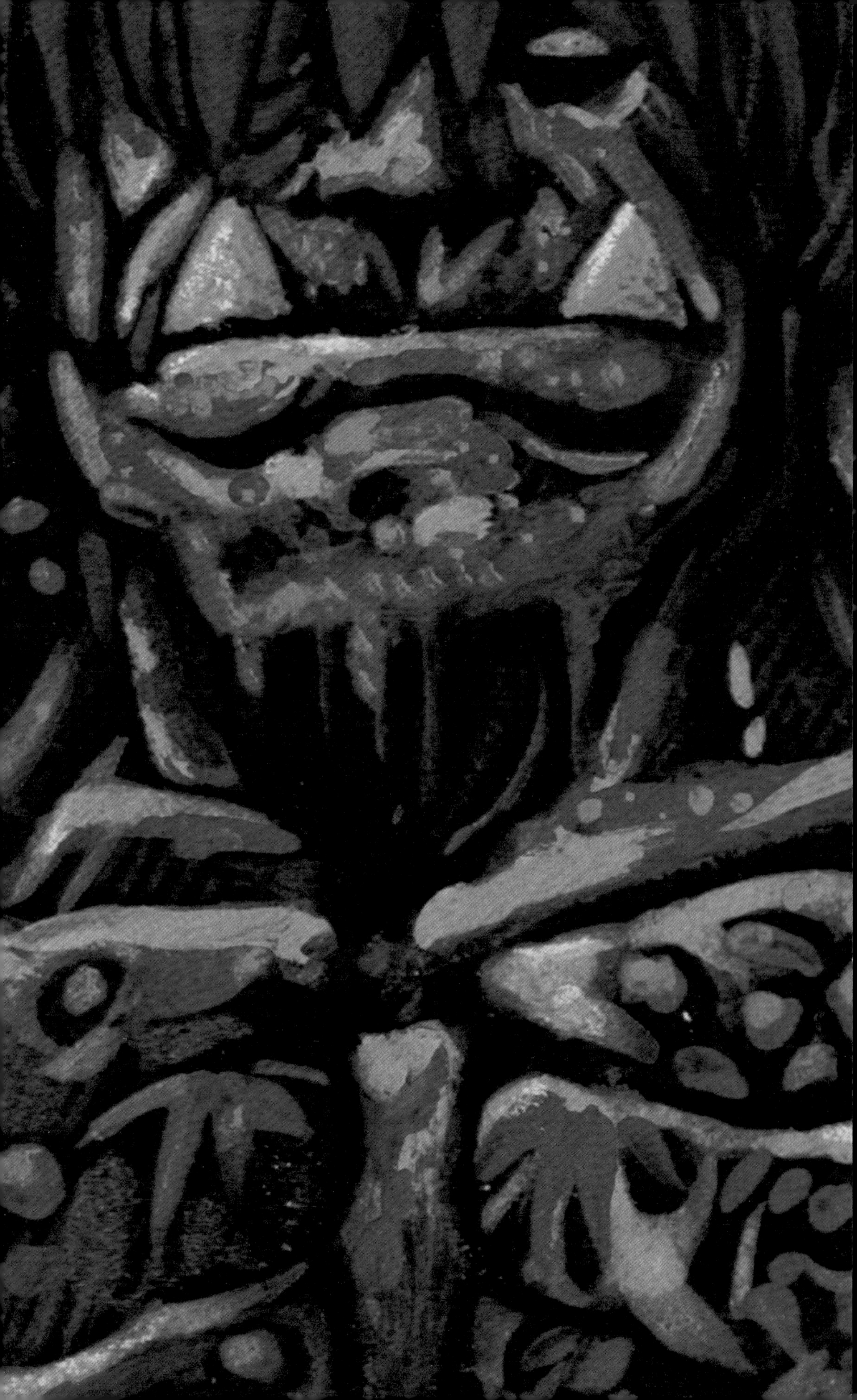

CHAPTER TWO

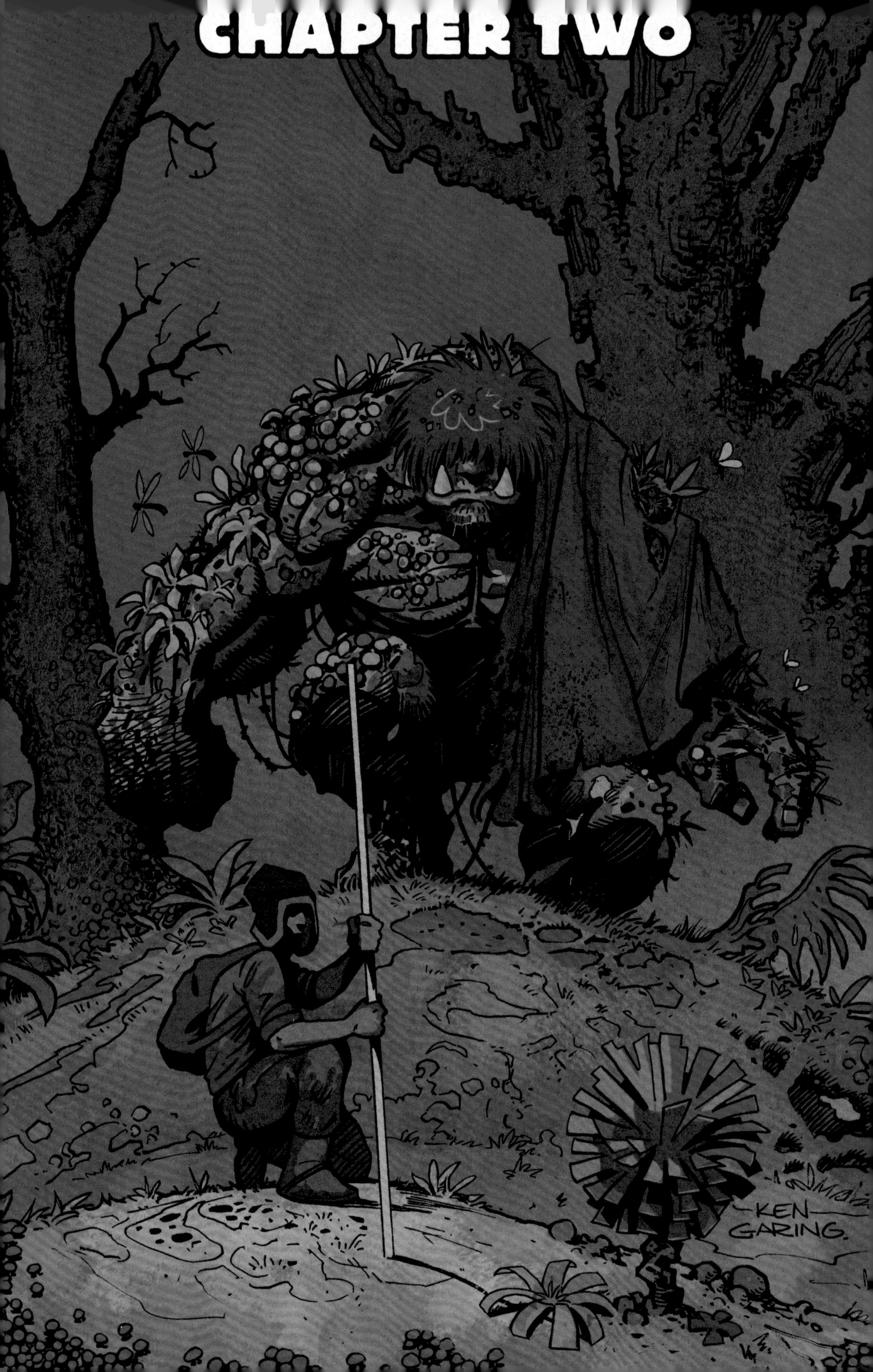

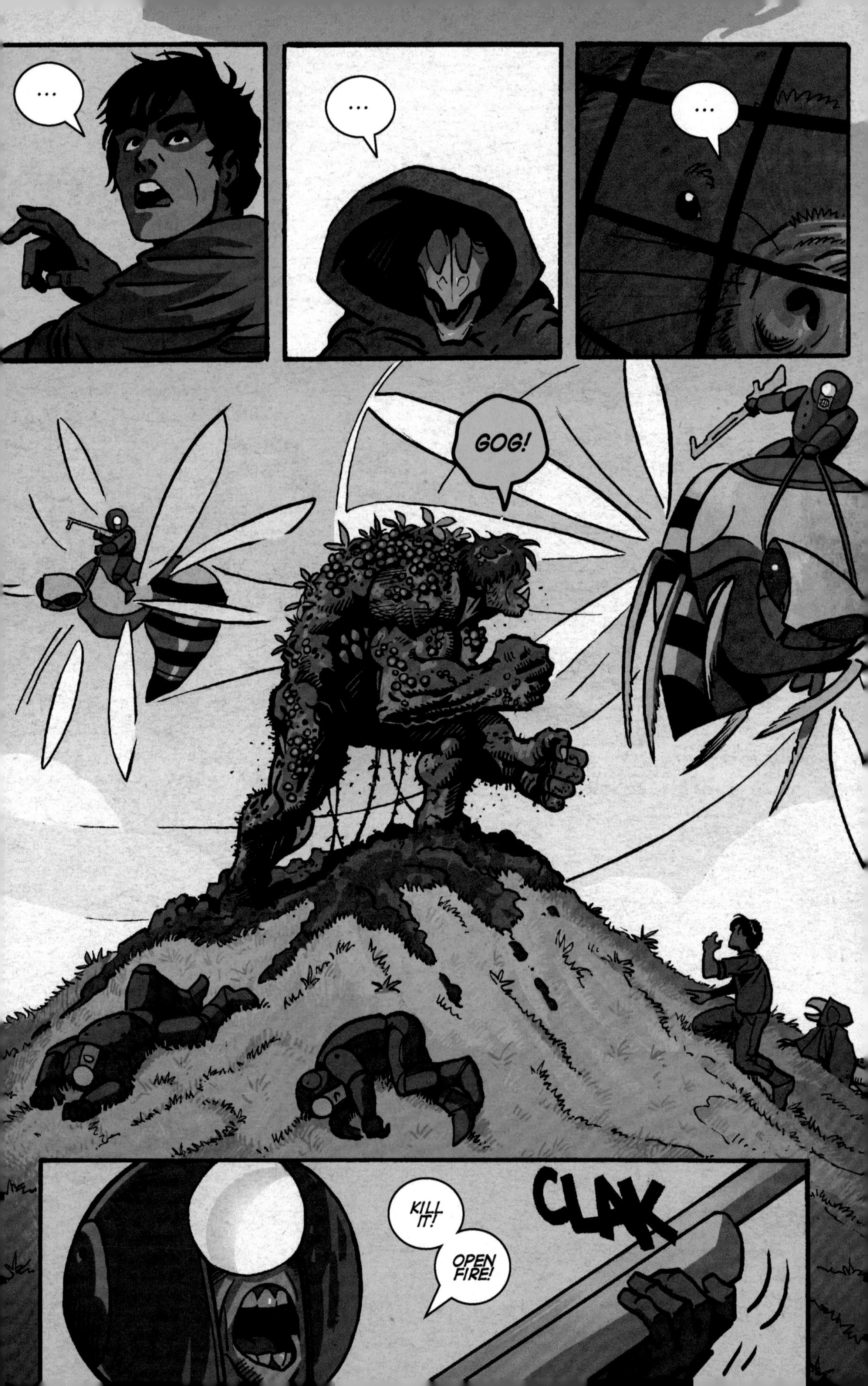
...
...
...
GOG!
KILL IT!
OPEN FIRE!
CLAK

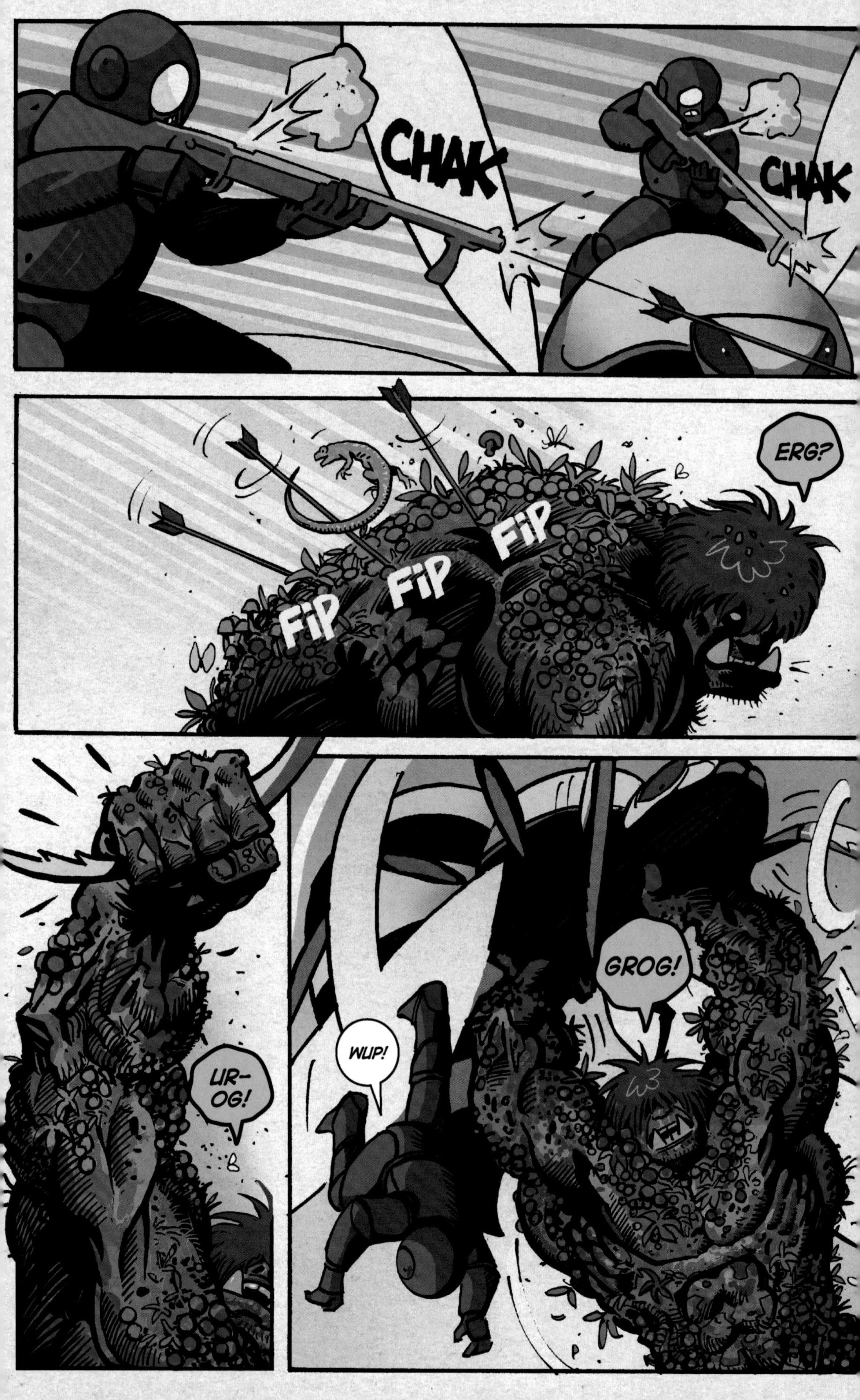
CHAK
CHAK
ERG?
FIP
FIP
FIP
UR-OG!
WUP!
GROG!

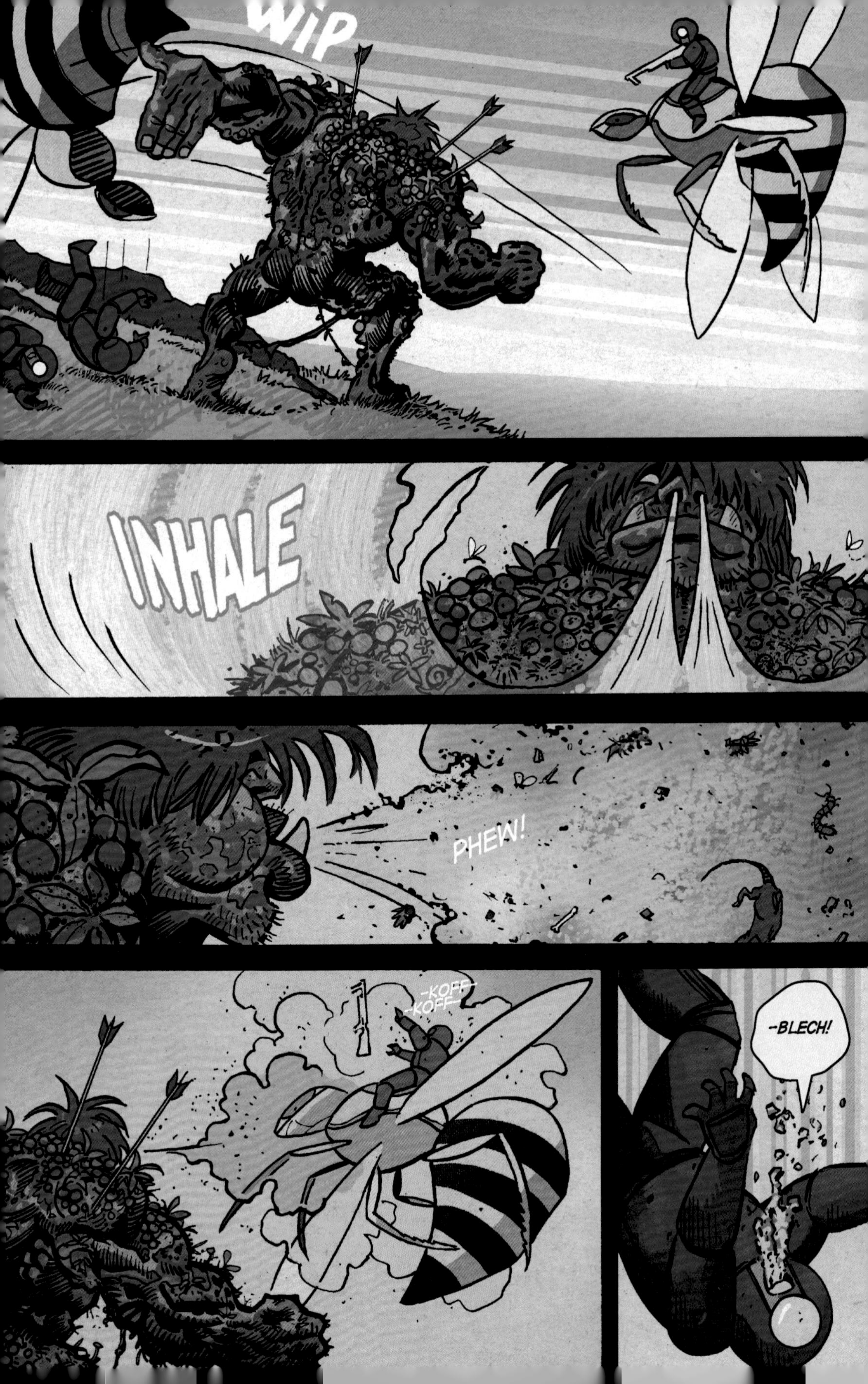
WIP
INHALE
PHEW!
-KOFF-
-KOFF-
-BLECH!

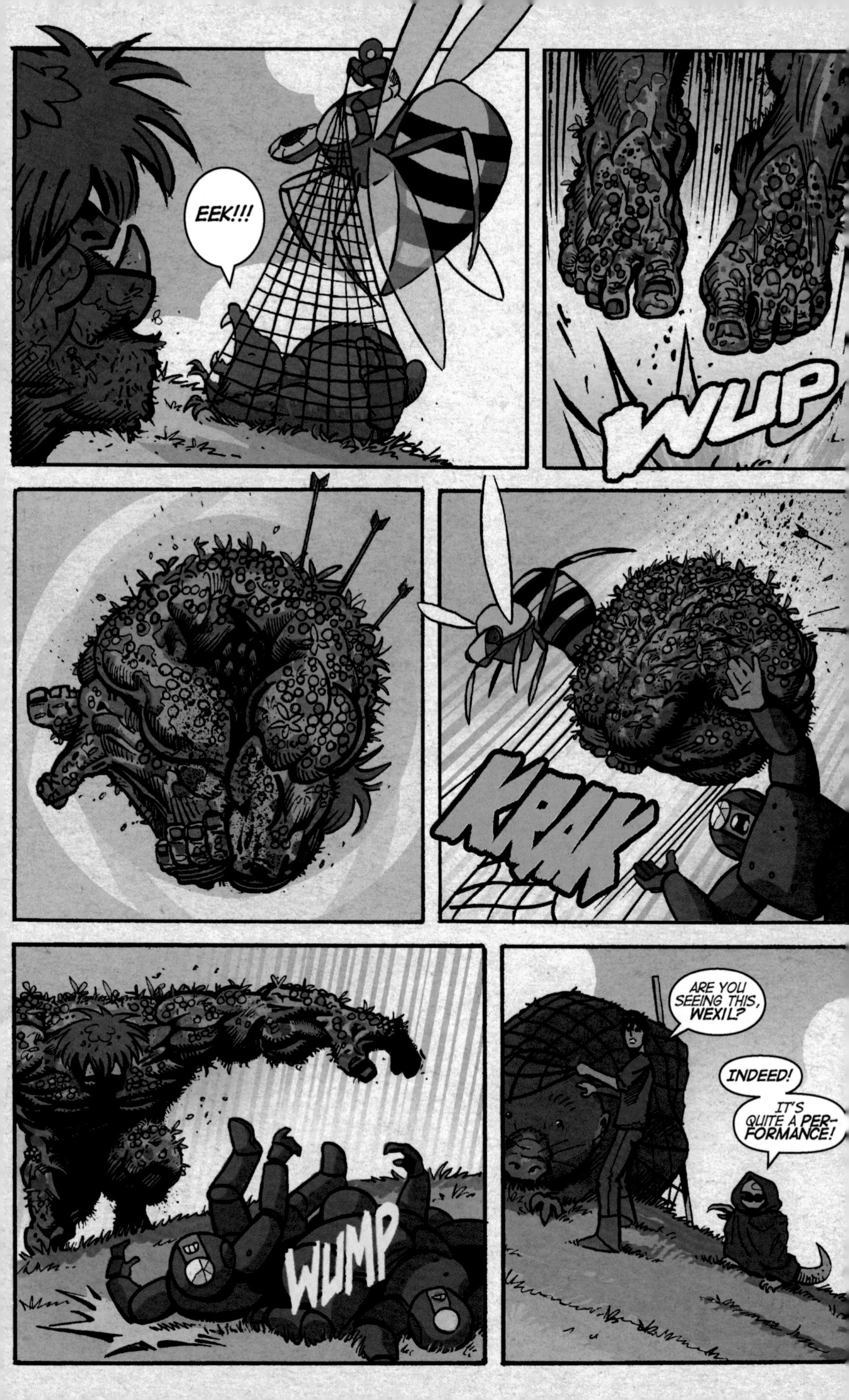
EEK!!!
WUP
KRAK
WUMP
ARE YOU SEEING THIS, WEXIL?
INDEED!
IT'S QUITE A PER-FORMANCE!

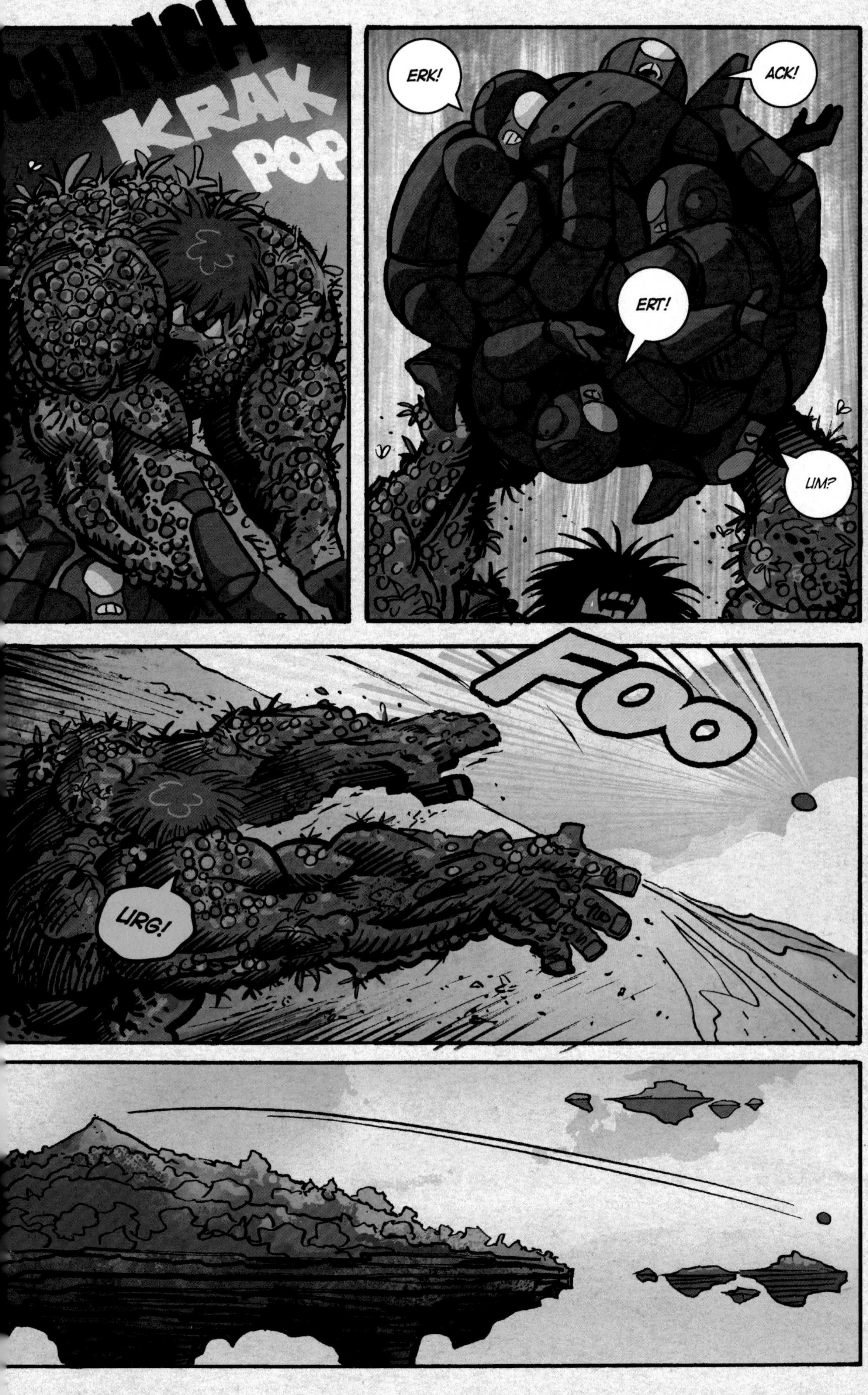
CRUNCH
KRAK
POP
ERK!
ACK!
ERT!
UM?
FOO
URG!

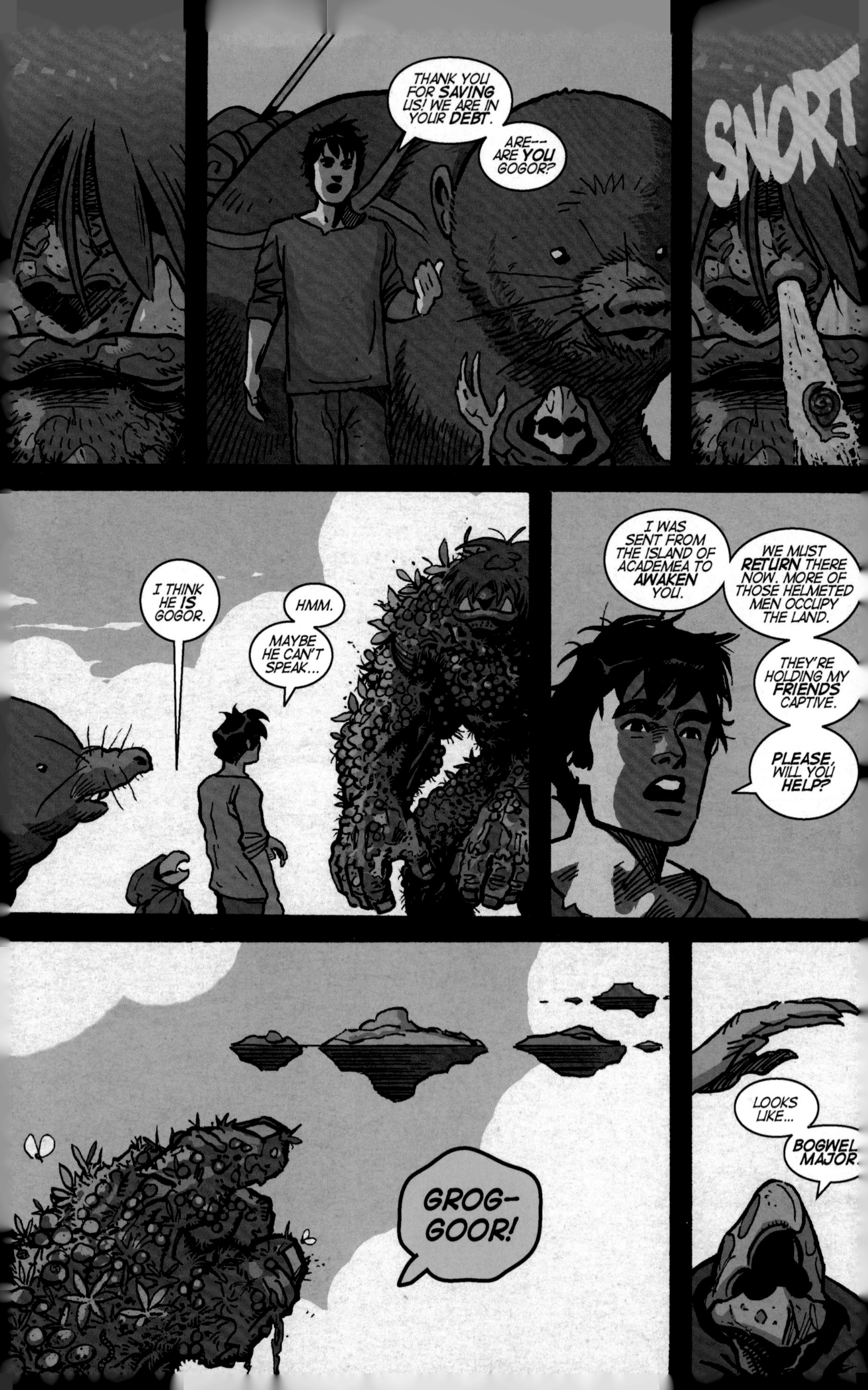
THANK YOU FOR SAVING US! WE ARE IN YOUR DEBT.
ARE-- ARE YOU GOGOR?
SNORT
I THINK HE IS GOGOR.
HMM.
MAYBE HE CAN'T SPEAK...
I WAS SENT FROM THE ISLAND OF ACADEMEA TO AWAKEN YOU.
WE MUST RETURN THERE NOW. MORE OF THOSE HELMETED MEN OCCUPY THE LAND.
THEY'RE HOLDING MY FRIENDS CAPTIVE.
PLEASE, WILL YOU HELP?
GROG-GOOR!
LOOKS LIKE...
BOGWEL MAJOR.

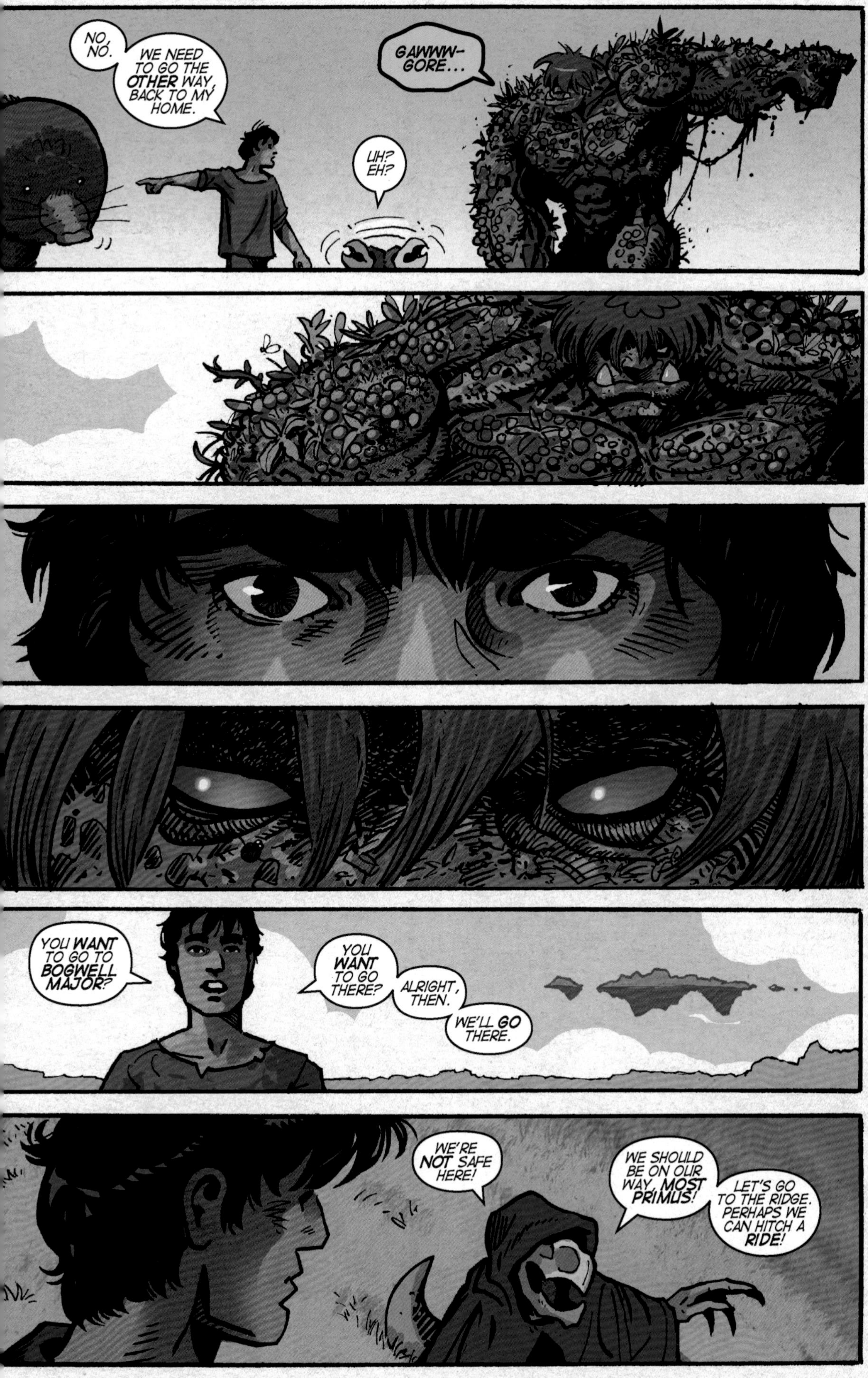
NO, NO.
WE NEED TO GO THE OTHER WAY, BACK TO MY HOME.
UH? EH?
GAWWW-GORE...
YOU WANT TO GO TO BOGWELL MAJOR?
YOU WANT TO GO THERE?
ALRIGHT, THEN.
WE'LL GO THERE.
WE'RE NOT SAFE HERE!
WE SHOULD BE ON OUR WAY, MOST PRIMUS!
LET'S GO TO THE RIDGE. PERHAPS WE CAN HITCH A RIDE!

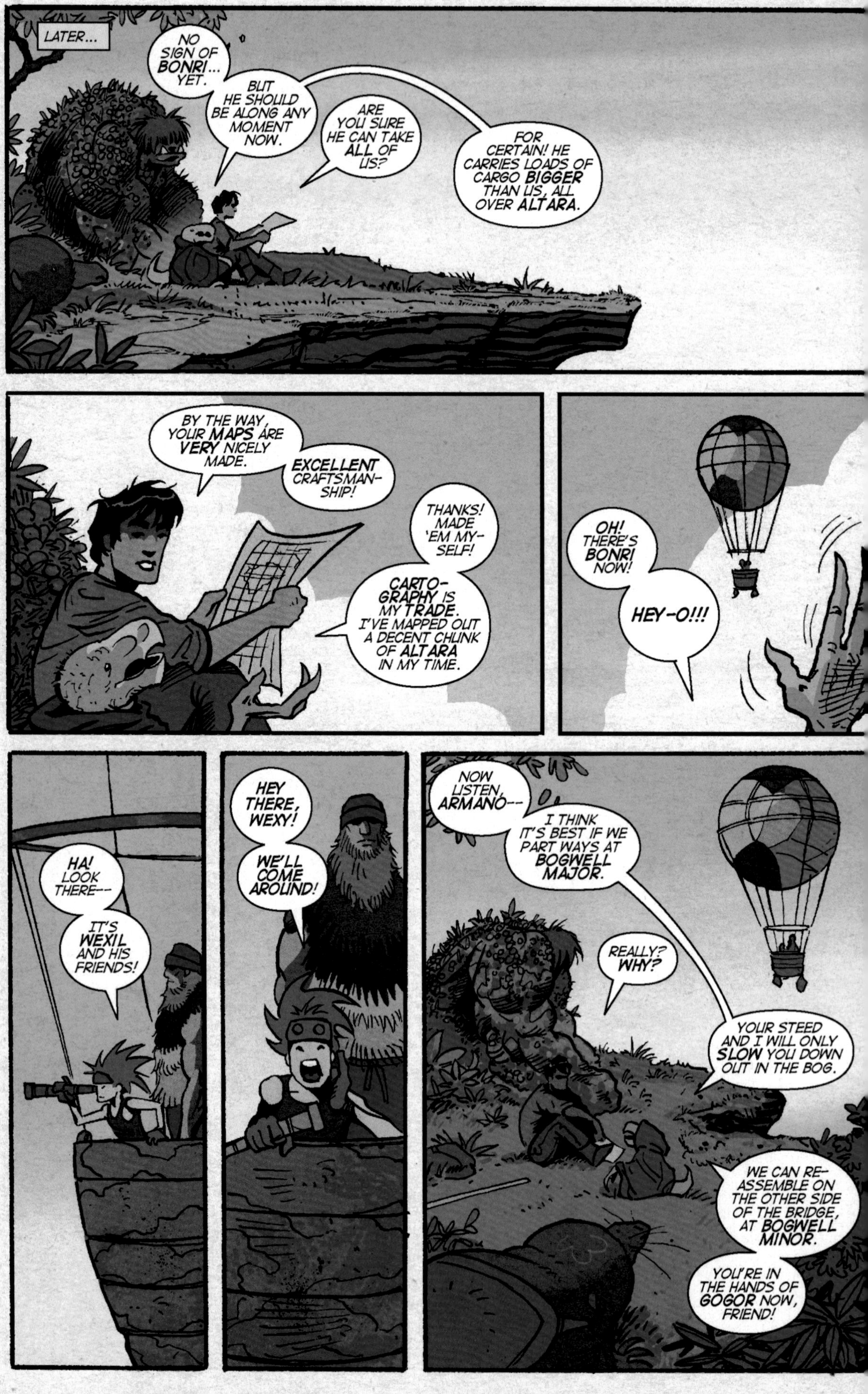
LATER...
NO SIGN OF BONRI... YET.
BUT HE SHOULD BE ALONG ANY MOMENT NOW.
ARE YOU SURE HE CAN TAKE ALL OF US?
FOR CERTAIN! HE CARRIES LOADS OF CARGO BIGGER THAN US, ALL OVER ALTARA.
BY THE WAY, YOUR MAPS ARE VERY NICELY MADE.
EXCELLENT CRAFTSMANSHIP!
THANKS! MADE 'EM MYSELF!
CARTOGRAPHY IS MY TRADE. I'VE MAPPED OUT A DECENT CHUNK OF ALTARA IN MY TIME.
OH! THERE'S BONRI NOW!
HEY-O!!!
HA! LOOK THERE--
IT'S WEXIL AND HIS FRIENDS!
HEY THERE, WEXY!
WE'LL COME AROUND!
NOW LISTEN, ARMANO--
I THINK IT'S BEST IF WE PART WAYS AT BOGWELL MAJOR.
REALLY? WHY?
YOUR STEED AND I WILL ONLY SLOW YOU DOWN OUT IN THE BOG.
WE CAN REASSEMBLE ON THE OTHER SIDE OF THE BRIDGE, AT BOGWELL MINOR.
YOU'RE IN THE HANDS OF GOGOR NOW, FRIEND!

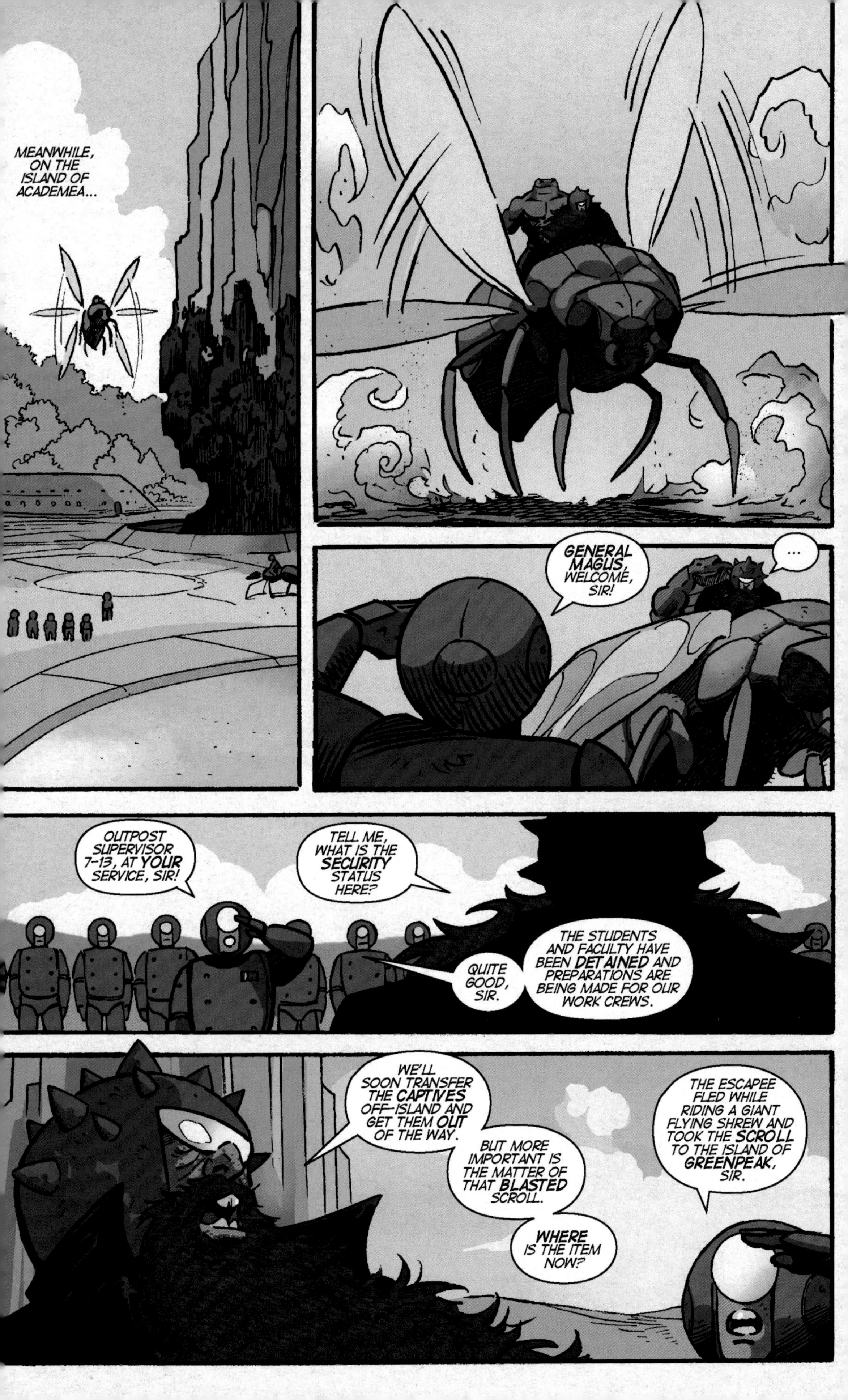
MEANWHILE, ON THE ISLAND OF ACADEMEA...
GENERAL MAGUS, WELCOME, SIR!
...
OUTPOST SUPERVISOR 7-13, AT YOUR SERVICE, SIR!
TELL ME, WHAT IS THE SECURITY STATUS HERE?
QUITE GOOD, SIR.
THE STUDENTS AND FACULTY HAVE BEEN DETAINED AND PREPARATIONS ARE BEING MADE FOR OUR WORK CREWS.
WE'LL SOON TRANSFER THE CAPTIVES OFF-ISLAND AND GET THEM OUT OF THE WAY.
BUT MORE IMPORTANT IS THE MATTER OF THAT BLASTED SCROLL.
WHERE IS THE ITEM NOW?
THE ESCAPEE FLED WHILE RIDING A GIANT FLYING SHREW AND TOOK THE SCROLL TO THE ISLAND OF GREENPEAK, SIR.

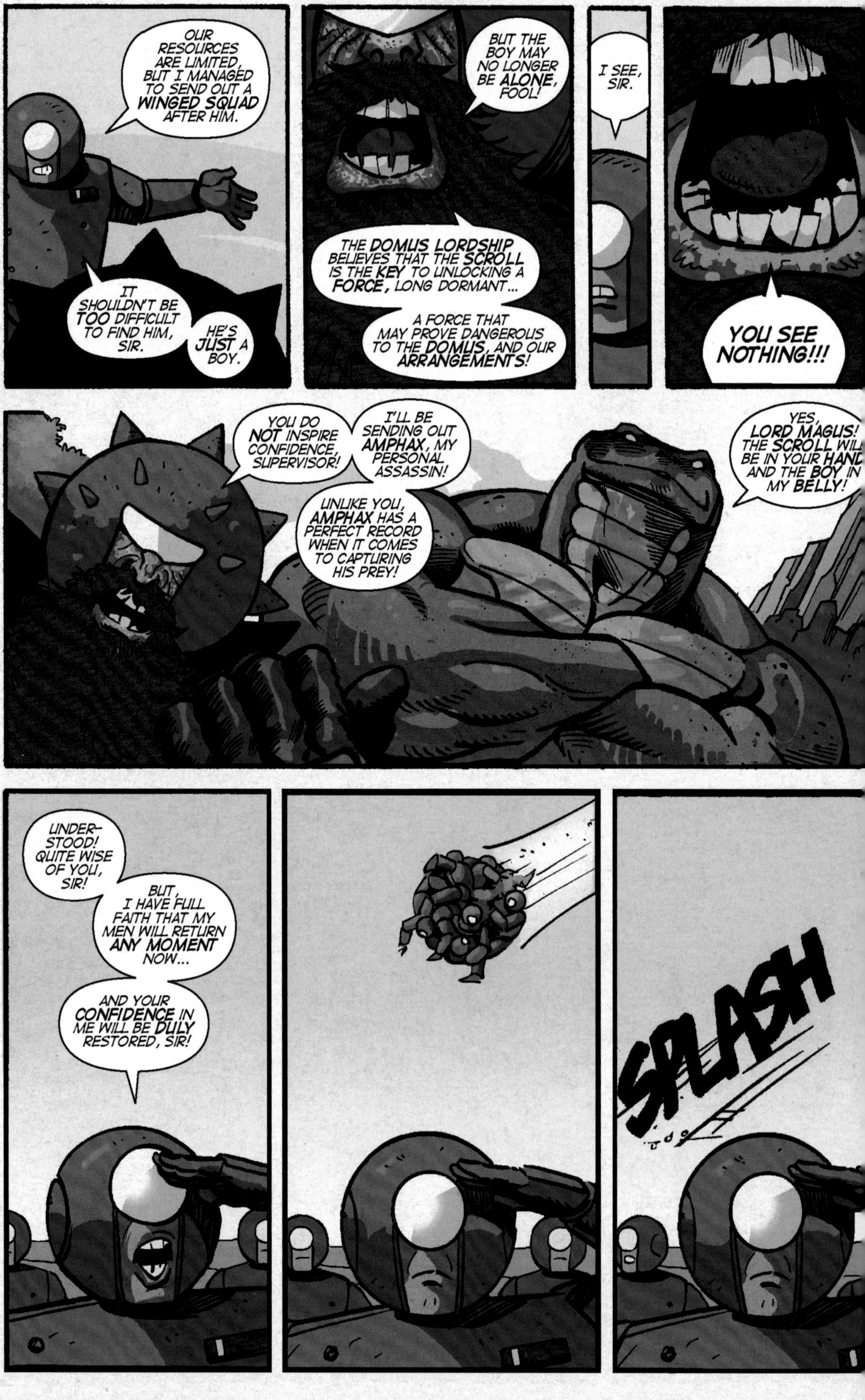
OUR RESOURCES ARE LIMITED, BUT I MANAGED TO SEND OUT A WINGED SQUAD AFTER HIM.
IT SHOULDN'T BE TOO DIFFICULT TO FIND HIM, SIR.
HE'S JUST A BOY.
BUT THE BOY MAY NO LONGER BE ALONE, FOOL!
THE DOMUS LORDSHIP BELIEVES THAT THE SCROLL IS THE KEY TO UNLOCKING A FORCE, LONG DORMANT...
A FORCE THAT MAY PROVE DANGEROUS TO THE DOMUS, AND OUR ARRANGEMENTS!
I SEE, SIR.
YOU SEE NOTHING!!!
YOU DO NOT INSPIRE CONFIDENCE, SUPERVISOR!
I'LL BE SENDING OUT AMPHAX, MY PERSONAL ASSASSIN!
UNLIKE YOU, AMPHAX HAS A PERFECT RECORD WHEN IT COMES TO CAPTURING HIS PREY!
YES, LORD MAGUS! THE SCROLL WILL BE IN YOUR HAND AND THE BOY IN MY BELLY!
UNDER-STOOD! QUITE WISE OF YOU, SIR!
BUT, I HAVE FULL FAITH THAT MY MEN WILL RETURN ANY MOMENT NOW...
AND YOUR CONFIDENCE IN ME WILL BE DULY RESTORED, SIR!
SPLASH

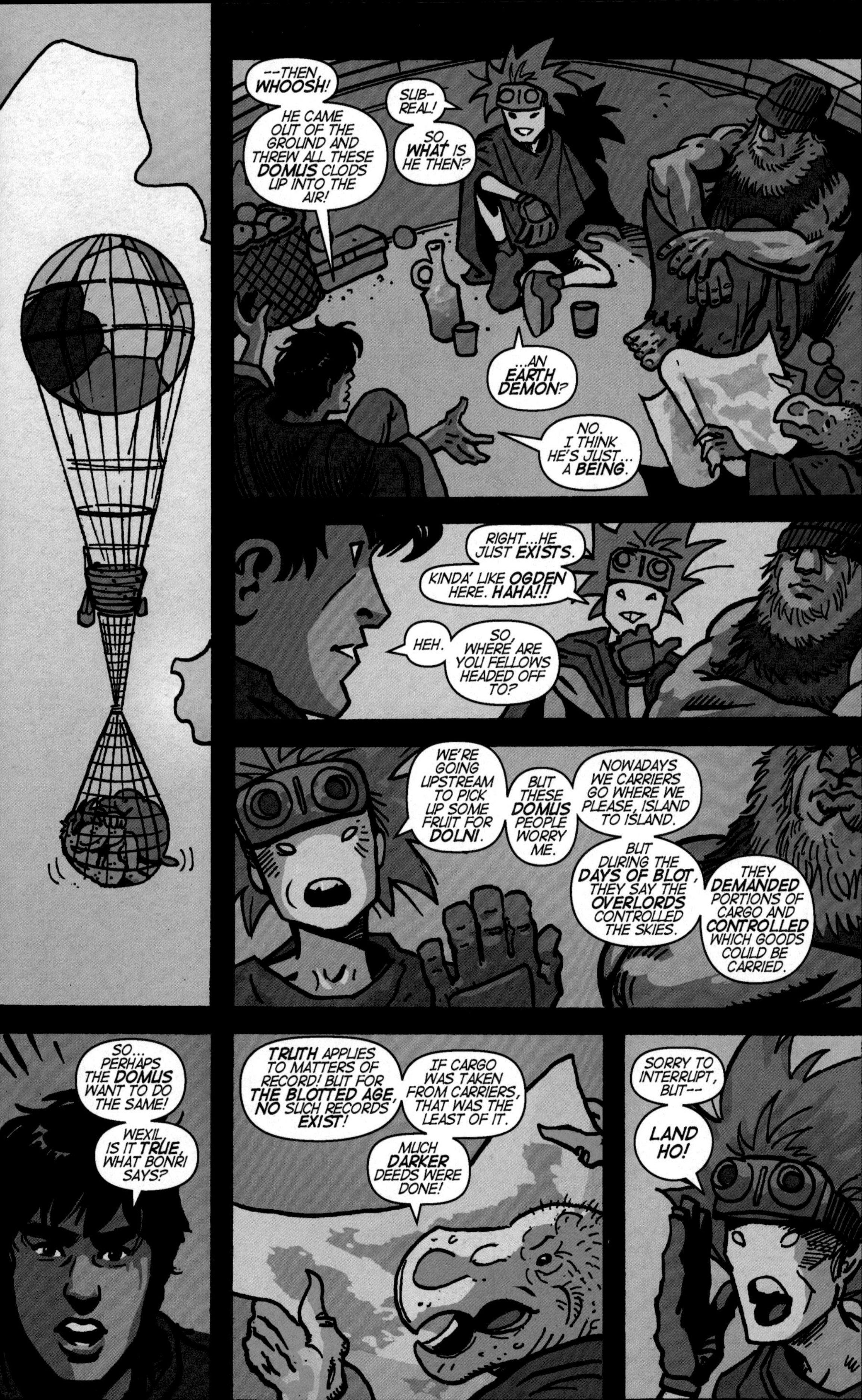
--THEN, WHOOSH!
HE CAME OUT OF THE GROUND AND THREW ALL THESE DOMUS CLODS UP INTO THE AIR!
SUB-REAL!
SO, WHAT IS HE THEN?
...AN EARTH DEMON?
NO. I THINK HE'S JUST... A BEING.
RIGHT...HE JUST EXISTS.
KINDA' LIKE OGDEN HERE. HAHA!!!
HEH.
SO, WHERE ARE YOU FELLOWS HEADED OFF TO?
WE'RE GOING UPSTREAM TO PICK UP SOME FRUIT FOR DOLNI.
BUT THESE DOMUS PEOPLE WORRY ME.
NOWADAYS WE CARRIERS GO WHERE WE PLEASE, ISLAND TO ISLAND.
BUT DURING THE DAYS OF BLOT, THEY SAY THE OVERLORDS CONTROLLED THE SKIES.
THEY DEMANDED PORTIONS OF CARGO AND CONTROLLED WHICH GOODS COULD BE CARRIED.
SO... PERHAPS THE DOMUS WANT TO DO THE SAME!
WEXIL, IS IT TRUE, WHAT BONRI SAYS?
TRUTH APPLIES TO MATTERS OF RECORD! BUT FOR THE BLOTTED AGE, NO SUCH RECORDS EXIST!
IF CARGO WAS TAKEN FROM CARRIERS, THAT WAS THE LEAST OF IT.
MUCH DARKER DEEDS WERE DONE!
SORRY TO INTERRUPT, BUT--
LAND HO!

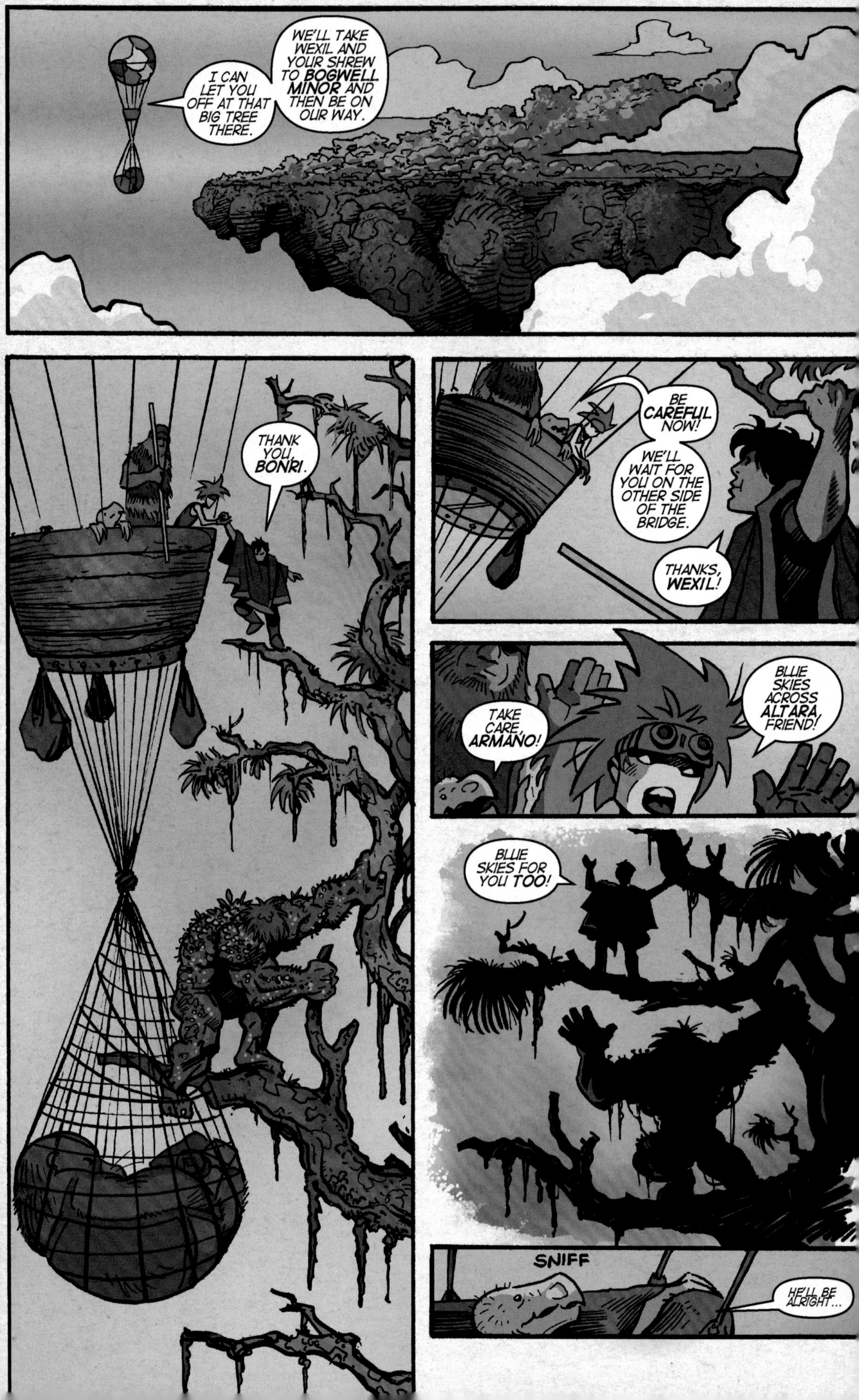
I CAN LET YOU OFF AT THAT BIG TREE THERE.
WE'LL TAKE WEXIL AND YOUR SHREW TO BOGWELL MINOR AND THEN BE ON OUR WAY.
THANK YOU, BONRI.
BE CAREFUL NOW!
WE'LL WAIT FOR YOU ON THE OTHER SIDE OF THE BRIDGE.
THANKS, WEXIL!
TAKE CARE, ARMANO!
BLUE SKIES ACROSS ALTARA, FRIEND!
BLUE SKIES FOR YOU TOO!
SNIFF
HE'LL BE ALRIGHT...

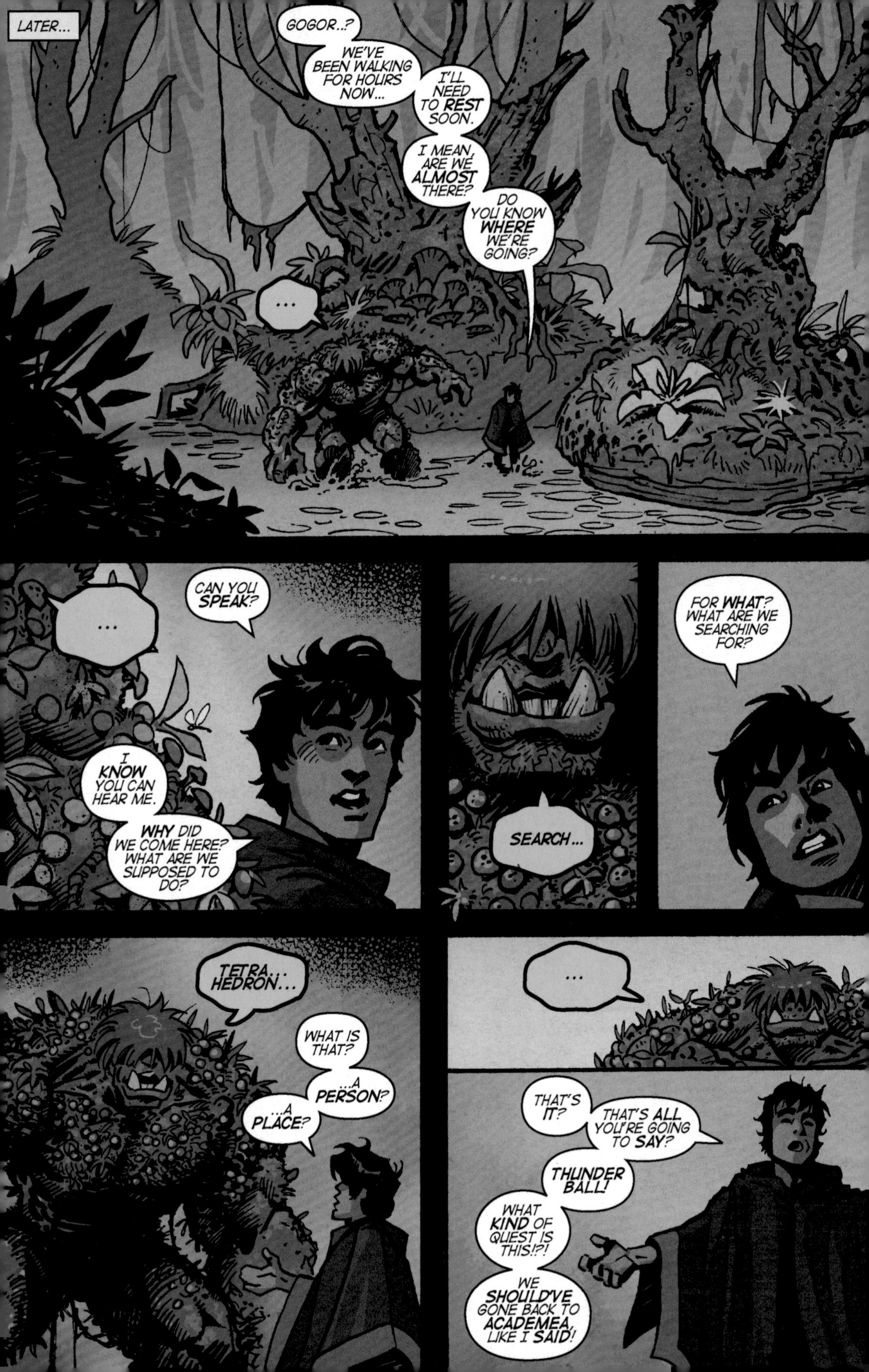
LATER...
GOGOR..?
WE'VE BEEN WALKING FOR HOURS NOW...
I'LL NEED TO REST SOON.
I MEAN, ARE WE ALMOST THERE?
DO YOU KNOW WHERE WE'RE GOING?
...
...
CAN YOU SPEAK?
I KNOW YOU CAN HEAR ME.
WHY DID WE COME HERE? WHAT ARE WE SUPPOSED TO DO?
SEARCH...
FOR WHAT? WHAT ARE WE SEARCHING FOR?
TETRA... HEDRON...
WHAT IS THAT?
...A PERSON?
...A PLACE?
...
THAT'S IT?
THAT'S ALL YOU'RE GOING TO SAY?
THUNDER BALL!
WHAT KIND OF QUEST IS THIS!?!
WE SHOULD'VE GONE BACK TO ACADEMEA, LIKE I SAID!

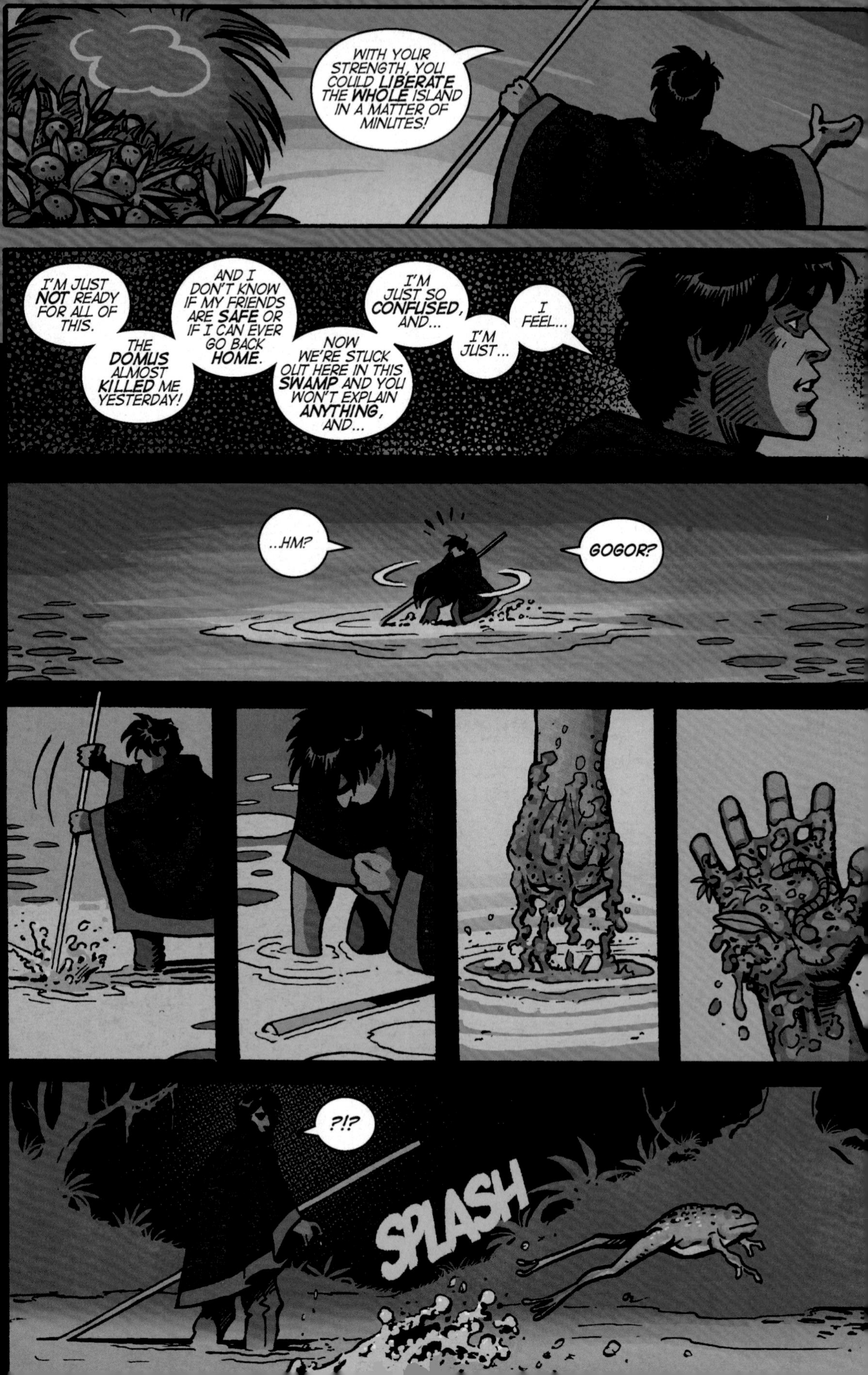
WITH YOUR STRENGTH, YOU COULD LIBERATE THE WHOLE ISLAND IN A MATTER OF MINUTES!
I'M JUST NOT READY FOR ALL OF THIS.
THE DOMUS ALMOST KILLED ME YESTERDAY!
AND I DON'T KNOW IF MY FRIENDS ARE SAFE OR IF I CAN EVER GO BACK HOME.
NOW WE'RE STUCK OUT HERE IN THIS SWAMP AND YOU WON'T EXPLAIN ANYTHING, AND...
I'M JUST SO CONFUSED, AND...
I'M JUST...
I FEEL...
...HM?
GOGOR?
?!?
SPLASH

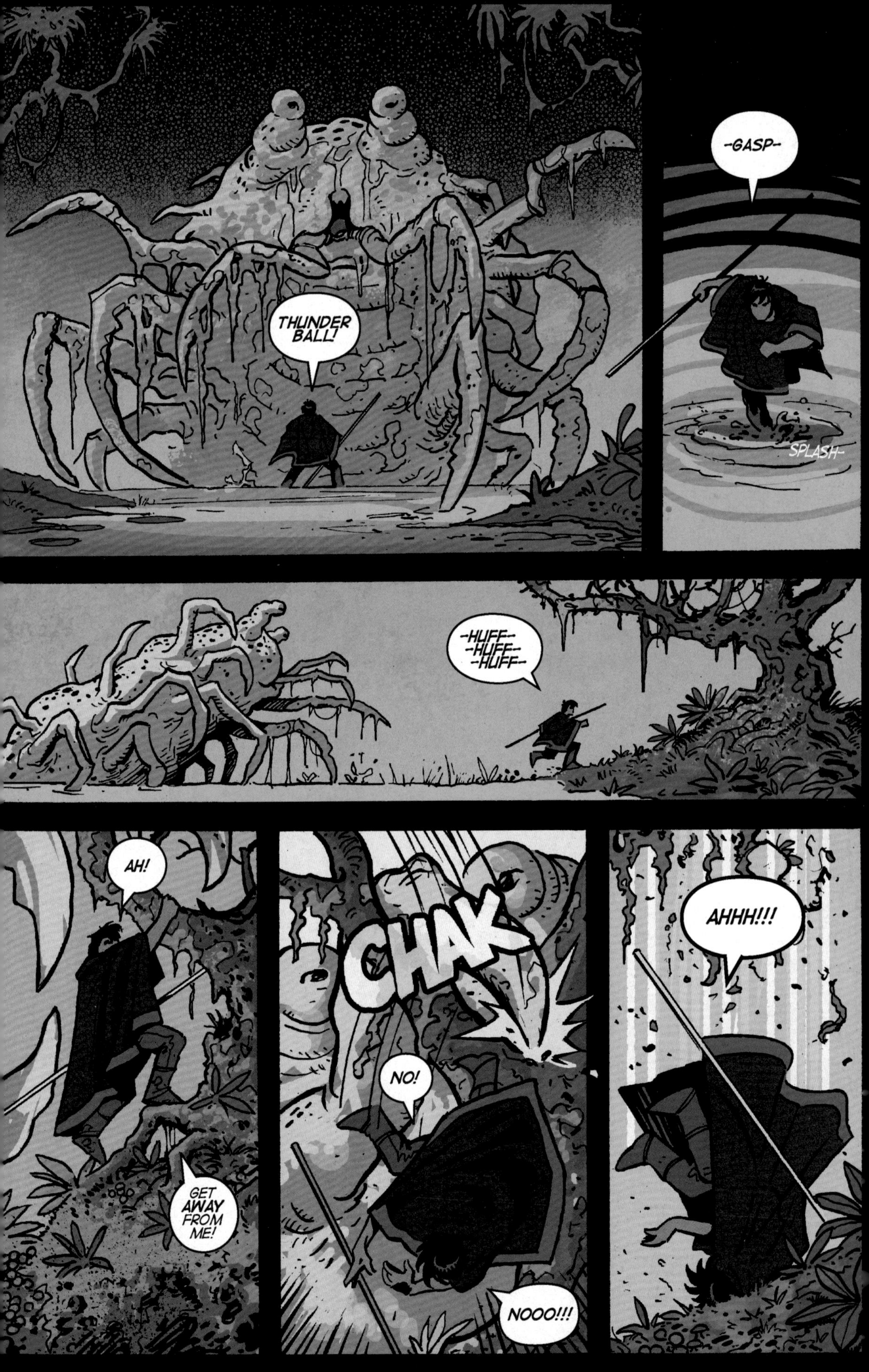
THUNDER BALL!
-GASP-
SPLASH-
-HUFF-
-HUFF-
-HUFF-
AH!
GET AWAY FROM ME!
CHAK
NO!
NOOO!!!
AHHH!!!

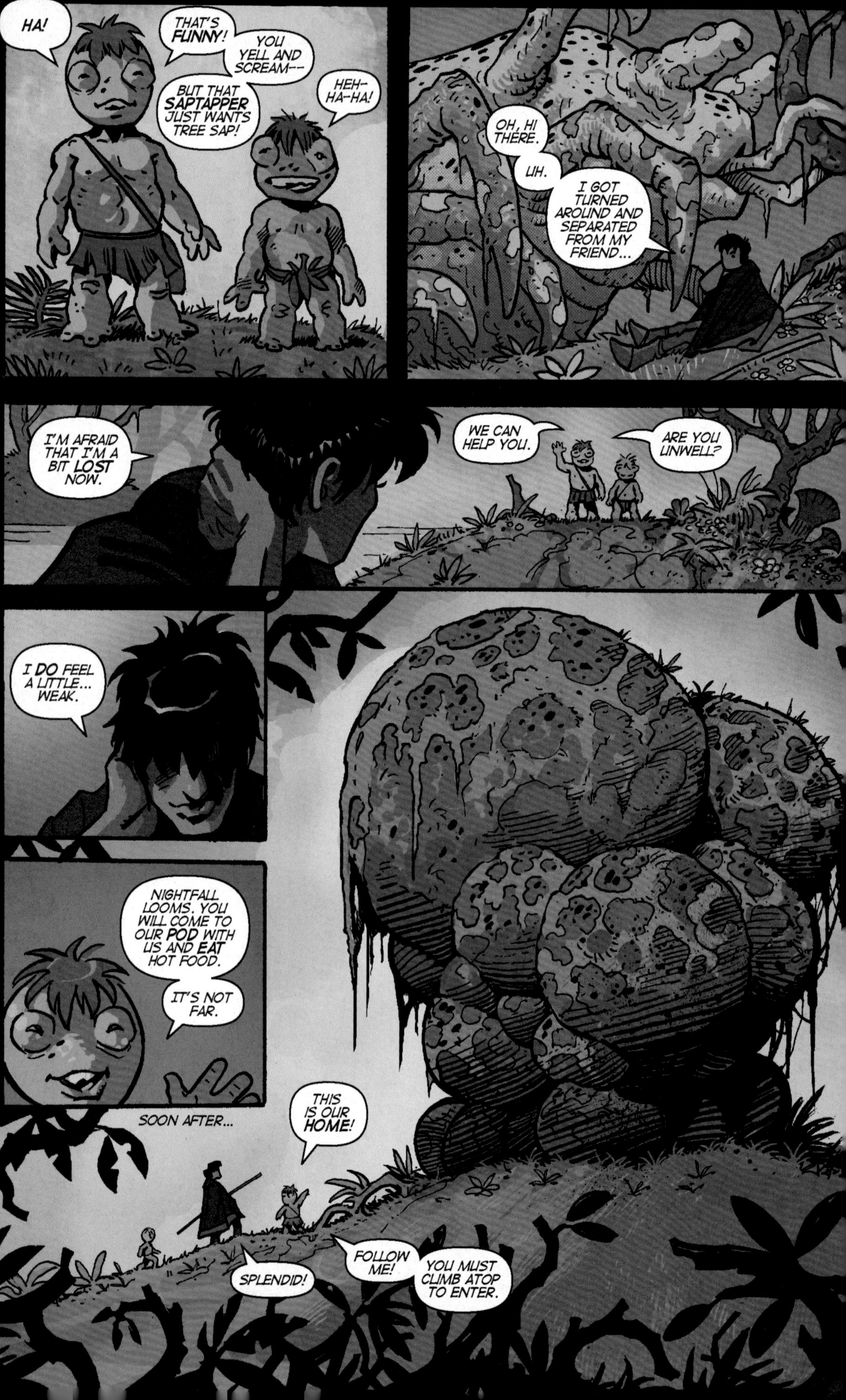
HA!
THAT'S FUNNY!
YOU YELL AND SCREAM--
BUT THAT SAPTAPPER JUST WANTS TREE SAP!
HEH-HA-HA!
OH, HI THERE.
UH.
I GOT TURNED AROUND AND SEPARATED FROM MY FRIEND...
I'M AFRAID THAT I'M A BIT LOST NOW.
WE CAN HELP YOU.
ARE YOU UNWELL?
I DO FEEL A LITTLE... WEAK.
NIGHTFALL LOOMS. YOU WILL COME TO OUR POD WITH US AND EAT HOT FOOD.
IT'S NOT FAR.
SOON AFTER...
THIS IS OUR HOME!
SPLENDID!
FOLLOW ME!
YOU MUST CLIMB ATOP TO ENTER.

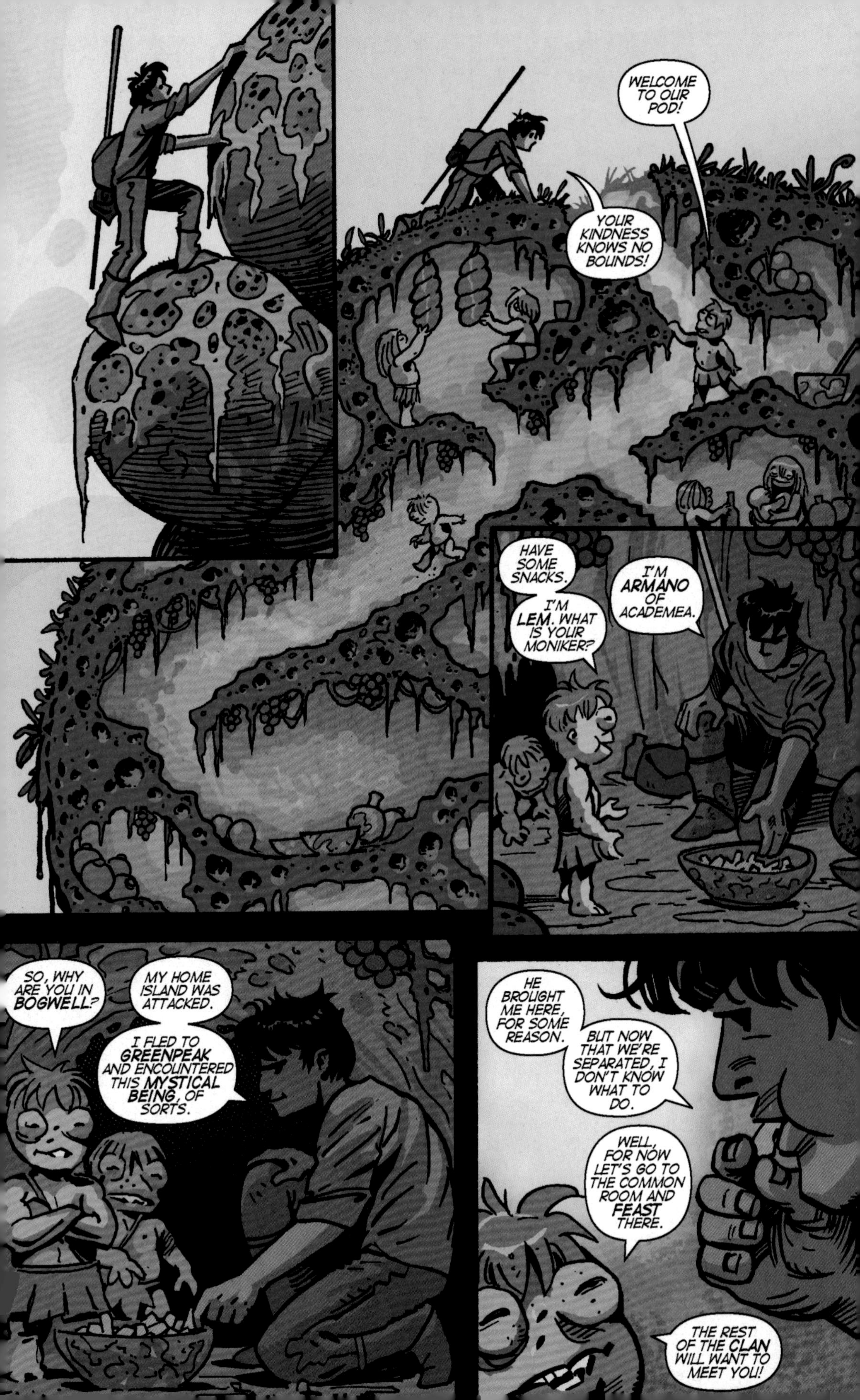
WELCOME TO OUR POD!
YOUR KINDNESS KNOWS NO BOUNDS!
HAVE SOME SNACKS.
I'M LEM. WHAT IS YOUR MONIKER?
I'M ARMANO OF ACADEMEA.
SO, WHY ARE YOU IN BOGWELL?
MY HOME ISLAND WAS ATTACKED.
I FLED TO GREENPEAK AND ENCOUNTERED THIS MYSTICAL BEING, OF SORTS.
HE BROUGHT ME HERE, FOR SOME REASON.
BUT NOW THAT WE'RE SEPARATED, I DON'T KNOW WHAT TO DO.
WELL, FOR NOW LET'S GO TO THE COMMON ROOM AND FEAST THERE.
THE REST OF THE CLAN WILL WANT TO MEET YOU!

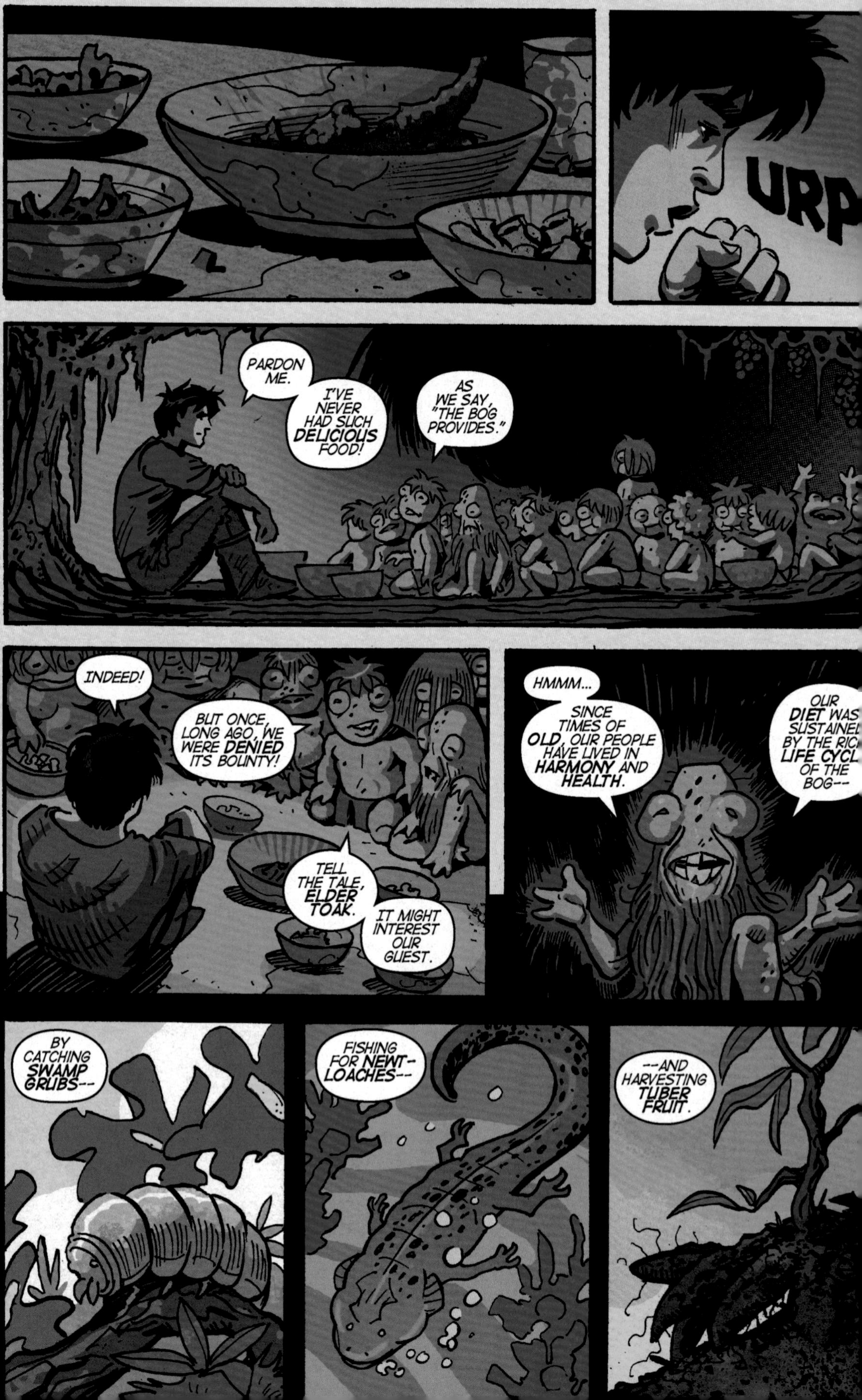
URP
PARDON ME.
I'VE NEVER HAD SUCH DELICIOUS FOOD!
AS WE SAY, "THE BOG PROVIDES."
INDEED!
BUT ONCE, LONG AGO, WE WERE DENIED ITS BOUNTY!
TELL THE TALE, ELDER TOAK.
IT MIGHT INTEREST OUR GUEST.
HMMM...
SINCE TIMES OF OLD, OUR PEOPLE HAVE LIVED IN HARMONY AND HEALTH.
BY CATCHING SWAMP GRUBS--
FISHING FOR NEWT-LOACHES--
--AND HARVESTING TUBER FRUIT.

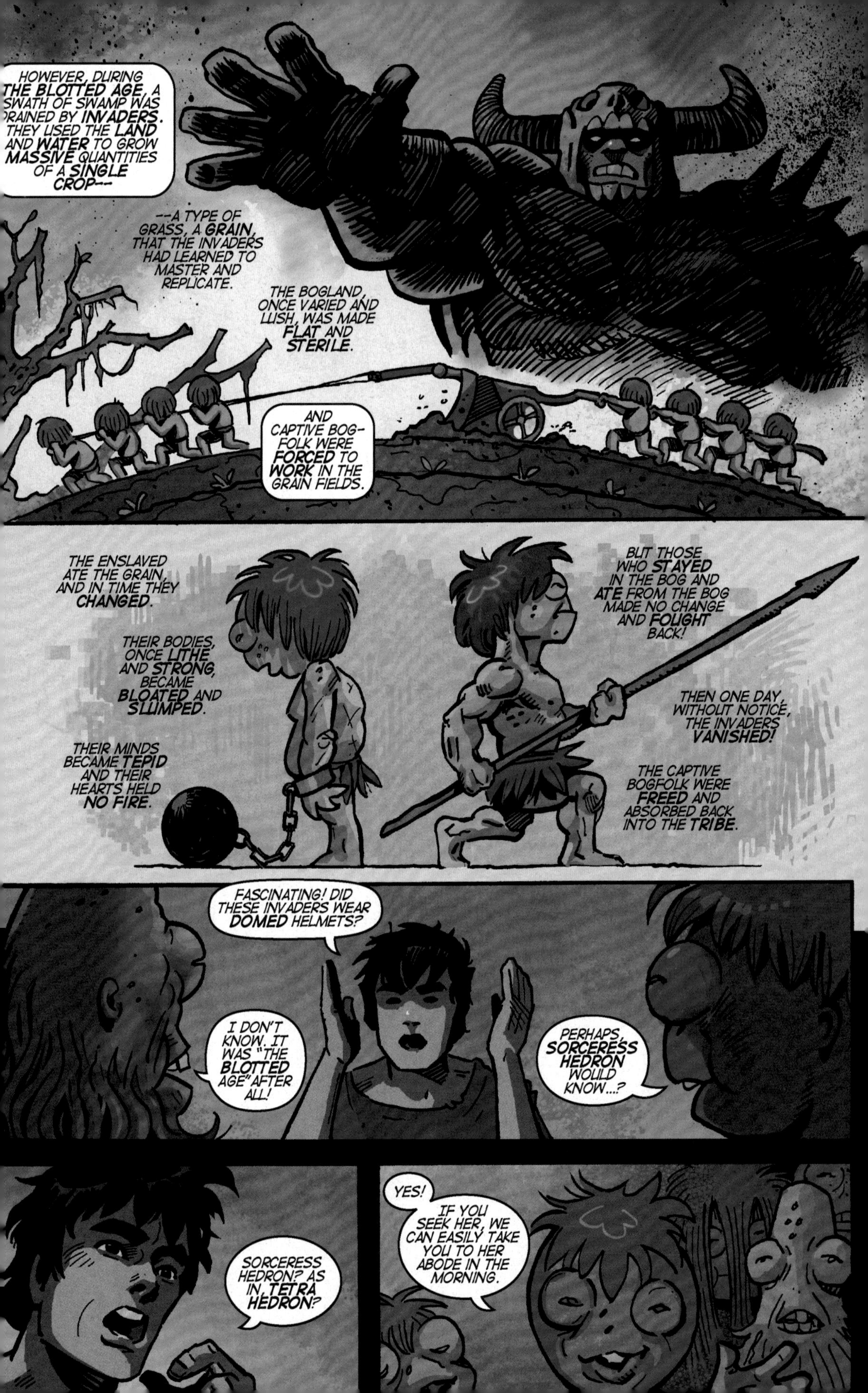
HOWEVER, DURING THE BLOTTED AGE, A SWATH OF SWAMP WAS DRAINED BY INVADERS. THEY USED THE LAND AND WATER TO GROW MASSIVE QUANTITIES OF A SINGLE CROP--
--A TYPE OF GRASS, A GRAIN, THAT THE INVADERS HAD LEARNED TO MASTER AND REPLICATE.
THE BOGLAND, ONCE VARIED AND LUSH, WAS MADE FLAT AND STERILE.
AND CAPTIVE BOG-FOLK WERE FORCED TO WORK IN THE GRAIN FIELDS.
THE ENSLAVED ATE THE GRAIN, AND IN TIME THEY CHANGED.
THEIR BODIES, ONCE LITHE AND STRONG, BECAME BLOATED AND SLUMPED.
THEIR MINDS BECAME TEPID AND THEIR HEARTS HELD NO FIRE.
BUT THOSE WHO STAYED IN THE BOG AND ATE FROM THE BOG MADE NO CHANGE AND FOUGHT BACK!
THEN ONE DAY, WITHOUT NOTICE, THE INVADERS VANISHED!
THE CAPTIVE BOGFOLK WERE FREED AND ABSORBED BACK INTO THE TRIBE.
FASCINATING! DID THESE INVADERS WEAR DOMED HELMETS?
I DON'T KNOW. IT WAS "THE BLOTTED AGE" AFTER ALL!
PERHAPS, SORCERESS HEDRON WOULD KNOW...?
SORCERESS HEDRON? AS IN, TETRA HEDRON?
YES!
IF YOU SEEK HER, WE CAN EASILY TAKE YOU TO HER ABODE IN THE MORNING.

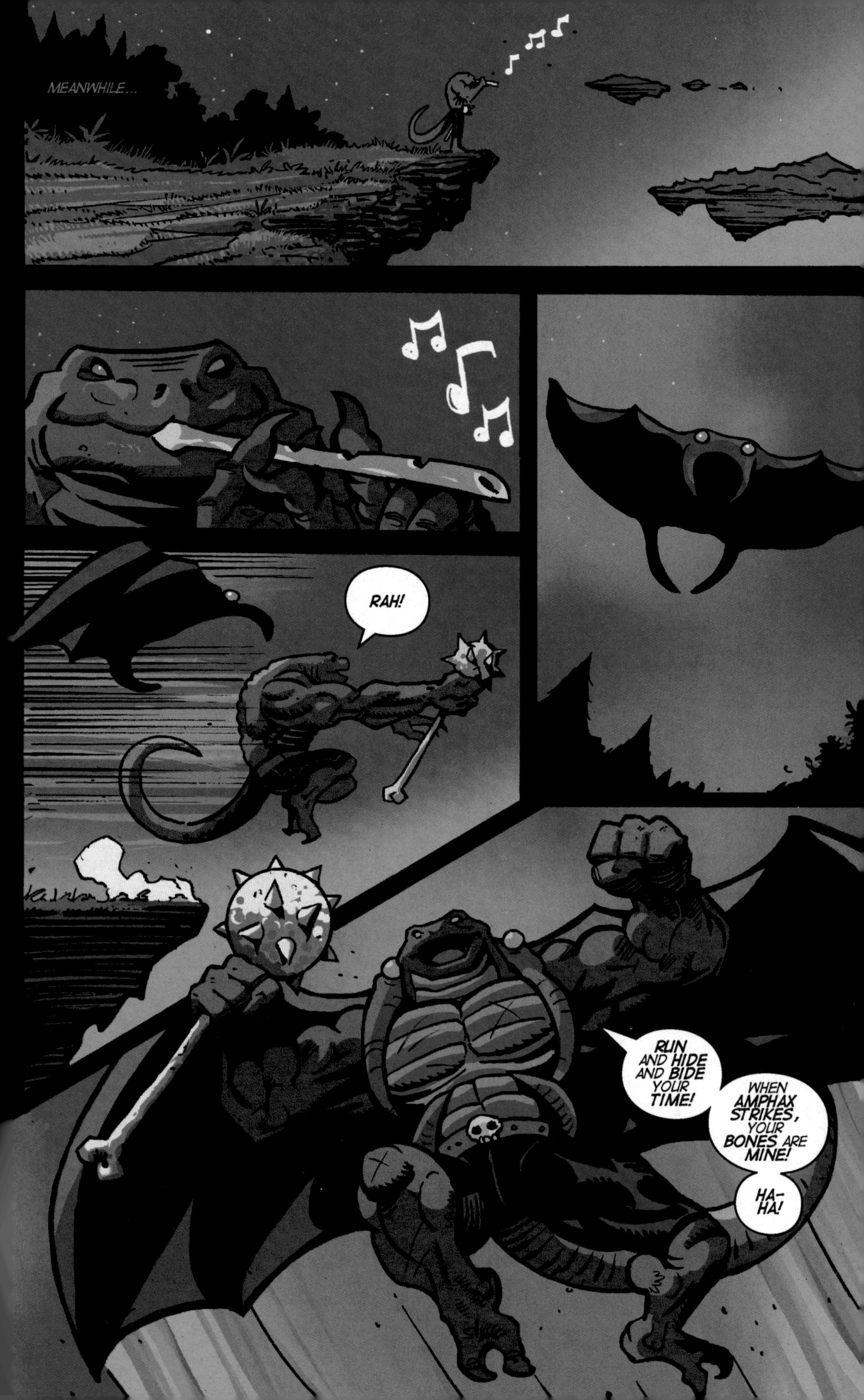
MEANWHILE...
RAH!
RUN AND HIDE AND BIDE YOUR TIME!
WHEN AMPHAX STRIKES, YOUR BONES ARE MINE!
HA-HA!

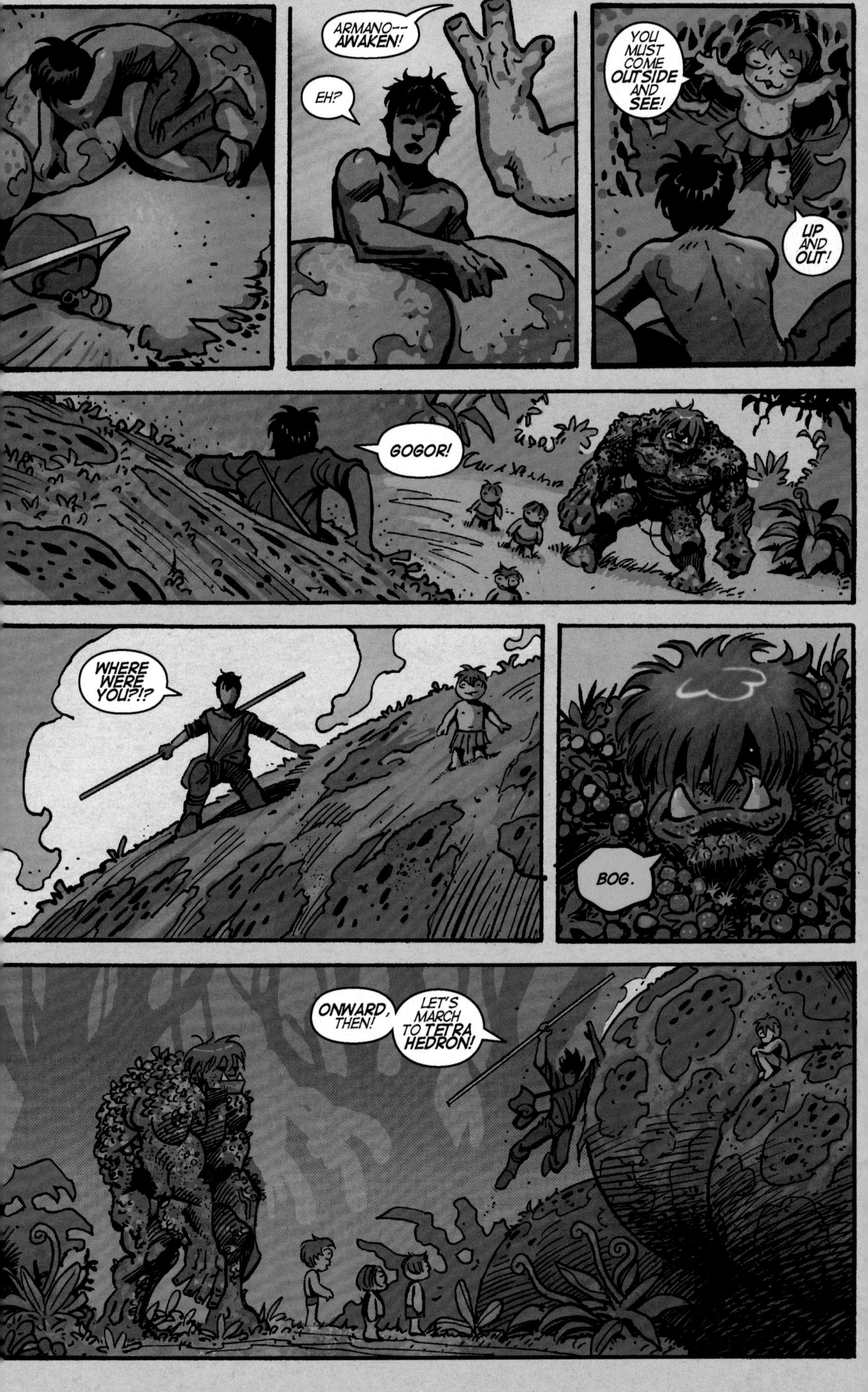
ARMANO-- AWAKEN!
EH?
YOU MUST COME OUTSIDE AND SEE!
UP AND OUT!
GOGOR!
WHERE WERE YOU?!?
BOG.
ONWARD, THEN!
LET'S MARCH TO TETRAHEDRON!

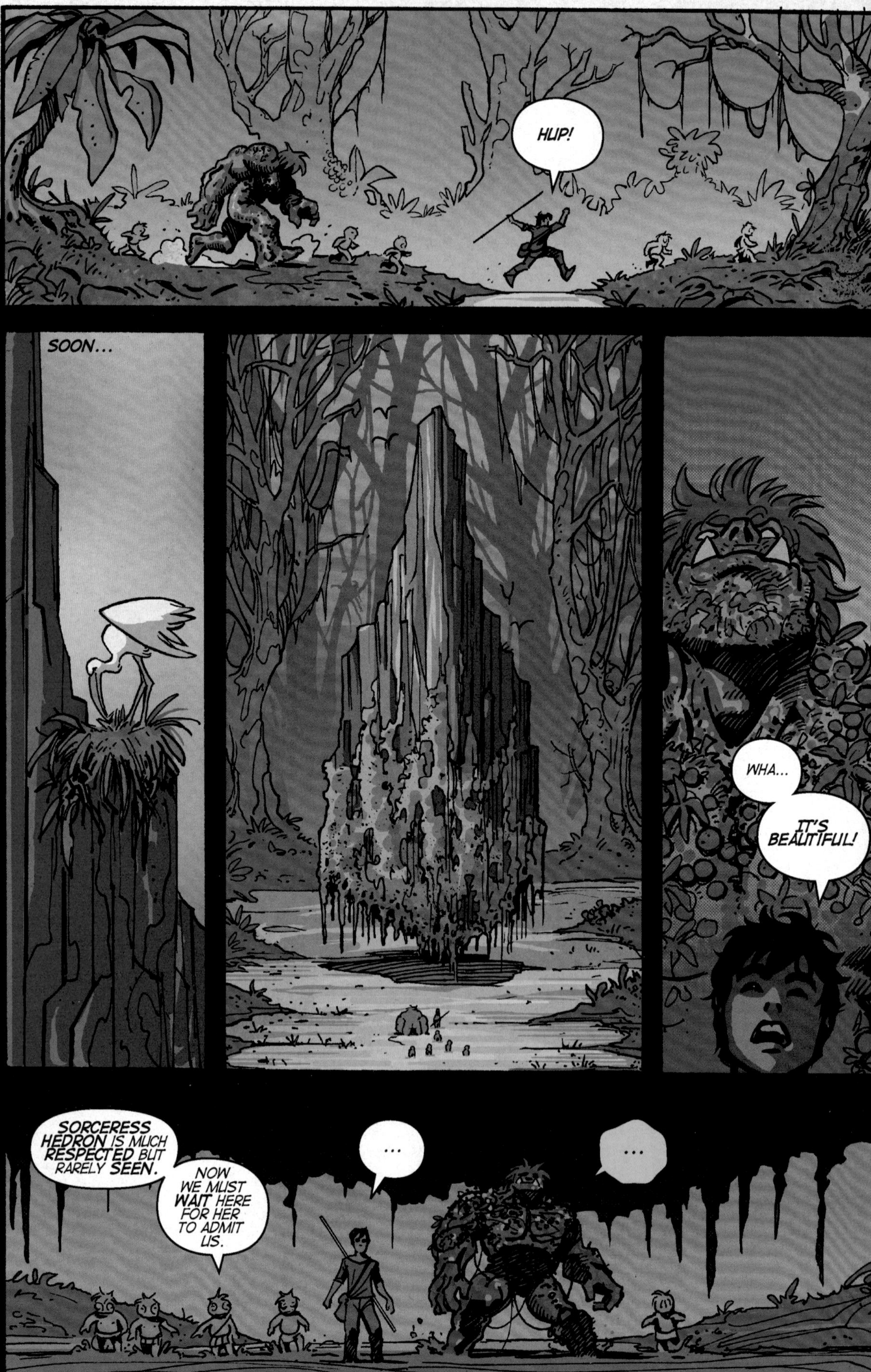
HUP!
SOON...
WHA...
IT'S BEAUTIFUL!
SORCERESS HEDRON IS MUCH RESPECTED BUT RARELY SEEN.
NOW WE MUST WAIT HERE FOR HER TO ADMIT US.
...
...

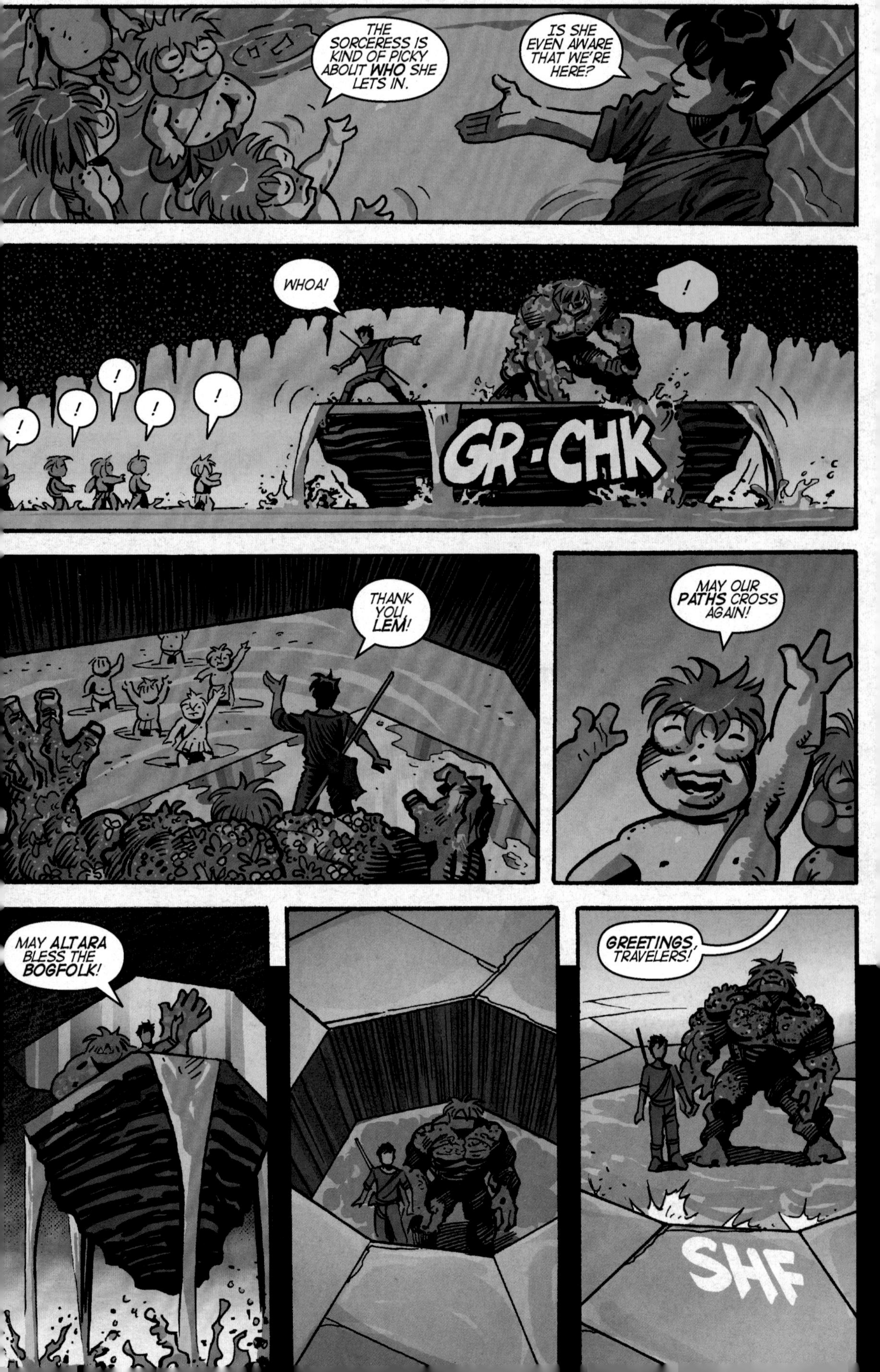
THE SORCERESS IS KIND OF PICKY ABOUT WHO SHE LETS IN.
IS SHE EVEN AWARE THAT WE'RE HERE?
WHOA!
!
!
!
!
!
!
GR-CHK
THANK YOU, LEM!
MAY OUR PATHS CROSS AGAIN!
MAY ALTARA BLESS THE BOGFOLK!
GREETINGS, TRAVELERS!
SHF

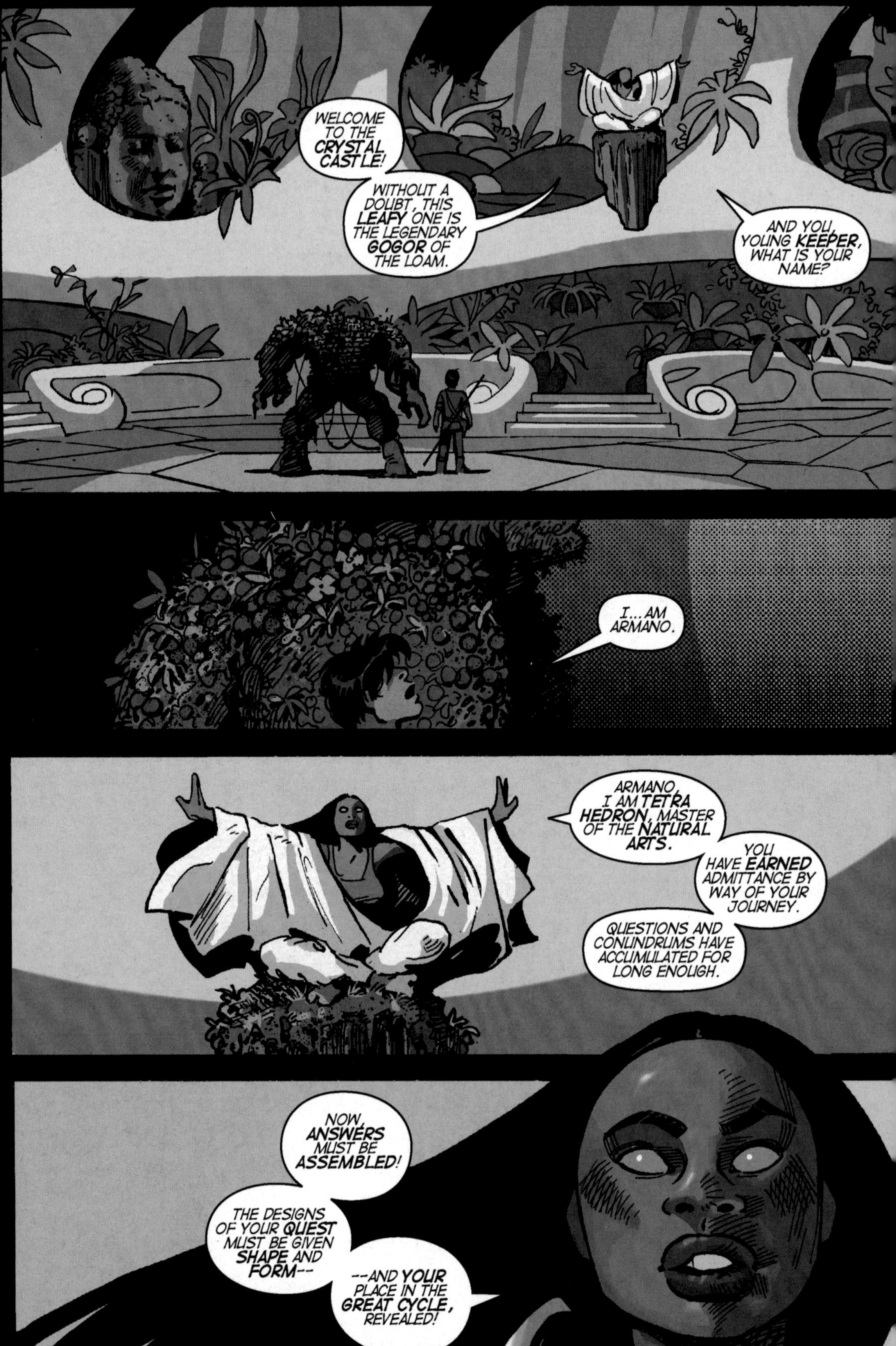
WELCOME TO THE CRYSTAL CASTLE!
WITHOUT A DOUBT, THIS LEAFY ONE IS THE LEGENDARY GOGOR OF THE LOAM.
AND YOU, YOUNG KEEPER, WHAT IS YOUR NAME?
I... AM ARMANO.
ARMANO, I AM TETRA HEDRON, MASTER OF THE NATURAL ARTS.
YOU HAVE EARNED ADMITTANCE BY WAY OF YOUR JOURNEY.
QUESTIONS AND CONUNDRUMS HAVE ACCUMULATED FOR LONG ENOUGH.
NOW, ANSWERS MUST BE ASSEMBLED!
THE DESIGNS OF YOUR QUEST MUST BE GIVEN SHAPE AND FORM--
--AND YOUR PLACE IN THE GREAT CYCLE, REVEALED!

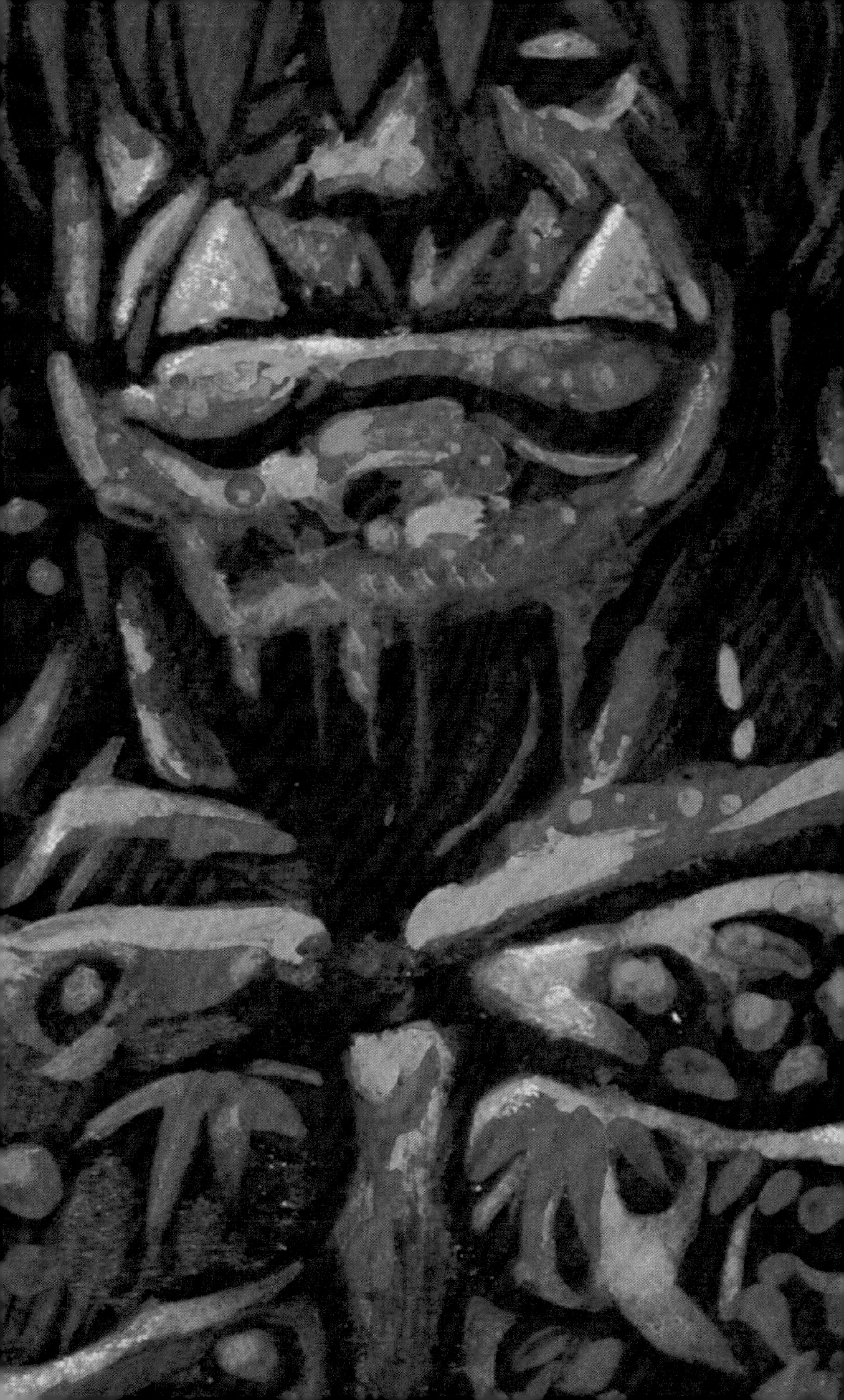

CHAPTER THREE

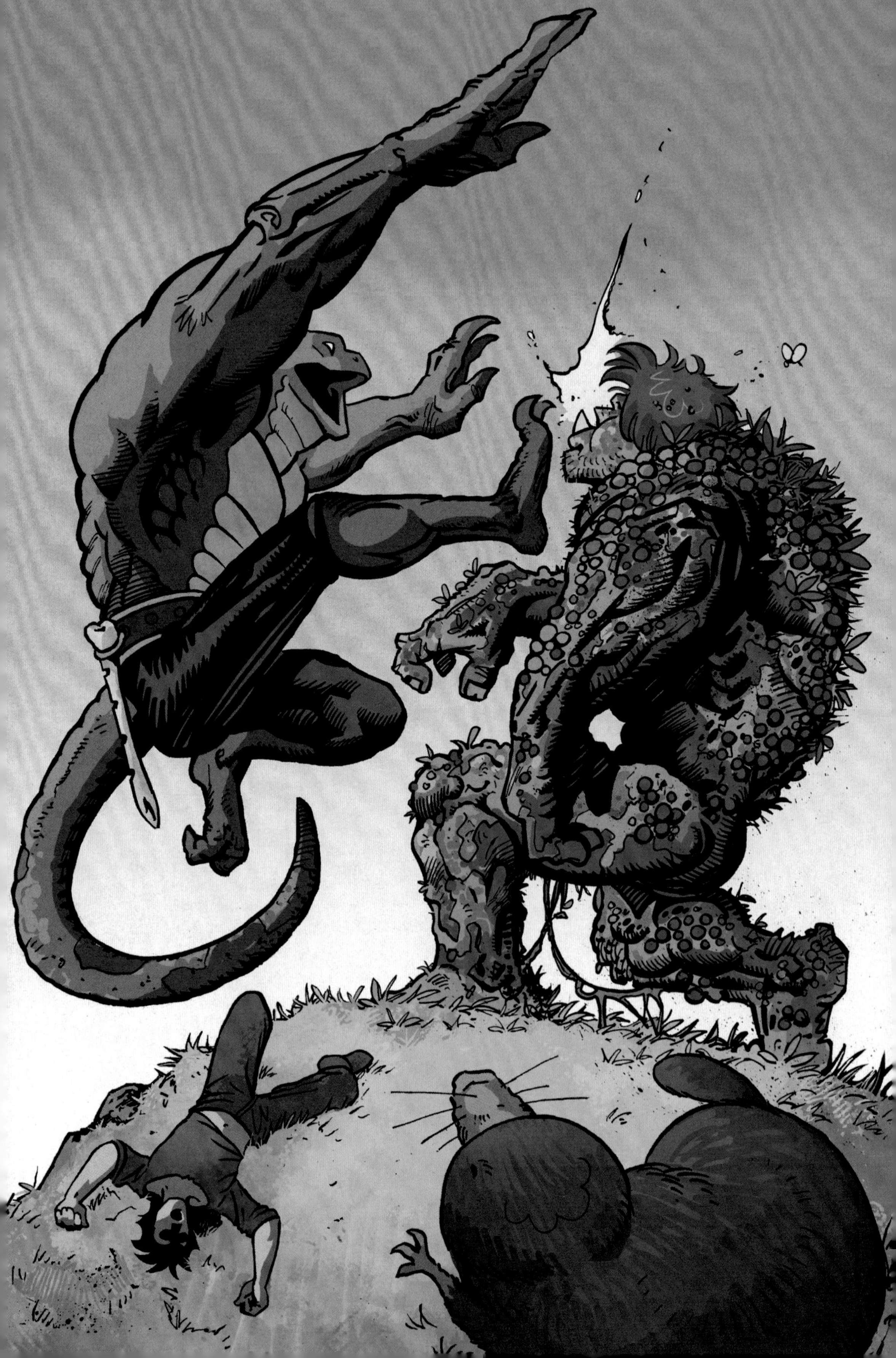

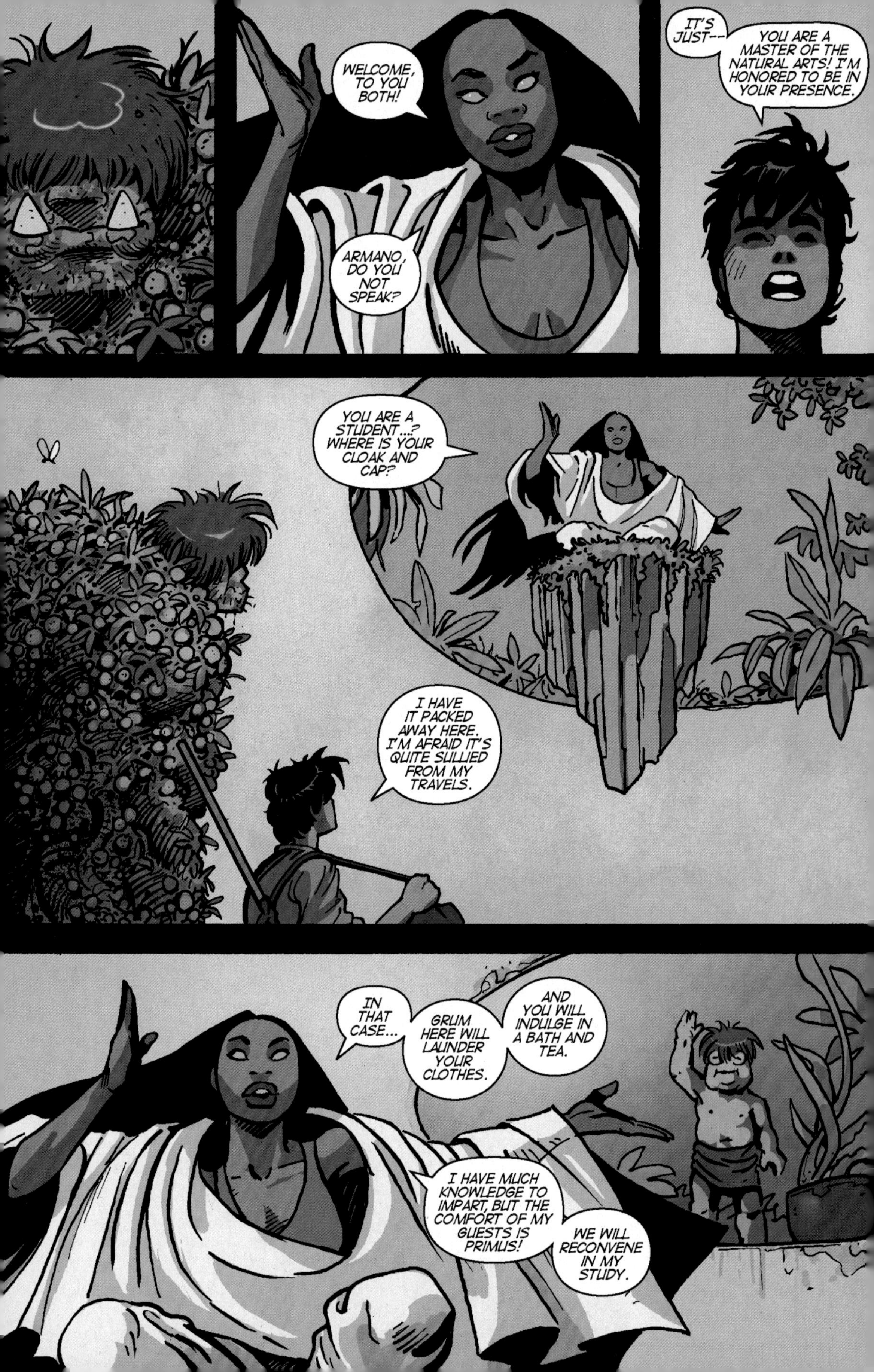
WELCOME, TO YOU BOTH!
ARMANO, DO YOU NOT SPEAK?
IT'S JUST--
YOU ARE A MASTER OF THE NATURAL ARTS! I'M HONORED TO BE IN YOUR PRESENCE.
YOU ARE A STUDENT...? WHERE IS YOUR CLOAK AND CAP?
I HAVE IT PACKED AWAY HERE. I'M AFRAID IT'S QUITE SULLIED FROM MY TRAVELS.
IN THAT CASE...
GRUM HERE WILL LAUNDER YOUR CLOTHES.
AND YOU WILL INDULGE IN A BATH AND TEA.
I HAVE MUCH KNOWLEDGE TO IMPART, BUT THE COMFORT OF MY GUESTS IS PRIMUS!
WE WILL RECONVENE IN MY STUDY.

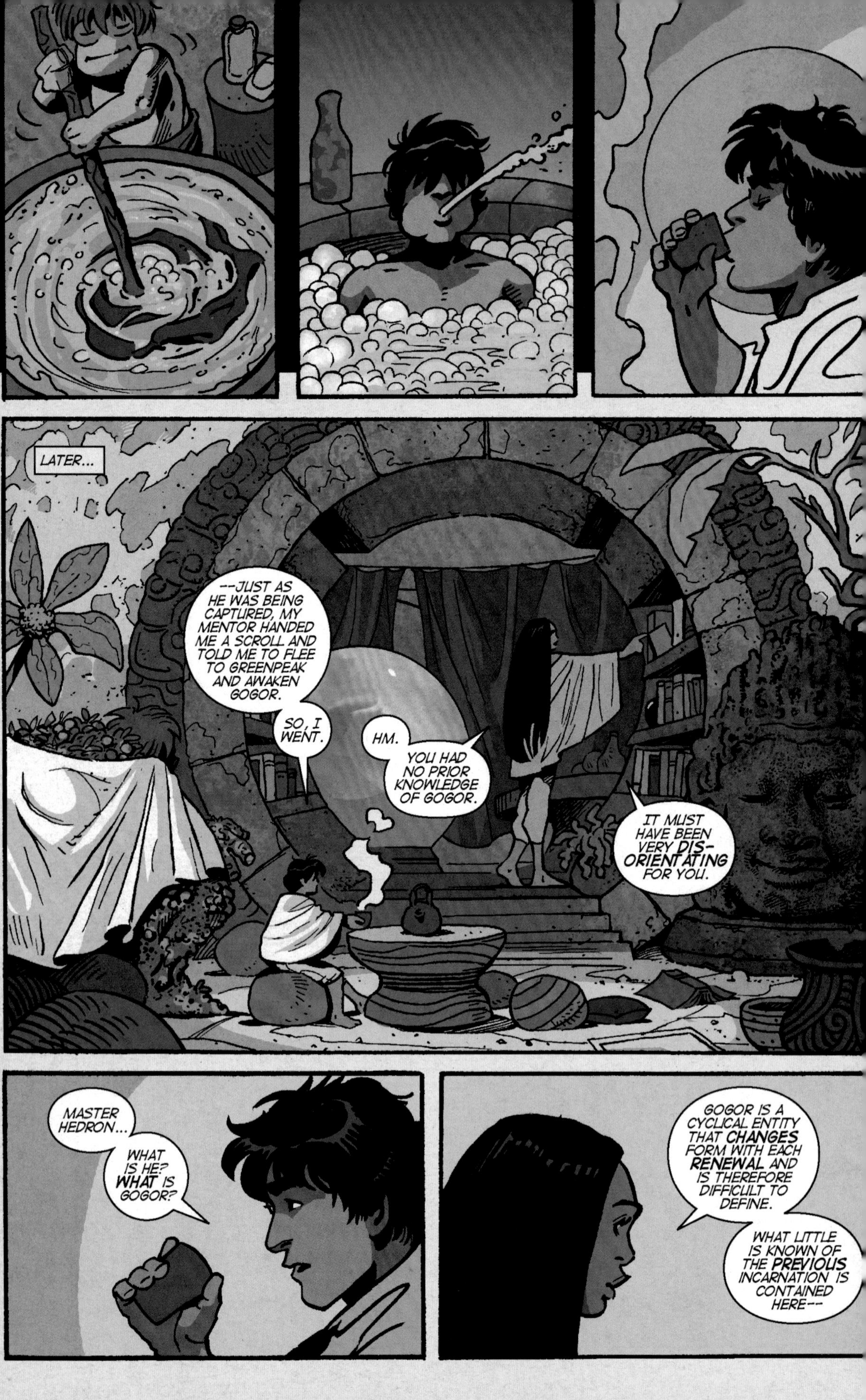

LATER...
--JUST AS HE WAS BEING CAPTURED, MY MENTOR HANDED ME A SCROLL AND TOLD ME TO FLEE TO GREENPEAK AND AWAKEN GOGOR.
SO, I WENT.
HM.
YOU HAD NO PRIOR KNOWLEDGE OF GOGOR.
IT MUST HAVE BEEN VERY DIS-ORIENTATING FOR YOU.
MASTER HEDRON...
WHAT IS HE? WHAT IS GOGOR?
GOGOR IS A CYCLICAL ENTITY THAT CHANGES FORM WITH EACH RENEWAL AND IS THEREFORE DIFFICULT TO DEFINE.
WHAT LITTLE IS KNOWN OF THE PREVIOUS INCARNATION IS CONTAINED HERE--

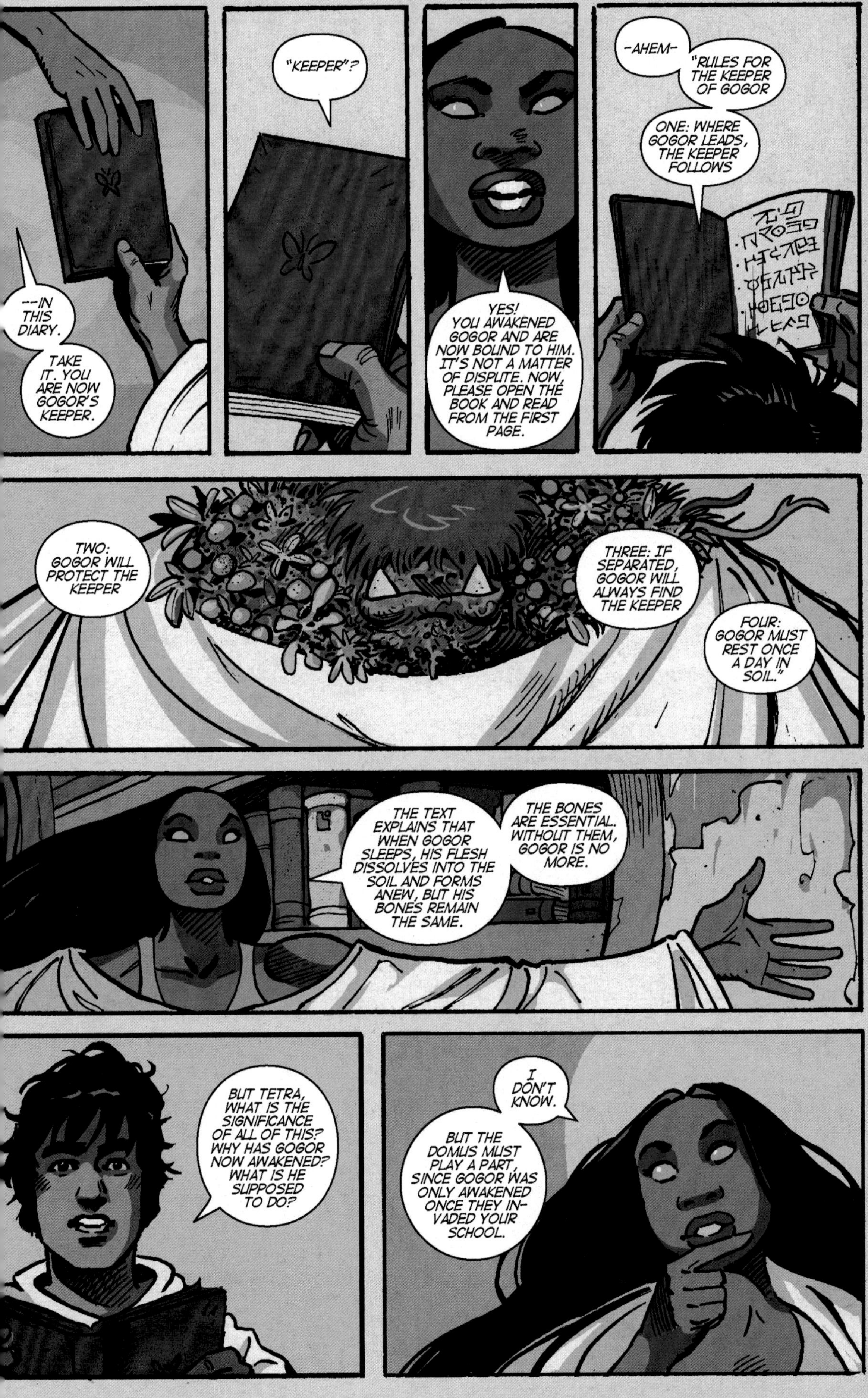
--IN THIS DIARY.
TAKE IT. YOU ARE NOW GOGOR'S KEEPER.
"KEEPER"?
YES! YOU AWAKENED GOGOR AND ARE NOW BOUND TO HIM. IT'S NOT A MATTER OF DISPUTE. NOW, PLEASE OPEN THE BOOK AND READ FROM THE FIRST PAGE.
-AHEM-
"RULES FOR THE KEEPER OF GOGOR
ONE: WHERE GOGOR LEADS, THE KEEPER FOLLOWS
TWO: GOGOR WILL PROTECT THE KEEPER
THREE: IF SEPARATED, GOGOR WILL ALWAYS FIND THE KEEPER
FOUR: GOGOR MUST REST ONCE A DAY IN SOIL."
THE TEXT EXPLAINS THAT WHEN GOGOR SLEEPS, HIS FLESH DISSOLVES INTO THE SOIL AND FORMS ANEW, BUT HIS BONES REMAIN THE SAME.
THE BONES ARE ESSENTIAL. WITHOUT THEM, GOGOR IS NO MORE.
BUT TETRA, WHAT IS THE SIGNIFICANCE OF ALL OF THIS? WHY HAS GOGOR NOW AWAKENED? WHAT IS HE SUPPOSED TO DO?
I DON'T KNOW.
BUT THE DOMUS MUST PLAY A PART, SINCE GOGOR WAS ONLY AWAKENED ONCE THEY IN-VADED YOUR SCHOOL.

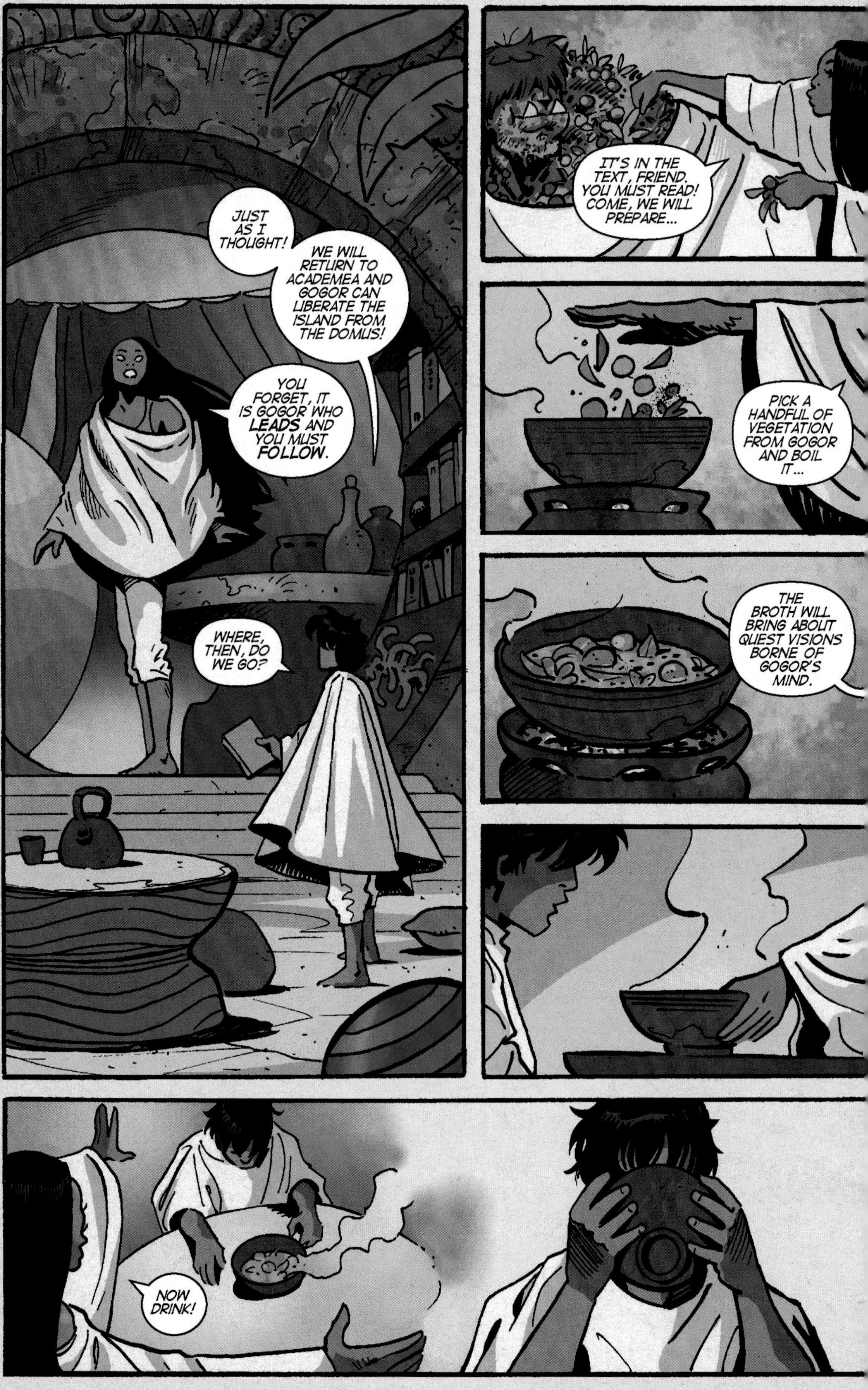
JUST AS I THOUGHT!
WE WILL RETURN TO ACADEMEA AND GOGOR CAN LIBERATE THE ISLAND FROM THE DOMUS!
YOU FORGET, IT IS GOGOR WHO **LEADS** AND YOU MUST **FOLLOW**.
WHERE, THEN, DO WE GO?
IT'S IN THE TEXT, FRIEND. YOU MUST READ! COME, WE WILL PREPARE...
PICK A HANDFUL OF VEGETATION FROM GOGOR AND BOIL IT...
THE BROTH WILL BRING ABOUT QUEST VISIONS BORNE OF GOGOR'S MIND.
NOW DRINK!

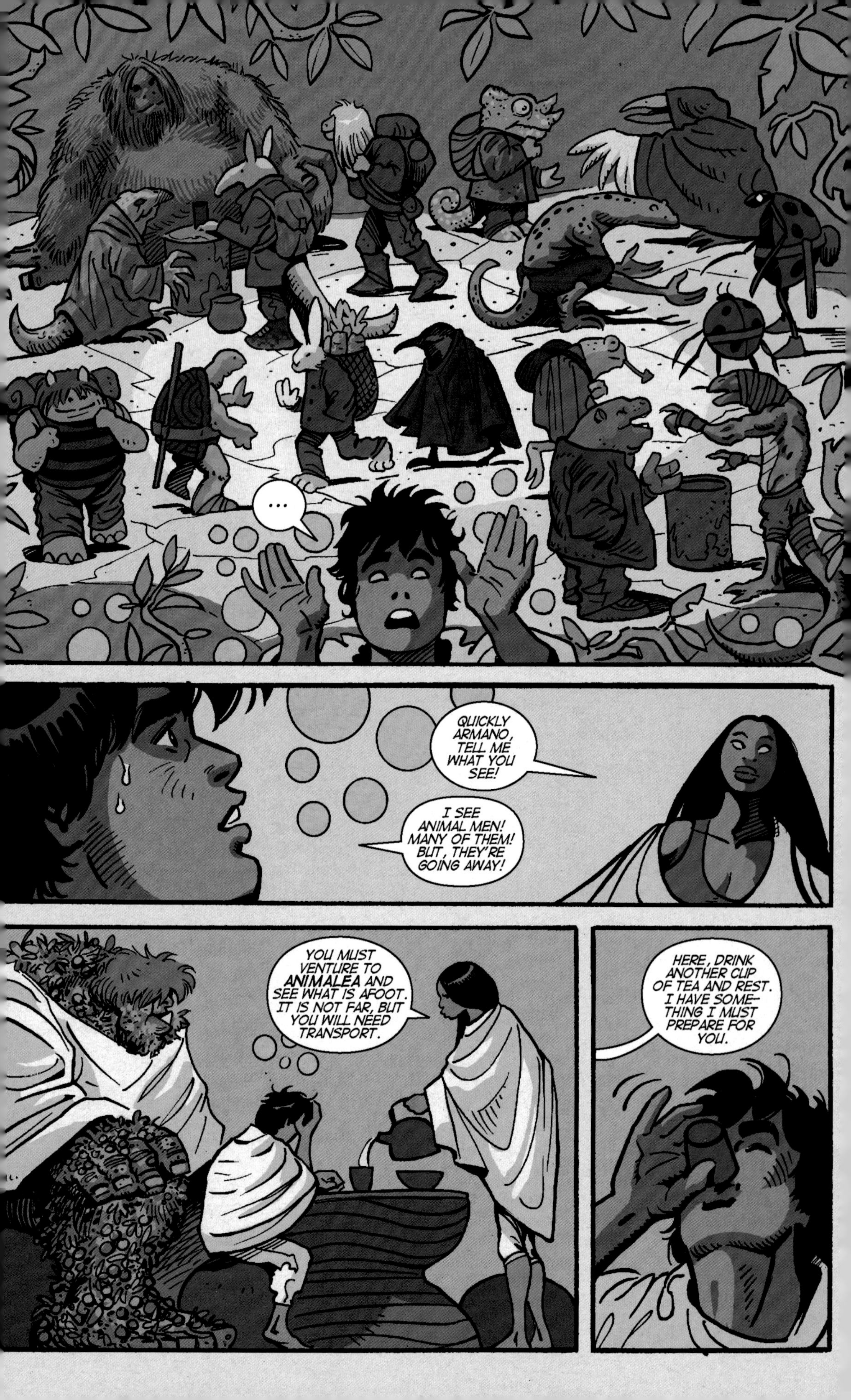
...
QUICKLY ARMANO, TELL ME WHAT YOU SEE!
I SEE ANIMAL MEN! MANY OF THEM! BUT, THEY'RE GOING AWAY!
YOU MUST VENTURE TO ANIMALEA AND SEE WHAT IS AFOOT. IT IS NOT FAR, BUT YOU WILL NEED TRANSPORT.
HERE, DRINK ANOTHER CUP OF TEA AND REST. I HAVE SOME-THING I MUST PREPARE FOR YOU.

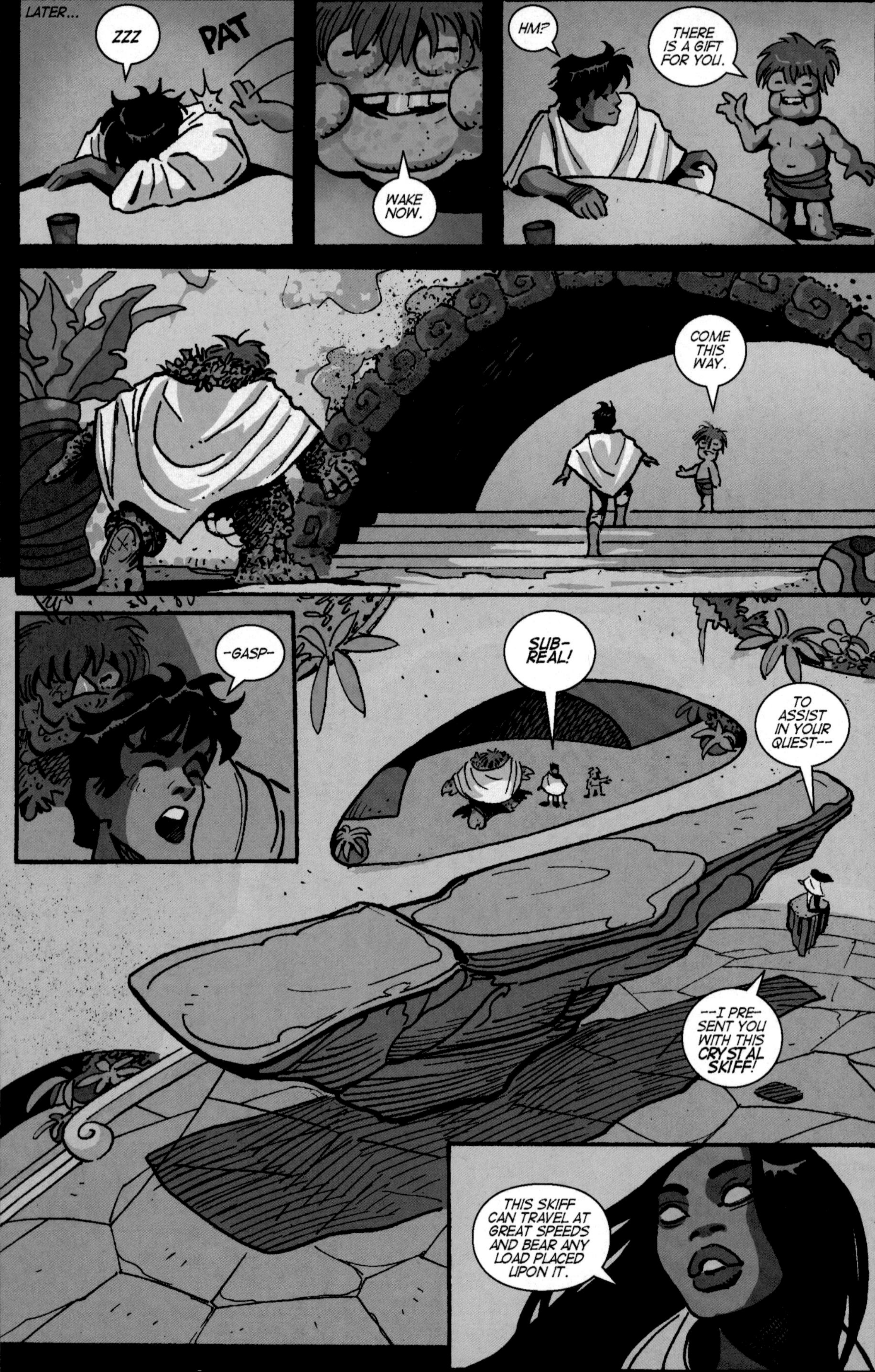
LATER...
ZZZ
PAT
WAKE NOW.
HM?
THERE IS A GIFT FOR YOU.
COME THIS WAY.
-GASP-
SUB-REAL!
TO ASSIST IN YOUR QUEST--
--I PRESENT YOU WITH THIS CRYSTAL SKIFF!
THIS SKIFF CAN TRAVEL AT GREAT SPEEDS AND BEAR ANY LOAD PLACED UPON IT.

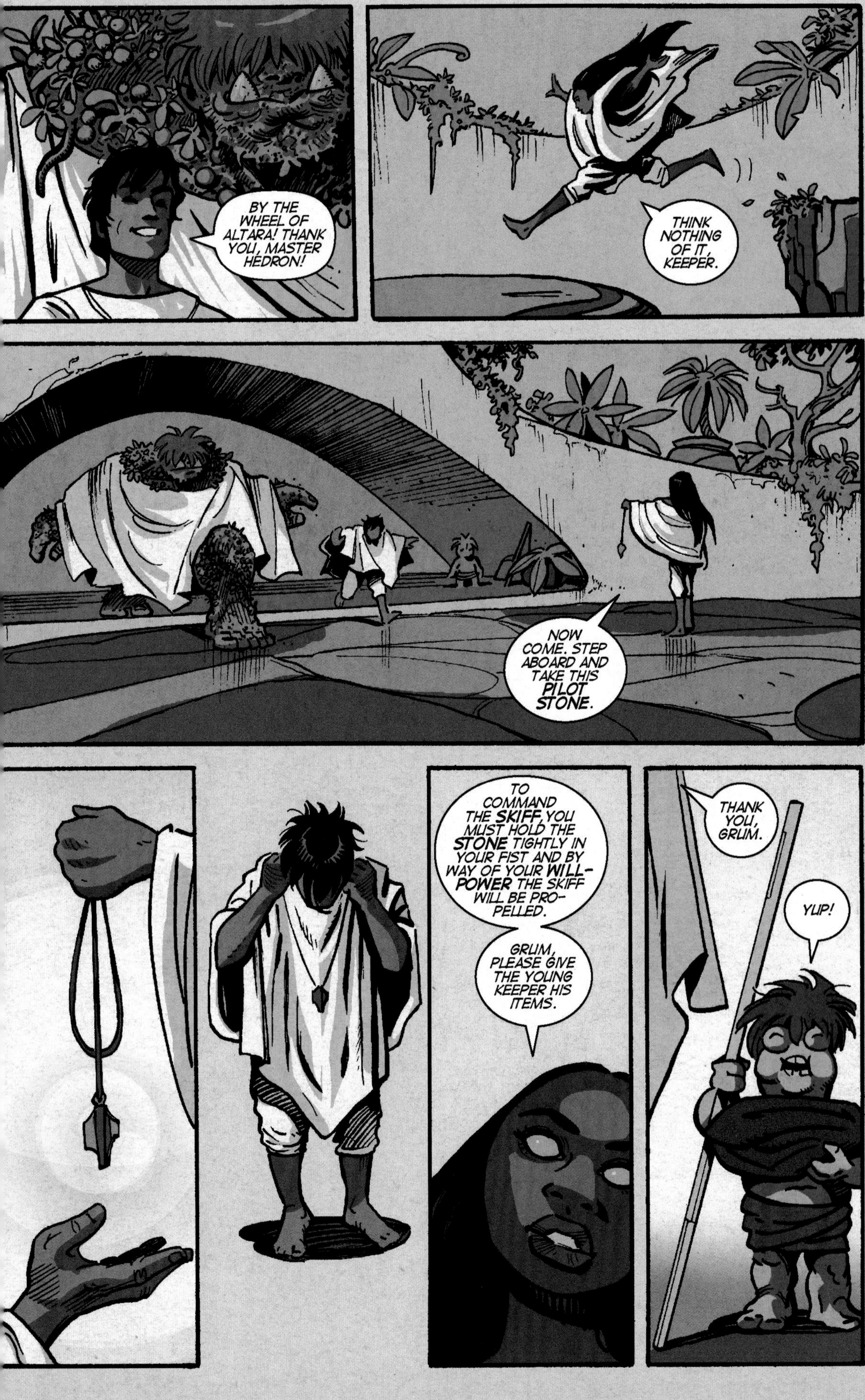
BY THE WHEEL OF ALTARA! THANK YOU, MASTER HEDRON!
THINK NOTHING OF IT, KEEPER.
NOW COME. STEP ABOARD AND TAKE THIS PILOT STONE.
TO COMMAND THE SKIFF, YOU MUST HOLD THE STONE TIGHTLY IN YOUR FIST AND BY WAY OF YOUR WILL-POWER THE SKIFF WILL BE PRO-PELLED.
GRUM, PLEASE GIVE THE YOUNG KEEPER HIS ITEMS.
THANK YOU, GRUM.
YUP!

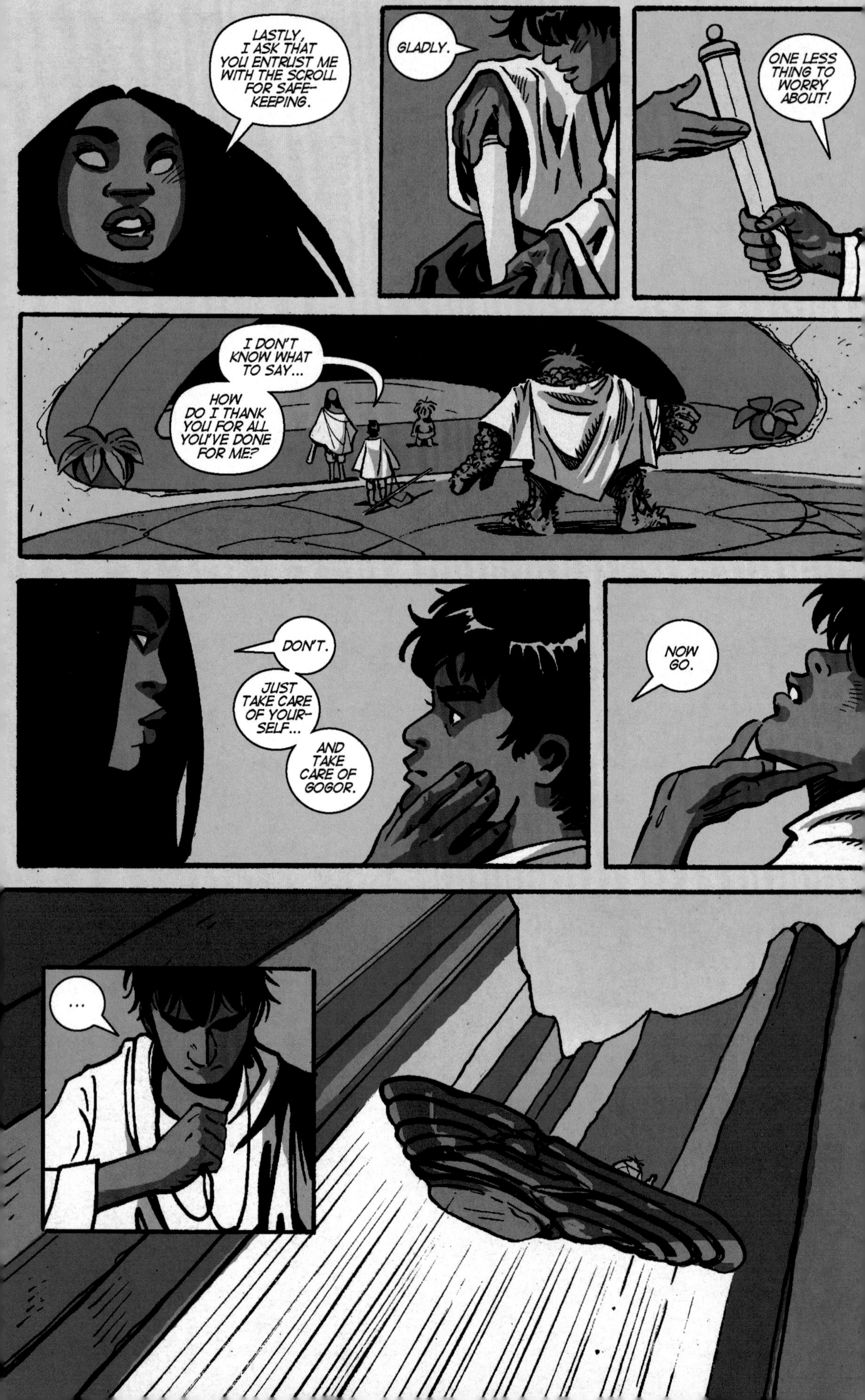
LASTLY, I ASK THAT YOU ENTRUST ME WITH THE SCROLL FOR SAFE-KEEPING.
GLADLY.
ONE LESS THING TO WORRY ABOUT!
I DON'T KNOW WHAT TO SAY...
HOW DO I THANK YOU FOR ALL YOU'VE DONE FOR ME?
DON'T.
JUST TAKE CARE OF YOUR-SELF...
AND TAKE CARE OF GOGOR.
NOW GO.
...

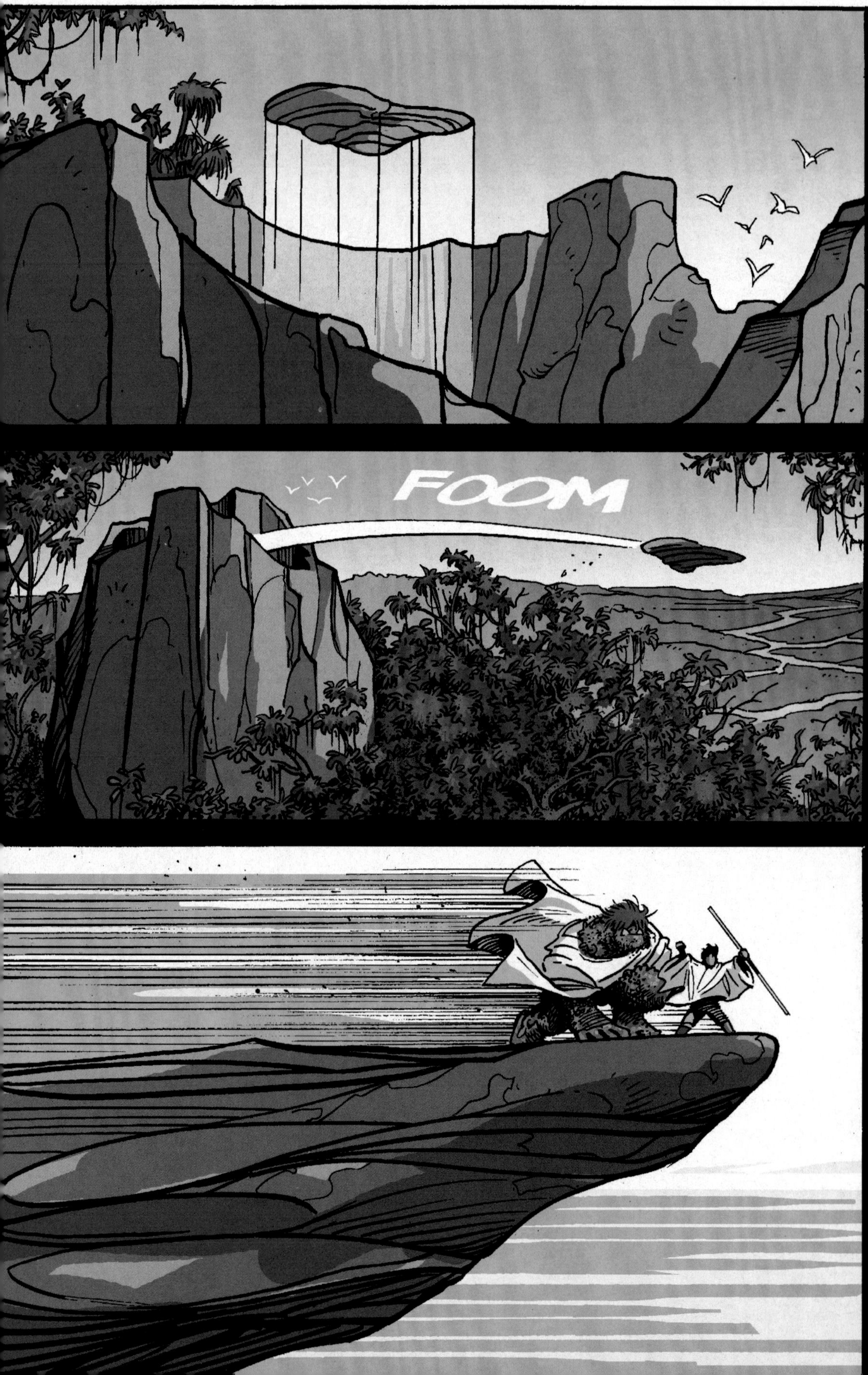
FOOM

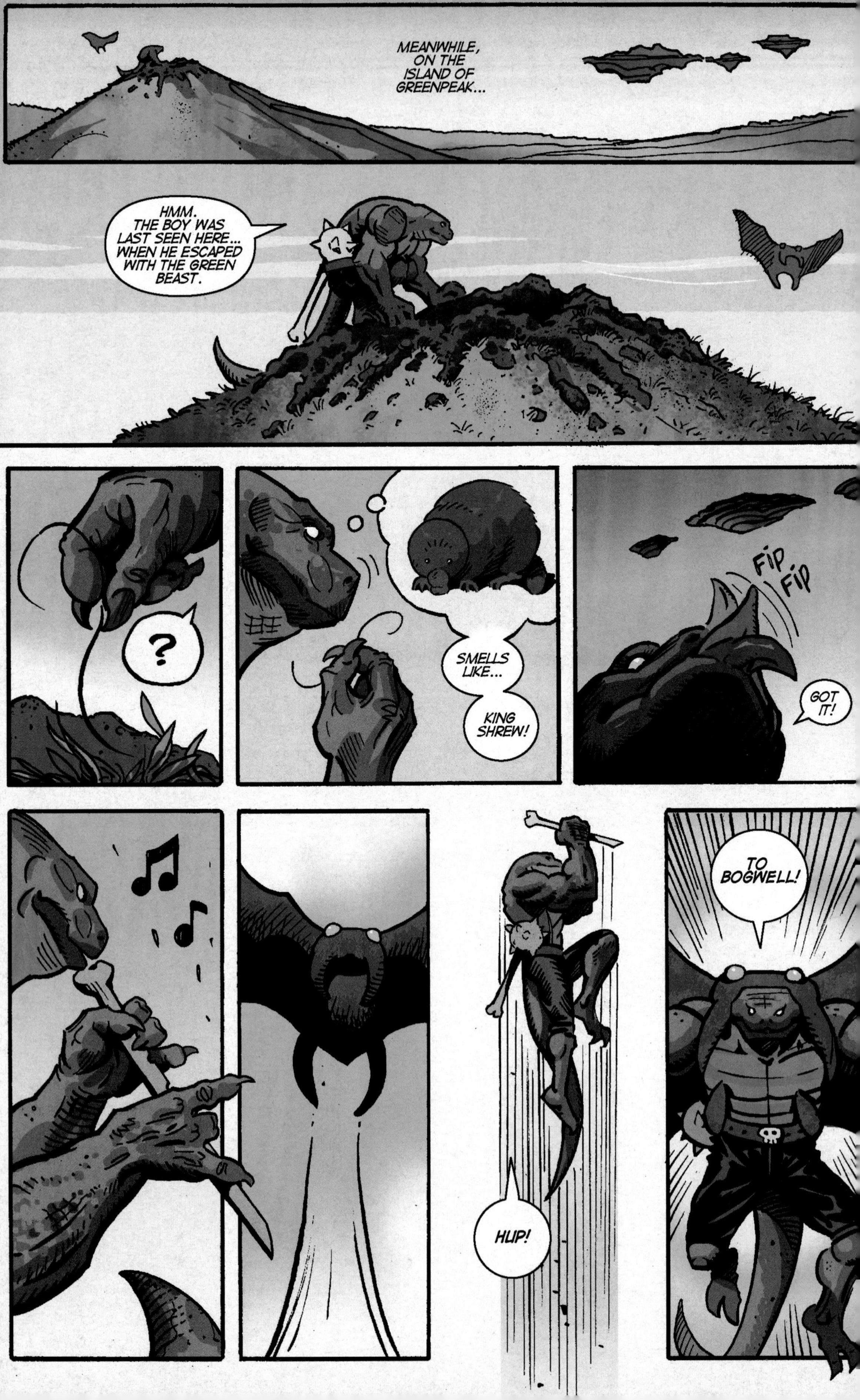
MEANWHILE, ON THE ISLAND OF GREENPEAK...
HMM. THE BOY WAS LAST SEEN HERE... WHEN HE ESCAPED WITH THE GREEN BEAST.
?
SMELLS LIKE...
KING SHREW!
FIP FIP
GOT IT!
HUP!
TO BOGWELL!

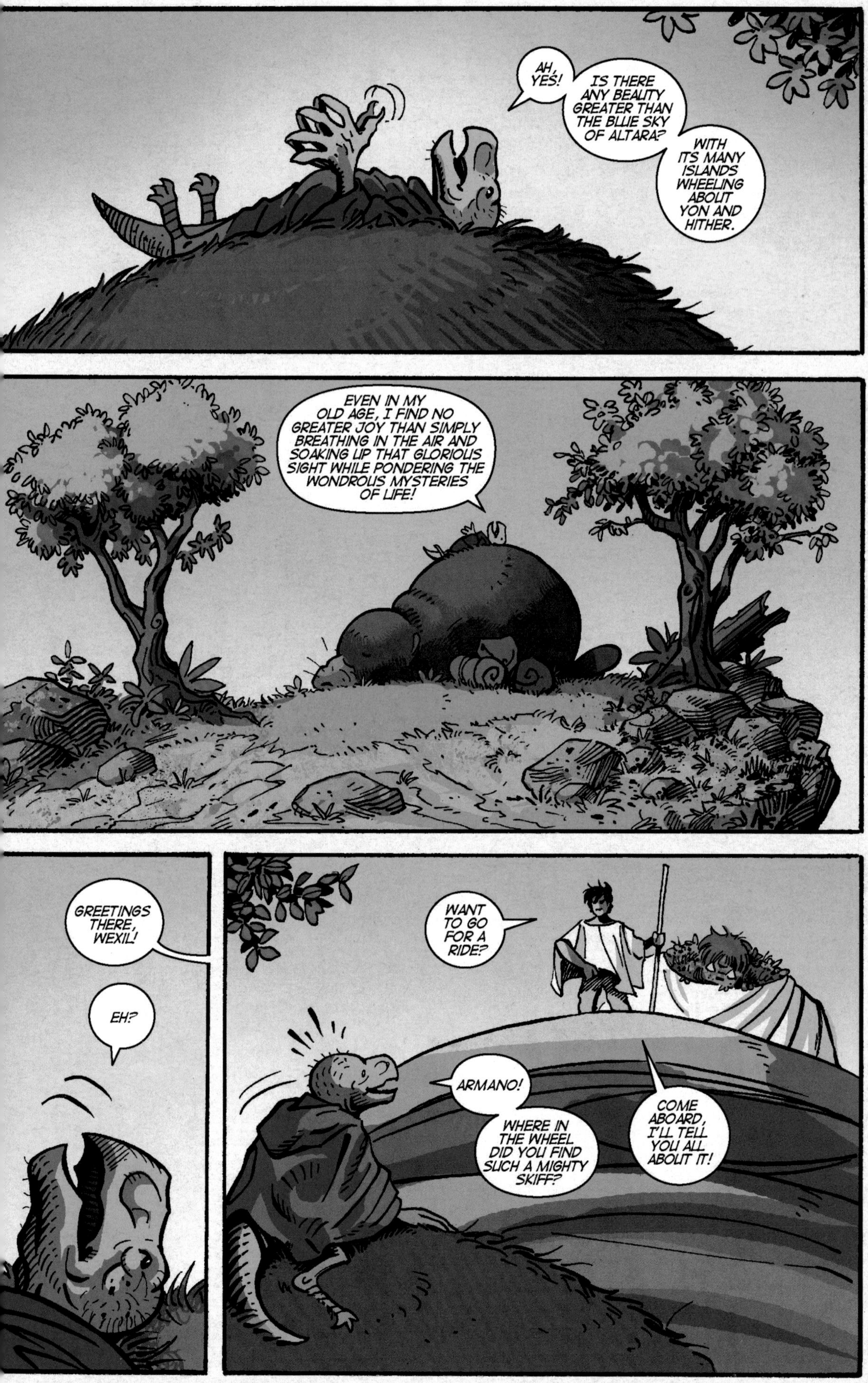
AH, YES!
IS THERE ANY BEAUTY GREATER THAN THE BLUE SKY OF ALTARA?
WITH ITS MANY ISLANDS WHEELING ABOUT YON AND HITHER.
EVEN IN MY OLD AGE, I FIND NO GREATER JOY THAN SIMPLY BREATHING IN THE AIR AND SOAKING UP THAT GLORIOUS SIGHT WHILE PONDERING THE WONDROUS MYSTERIES OF LIFE!
GREETINGS THERE, WEXIL!
EH?
WANT TO GO FOR A RIDE?
ARMANO!
WHERE IN THE WHEEL DID YOU FIND SUCH A MIGHTY SKIFF?
COME ABOARD, I'LL TELL YOU ALL ABOUT IT!

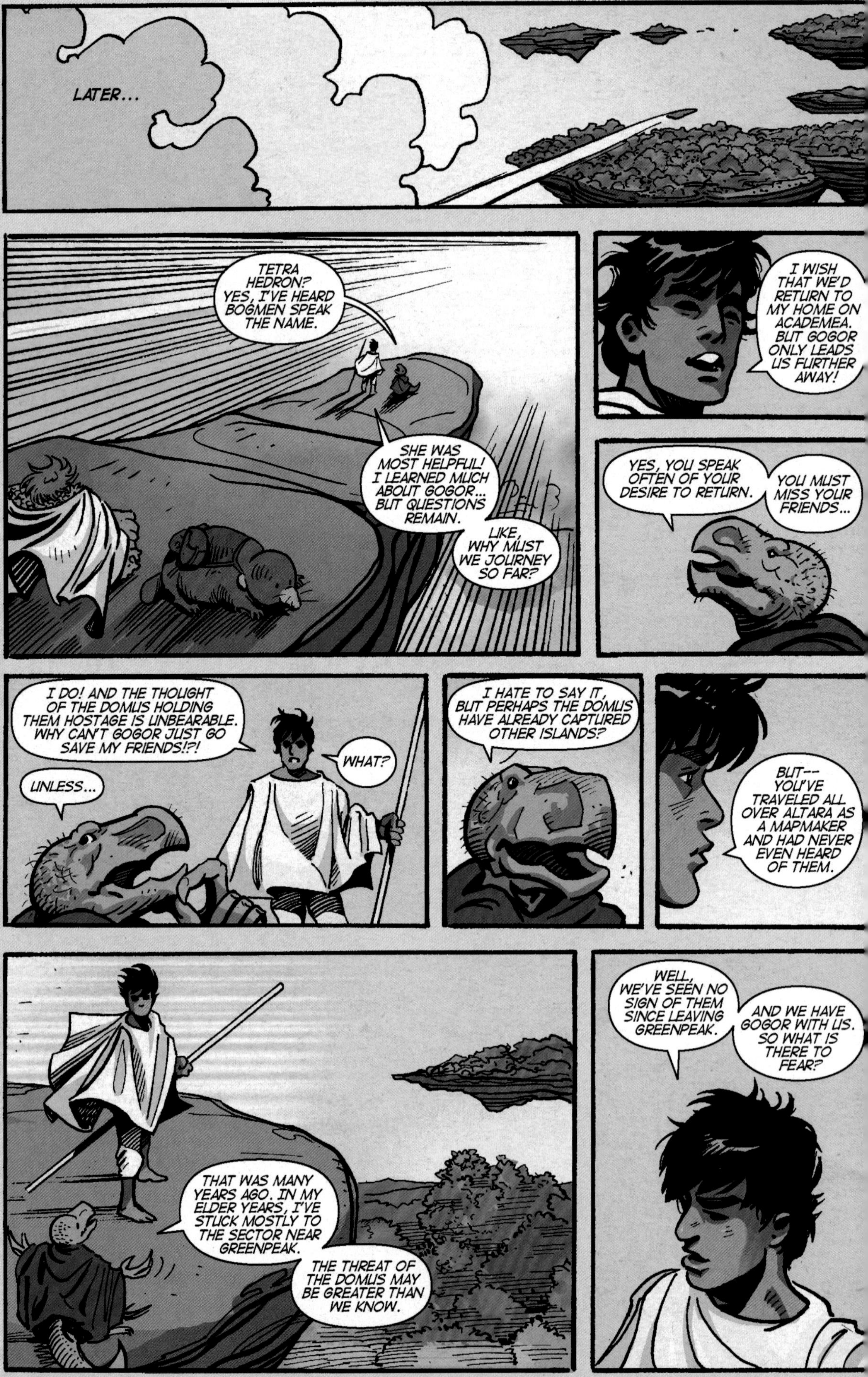
LATER...
TETRA HEDRON? YES, I'VE HEARD BOGMEN SPEAK THE NAME.
SHE WAS MOST HELPFUL! I LEARNED MUCH ABOUT GOGOR... BUT QUESTIONS REMAIN.
LIKE, WHY MUST WE JOURNEY SO FAR?
I WISH THAT WE'D RETURN TO MY HOME ON ACADEMEA. BUT GOGOR ONLY LEADS US FURTHER AWAY!
YES, YOU SPEAK OFTEN OF YOUR DESIRE TO RETURN.
YOU MUST MISS YOUR FRIENDS...
I DO! AND THE THOUGHT OF THE DOMUS HOLDING THEM HOSTAGE IS UNBEARABLE. WHY CAN'T GOGOR JUST GO SAVE MY FRIENDS!?!
UNLESS...
WHAT?
I HATE TO SAY IT, BUT PERHAPS THE DOMUS HAVE ALREADY CAPTURED OTHER ISLANDS?
BUT-- YOU'VE TRAVELED ALL OVER ALTARA AS A MAPMAKER AND HAD NEVER EVEN HEARD OF THEM.
THAT WAS MANY YEARS AGO. IN MY ELDER YEARS, I'VE STUCK MOSTLY TO THE SECTOR NEAR GREENPEAK.
THE THREAT OF THE DOMUS MAY BE GREATER THAN WE KNOW.
WELL, WE'VE SEEN NO SIGN OF THEM SINCE LEAVING GREENPEAK.
AND WE HAVE GOGOR WITH US. SO WHAT IS THERE TO FEAR?

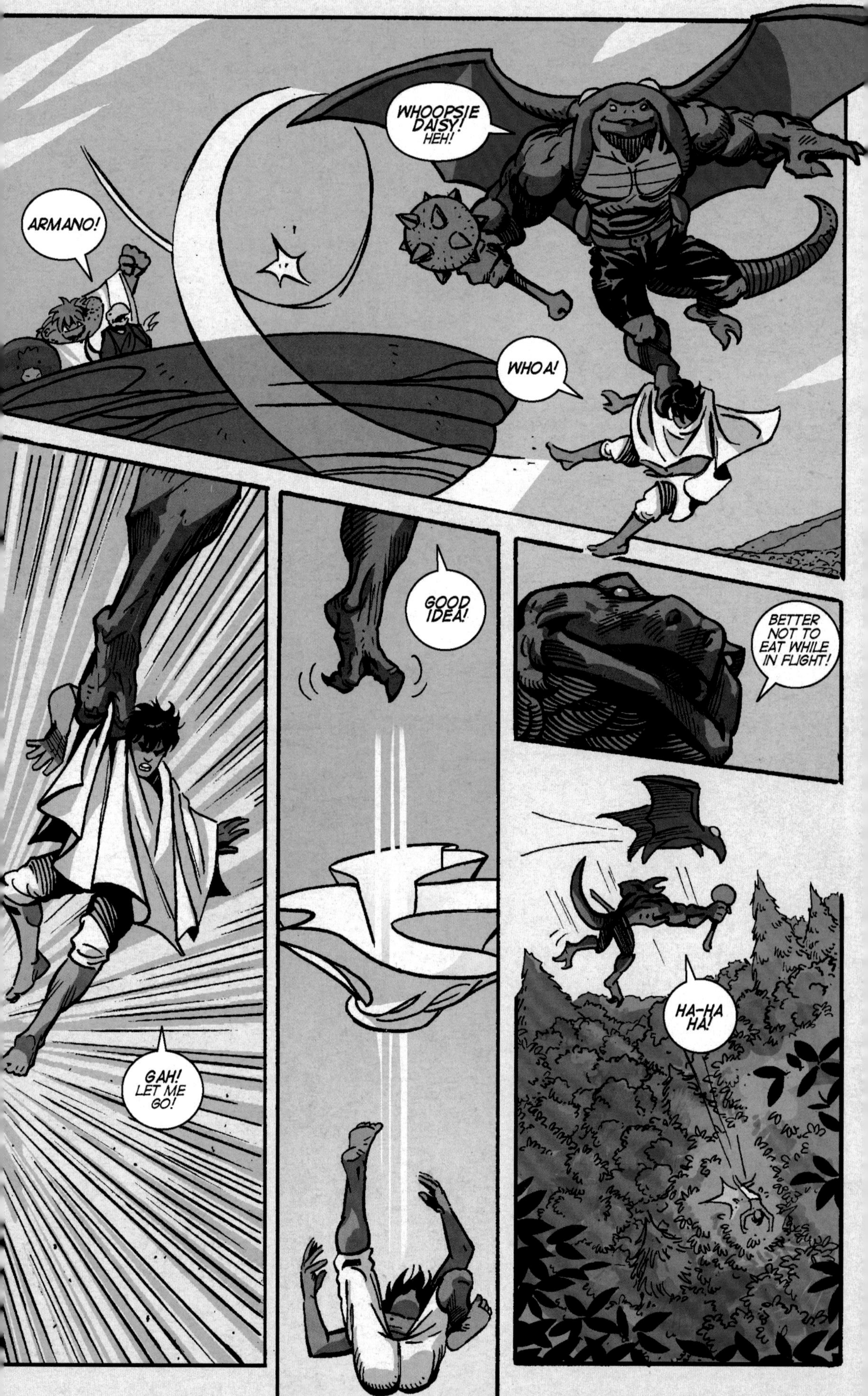
ARMANO!
WHOOPSIE DAISY! HEH!
WHOA!
GAH! LET ME GO!
GOOD IDEA!
BETTER NOT TO EAT WHILE IN FLIGHT!
HA-HA HA!

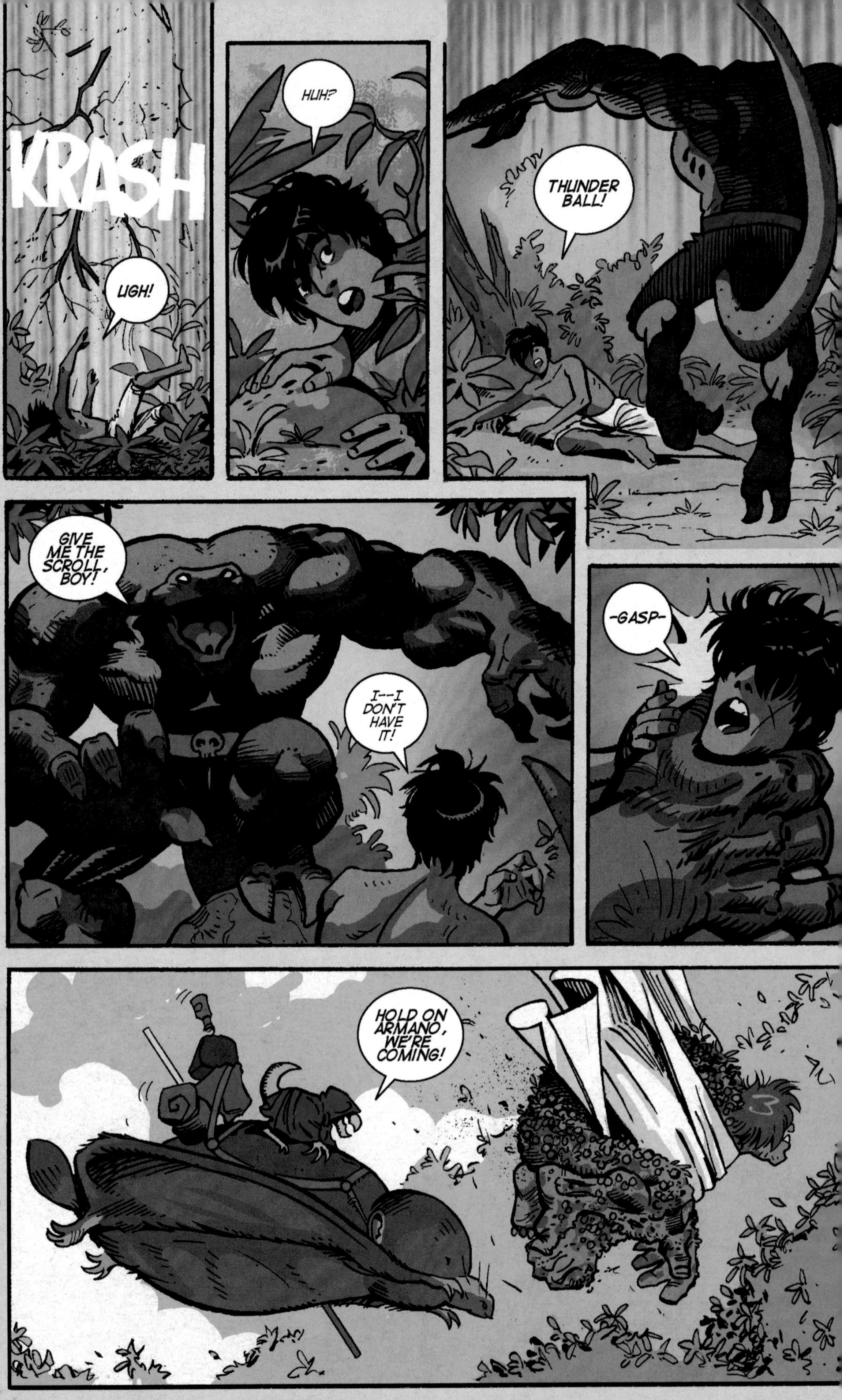
KRASH
UGH!
HUH?
THUNDER BALL!
GIVE ME THE SCROLL, BOY!
I--I DON'T HAVE IT!
-GASP-
HOLD ON ARMANO, WE'RE COMING!

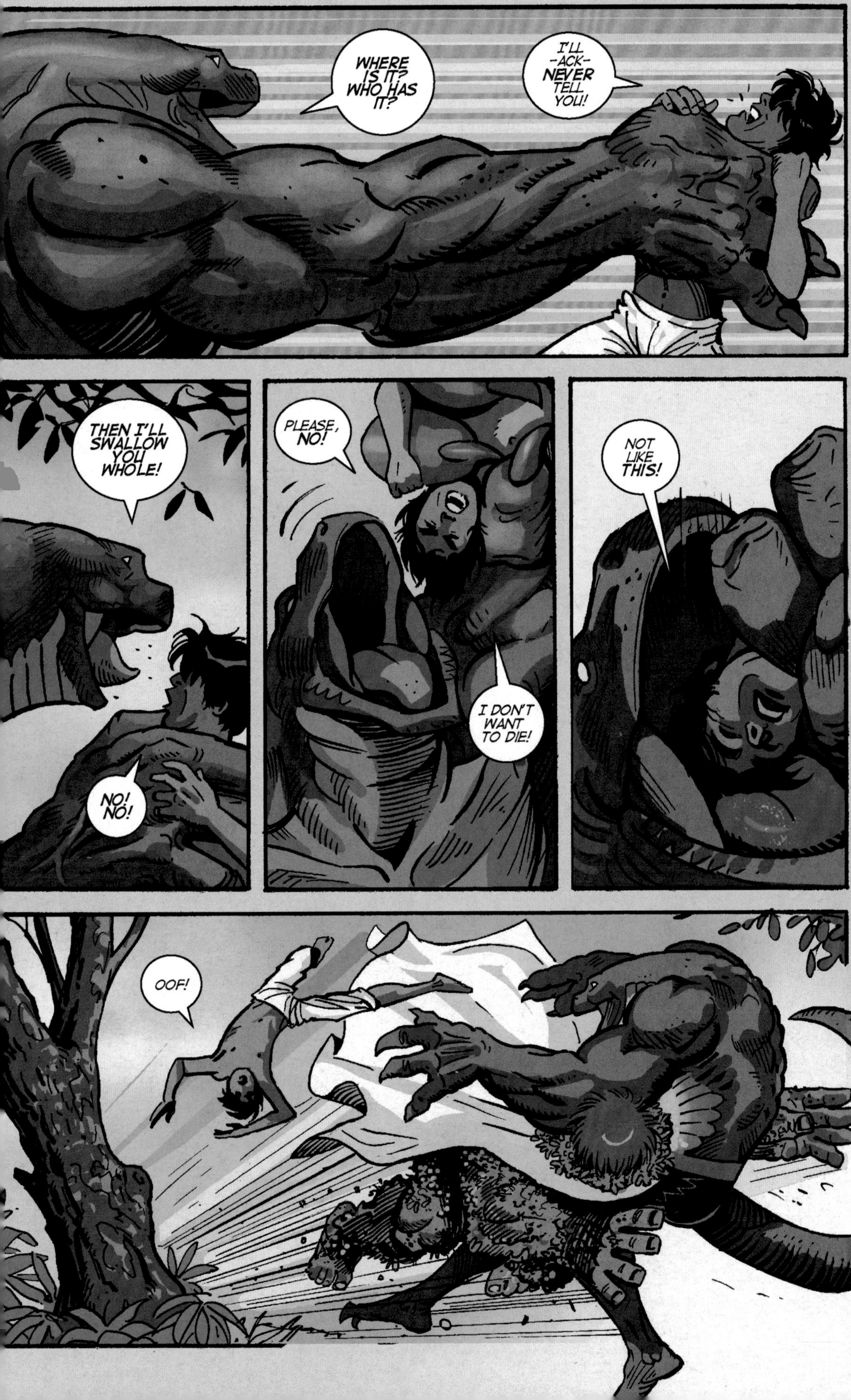
WHERE IS IT? WHO HAS IT?
I'LL -ACK- NEVER TELL YOU!
THEN I'LL SWALLOW YOU WHOLE!
NO! NO!
PLEASE, NO!
I DON'T WANT TO DIE!
NOT LIKE THIS!
OOF!

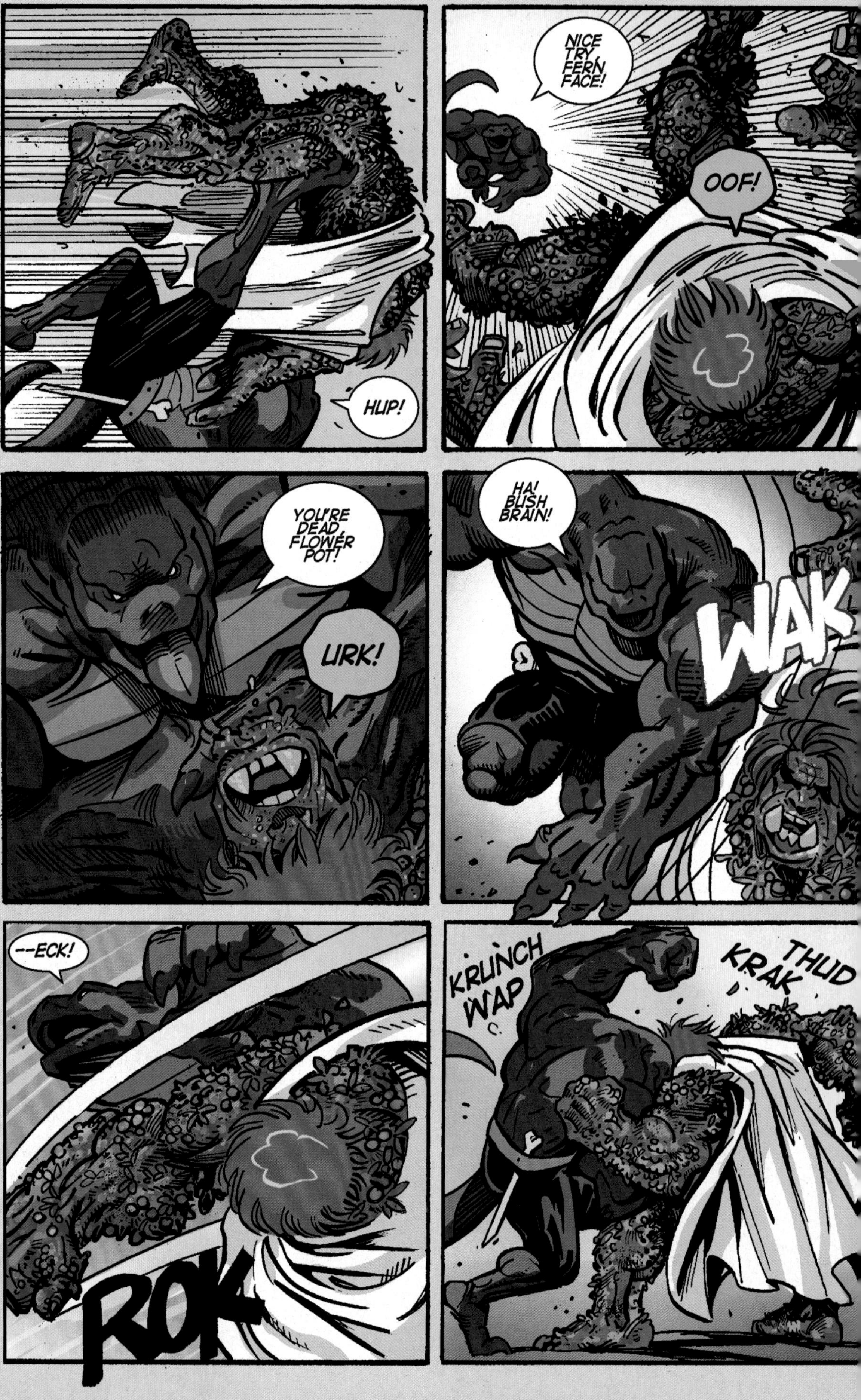
HUP!
NICE TRY, FERN FACE!
OOF!
YOU'RE DEAD, FLOWER POT!
URK!
HA! BUSH BRAIN!
WAK
--ECK!
ROK
KRUNCH
WAP
THUD
KRAK

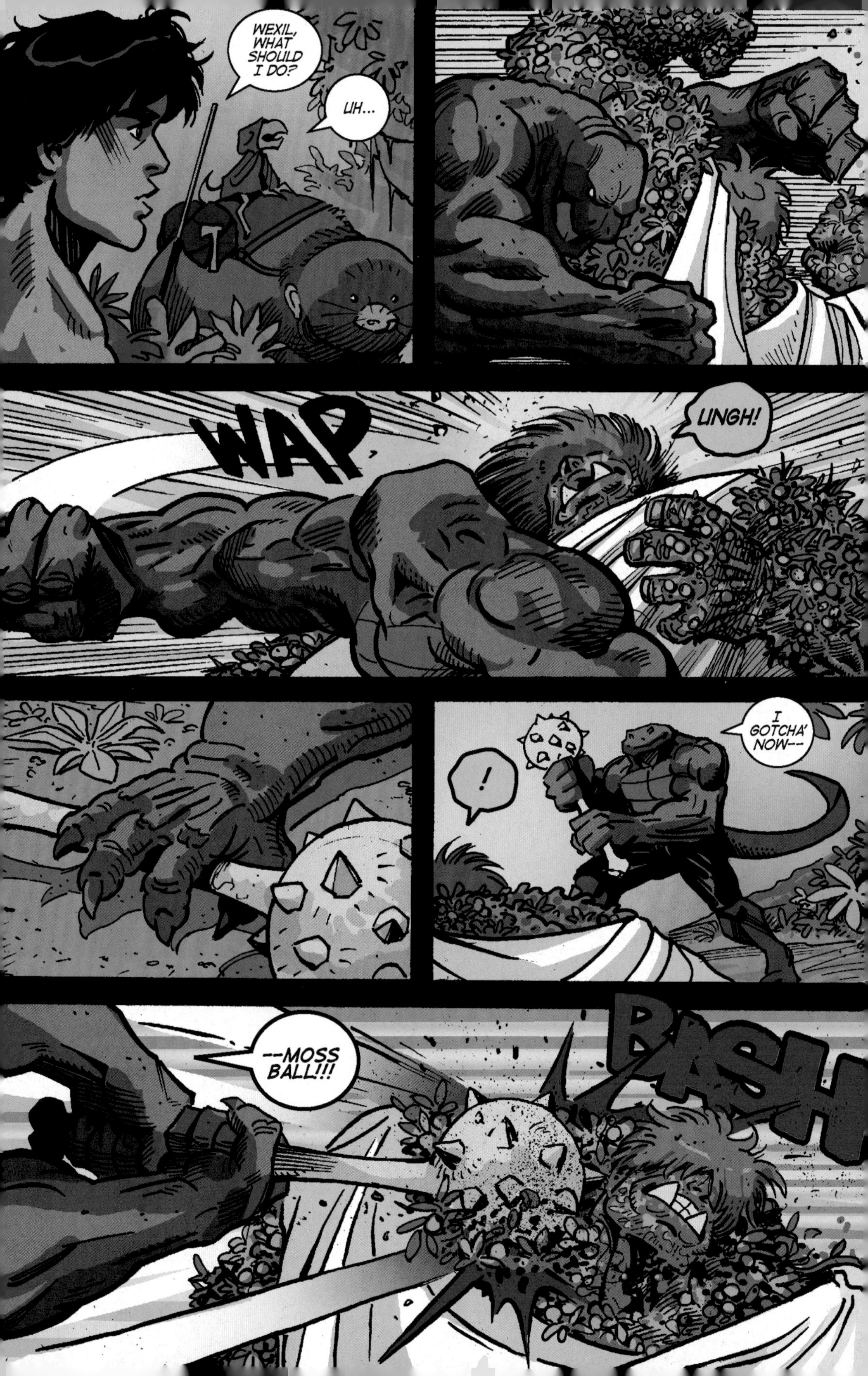
WEXIL, WHAT SHOULD I DO?
UH...
WAP
UNGH!
!
I GOTCHA' NOW--
--MOSS BALL!!!
BASH

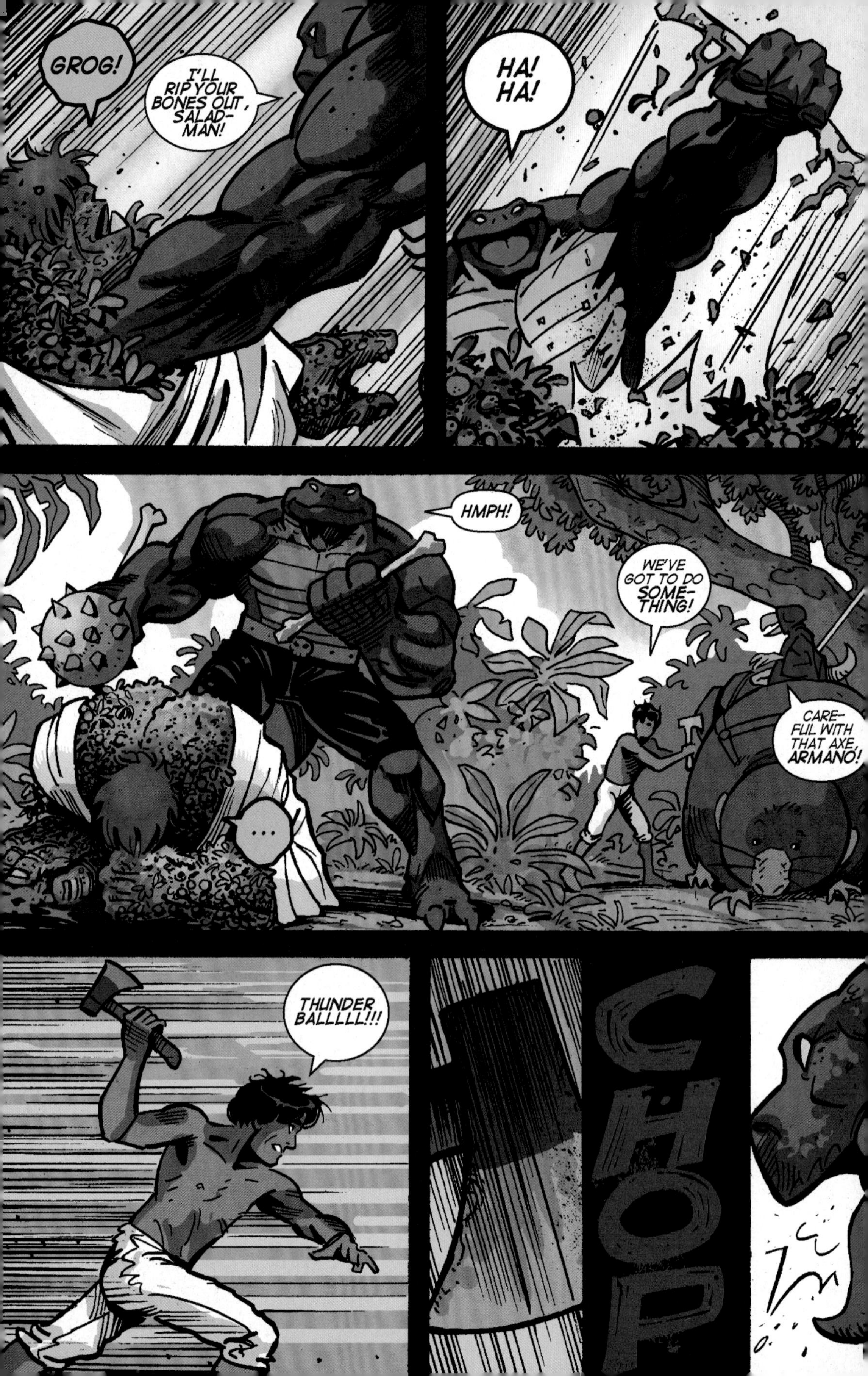
GROG!
I'LL RIP YOUR BONES OUT, SALAD-MAN!
HA! HA!
HMPH!
WE'VE GOT TO DO SOME-THING!
CARE-FUL WITH THAT AXE, ARMANO!
...
THUNDER BALLLLL!!!
CHOP

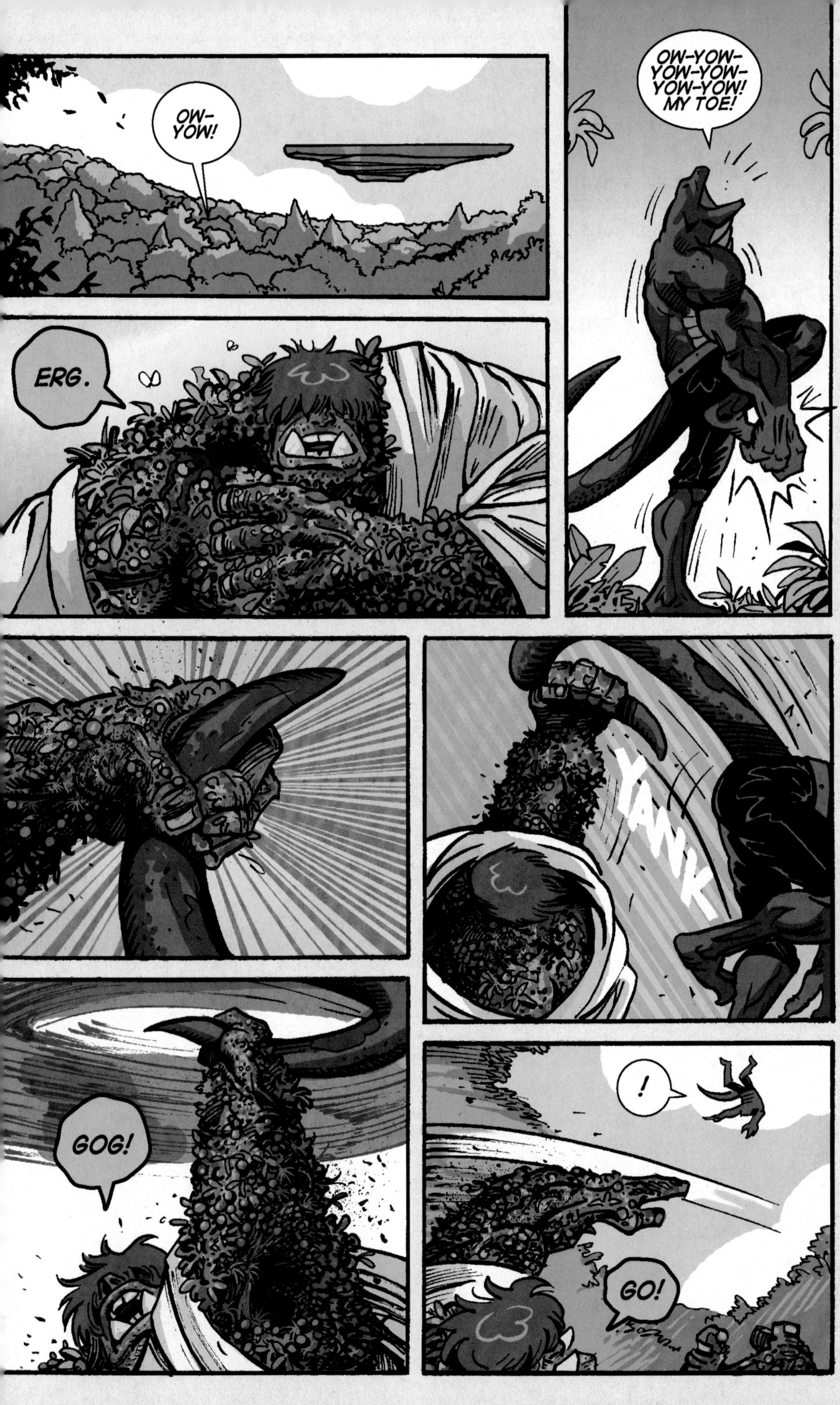
OW-
YOW!
OW-YOW-
YOW-YOW-
YOW-YOW!
MY TOE!
ERG.
YANK
!
GOG!
GO!

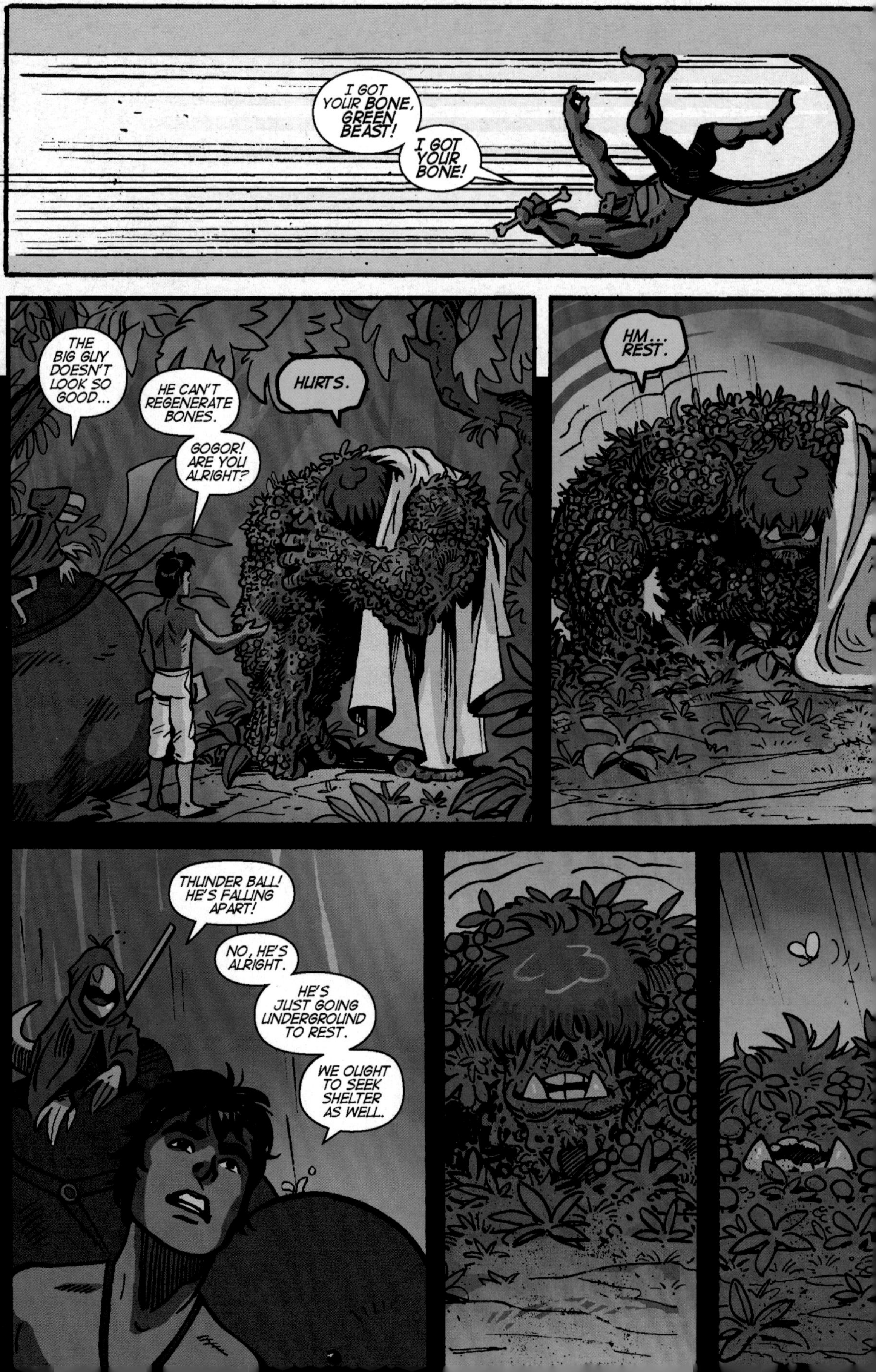
I GOT YOUR BONE, GREEN BEAST!
I GOT YOUR BONE!
THE BIG GUY DOESN'T LOOK SO GOOD...
HE CAN'T REGENERATE BONES.
GOGOR! ARE YOU ALRIGHT?
HURTS.
HM... REST.
THUNDER BALL! HE'S FALLING APART!
NO, HE'S ALRIGHT.
HE'S JUST GOING UNDERGROUND TO REST.
WE OUGHT TO SEEK SHELTER AS WELL.

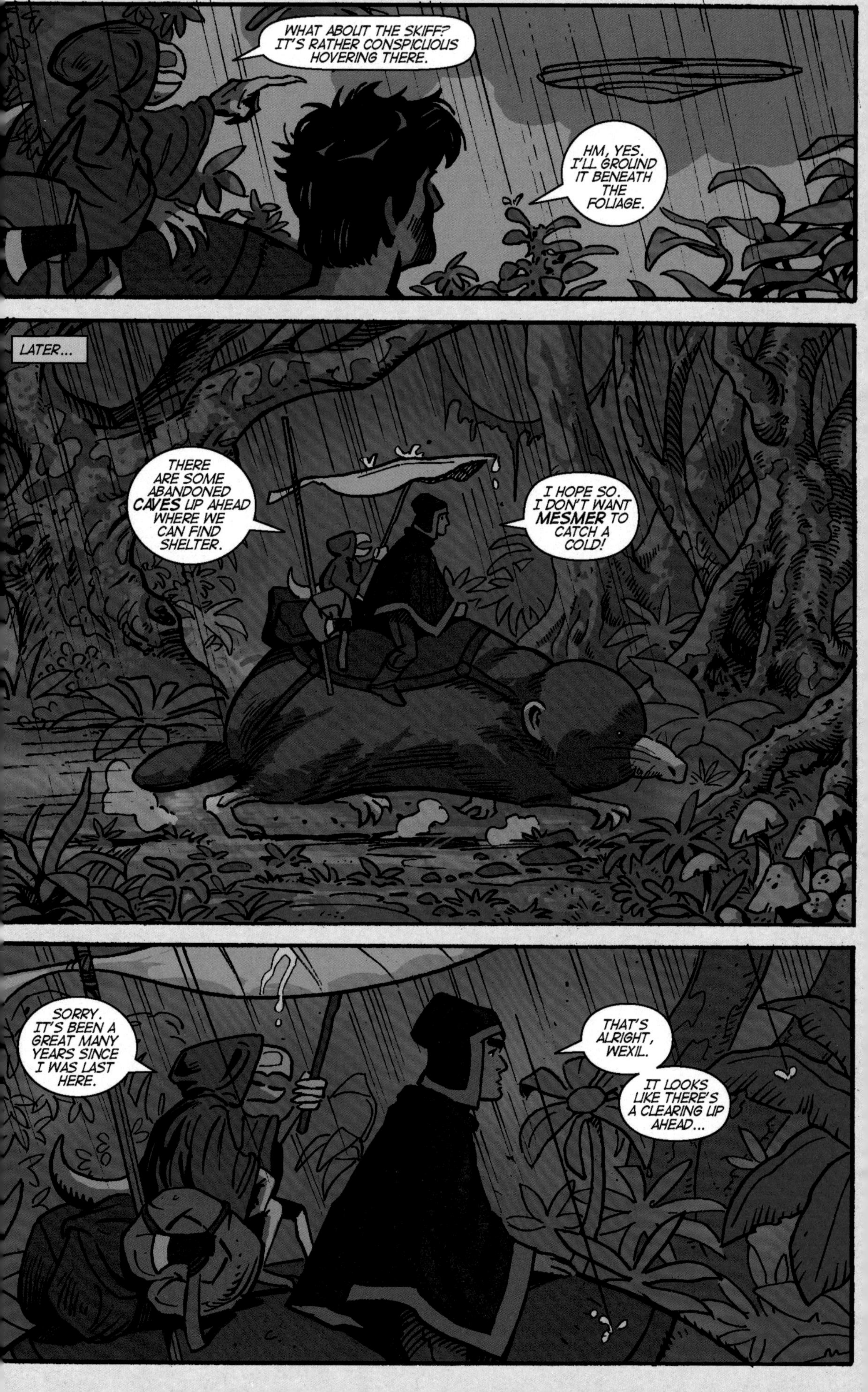
WHAT ABOUT THE SKIFF? IT'S RATHER CONSPICUOUS HOVERING THERE.
HM, YES. I'LL GROUND IT BENEATH THE FOLIAGE.
LATER...
THERE ARE SOME ABANDONED CAVES UP AHEAD WHERE WE CAN FIND SHELTER.
I HOPE SO. I DON'T WANT MESMER TO CATCH A COLD!
SORRY. IT'S BEEN A GREAT MANY YEARS SINCE I WAS LAST HERE.
THAT'S ALRIGHT, WEXIL.
IT LOOKS LIKE THERE'S A CLEARING UP AHEAD...

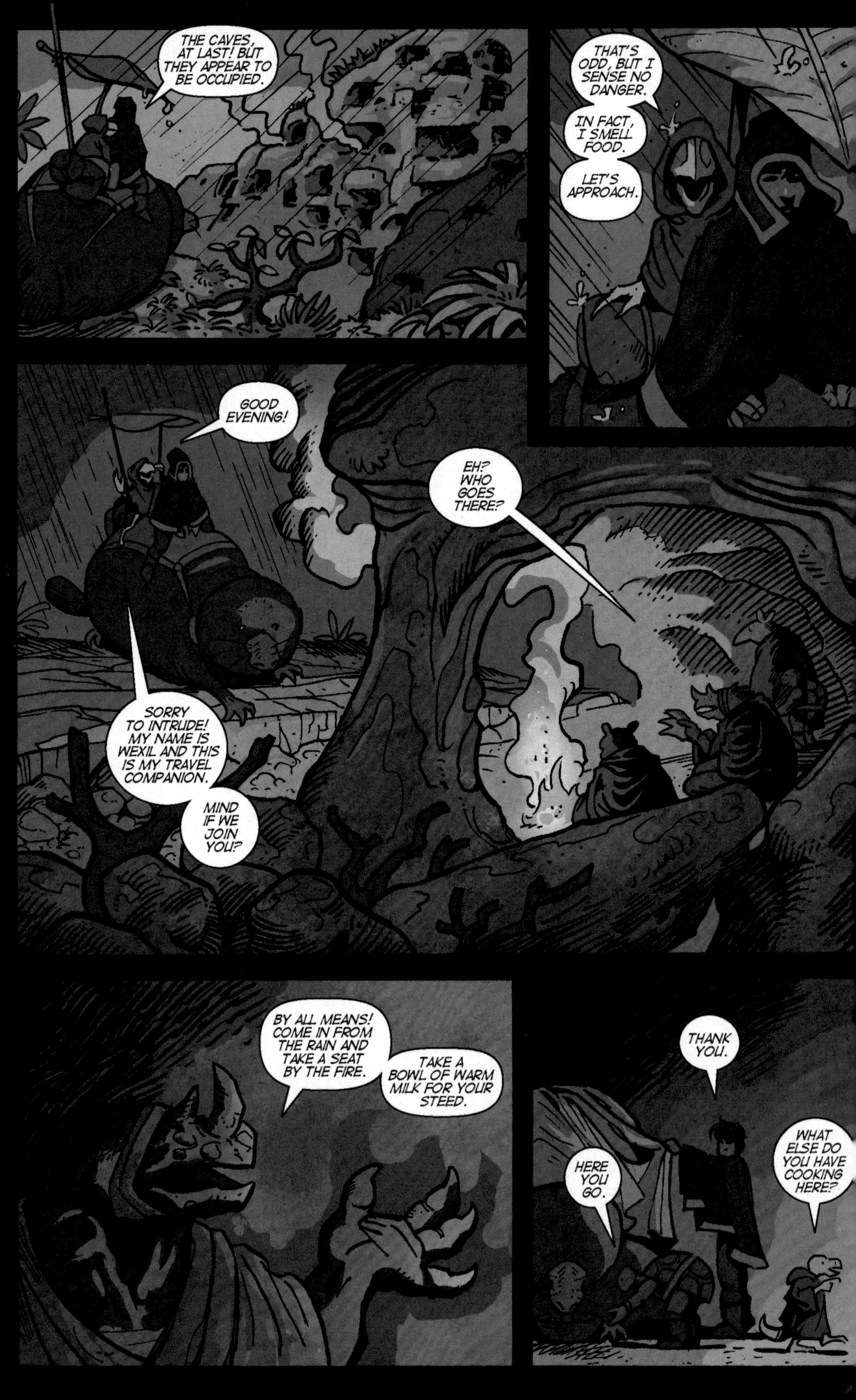
THE CAVES, AT LAST! BUT THEY APPEAR TO BE OCCUPIED.
THAT'S ODD, BUT I SENSE NO DANGER.
IN FACT, I SMELL FOOD.
LET'S APPROACH.
GOOD EVENING!
EH? WHO GOES THERE?
SORRY TO INTRUDE! MY NAME IS WEXIL AND THIS IS MY TRAVEL COMPANION.
MIND IF WE JOIN YOU?
BY ALL MEANS! COME IN FROM THE RAIN AND TAKE A SEAT BY THE FIRE.
TAKE A BOWL OF WARM MILK FOR YOUR STEED.
THANK YOU.
HERE YOU GO.
WHAT ELSE DO YOU HAVE COOKING HERE?

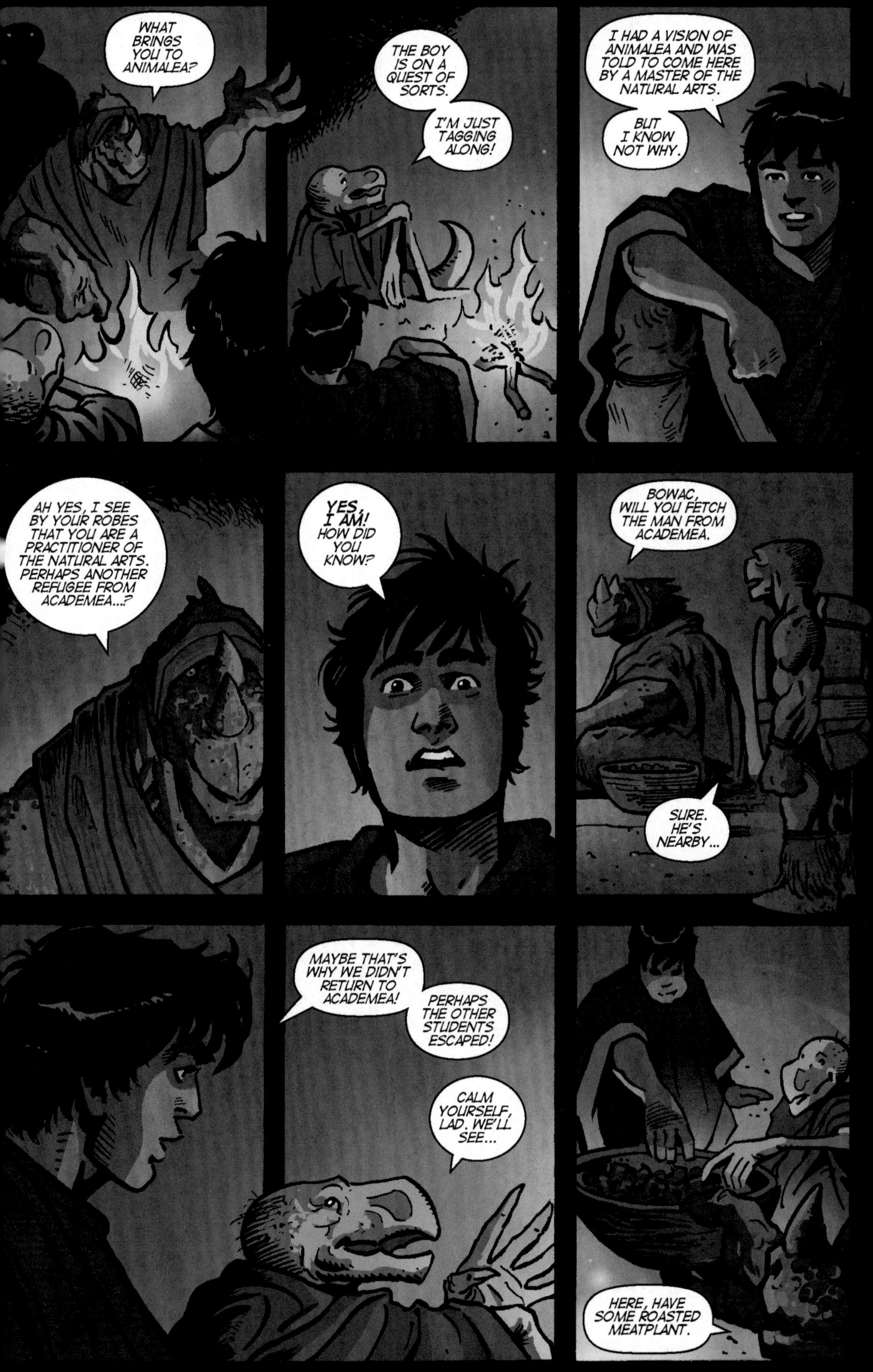
WHAT BRINGS YOU TO ANIMALEA?
THE BOY IS ON A QUEST OF SORTS.
I'M JUST TAGGING ALONG!
I HAD A VISION OF ANIMALEA AND WAS TOLD TO COME HERE BY A MASTER OF THE NATURAL ARTS.
BUT I KNOW NOT WHY.
AH YES, I SEE BY YOUR ROBES THAT YOU ARE A PRACTITIONER OF THE NATURAL ARTS. PERHAPS ANOTHER REFUGEE FROM ACADEMEA...?
YES, I AM! HOW DID YOU KNOW?
BOWAC, WILL YOU FETCH THE MAN FROM ACADEMEA.
SURE. HE'S NEARBY...
MAYBE THAT'S WHY WE DIDN'T RETURN TO ACADEMEA!
PERHAPS THE OTHER STUDENTS ESCAPED!
CALM YOURSELF, LAD. WE'LL SEE...
HERE, HAVE SOME ROASTED MEATPLANT.

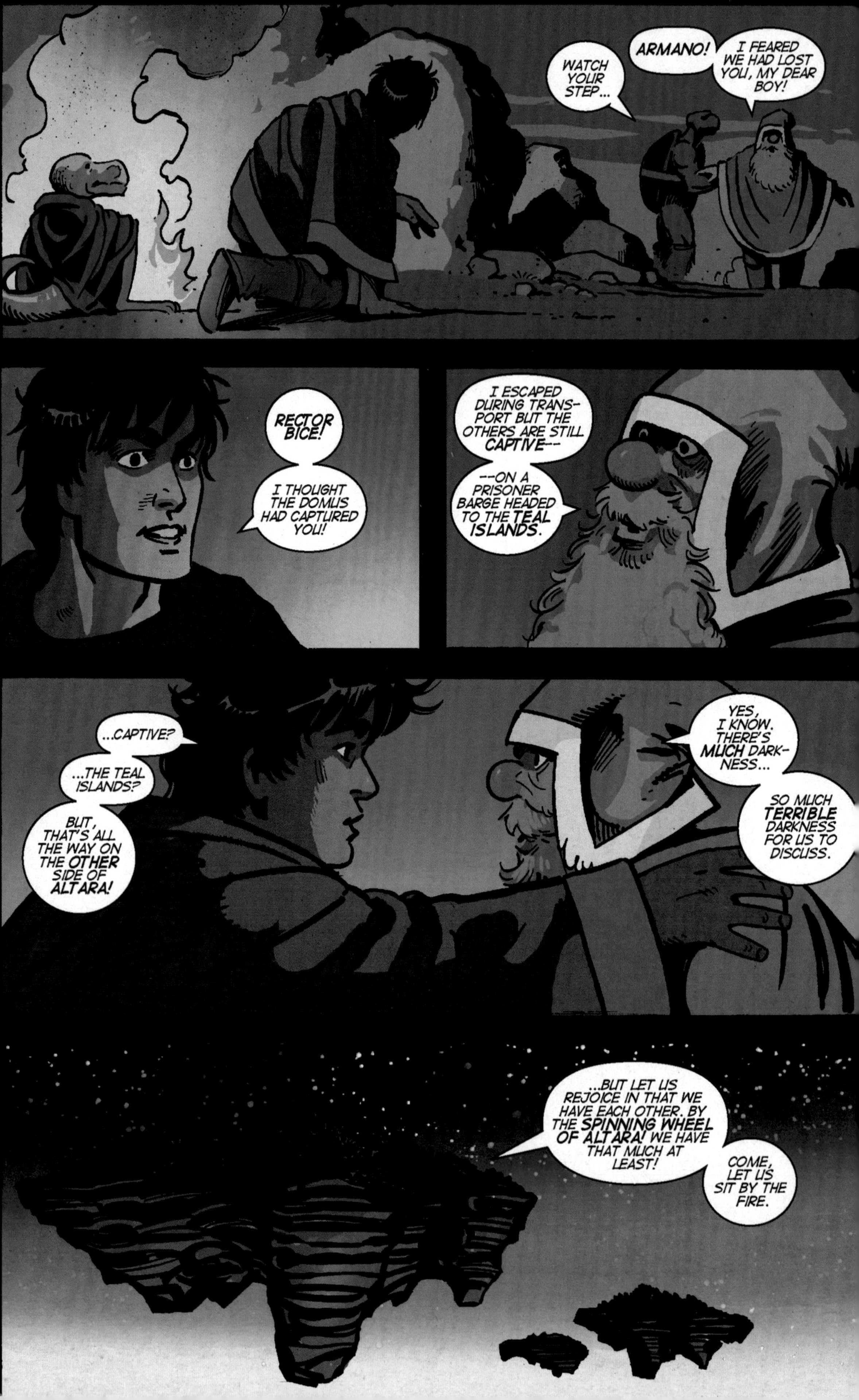
WATCH YOUR STEP...
ARMANO!
I FEARED WE HAD LOST YOU, MY DEAR BOY!
RECTOR BICE!
I THOUGHT THE DOMUS HAD CAPTURED YOU!
I ESCAPED DURING TRANSPORT BUT THE OTHERS ARE STILL CAPTIVE--
--ON A PRISONER BARGE HEADED TO THE TEAL ISLANDS.
...CAPTIVE?
...THE TEAL ISLANDS?
BUT, THAT'S ALL THE WAY ON THE OTHER SIDE OF ALTARA!
YES, I KNOW. THERE'S MUCH DARKNESS...
SO MUCH TERRIBLE DARKNESS FOR US TO DISCUSS.
...BUT LET US REJOICE IN THAT WE HAVE EACH OTHER. BY THE SPINNING WHEEL OF ALTARA! WE HAVE THAT MUCH AT LEAST!
COME, LET US SIT BY THE FIRE.

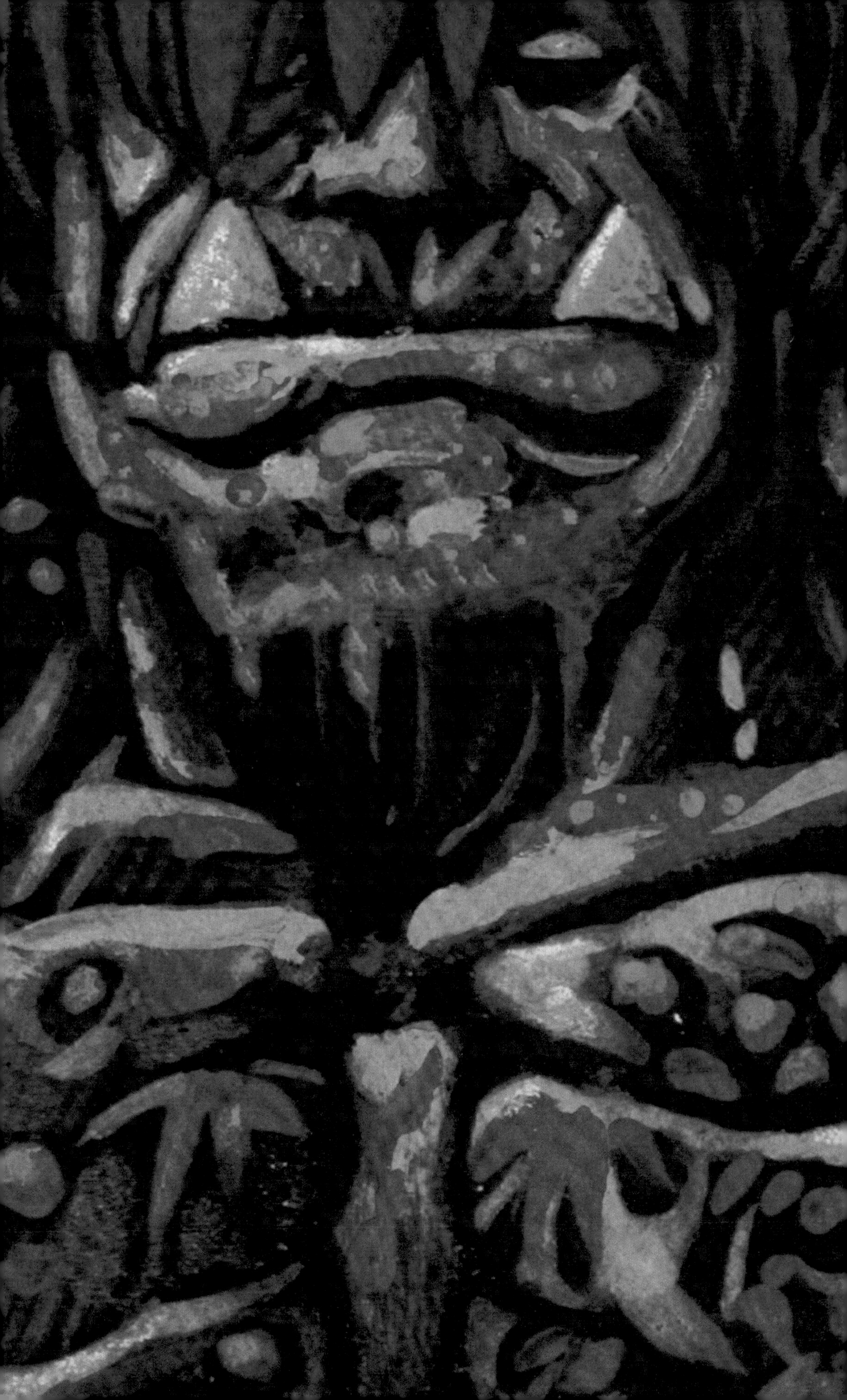

CHAPTER FOUR

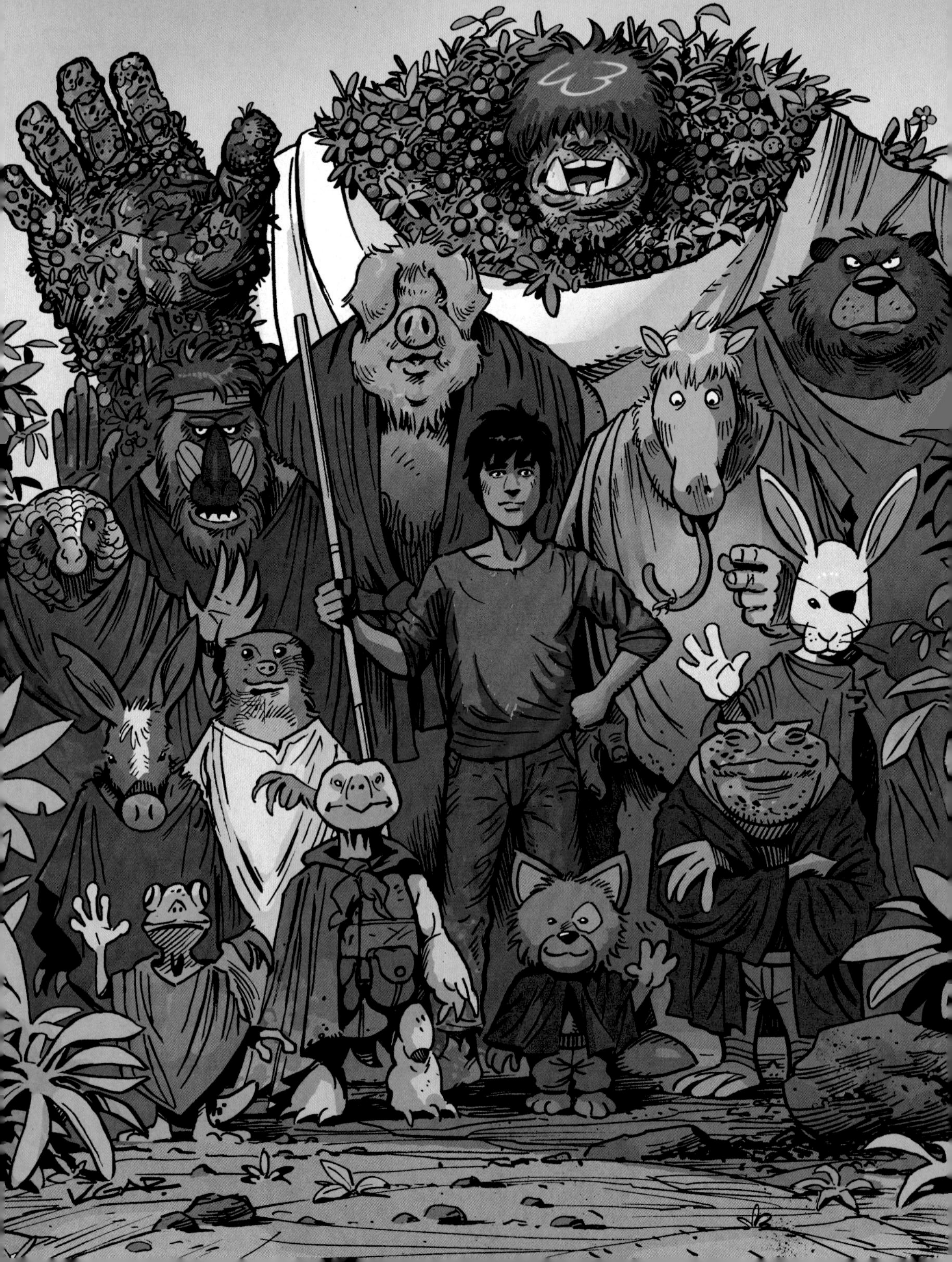

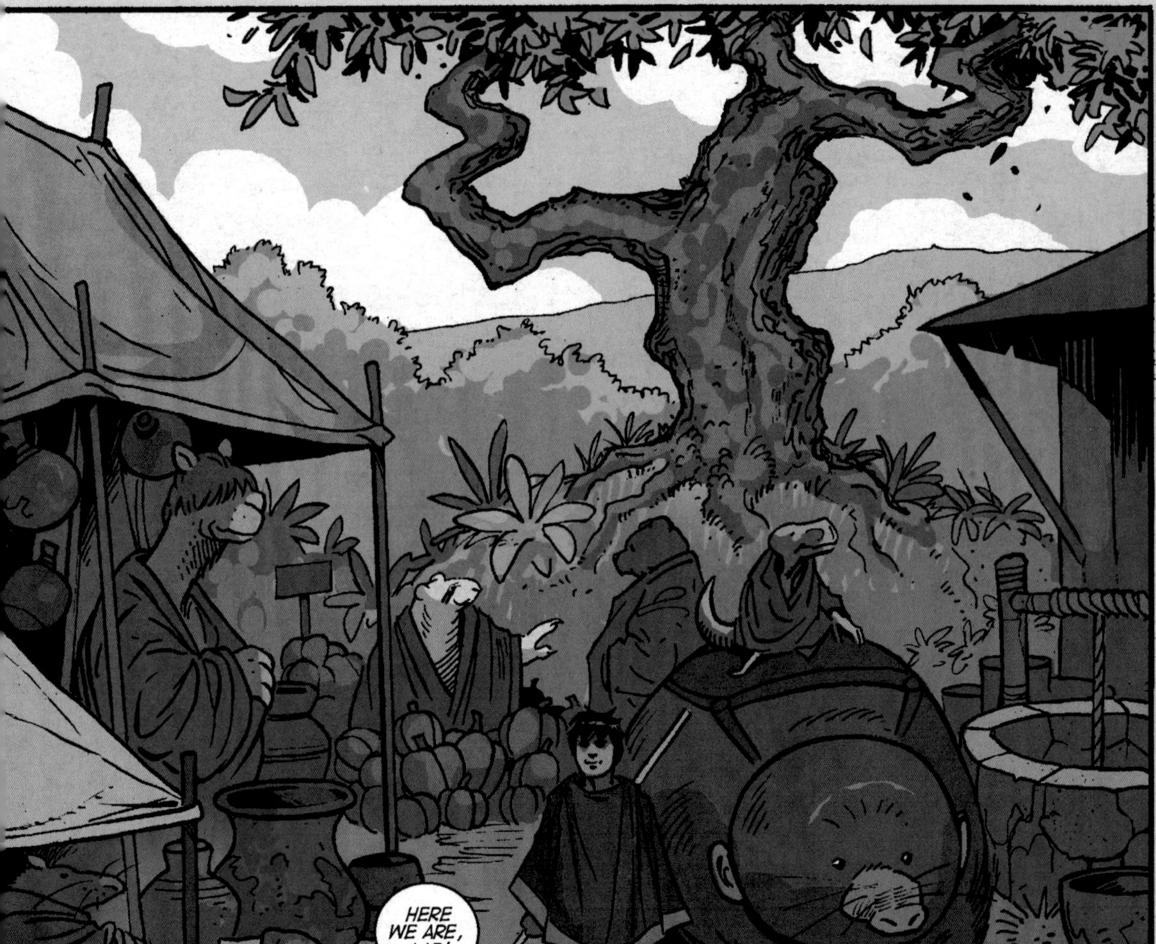
HERE WE ARE, LAD!
THIS IS THE CAMP WHERE THE ANIMAL MEN CONVENE. DOES IT LOOK FAMILIAR?

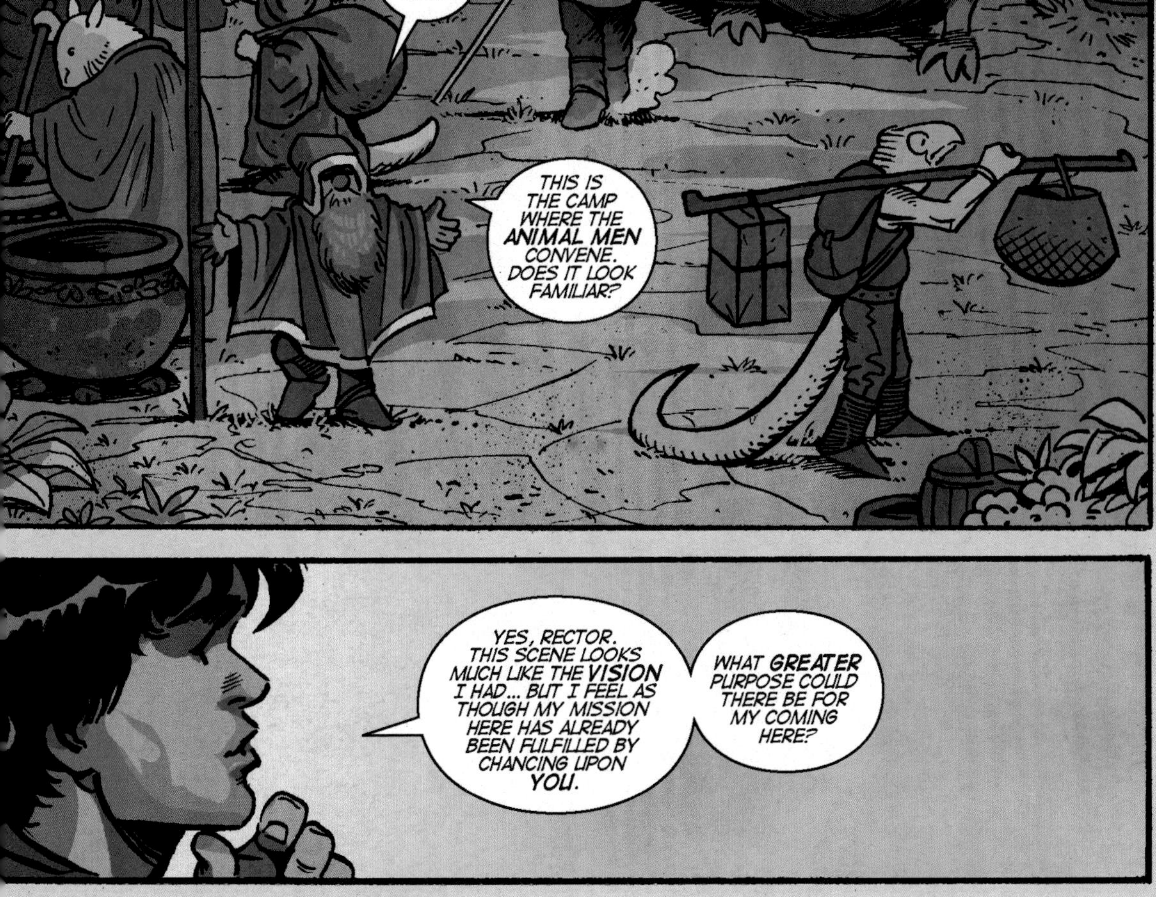
YES, RECTOR. THIS SCENE LOOKS MUCH LIKE THE VISION I HAD... BUT I FEEL AS THOUGH MY MISSION HERE HAS ALREADY BEEN FULFILLED BY CHANCING UPON YOU.
WHAT GREATER PURPOSE COULD THERE BE FOR MY COMING HERE?

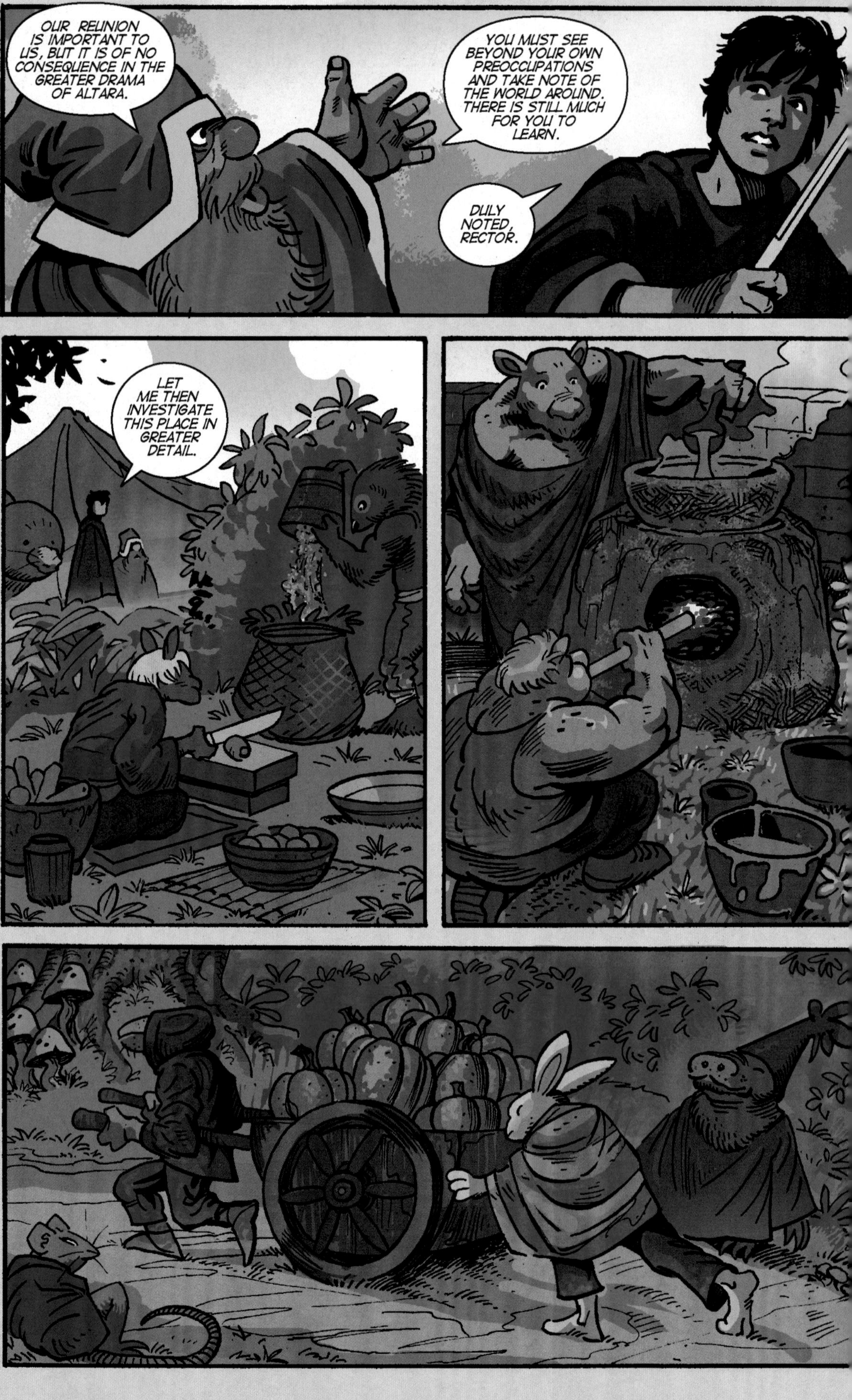
OUR REUNION IS IMPORTANT TO US, BUT IT IS OF NO CONSEQUENCE IN THE GREATER DRAMA OF ALTARA.
YOU MUST SEE BEYOND YOUR OWN PREOCCUPATIONS AND TAKE NOTE OF THE WORLD AROUND. THERE IS STILL MUCH FOR YOU TO LEARN.
DULY NOTED, RECTOR.
LET ME THEN INVESTIGATE THIS PLACE IN GREATER DETAIL.

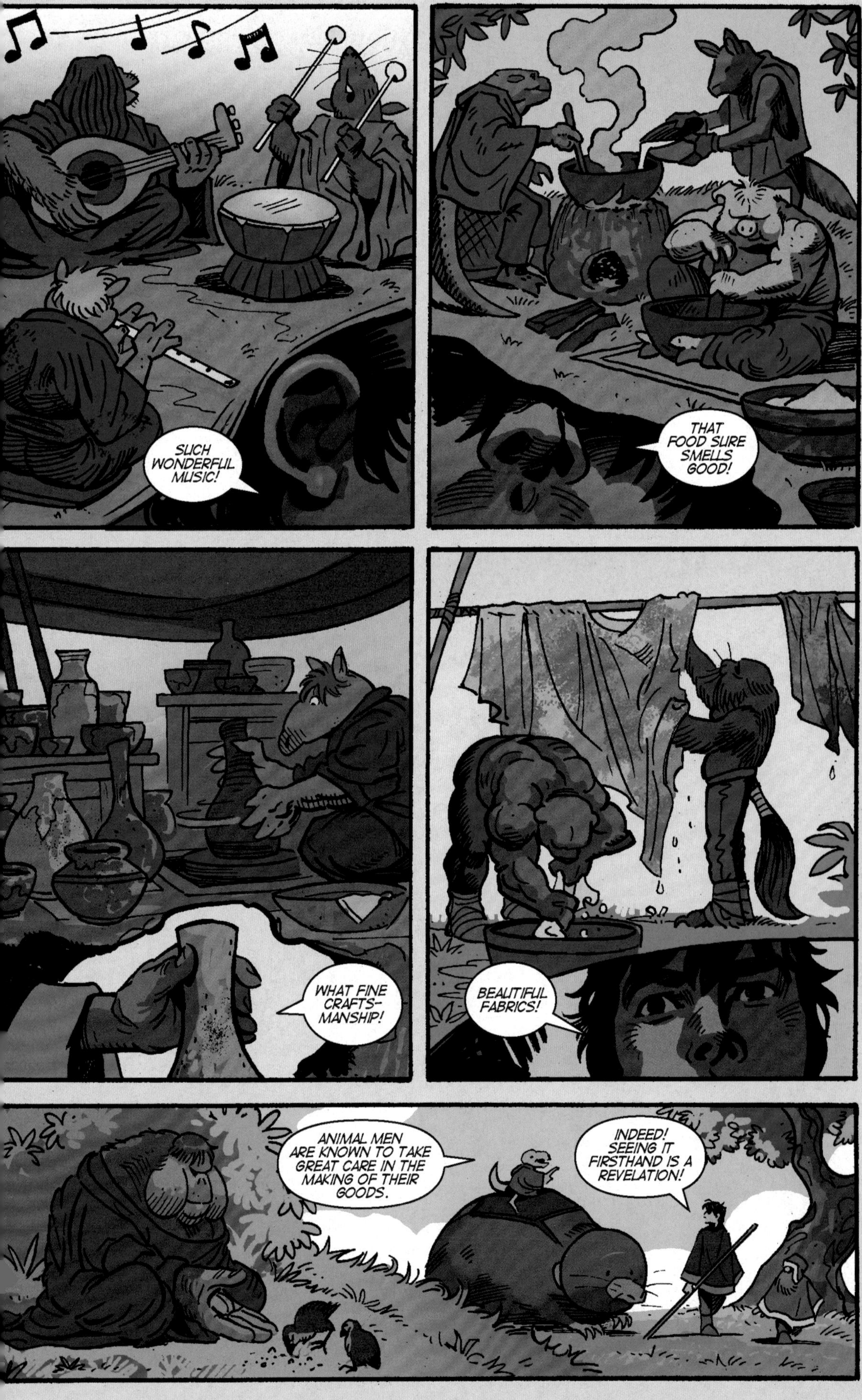
SUCH WONDERFUL MUSIC!
THAT FOOD SURE SMELLS GOOD!
WHAT FINE CRAFTS-MANSHIP!
BEAUTIFUL FABRICS!
ANIMAL MEN ARE KNOWN TO TAKE GREAT CARE IN THE MAKING OF THEIR GOODS.
INDEED! SEEING IT FIRSTHAND IS A REVELATION!

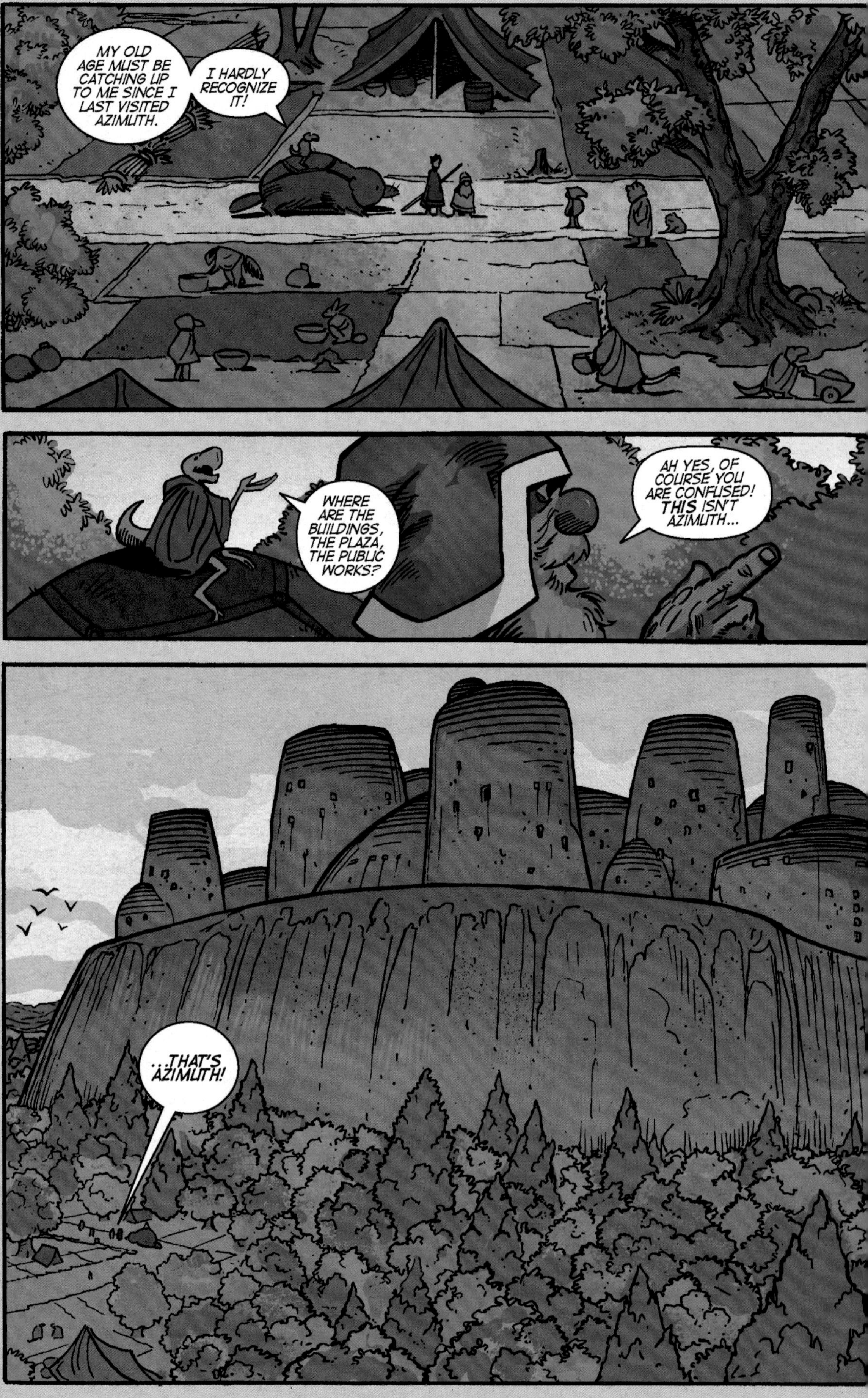
MY OLD AGE MUST BE CATCHING UP TO ME SINCE I LAST VISITED AZIMUTH.
I HARDLY RECOGNIZE IT!
WHERE ARE THE BUILDINGS, THE PLAZA, THE PUBLIC WORKS?
AH YES, OF COURSE YOU ARE CONFUSED! THIS ISN'T AZIMUTH...
...THAT'S AZIMUTH!

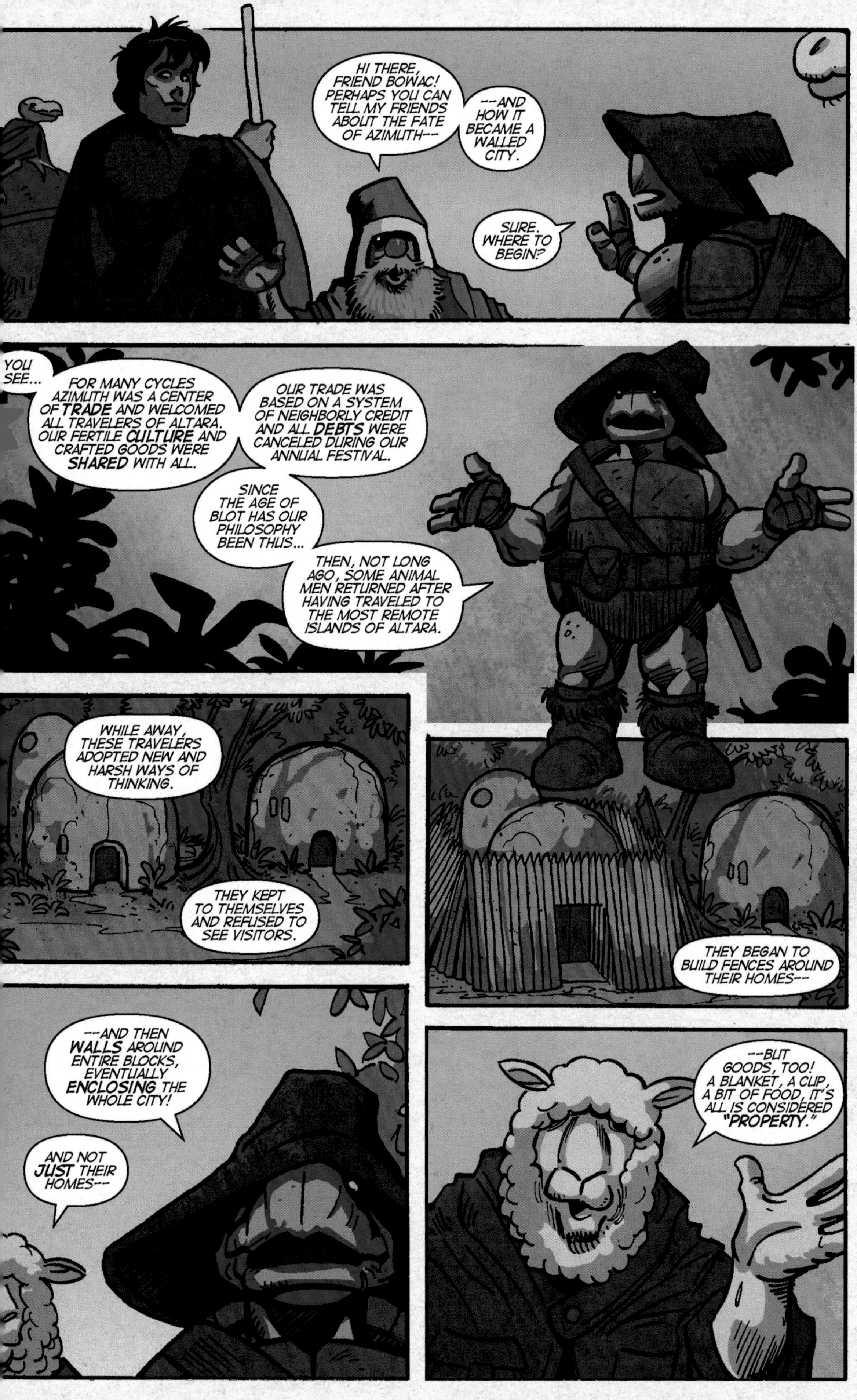
HI THERE, FRIEND BOWAC! PERHAPS YOU CAN TELL MY FRIENDS ABOUT THE FATE OF AZIMUTH--
--AND HOW IT BECAME A WALLED CITY.
SURE. WHERE TO BEGIN?
YOU SEE...
FOR MANY CYCLES AZIMUTH WAS A CENTER OF TRADE AND WELCOMED ALL TRAVELERS OF ALTARA. OUR FERTILE CULTURE AND CRAFTED GOODS WERE SHARED WITH ALL.
OUR TRADE WAS BASED ON A SYSTEM OF NEIGHBORLY CREDIT AND ALL DEBTS WERE CANCELED DURING OUR ANNUAL FESTIVAL.
SINCE THE AGE OF BLOT HAS OUR PHILOSOPHY BEEN THUS...
THEN, NOT LONG AGO, SOME ANIMAL MEN RETURNED AFTER HAVING TRAVELED TO THE MOST REMOTE ISLANDS OF ALTARA.
WHILE AWAY, THESE TRAVELERS ADOPTED NEW AND HARSH WAYS OF THINKING.
THEY KEPT TO THEMSELVES AND REFUSED TO SEE VISITORS.
THEY BEGAN TO BUILD FENCES AROUND THEIR HOMES--
--AND THEN WALLS AROUND ENTIRE BLOCKS, EVENTUALLY ENCLOSING THE WHOLE CITY!
AND NOT JUST THEIR HOMES--
--BUT GOODS, TOO! A BLANKET, A CUP, A BIT OF FOOD, IT'S ALL IS CONSIDERED "PROPERTY."

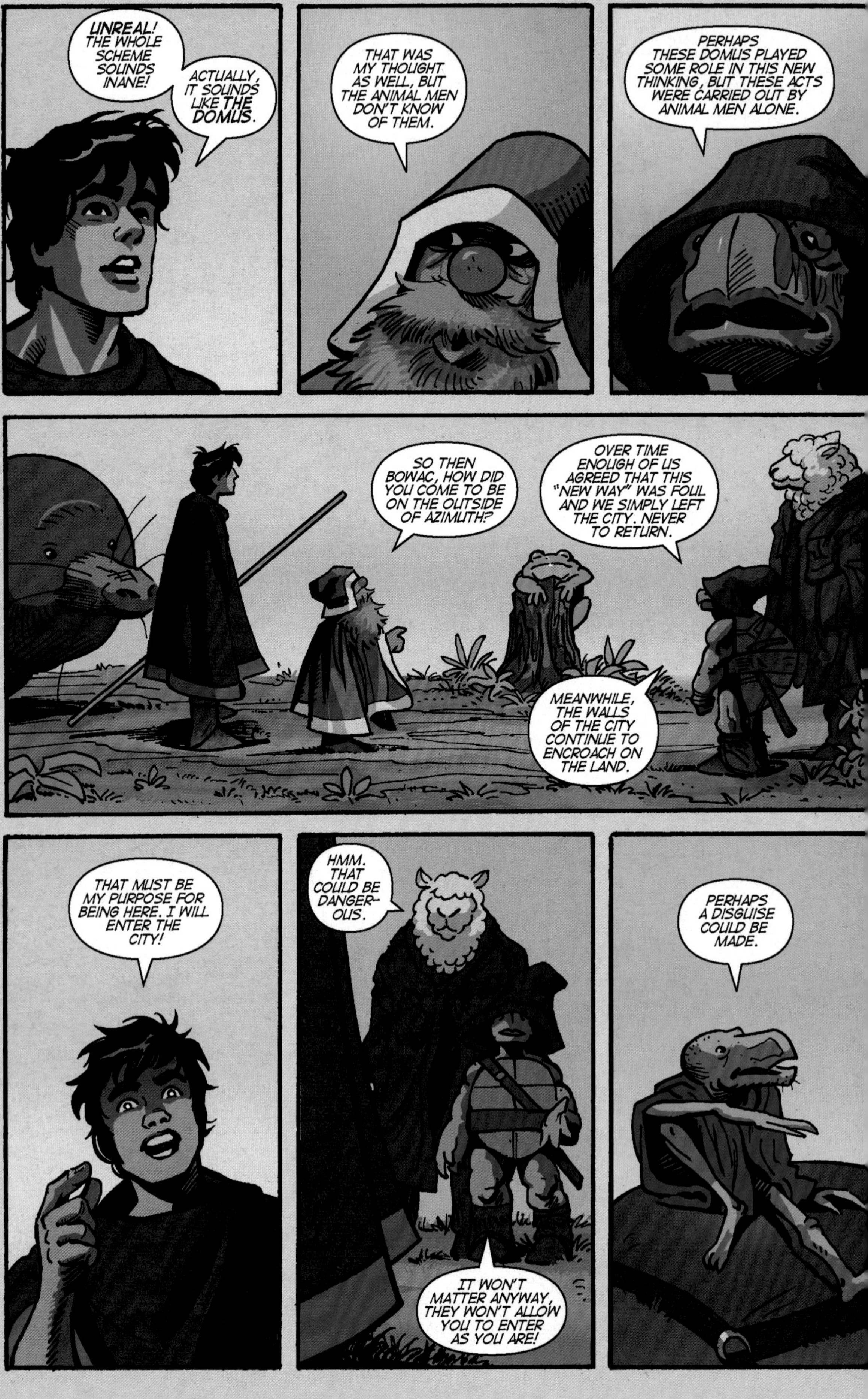
UNREAL! THE WHOLE SCHEME SOUNDS INANE!
ACTUALLY, IT SOUNDS LIKE THE DOMUS.
THAT WAS MY THOUGHT AS WELL, BUT THE ANIMAL MEN DON'T KNOW OF THEM.
PERHAPS THESE DOMUS PLAYED SOME ROLE IN THIS NEW THINKING, BUT THESE ACTS WERE CARRIED OUT BY ANIMAL MEN ALONE.
SO THEN BOWAC, HOW DID YOU COME TO BE ON THE OUTSIDE OF AZIMUTH?
OVER TIME ENOUGH OF US AGREED THAT THIS "NEW WAY" WAS FOUL AND WE SIMPLY LEFT THE CITY. NEVER TO RETURN.
MEANWHILE, THE WALLS OF THE CITY CONTINUE TO ENCROACH ON THE LAND.
THAT MUST BE MY PURPOSE FOR BEING HERE. I WILL ENTER THE CITY!
HMM. THAT COULD BE DANGER-OUS.
IT WON'T MATTER ANYWAY, THEY WON'T ALLOW YOU TO ENTER AS YOU ARE!
PERHAPS A DISGUISE COULD BE MADE.

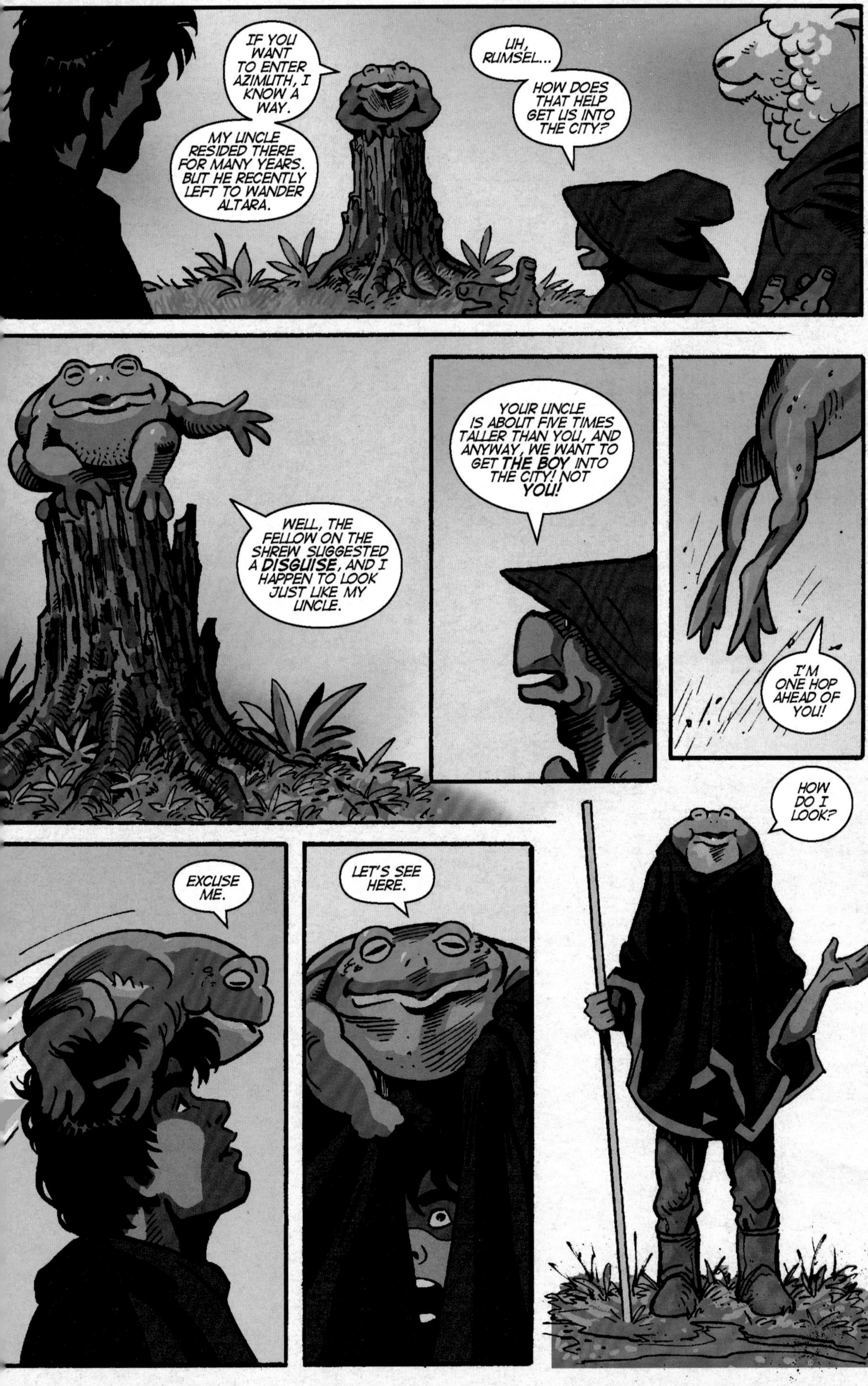
IF YOU WANT TO ENTER AZIMUTH, I KNOW A WAY.
MY UNCLE RESIDED THERE FOR MANY YEARS. BUT HE RECENTLY LEFT TO WANDER ALTARA.
UH, RUMSEL...
HOW DOES THAT HELP GET US INTO THE CITY?
WELL, THE FELLOW ON THE SHREW SUGGESTED A DISGUISE, AND I HAPPEN TO LOOK JUST LIKE MY UNCLE.
YOUR UNCLE IS ABOUT FIVE TIMES TALLER THAN YOU, AND ANYWAY, WE WANT TO GET THE BOY INTO THE CITY! NOT YOU!
I'M ONE HOP AHEAD OF YOU!
EXCUSE ME.
LET'S SEE HERE.
HOW DO I LOOK?

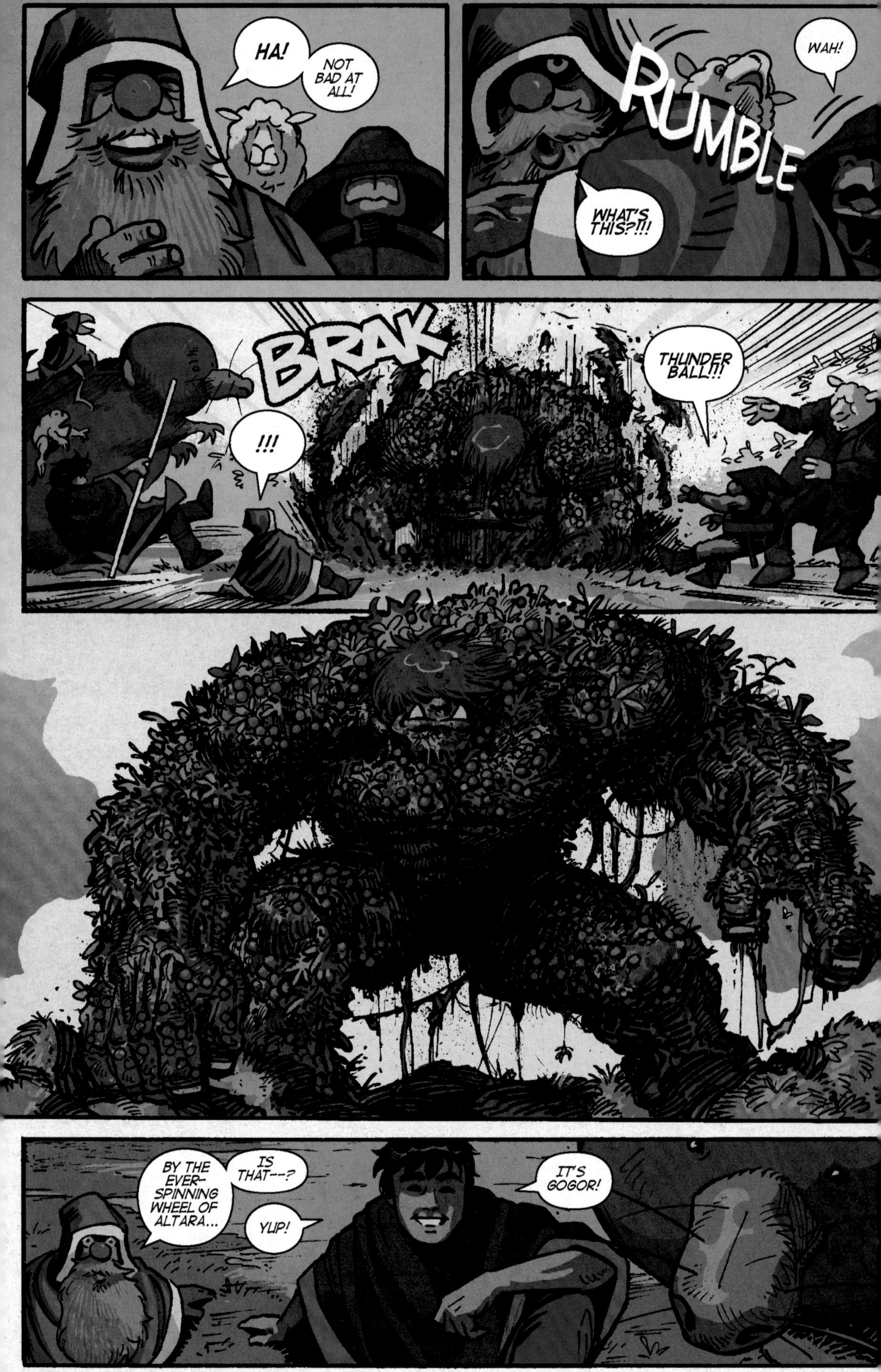
HA!
NOT BAD AT ALL!
WAH!
RUMBLE
WHAT'S THIS?!!!
BRAK
!!!
THUNDER BALL!!!
BY THE EVER-SPINNING WHEEL OF ALTARA...
IS THAT--?
YUP!
IT'S GOGOR!

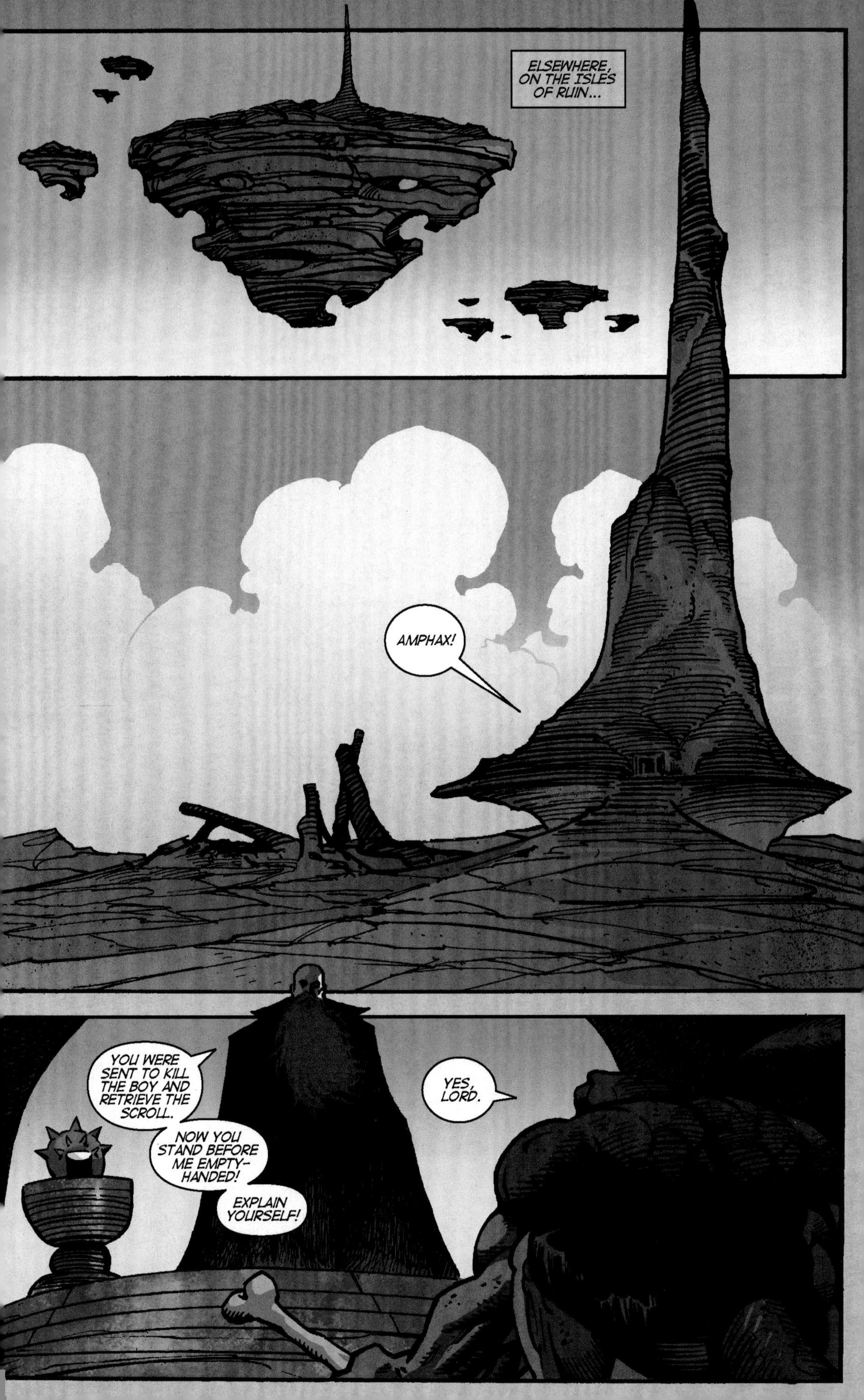
ELSEWHERE, ON THE ISLES OF RUIN...
AMPHAX!
YOU WERE SENT TO KILL THE BOY AND RETRIEVE THE SCROLL.
NOW YOU STAND BEFORE ME EMPTY-HANDED!
EXPLAIN YOURSELF!
YES, LORD.

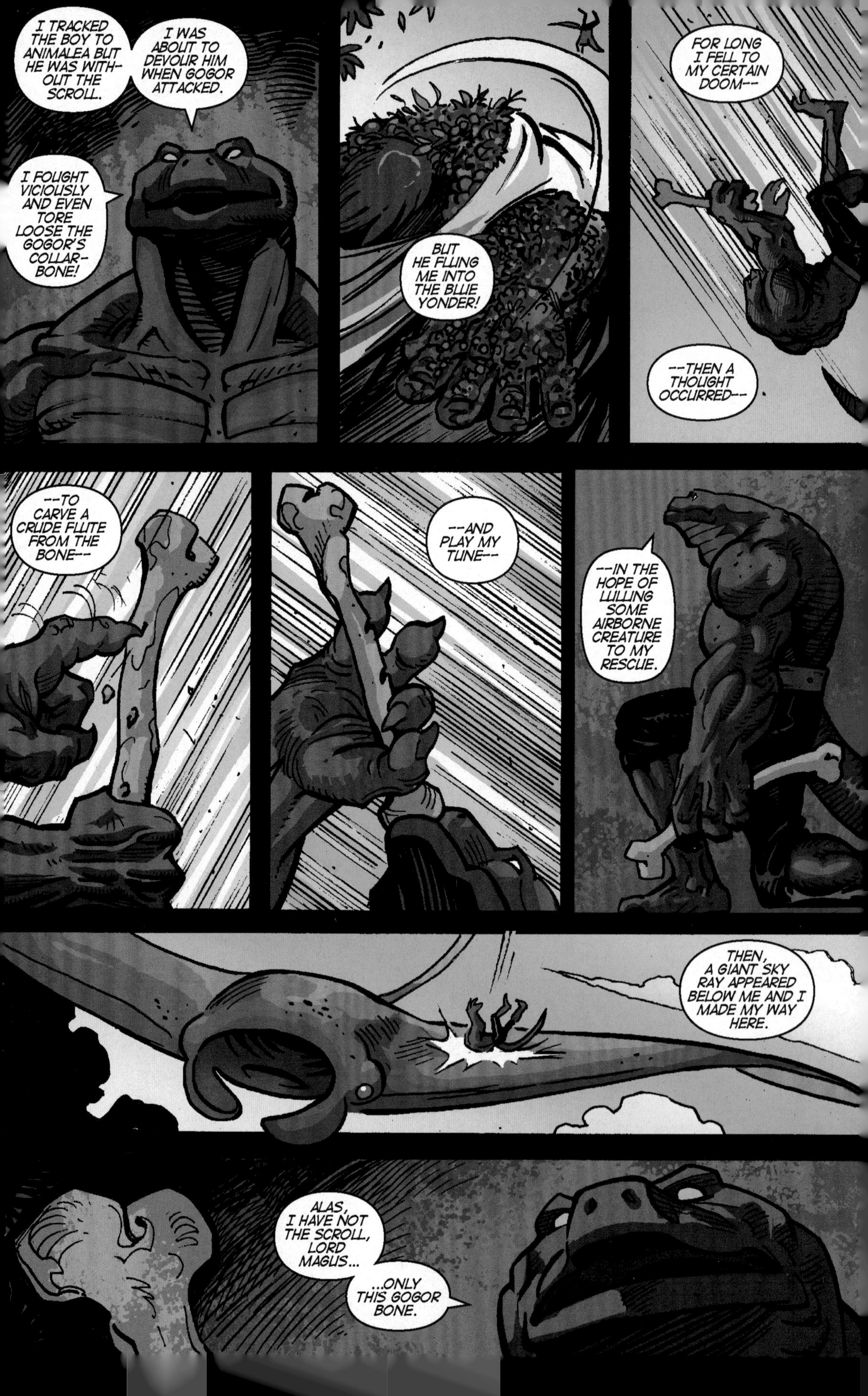
I TRACKED THE BOY TO ANIMALEA BUT HE WAS WITH-OUT THE SCROLL.
I WAS ABOUT TO DEVOUR HIM WHEN GOGOR ATTACKED.
I FOUGHT VICIOUSLY AND EVEN TORE LOOSE THE GOGOR'S COLLAR-BONE!
BUT HE FLUNG ME INTO THE BLUE YONDER!
FOR LONG I FELL TO MY CERTAIN DOOM--
--THEN A THOUGHT OCCURRED--
--TO CARVE A CRUDE FLUTE FROM THE BONE--
--AND PLAY MY TUNE--
--IN THE HOPE OF LULLING SOME AIRBORNE CREATURE TO MY RESCUE.
THEN, A GIANT SKY RAY APPEARED BELOW ME AND I MADE MY WAY HERE.
ALAS, I HAVE NOT THE SCROLL, LORD MAGUS...
...ONLY THIS GOGOR BONE.

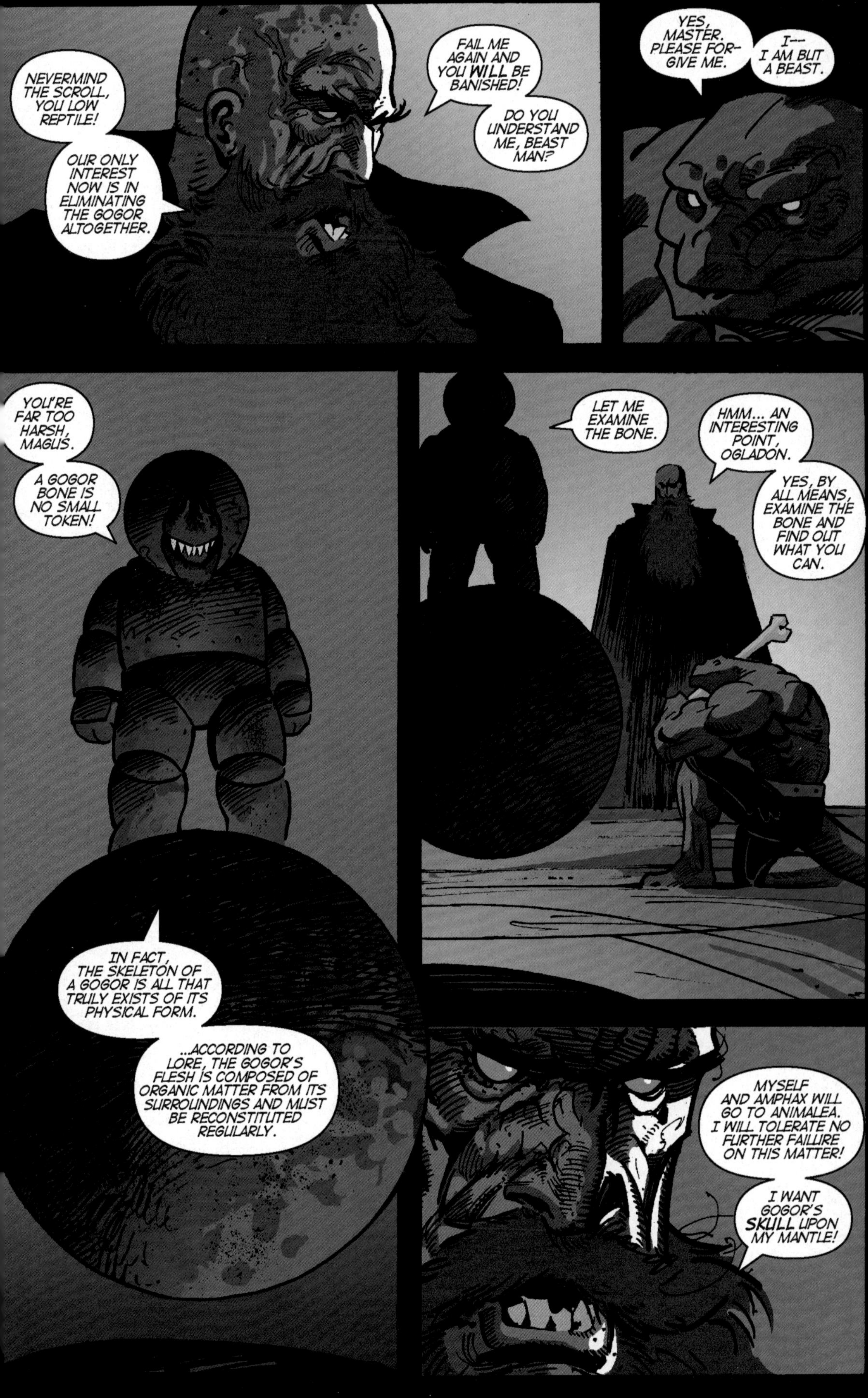

NEVERMIND THE SCROLL, YOU LOW REPTILE!
OUR ONLY INTEREST NOW IS IN ELIMINATING THE GOGOR ALTOGETHER.
FAIL ME AGAIN AND YOU WILL BE BANISHED!
DO YOU UNDERSTAND ME, BEAST MAN?
YES, MASTER. PLEASE FOR-GIVE ME.
I-- I AM BUT A BEAST.
YOU'RE FAR TOO HARSH, MAGUS.
A GOGOR BONE IS NO SMALL TOKEN!
LET ME EXAMINE THE BONE.
HMM... AN INTERESTING POINT, OGLADON.
YES, BY ALL MEANS, EXAMINE THE BONE AND FIND OUT WHAT YOU CAN.
IN FACT, THE SKELETON OF A GOGOR IS ALL THAT TRULY EXISTS OF ITS PHYSICAL FORM.
...ACCORDING TO LORE, THE GOGOR'S FLESH IS COMPOSED OF ORGANIC MATTER FROM ITS SURROUNDINGS AND MUST BE RECONSTITUTED REGULARLY.
MYSELF AND AMPHAX WILL GO TO ANIMALEA. I WILL TOLERATE NO FURTHER FAILURE ON THIS MATTER!
I WANT GOGOR'S SKULL UPON MY MANTLE!

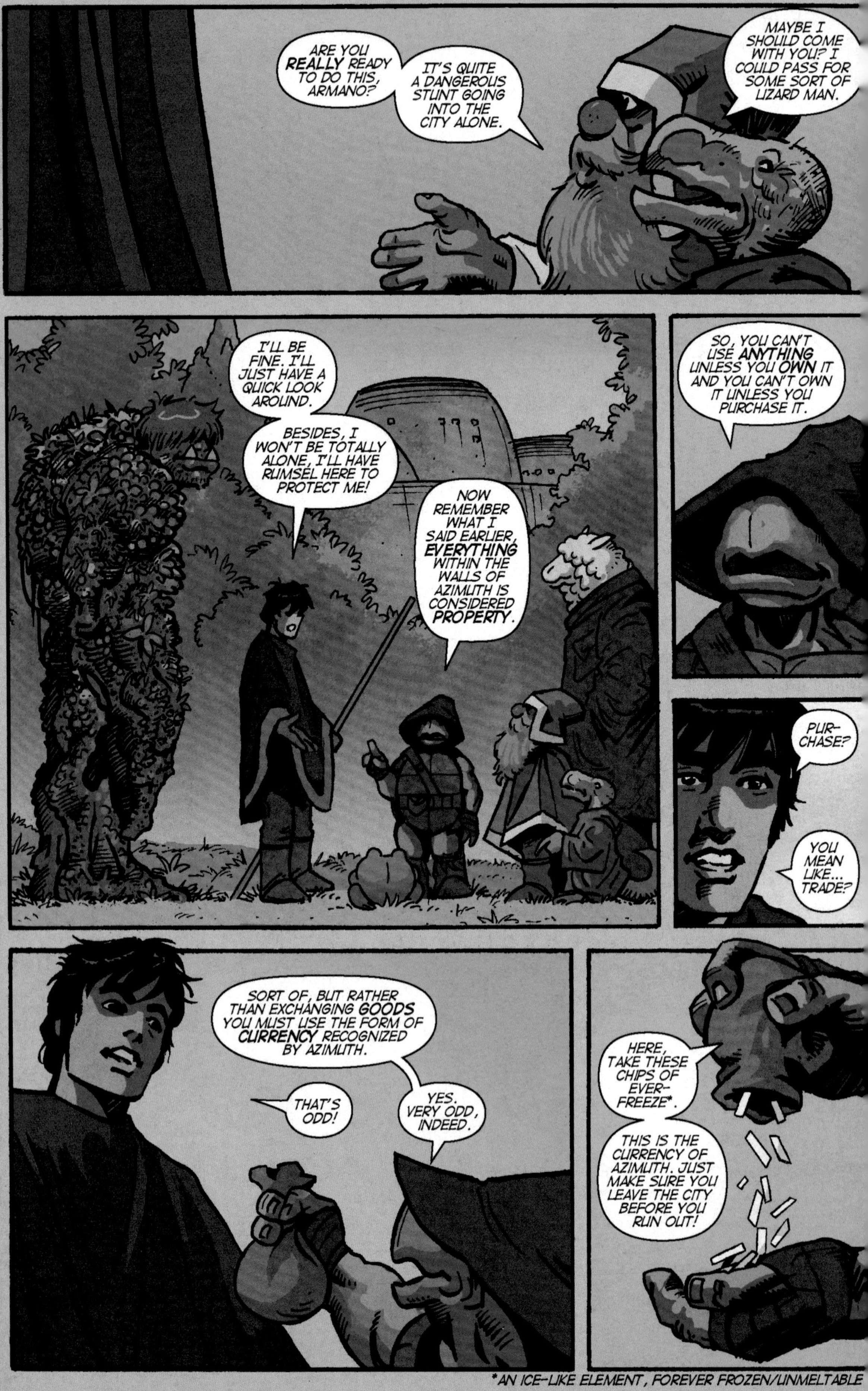
ARE YOU REALLY READY TO DO THIS, ARMANO?
IT'S QUITE A DANGEROUS STUNT GOING INTO THE CITY ALONE.
MAYBE I SHOULD COME WITH YOU? I COULD PASS FOR SOME SORT OF LIZARD MAN.
I'LL BE FINE. I'LL JUST HAVE A QUICK LOOK AROUND.
BESIDES, I WON'T BE TOTALLY ALONE, I'LL HAVE RUMSÉL HERE TO PROTECT ME!
NOW REMEMBER WHAT I SAID EARLIER, EVERYTHING WITHIN THE WALLS OF AZIMUTH IS CONSIDERED PROPERTY.
SO, YOU CAN'T USE ANYTHING UNLESS YOU OWN IT AND YOU CAN'T OWN IT UNLESS YOU PURCHASE IT.
PUR-CHASE?
YOU MEAN LIKE... TRADE?
SORT OF, BUT RATHER THAN EXCHANGING GOODS YOU MUST USE THE FORM OF CURRENCY RECOGNIZED BY AZIMUTH.
THAT'S ODD!
YES. VERY ODD, INDEED.
HERE, TAKE THESE CHIPS OF EVER-FREEZE*.
THIS IS THE CURRENCY OF AZIMUTH. JUST MAKE SURE YOU LEAVE THE CITY BEFORE YOU RUN OUT!

*AN ICE-LIKE ELEMENT, FOREVER FROZEN/UNMELTABLE

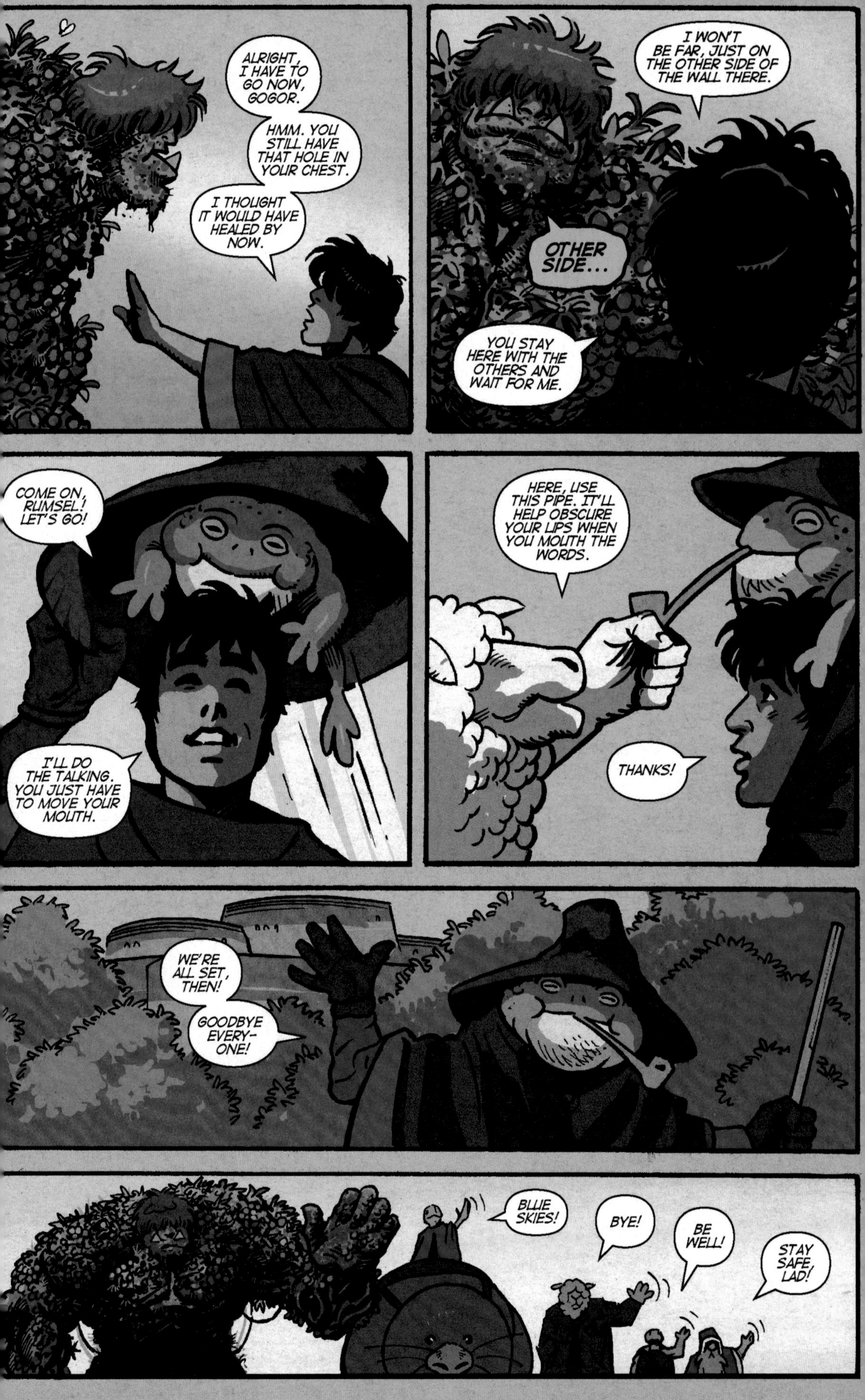
ALRIGHT, I HAVE TO GO NOW, GOGOR.
HMM. YOU STILL HAVE THAT HOLE IN YOUR CHEST.
I THOUGHT IT WOULD HAVE HEALED BY NOW.
I WON'T BE FAR, JUST ON THE OTHER SIDE OF THE WALL THERE.
OTHER SIDE...
YOU STAY HERE WITH THE OTHERS AND WAIT FOR ME.
COME ON, RUMSEL! LET'S GO!
I'LL DO THE TALKING. YOU JUST HAVE TO MOVE YOUR MOUTH.
HERE, USE THIS PIPE. IT'LL HELP OBSCURE YOUR LIPS WHEN YOU MOUTH THE WORDS.
THANKS!
WE'RE ALL SET, THEN!
GOODBYE EVERY-ONE!
BLUE SKIES!
BYE!
BE WELL!
STAY SAFE, LAD!

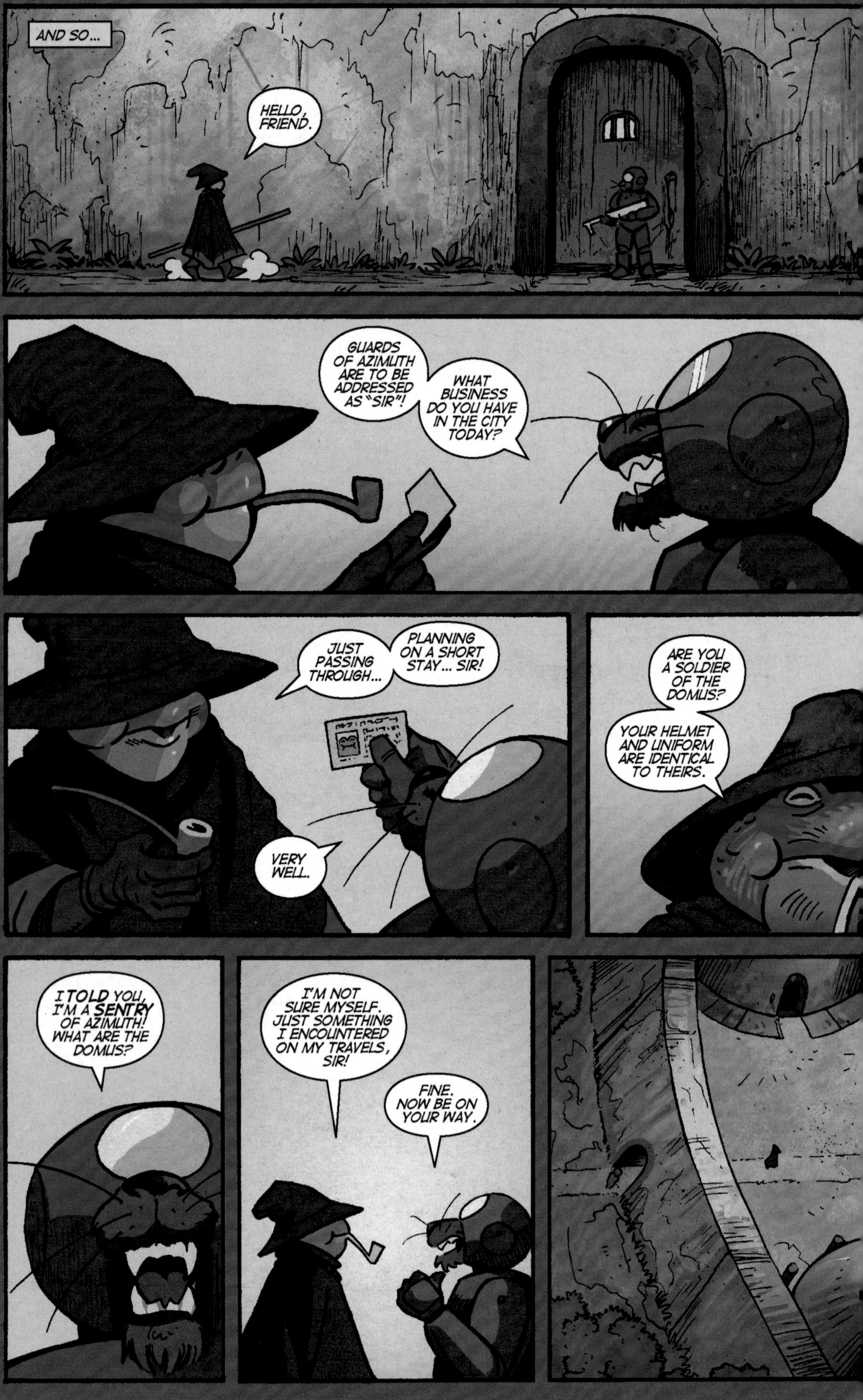
AND SO...
HELLO, FRIEND.
GUARDS OF AZIMUTH ARE TO BE ADDRESSED AS "SIR"!
WHAT BUSINESS DO YOU HAVE IN THE CITY TODAY?
JUST PASSING THROUGH...
PLANNING ON A SHORT STAY... SIR!
VERY WELL.
ARE YOU A SOLDIER OF THE DOMUS?
YOUR HELMET AND UNIFORM ARE IDENTICAL TO THEIRS.
I TOLD YOU, I'M A SENTRY OF AZIMUTH! WHAT ARE THE DOMUS?
I'M NOT SURE MYSELF. JUST SOMETHING I ENCOUNTERED ON MY TRAVELS, SIR!
FINE. NOW BE ON YOUR WAY.

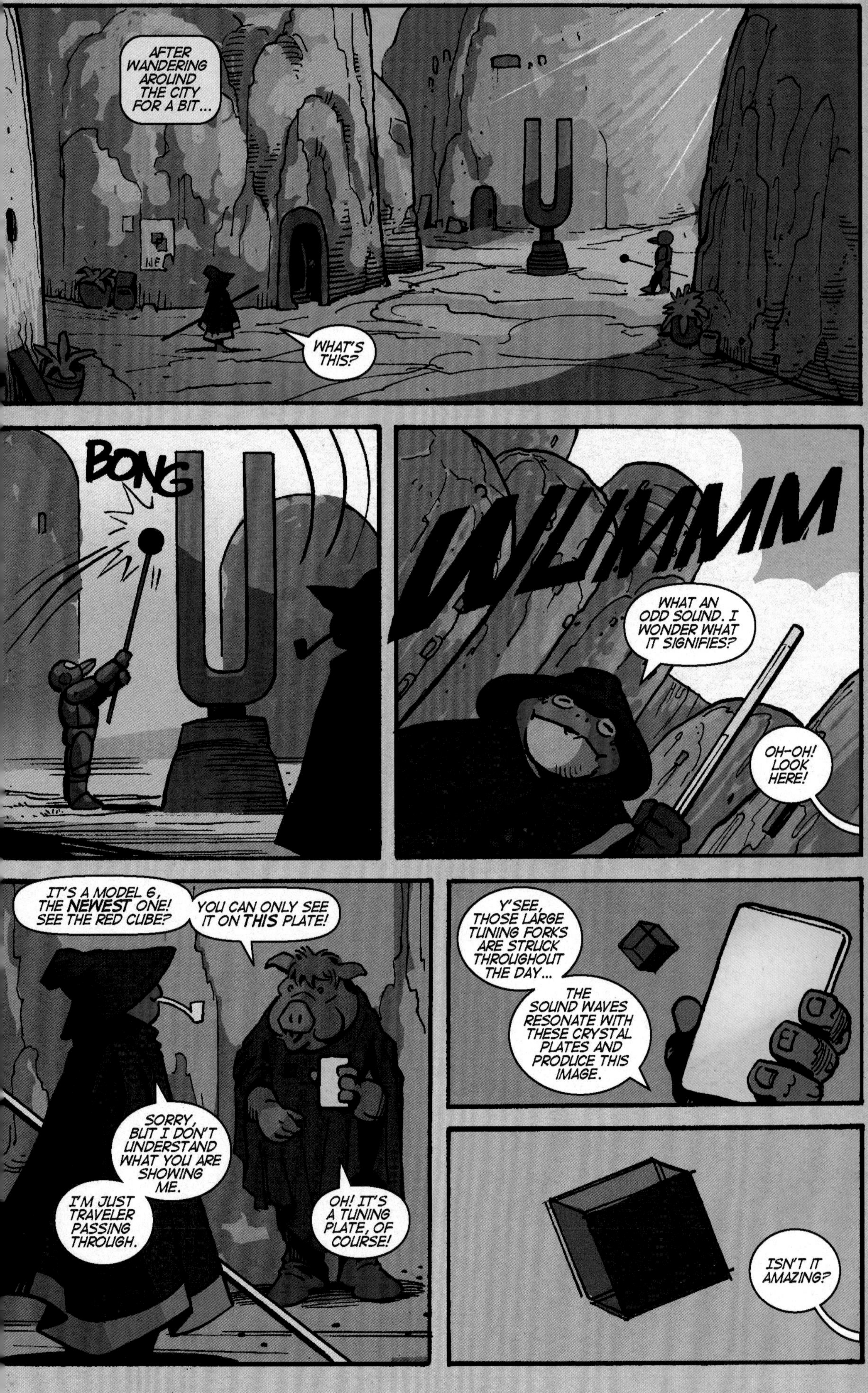
AFTER WANDERING AROUND THE CITY FOR A BIT...
WHAT'S THIS?
BONG
WUMMM
WHAT AN ODD SOUND. I WONDER WHAT IT SIGNIFIES?
OH-OH! LOOK HERE!
IT'S A MODEL 6, THE NEWEST ONE! SEE THE RED CUBE?
YOU CAN ONLY SEE IT ON THIS PLATE!
SORRY, BUT I DON'T UNDERSTAND WHAT YOU ARE SHOWING ME.
I'M JUST TRAVELER PASSING THROUGH.
OH! IT'S A TUNING PLATE, OF COURSE!
Y'SEE, THOSE LARGE TUNING FORKS ARE STRUCK THROUGHOUT THE DAY...
THE SOUND WAVES RESONATE WITH THESE CRYSTAL PLATES AND PRODUCE THIS IMAGE.
ISN'T IT AMAZING?

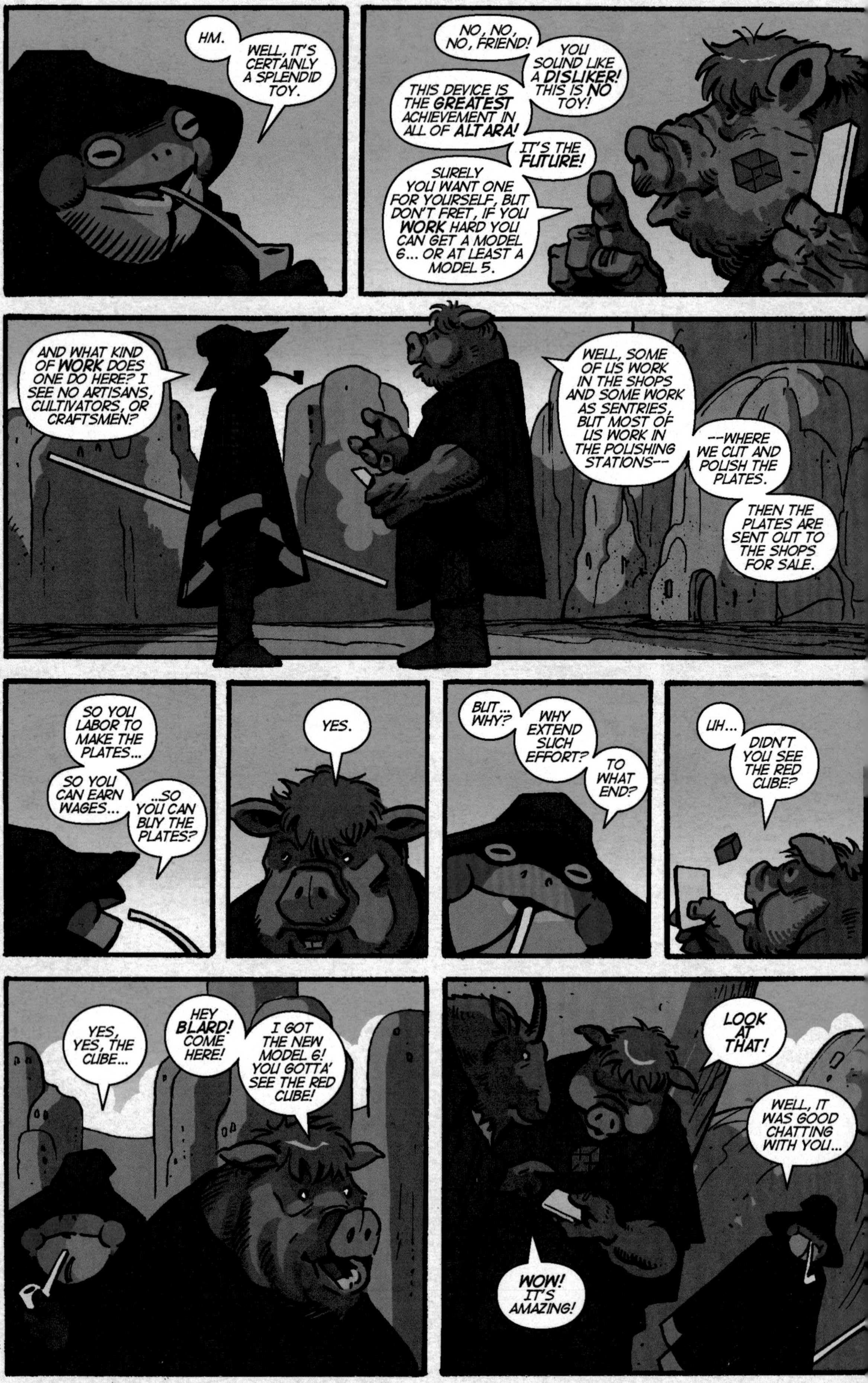
HM.
WELL, IT'S CERTAINLY A SPLENDID TOY.
NO, NO, NO, FRIEND!
YOU SOUND LIKE A DISLIKER! THIS IS NO TOY!
THIS DEVICE IS THE GREATEST ACHIEVEMENT IN ALL OF ALTARA!
IT'S THE FUTURE!
SURELY YOU WANT ONE FOR YOURSELF, BUT DON'T FRET, IF YOU WORK HARD YOU CAN GET A MODEL 6... OR AT LEAST A MODEL 5.
AND WHAT KIND OF WORK DOES ONE DO HERE? I SEE NO ARTISANS, CULTIVATORS, OR CRAFTSMEN?
WELL, SOME OF US WORK IN THE SHOPS AND SOME WORK AS SENTRIES, BUT MOST OF US WORK IN THE POLISHING STATIONS--
--WHERE WE CUT AND POLISH THE PLATES.
THEN THE PLATES ARE SENT OUT TO THE SHOPS FOR SALE.
SO YOU LABOR TO MAKE THE PLATES...
SO YOU CAN EARN WAGES...
...SO YOU CAN BUY THE PLATES?
YES.
BUT... WHY?
WHY EXTEND SUCH EFFORT?
TO WHAT END?
UH...
DIDN'T YOU SEE THE RED CUBE?
YES, YES, THE CUBE...
HEY BLARD! COME HERE!
I GOT THE NEW MODEL 6! YOU GOTTA' SEE THE RED CUBE!
LOOK AT THAT!
WOW! IT'S AMAZING!
WELL, IT WAS GOOD CHATTING WITH YOU...

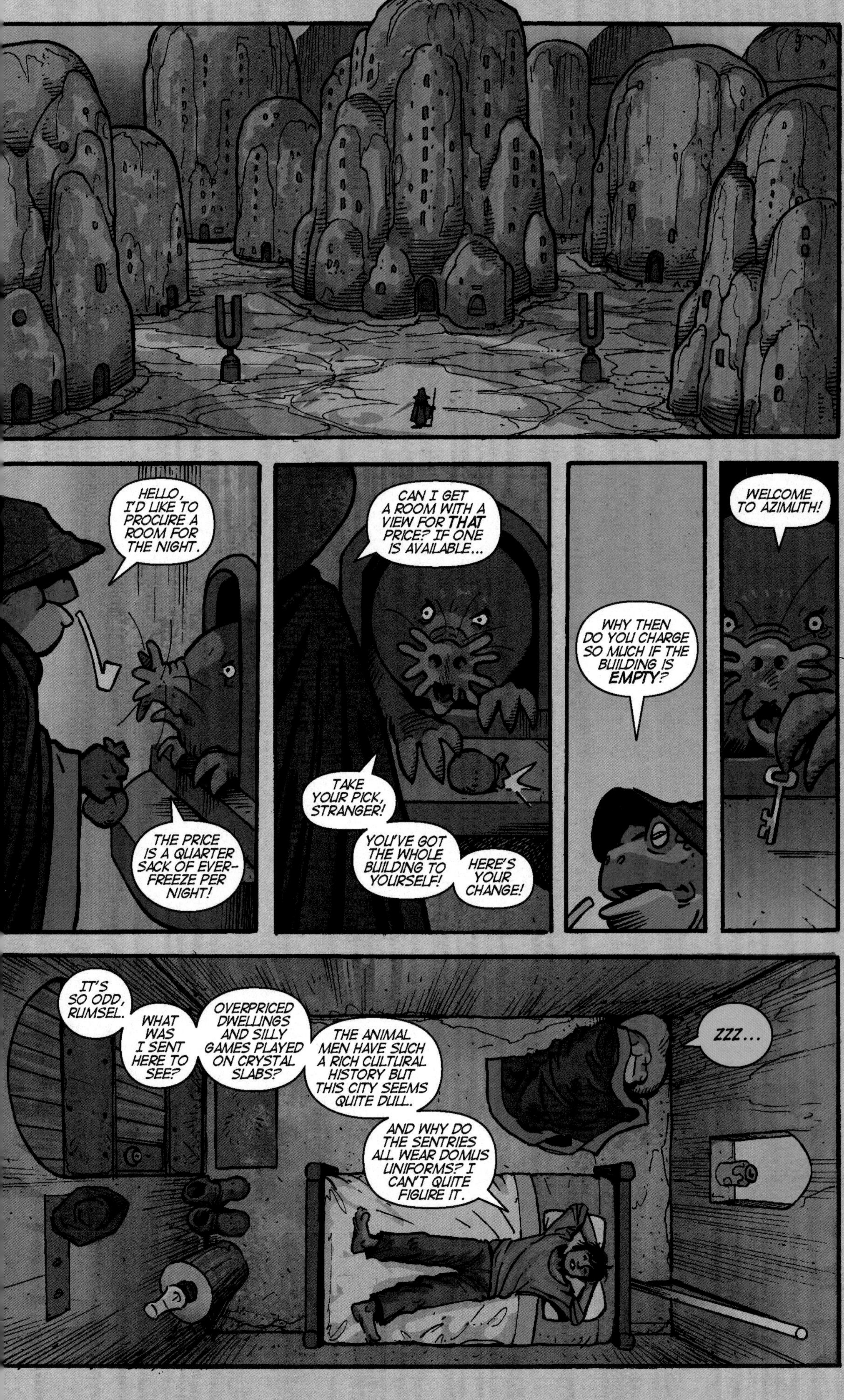
HELLO, I'D LIKE TO PROCURE A ROOM FOR THE NIGHT.
THE PRICE IS A QUARTER SACK OF EVER-FREEZE PER NIGHT!
CAN I GET A ROOM WITH A VIEW FOR THAT PRICE? IF ONE IS AVAILABLE...
TAKE YOUR PICK, STRANGER!
YOU'VE GOT THE WHOLE BUILDING TO YOURSELF!
HERE'S YOUR CHANGE!
WHY THEN DO YOU CHARGE SO MUCH IF THE BUILDING IS EMPTY?
WELCOME TO AZIMUTH!
IT'S SO ODD, RUMSEL.
WHAT WAS I SENT HERE TO SEE?
OVERPRICED DWELLINGS AND SILLY GAMES PLAYED ON CRYSTAL SLABS?
THE ANIMAL MEN HAVE SUCH A RICH CULTURAL HISTORY BUT THIS CITY SEEMS QUITE DULL.
AND WHY DO THE SENTRIES ALL WEAR DOMUS UNIFORMS? I CAN'T QUITE FIGURE IT.
ZZZ...

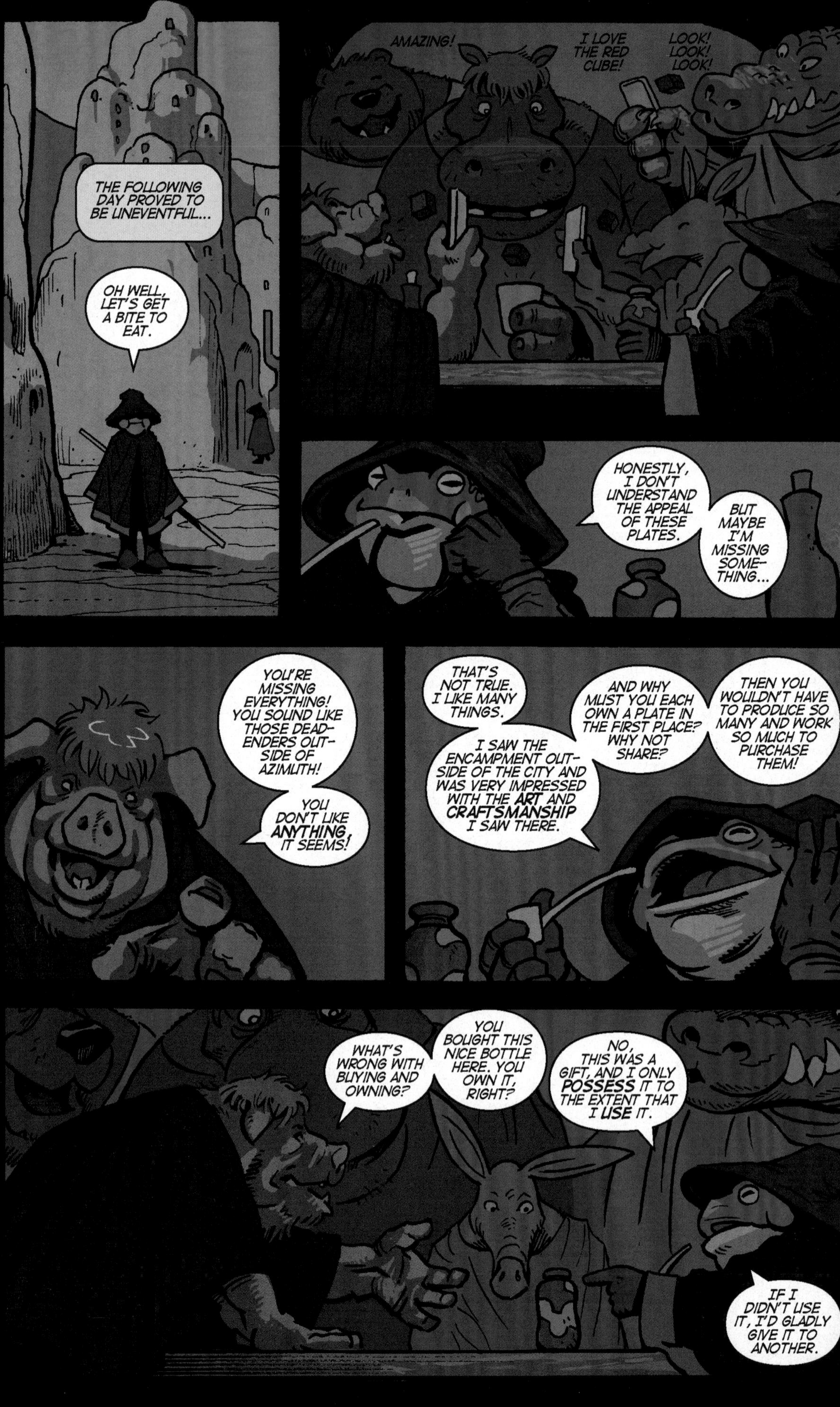
THE FOLLOWING DAY PROVED TO BE UNEVENTFUL...
OH WELL, LET'S GET A BITE TO EAT.
AMAZING!
I LOVE THE RED CUBE!
LOOK! LOOK! LOOK!
HONESTLY, I DON'T UNDERSTAND THE APPEAL OF THESE PLATES.
BUT MAYBE I'M MISSING SOME-THING...
YOU'RE MISSING EVERYTHING! YOU SOUND LIKE THOSE DEAD-ENDERS OUT-SIDE OF AZIMUTH!
YOU DON'T LIKE ANYTHING, IT SEEMS!
THAT'S NOT TRUE. I LIKE MANY THINGS.
I SAW THE ENCAMPMENT OUT-SIDE OF THE CITY AND WAS VERY IMPRESSED WITH THE ART AND CRAFTSMANSHIP I SAW THERE.
AND WHY MUST YOU EACH OWN A PLATE IN THE FIRST PLACE? WHY NOT SHARE?
THEN YOU WOULDN'T HAVE TO PRODUCE SO MANY AND WORK SO MUCH TO PURCHASE THEM!
WHAT'S WRONG WITH BUYING AND OWNING?
YOU BOUGHT THIS NICE BOTTLE HERE. YOU OWN IT, RIGHT?
NO, THIS WAS A GIFT, AND I ONLY POSSESS IT TO THE EXTENT THAT I USE IT.
IF I DIDN'T USE IT, I'D GLADLY GIVE IT TO ANOTHER.

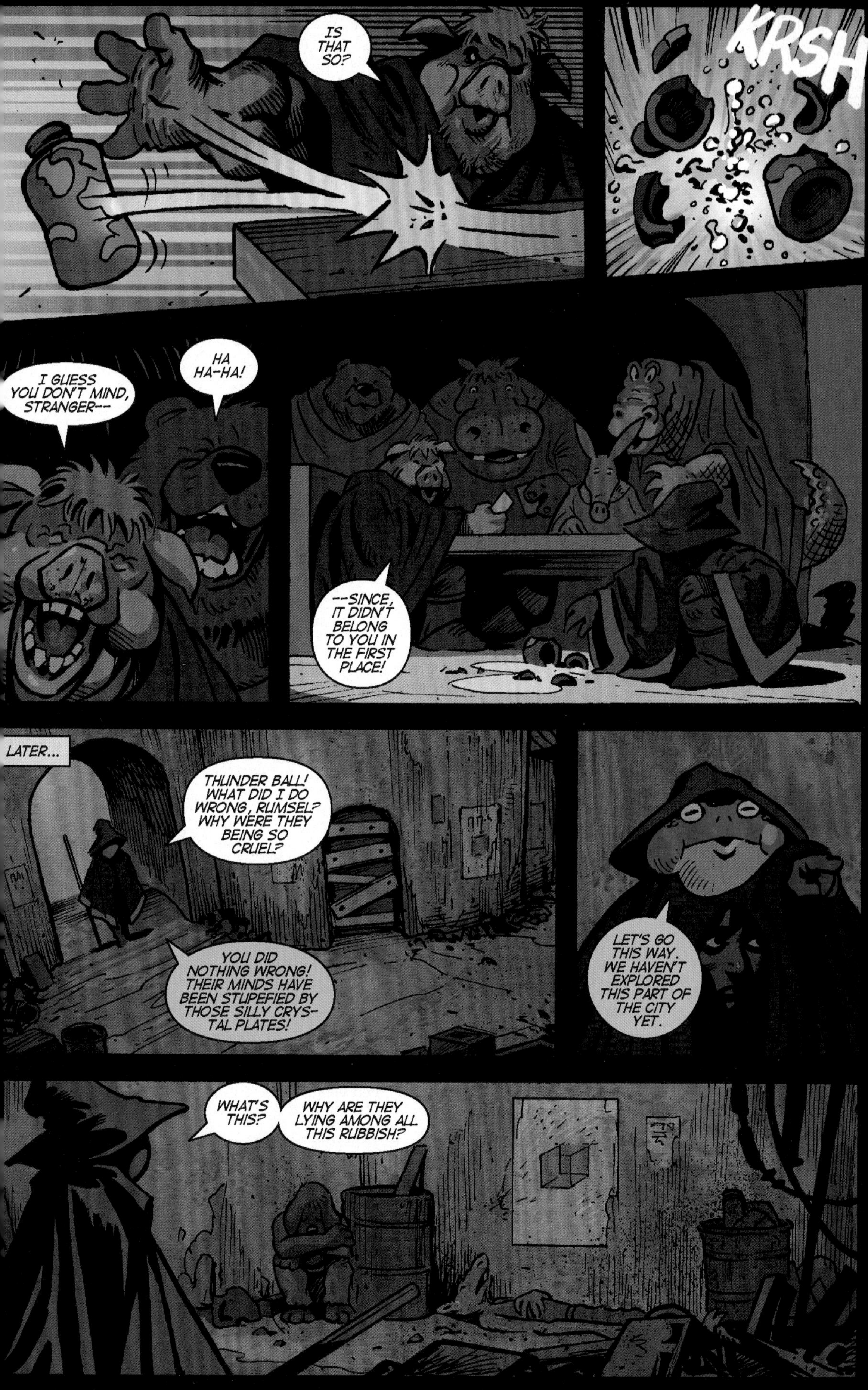
IS THAT SO?
KRSH
I GUESS YOU DON'T MIND, STRANGER--
HA HA-HA!
--SINCE, IT DIDN'T BELONG TO YOU IN THE FIRST PLACE!
LATER...
THUNDER BALL! WHAT DID I DO WRONG, RUMSEL? WHY WERE THEY BEING SO CRUEL?
YOU DID NOTHING WRONG! THEIR MINDS HAVE BEEN STUPEFIED BY THOSE SILLY CRYS-TAL PLATES!
LET'S GO THIS WAY. WE HAVEN'T EXPLORED THIS PART OF THE CITY YET.
WHAT'S THIS?
WHY ARE THEY LYING AMONG ALL THIS RUBBISH?

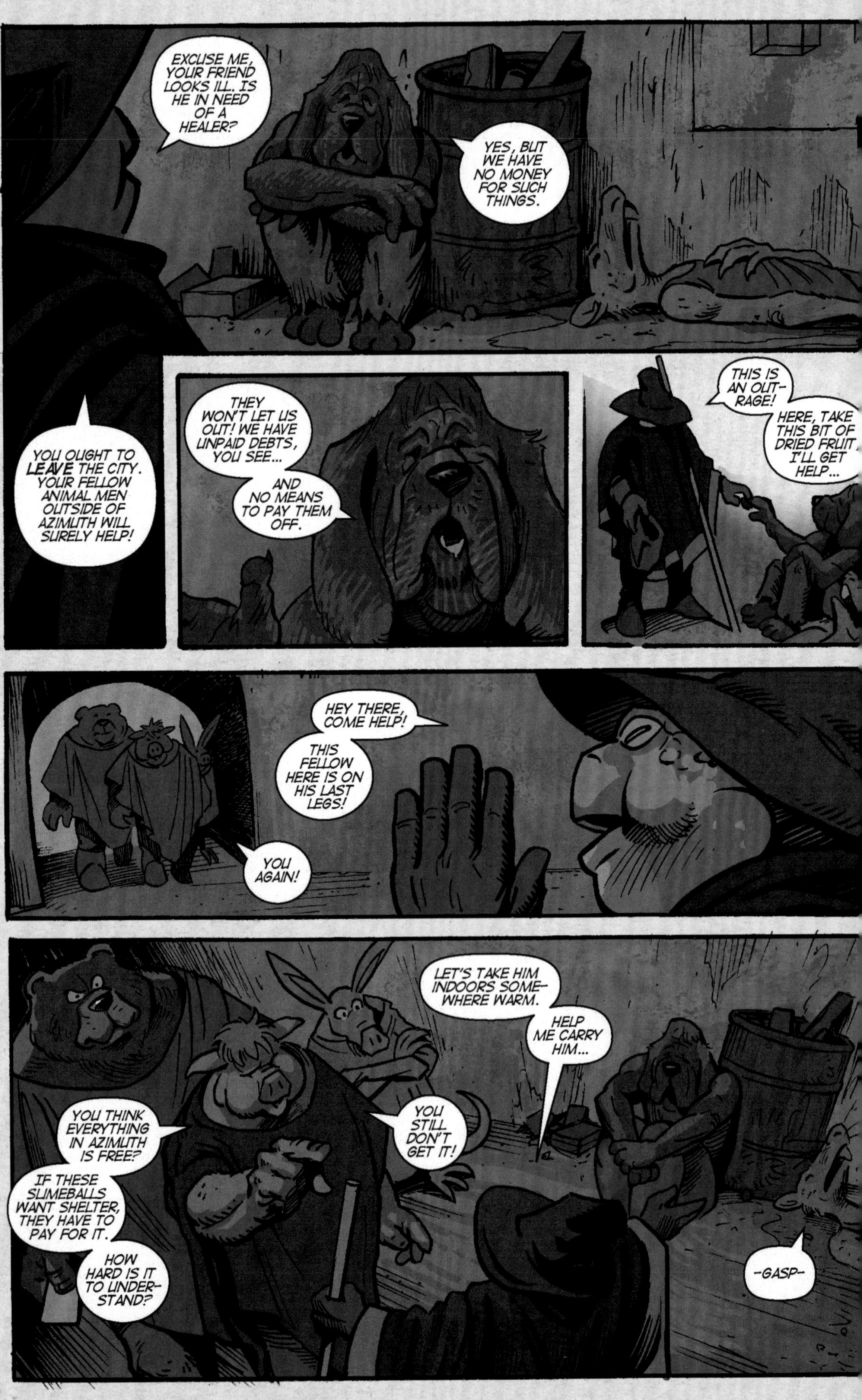
EXCUSE ME, YOUR FRIEND LOOKS ILL. IS HE IN NEED OF A HEALER?
YES, BUT WE HAVE NO MONEY FOR SUCH THINGS.
YOU OUGHT TO LEAVE THE CITY. YOUR FELLOW ANIMAL MEN OUTSIDE OF AZIMUTH WILL SURELY HELP!
THEY WON'T LET US OUT! WE HAVE UNPAID DEBTS, YOU SEE...
AND NO MEANS TO PAY THEM OFF.
THIS IS AN OUTRAGE!
HERE, TAKE THIS BIT OF DRIED FRUIT. I'LL GET HELP...
HEY THERE, COME HELP!
THIS FELLOW HERE IS ON HIS LAST LEGS!
YOU AGAIN!
LET'S TAKE HIM INDOORS SOMEWHERE WARM.
HELP ME CARRY HIM...
YOU THINK EVERYTHING IN AZIMUTH IS FREE?
IF THESE SLIMEBALLS WANT SHELTER, THEY HAVE TO PAY FOR IT.
HOW HARD IS IT TO UNDERSTAND?
YOU STILL DON'T GET IT!
-GASP-

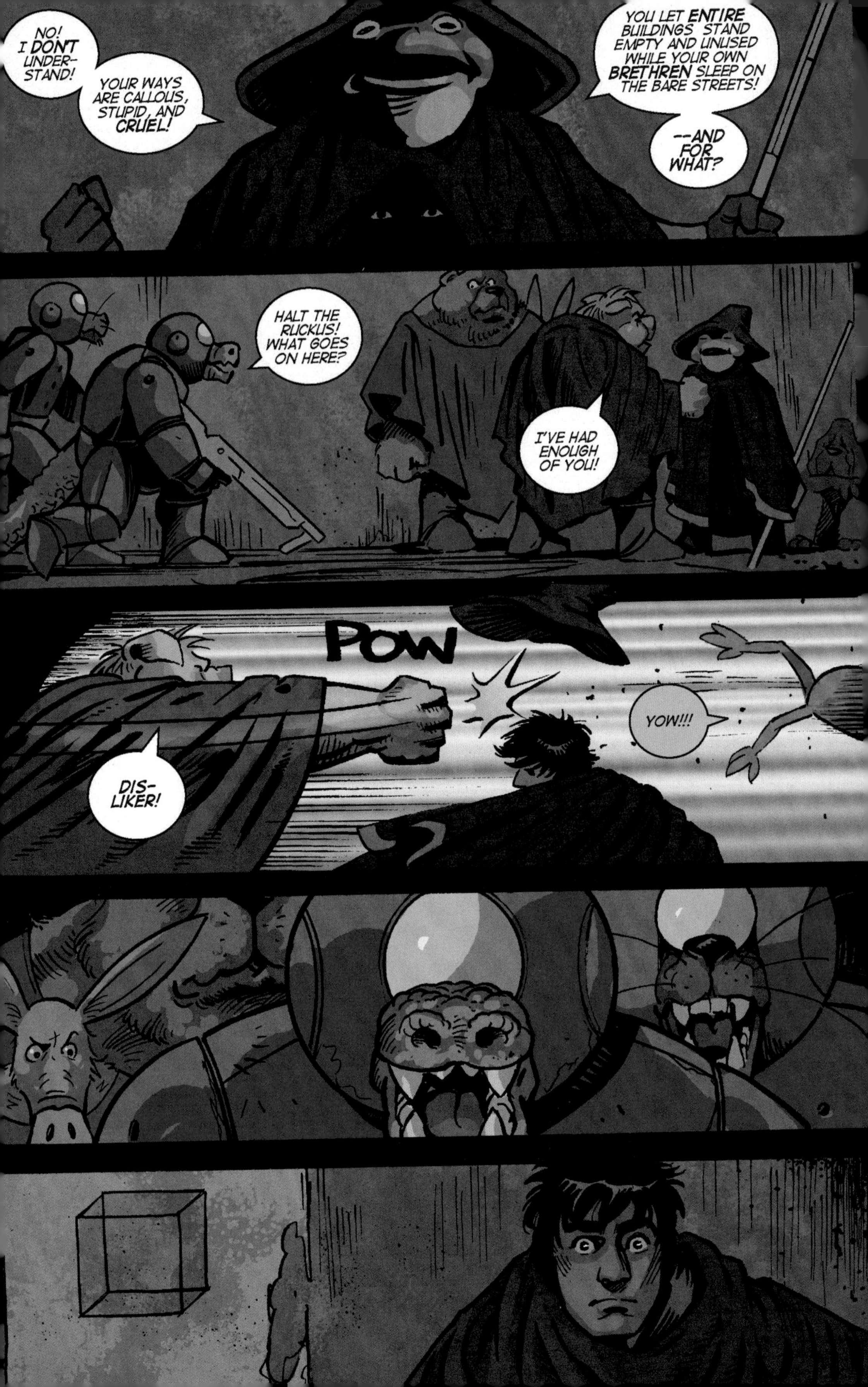
NO! I DON'T UNDER-STAND!
YOUR WAYS ARE CALLOUS, STUPID, AND CRUEL!
YOU LET ENTIRE BUILDINGS STAND EMPTY AND UNUSED WHILE YOUR OWN BRETHREN SLEEP ON THE BARE STREETS!
--AND FOR WHAT?
HALT THE RUCKUS! WHAT GOES ON HERE?
I'VE HAD ENOUGH OF YOU!
POW
DIS-LIKER!
YOW!!!

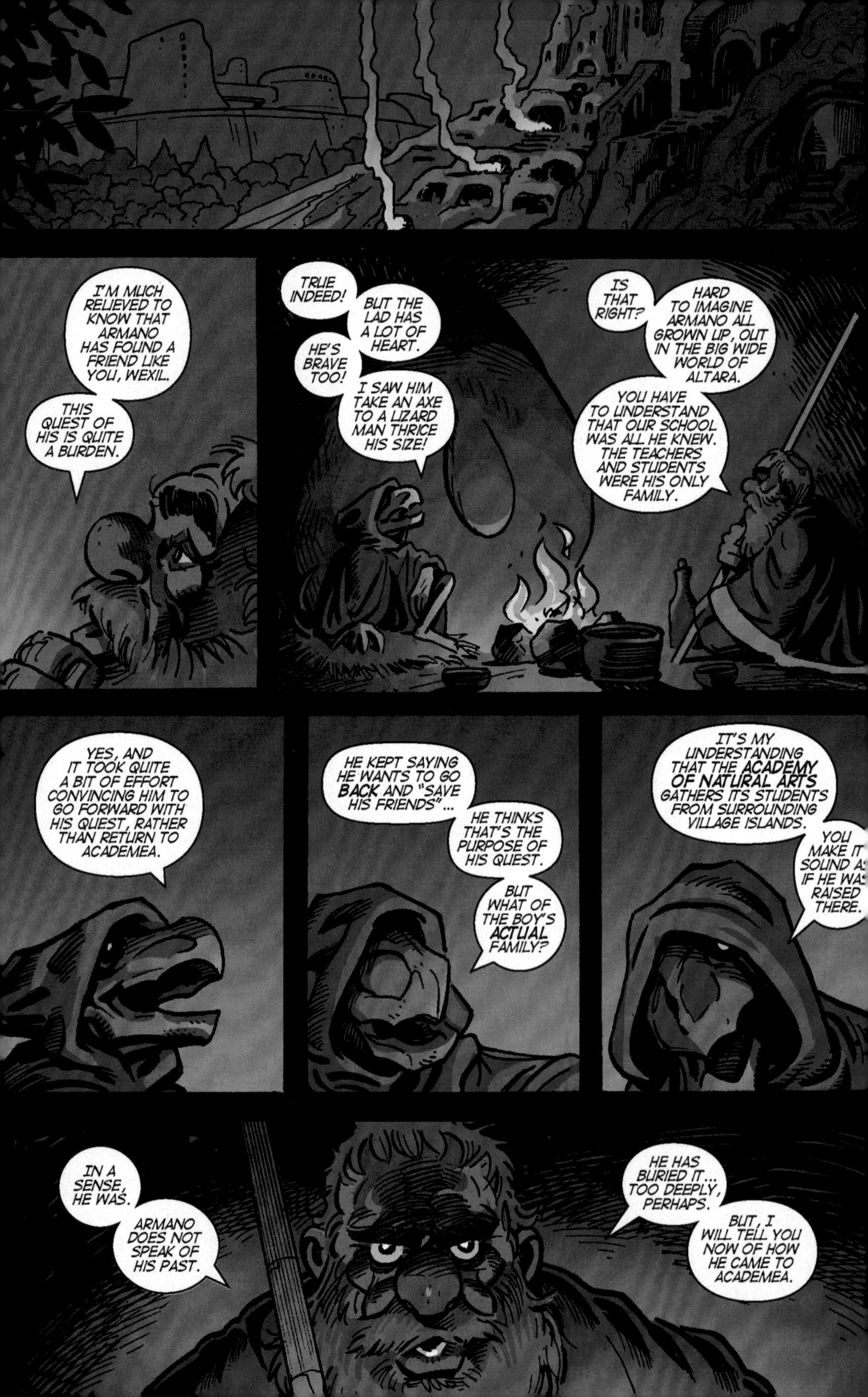
I'M MUCH RELIEVED TO KNOW THAT ARMANO HAS FOUND A FRIEND LIKE YOU, WEXIL.
THIS QUEST OF HIS IS QUITE A BURDEN.
TRUE INDEED!
BUT THE LAD HAS A LOT OF HEART.
HE'S BRAVE TOO!
I SAW HIM TAKE AN AXE TO A LIZARD MAN THRICE HIS SIZE!
IS THAT RIGHT?
HARD TO IMAGINE ARMANO ALL GROWN UP, OUT IN THE BIG WIDE WORLD OF ALTARA.
YOU HAVE TO UNDERSTAND THAT OUR SCHOOL WAS ALL HE KNEW. THE TEACHERS AND STUDENTS WERE HIS ONLY FAMILY.
YES, AND IT TOOK QUITE A BIT OF EFFORT CONVINCING HIM TO GO FORWARD WITH HIS QUEST, RATHER THAN RETURN TO ACADEMEA.
HE KEPT SAYING HE WANTS TO GO BACK AND "SAVE HIS FRIENDS"...
HE THINKS THAT'S THE PURPOSE OF HIS QUEST.
BUT WHAT OF THE BOY'S ACTUAL FAMILY?
IT'S MY UNDERSTANDING THAT THE ACADEMY OF NATURAL ARTS GATHERS ITS STUDENTS FROM SURROUNDING VILLAGE ISLANDS.
IN A SENSE, HE WAS.
ARMANO DOES NOT SPEAK OF HIS PAST.
HE HAS BURIED IT... TOO DEEPLY, PERHAPS.
BUT, I WILL TELL YOU NOW OF HOW HE CAME TO ACADEMEA.

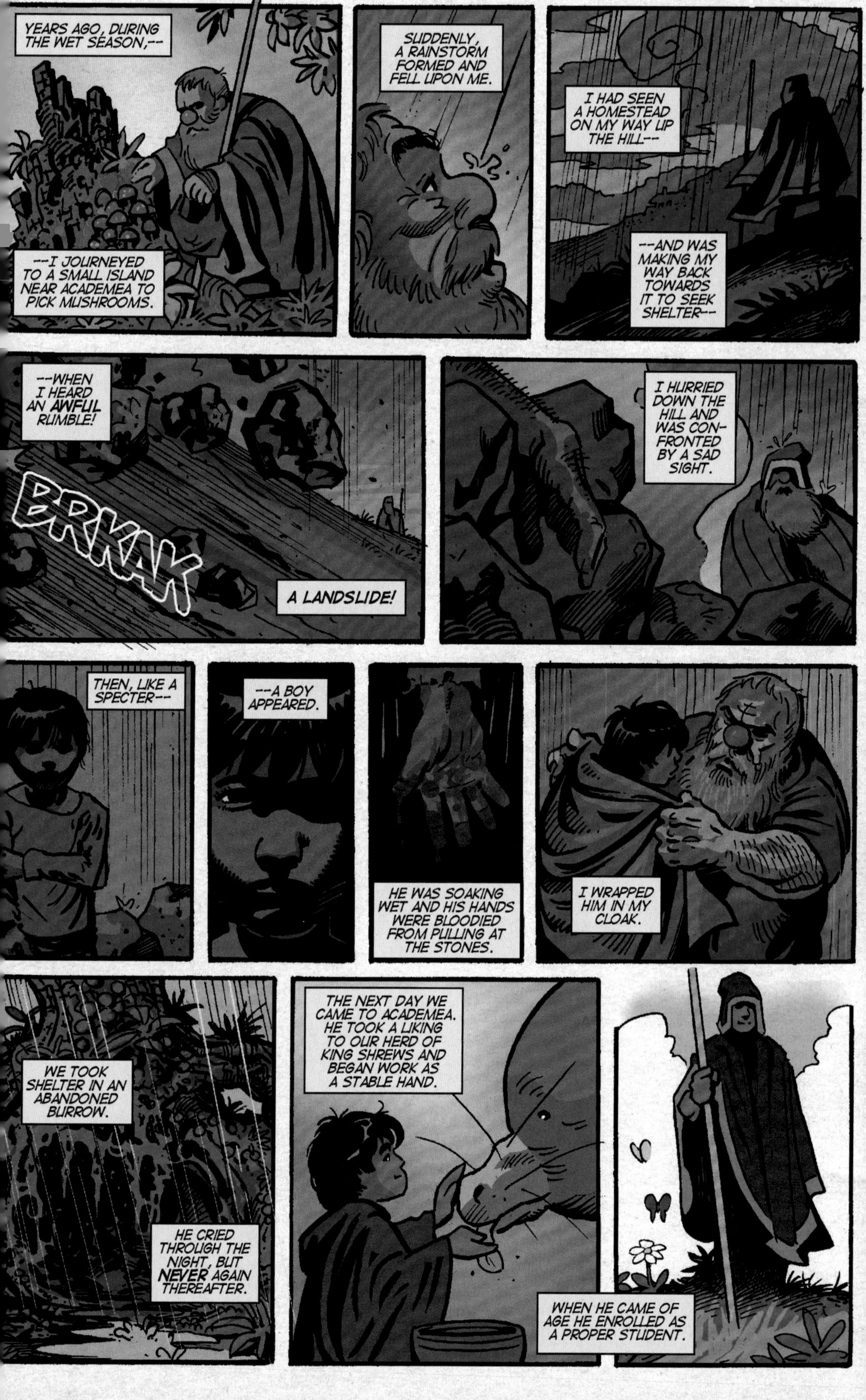
YEARS AGO, DURING THE WET SEASON,--
--I JOURNEYED TO A SMALL ISLAND NEAR ACADEMEA TO PICK MUSHROOMS.
SUDDENLY, A RAINSTORM FORMED AND FELL UPON ME.
I HAD SEEN A HOMESTEAD ON MY WAY UP THE HILL--
--AND WAS MAKING MY WAY BACK TOWARDS IT TO SEEK SHELTER--
--WHEN I HEARD AN AWFUL RUMBLE!
BRKAK
A LANDSLIDE!
I HURRIED DOWN THE HILL AND WAS CONFRONTED BY A SAD SIGHT.
THEN, LIKE A SPECTER--
--A BOY APPEARED.
HE WAS SOAKING WET AND HIS HANDS WERE BLOODIED FROM PULLING AT THE STONES.
I WRAPPED HIM IN MY CLOAK.
WE TOOK SHELTER IN AN ABANDONED BURROW.
HE CRIED THROUGH THE NIGHT, BUT NEVER AGAIN THEREAFTER.
THE NEXT DAY WE CAME TO ACADEMEA. HE TOOK A LIKING TO OUR HERD OF KING SHREWS AND BEGAN WORK AS A STABLE HAND.
WHEN HE CAME OF AGE HE ENROLLED AS A PROPER STUDENT.

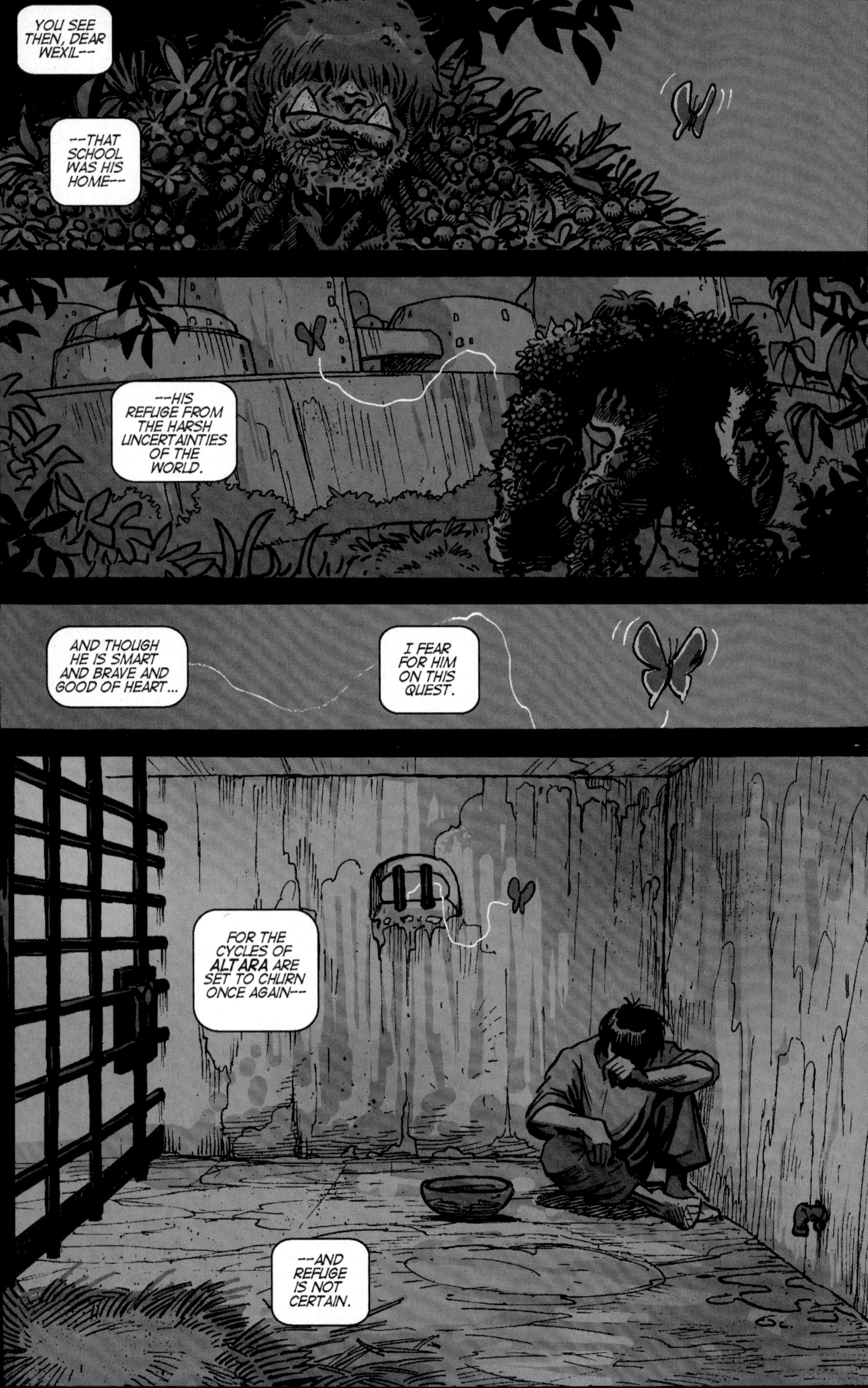
YOU SEE THEN, DEAR WEXIL--
--THAT SCHOOL WAS HIS HOME--
--HIS REFUGE FROM THE HARSH UNCERTAINTIES OF THE WORLD.
AND THOUGH HE IS SMART AND BRAVE AND GOOD OF HEART...
I FEAR FOR HIM ON THIS QUEST.
FOR THE CYCLES OF ALTARA ARE SET TO CHURN ONCE AGAIN--
--AND REFUGE IS NOT CERTAIN.

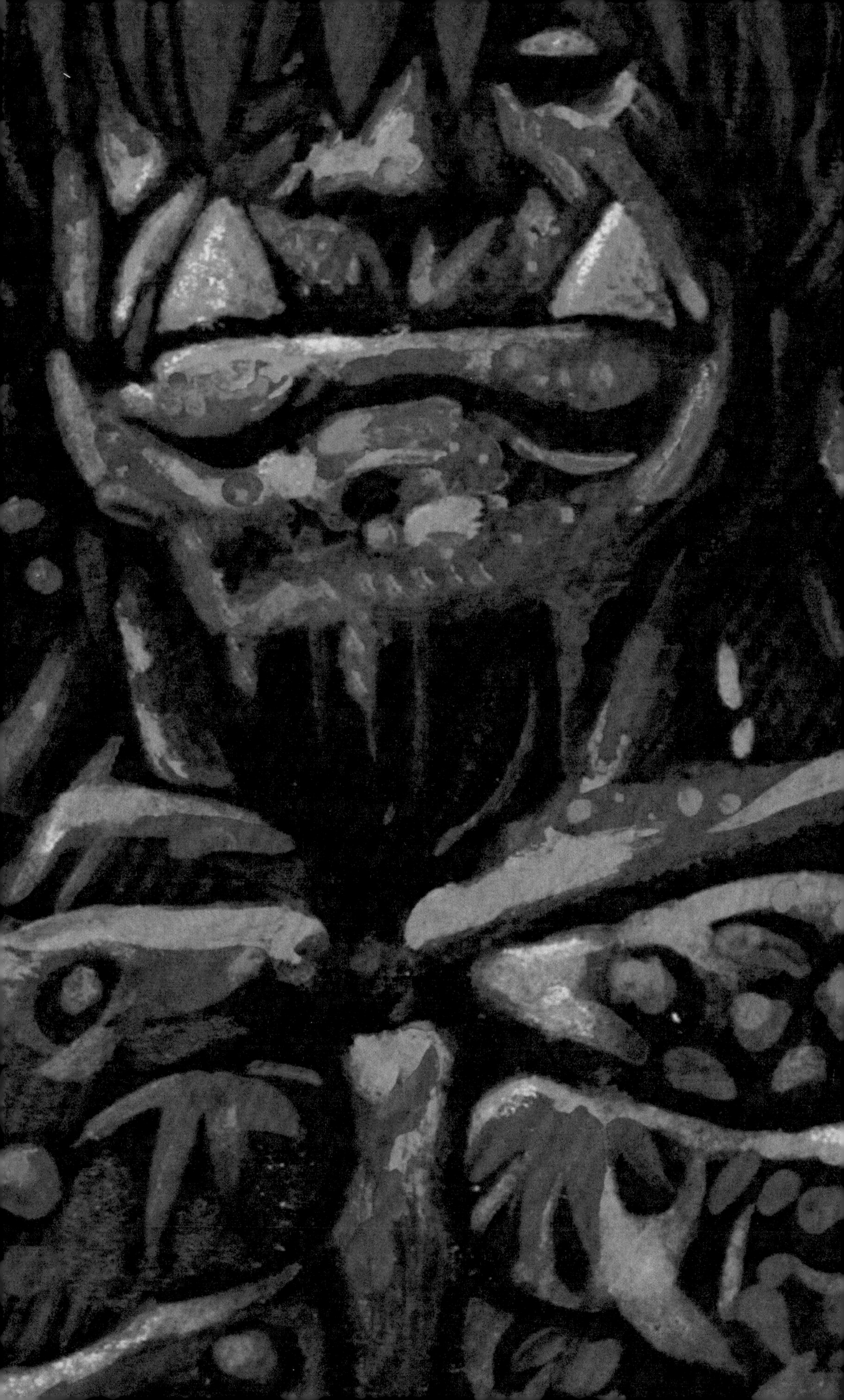

CHAPTER FIVE

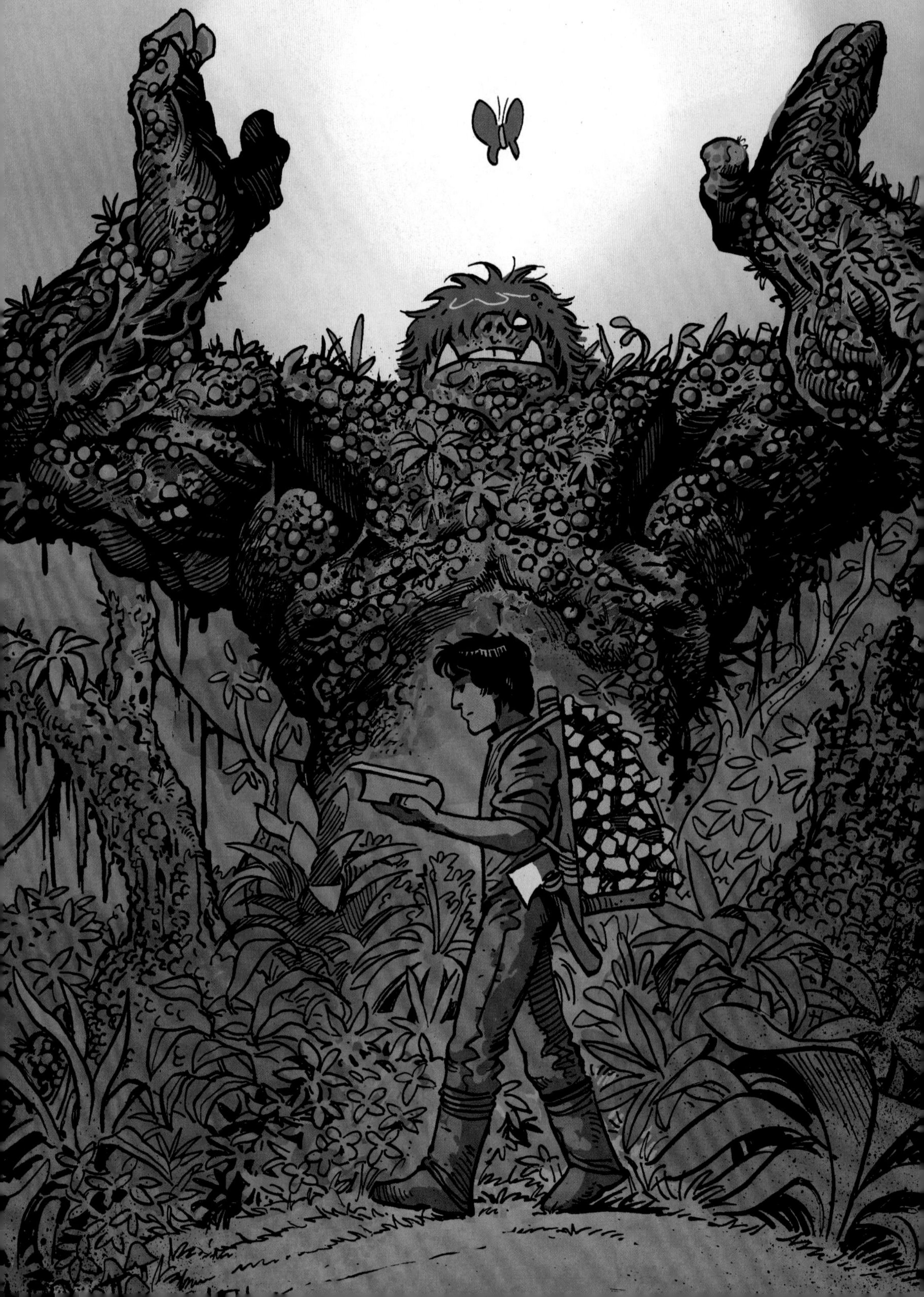

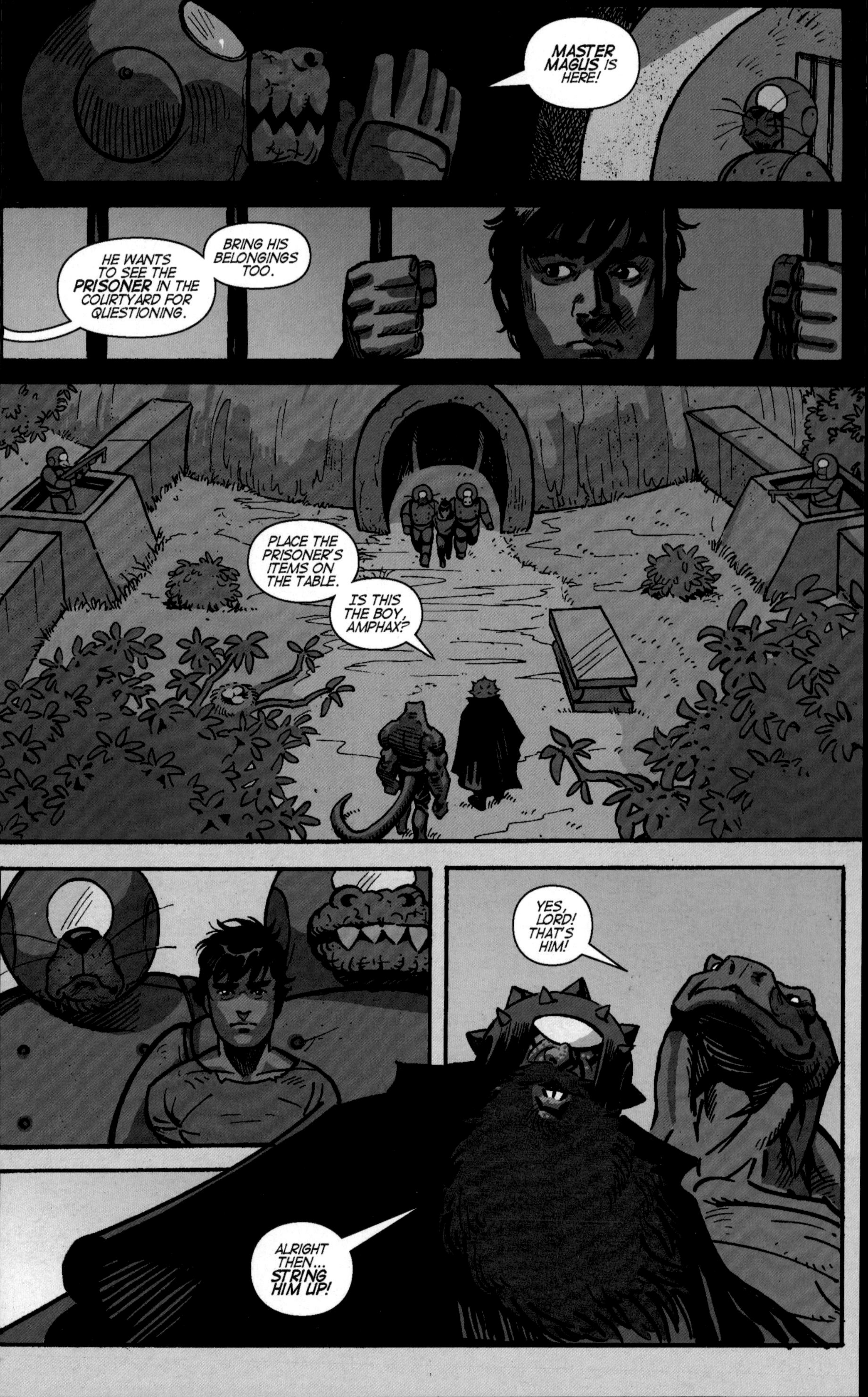
MASTER MAGUS IS HERE!
HE WANTS TO SEE THE PRISONER IN THE COURTYARD FOR QUESTIONING.
BRING HIS BELONGINGS TOO.
PLACE THE PRISONER'S ITEMS ON THE TABLE.
IS THIS THE BOY, AMPHAX?
YES, LORD! THAT'S HIM!
ALRIGHT THEN... STRING HIM UP!

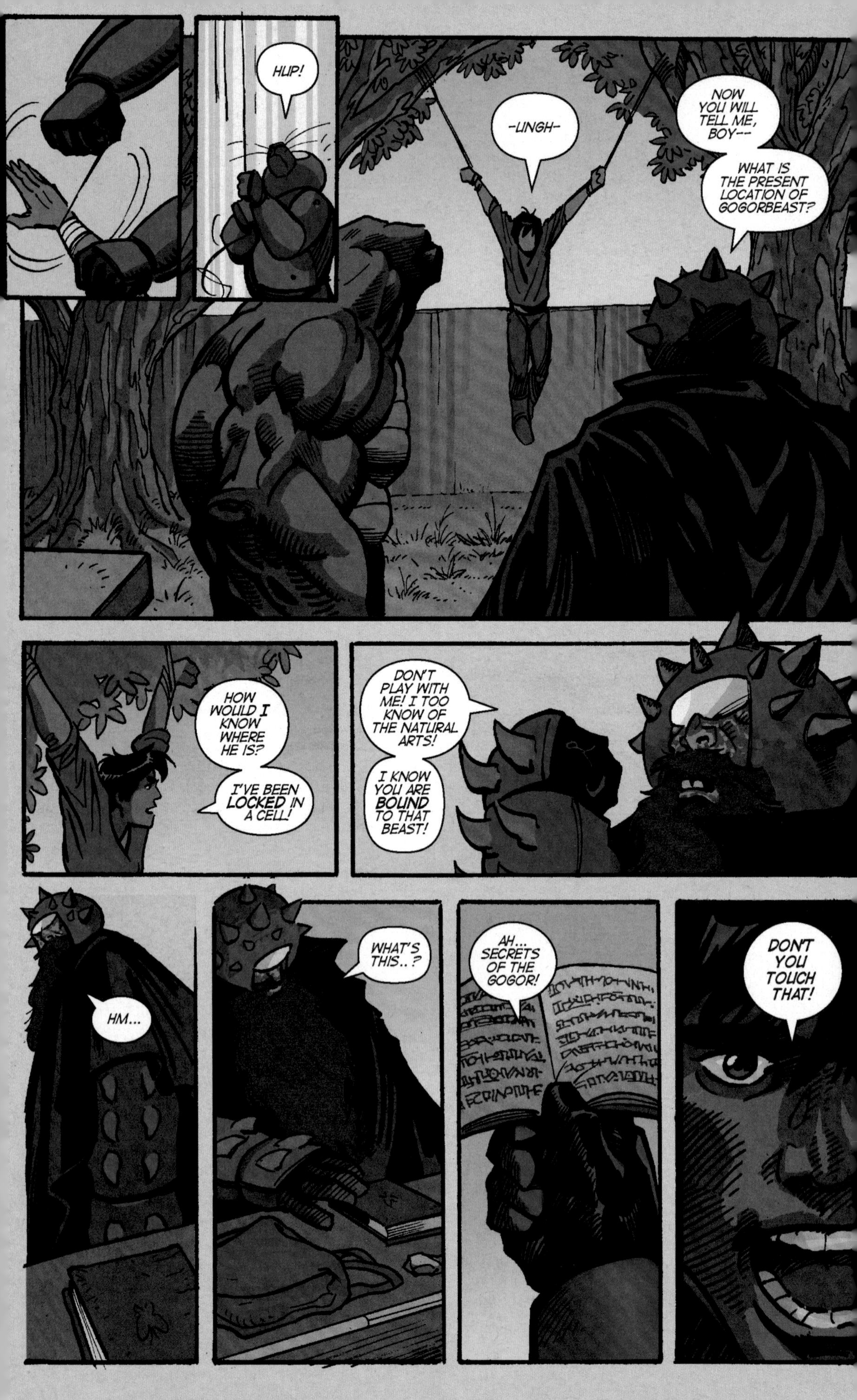
HUP!
-UNGH-
NOW YOU WILL TELL ME, BOY--
WHAT IS THE PRESENT LOCATION OF GOGORBEAST?
HOW WOULD I KNOW WHERE HE IS?
I'VE BEEN LOCKED IN A CELL!
DON'T PLAY WITH ME! I TOO KNOW OF THE NATURAL ARTS!
I KNOW YOU ARE BOUND TO THAT BEAST!
HM...
WHAT'S THIS..?
AH... SECRETS OF THE GOGOR!
DON'T YOU TOUCH THAT!

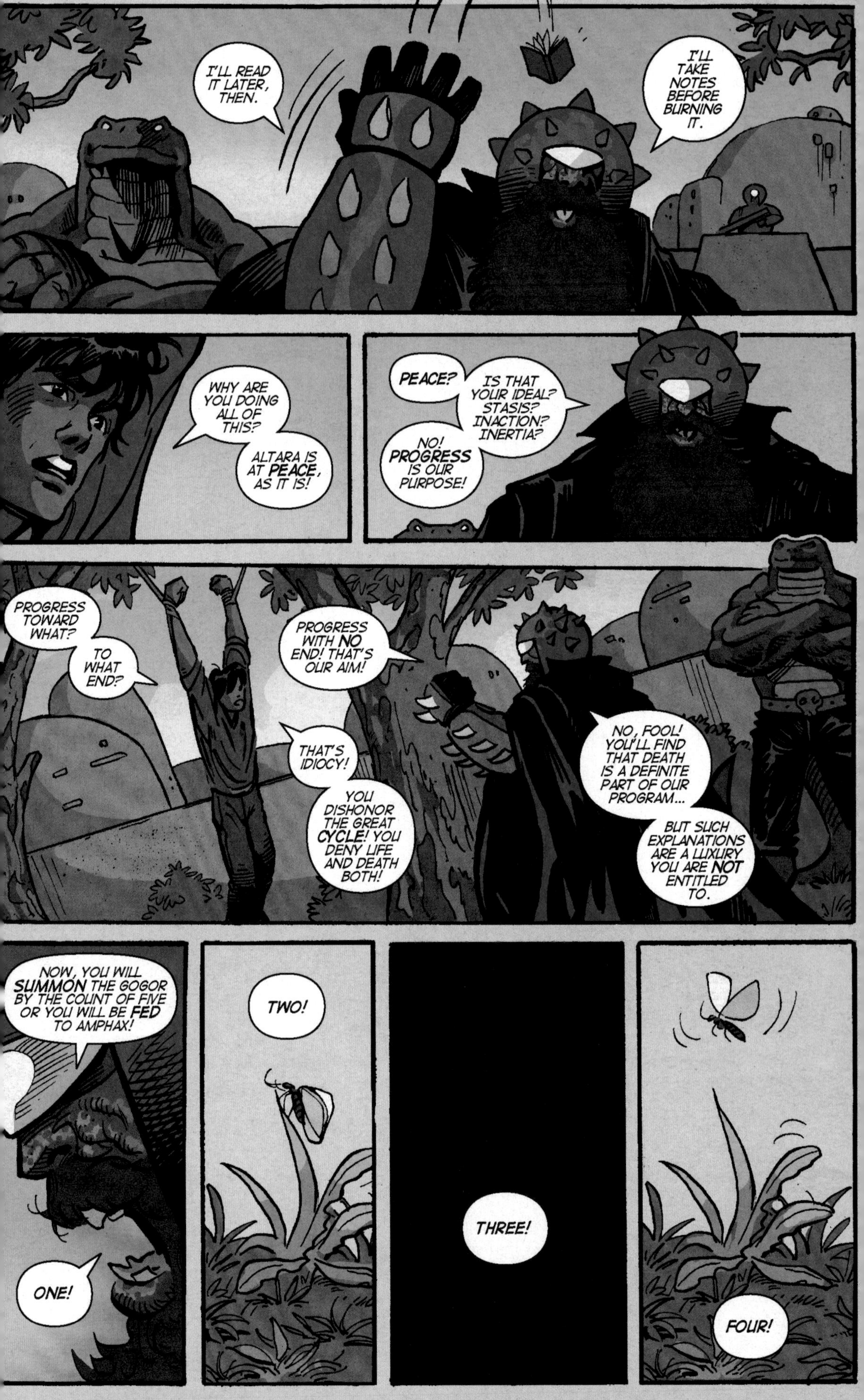
I'LL READ IT LATER, THEN.
I'LL TAKE NOTES BEFORE BURNING IT.
WHY ARE YOU DOING ALL OF THIS?
ALTARA IS AT PEACE, AS IT IS!
PEACE?
IS THAT YOUR IDEAL? STASIS? INACTION? INERTIA?
NO! PROGRESS IS OUR PURPOSE!
PROGRESS TOWARD WHAT?
TO WHAT END?
PROGRESS WITH NO END! THAT'S OUR AIM!
THAT'S IDIOCY!
YOU DISHONOR THE GREAT CYCLE! YOU DENY LIFE AND DEATH BOTH!
NO, FOOL! YOU'LL FIND THAT DEATH IS A DEFINITE PART OF OUR PROGRAM...
BUT SUCH EXPLANATIONS ARE A LUXURY YOU ARE NOT ENTITLED TO.
NOW, YOU WILL SUMMON THE GOGOR BY THE COUNT OF FIVE OR YOU WILL BE FED TO AMPHAX!
ONE!
TWO!
THREE!
FOUR!

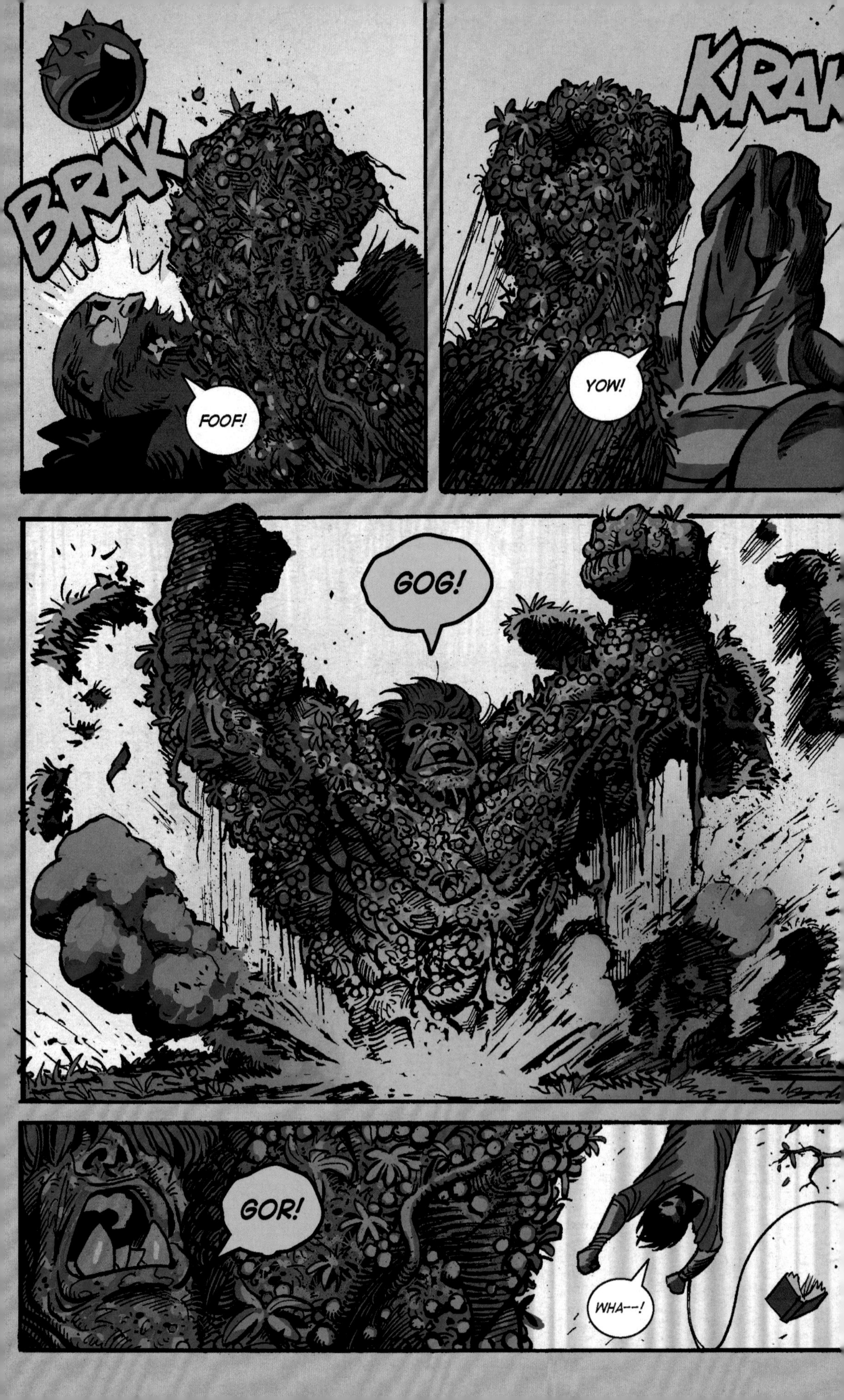
BRAK
FOOF!
KRAK
YOW!
GOG!
GOR!
WHA--!

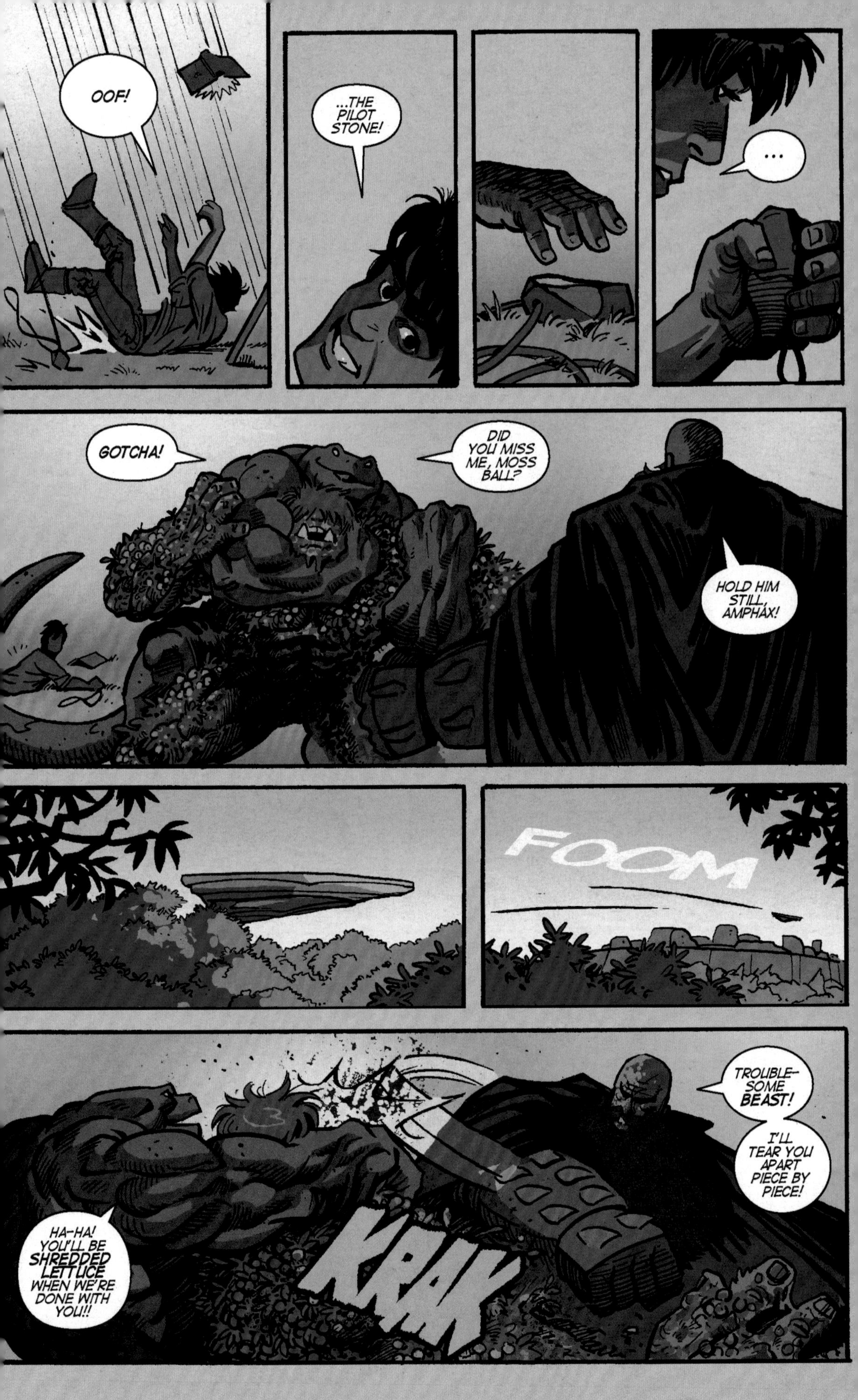
OOF!
...THE PILOT STONE!
...
GOTCHA!
DID YOU MISS ME, MOSS BALL?
HOLD HIM STILL, AMPHAX!
FOOM
TROUBLE-SOME BEAST!
I'LL TEAR YOU APART PIECE BY PIECE!
HA-HA! YOU'LL BE SHREDDED LETTUCE WHEN WE'RE DONE WITH YOU!!
KRAK

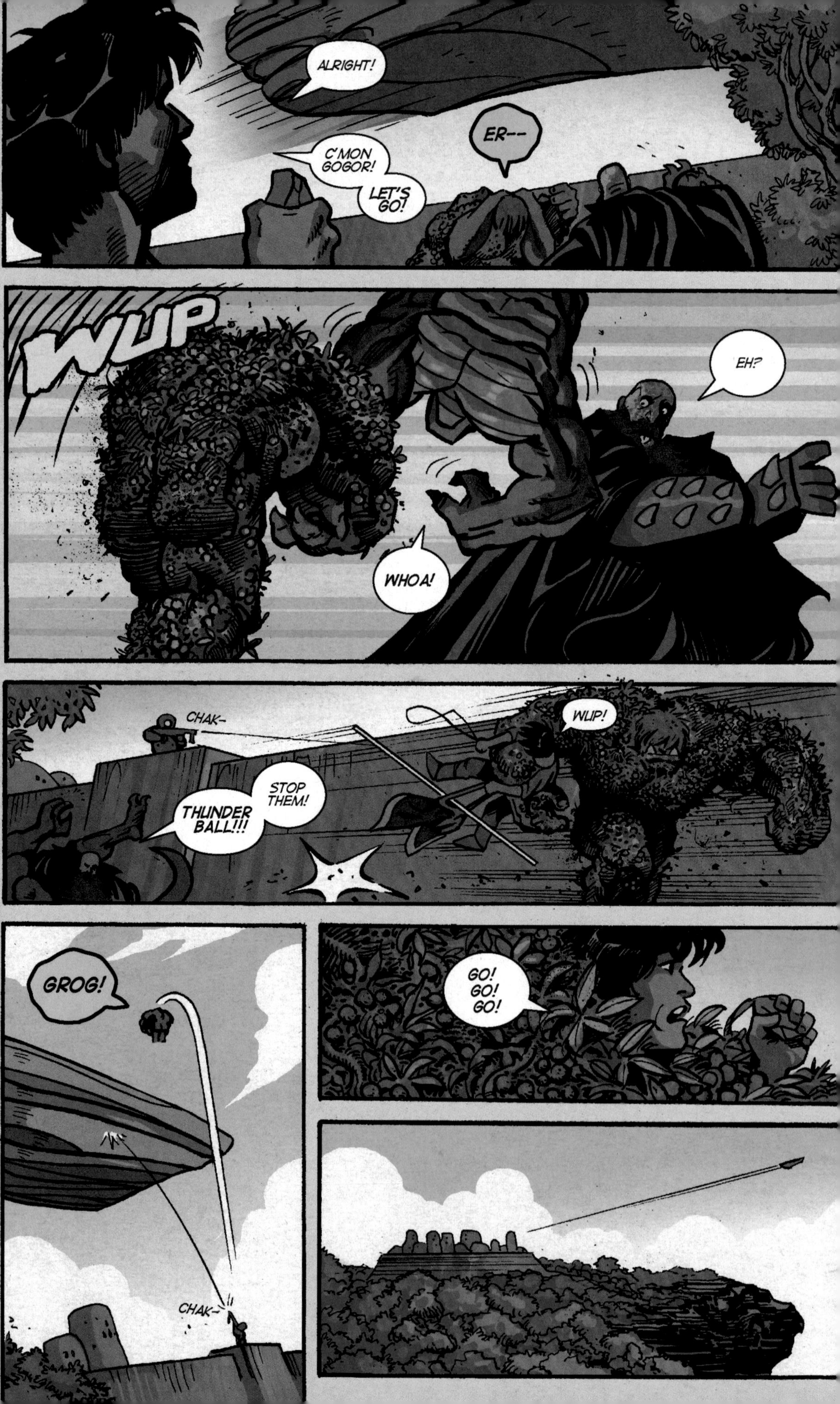

ALRIGHT!
C'MON GOGOR!
LET'S GO!
ER--
WUP
EH?
WHOA!
CHAK-
WUP!
STOP THEM!
THUNDER BALL!!!
GROG!
GO! GO! GO!
CHAK-

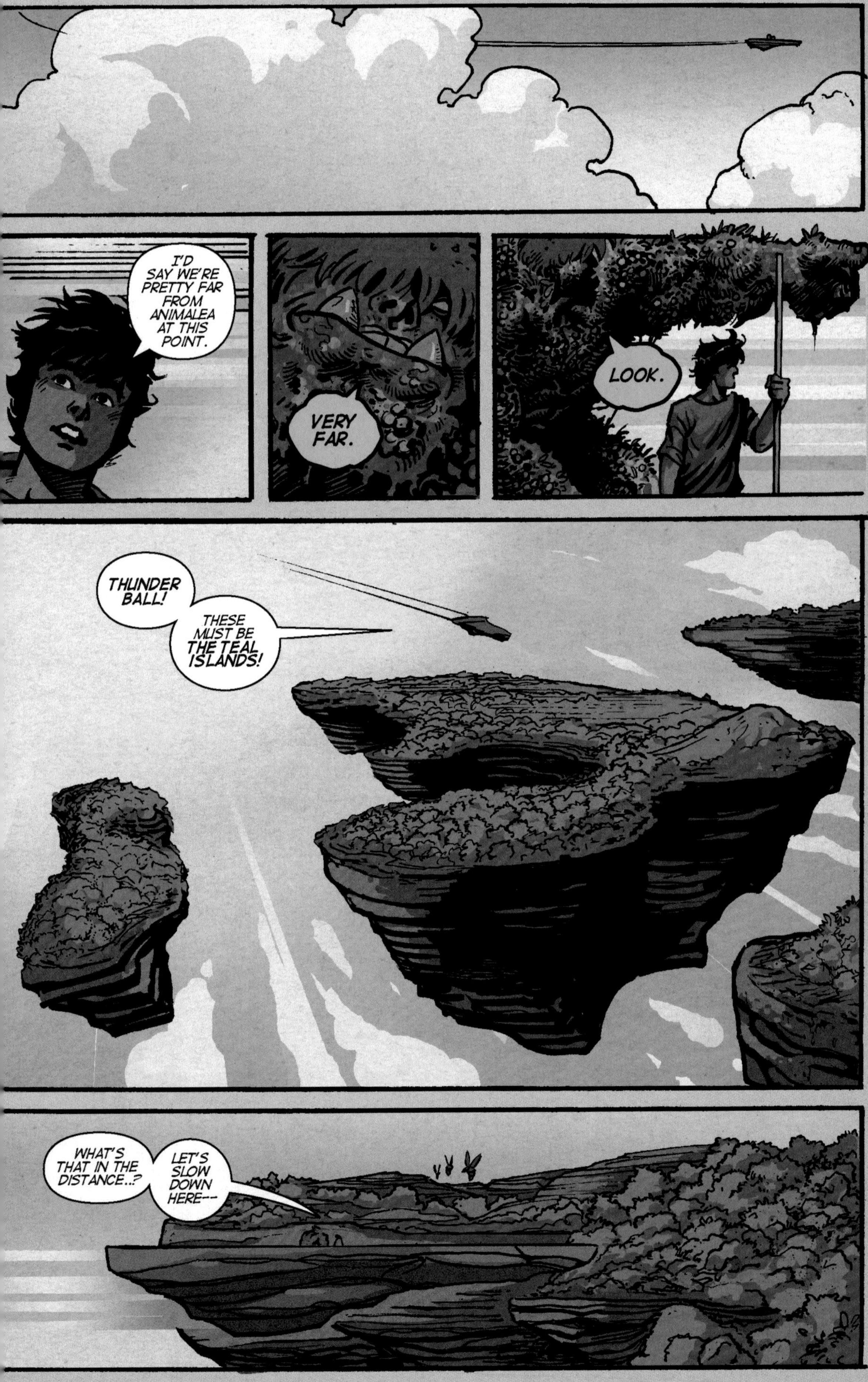
I'D SAY WE'RE PRETTY FAR FROM ANIMALEA AT THIS POINT.
VERY FAR.
LOOK.
THUNDER BALL!
THESE MUST BE THE TEAL ISLANDS!
WHAT'S THAT IN THE DISTANCE..?
LET'S SLOW DOWN HERE--

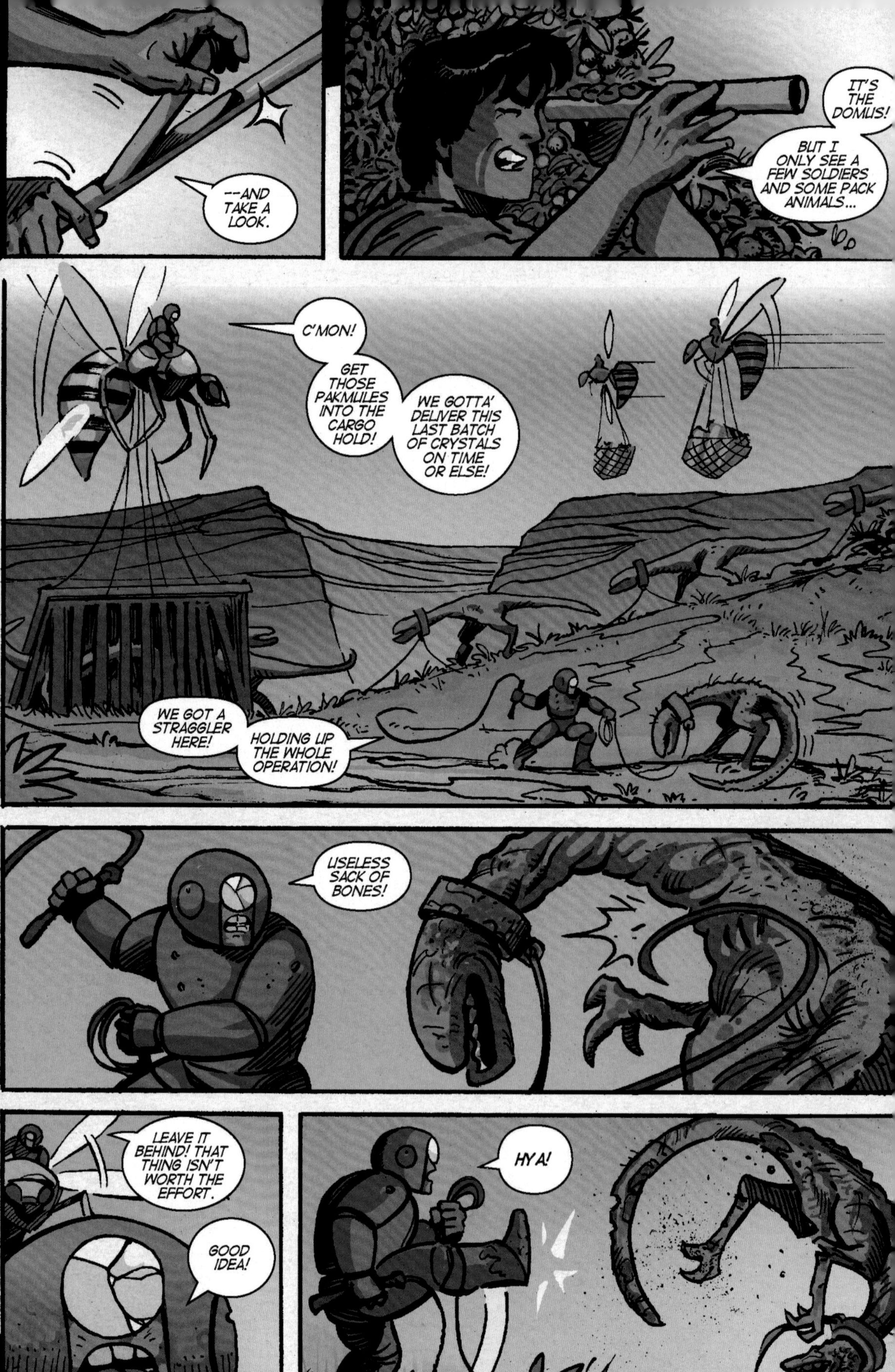
--AND TAKE A LOOK.
IT'S THE DOMUS!
BUT I ONLY SEE A FEW SOLDIERS AND SOME PACK ANIMALS...
C'MON!
GET THOSE PAKMULES INTO THE CARGO HOLD!
WE GOTTA' DELIVER THIS LAST BATCH OF CRYSTALS ON TIME OR ELSE!
WE GOT A STRAGGLER HERE!
HOLDING UP THE WHOLE OPERATION!
USELESS SACK OF BONES!
LEAVE IT BEHIND! THAT THING ISN'T WORTH THE EFFORT.
GOOD IDEA!
HYA!

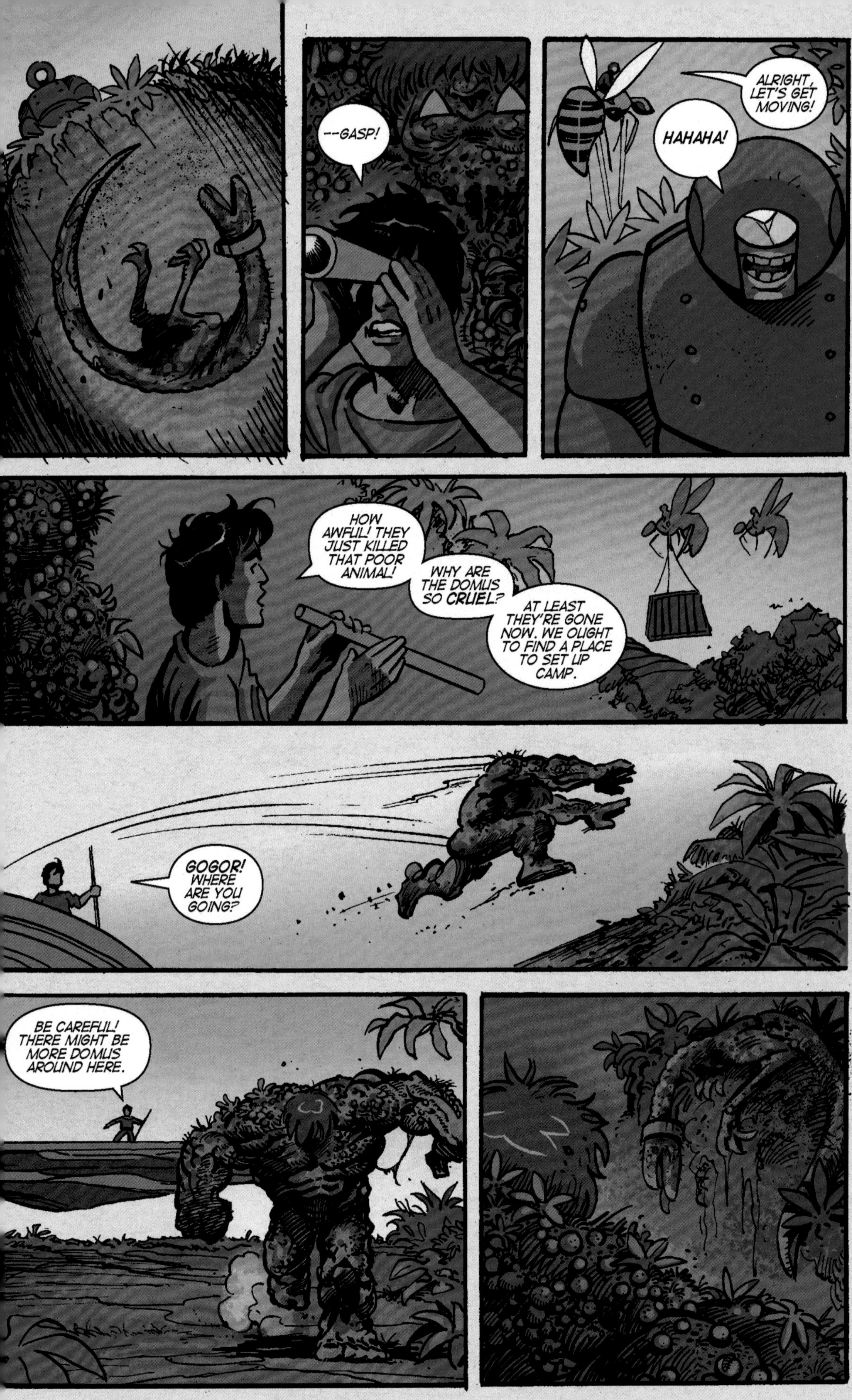
--GASP!
ALRIGHT, LET'S GET MOVING!
HAHAHA!
HOW AWFUL! THEY JUST KILLED THAT POOR ANIMAL!
WHY ARE THE DOMUS SO CRUEL?
AT LEAST THEY'RE GONE NOW. WE OUGHT TO FIND A PLACE TO SET UP CAMP.
GOGOR! WHERE ARE YOU GOING?
BE CAREFUL! THERE MIGHT BE MORE DOMUS AROUND HERE.

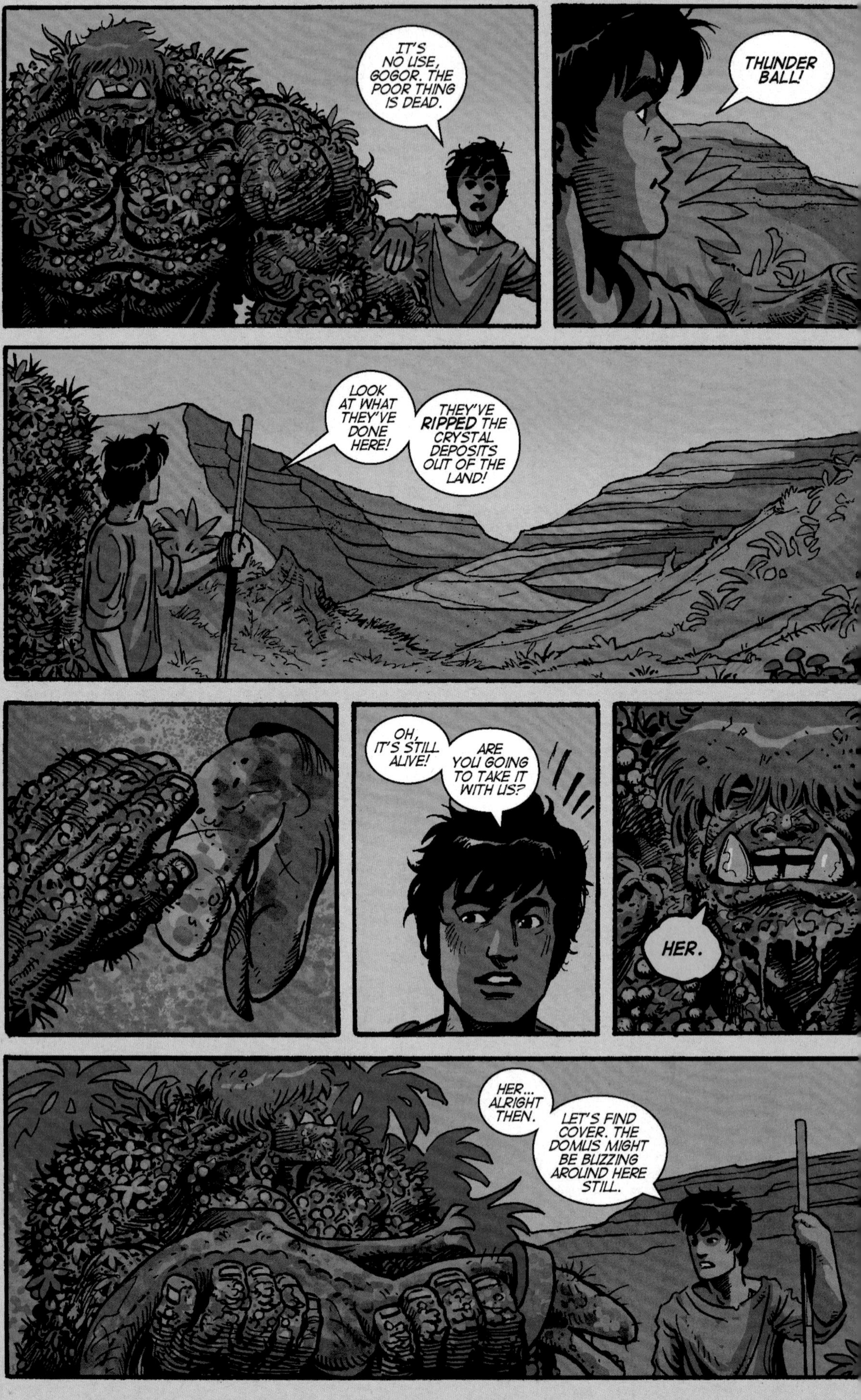
IT'S NO USE, GOGOR. THE POOR THING IS DEAD.
THUNDER BALL!
LOOK AT WHAT THEY'VE DONE HERE!
THEY'VE **RIPPED** THE CRYSTAL DEPOSITS OUT OF THE LAND!
OH, IT'S STILL ALIVE!
ARE YOU GOING TO TAKE IT WITH US?
HER.
HER... ALRIGHT THEN.
LET'S FIND COVER. THE DOMUS MIGHT BE BUZZING AROUND HERE STILL.

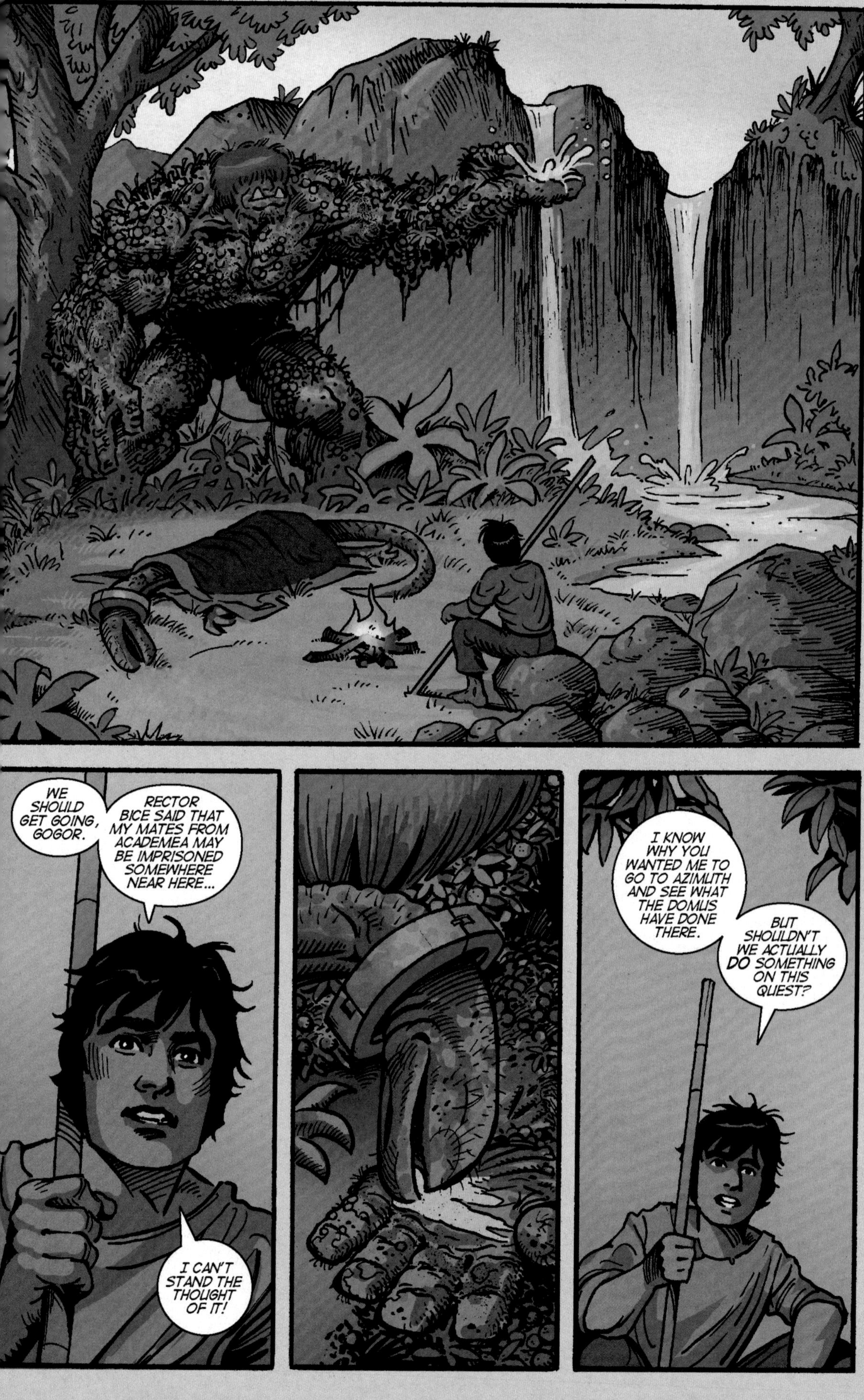
WE SHOULD GET GOING, GOGOR.
RECTOR BICE SAID THAT MY MATES FROM ACADEMEA MAY BE IMPRISONED SOMEWHERE NEAR HERE...
I CAN'T STAND THE THOUGHT OF IT!
I KNOW WHY YOU WANTED ME TO GO TO AZIMUTH AND SEE WHAT THE DOMUS HAVE DONE THERE.
BUT SHOULDN'T WE ACTUALLY DO SOMETHING ON THIS QUEST?

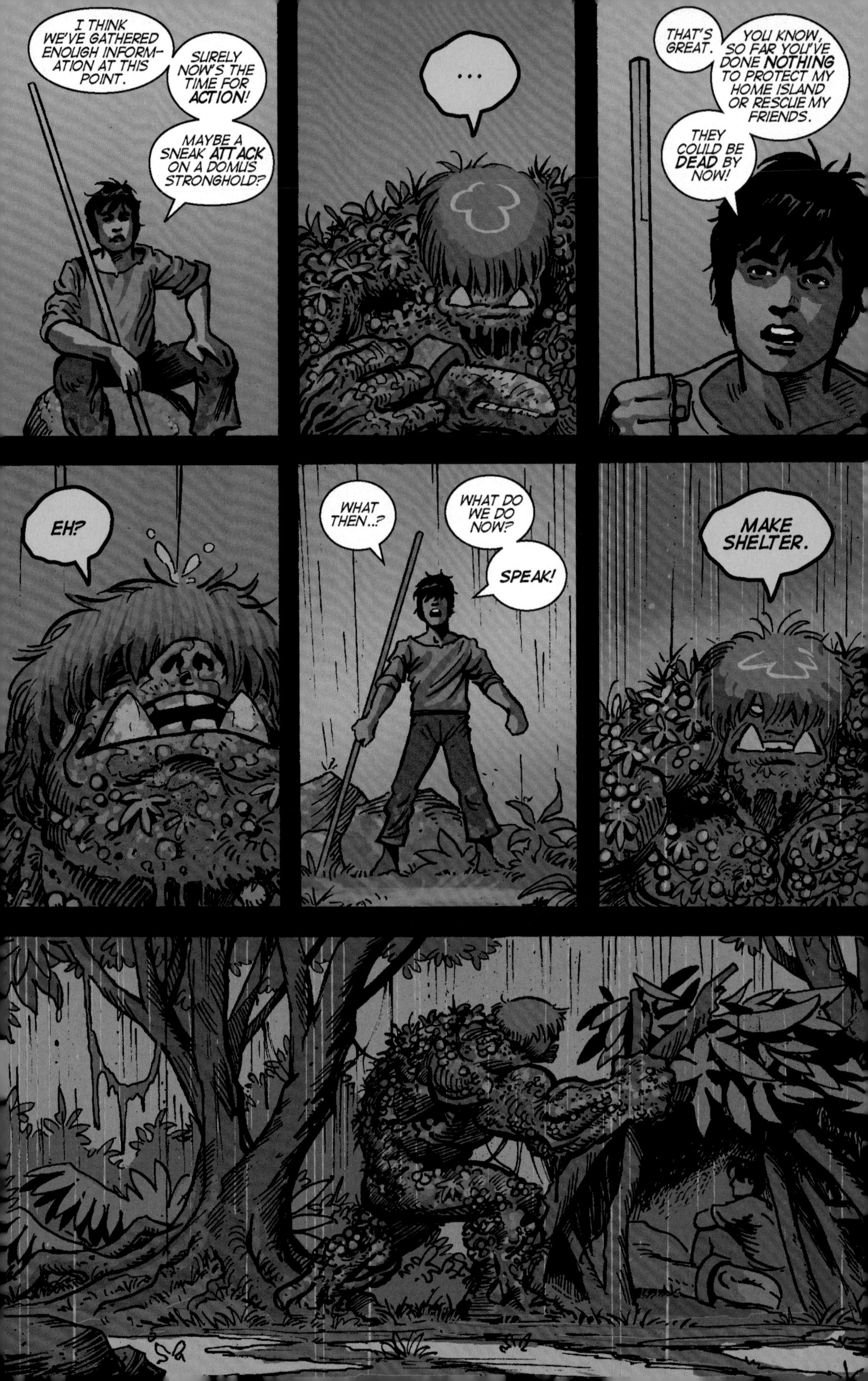
I THINK WE'VE GATHERED ENOUGH INFORMATION AT THIS POINT.
SURELY NOW'S THE TIME FOR ACTION!
MAYBE A SNEAK ATTACK ON A DOMUS STRONGHOLD?
...
THAT'S GREAT.
YOU KNOW, SO FAR YOU'VE DONE NOTHING TO PROTECT MY HOME ISLAND OR RESCUE MY FRIENDS.
THEY COULD BE DEAD BY NOW!
EH?
WHAT THEN..?
WHAT DO WE DO NOW?
SPEAK!
MAKE SHELTER.

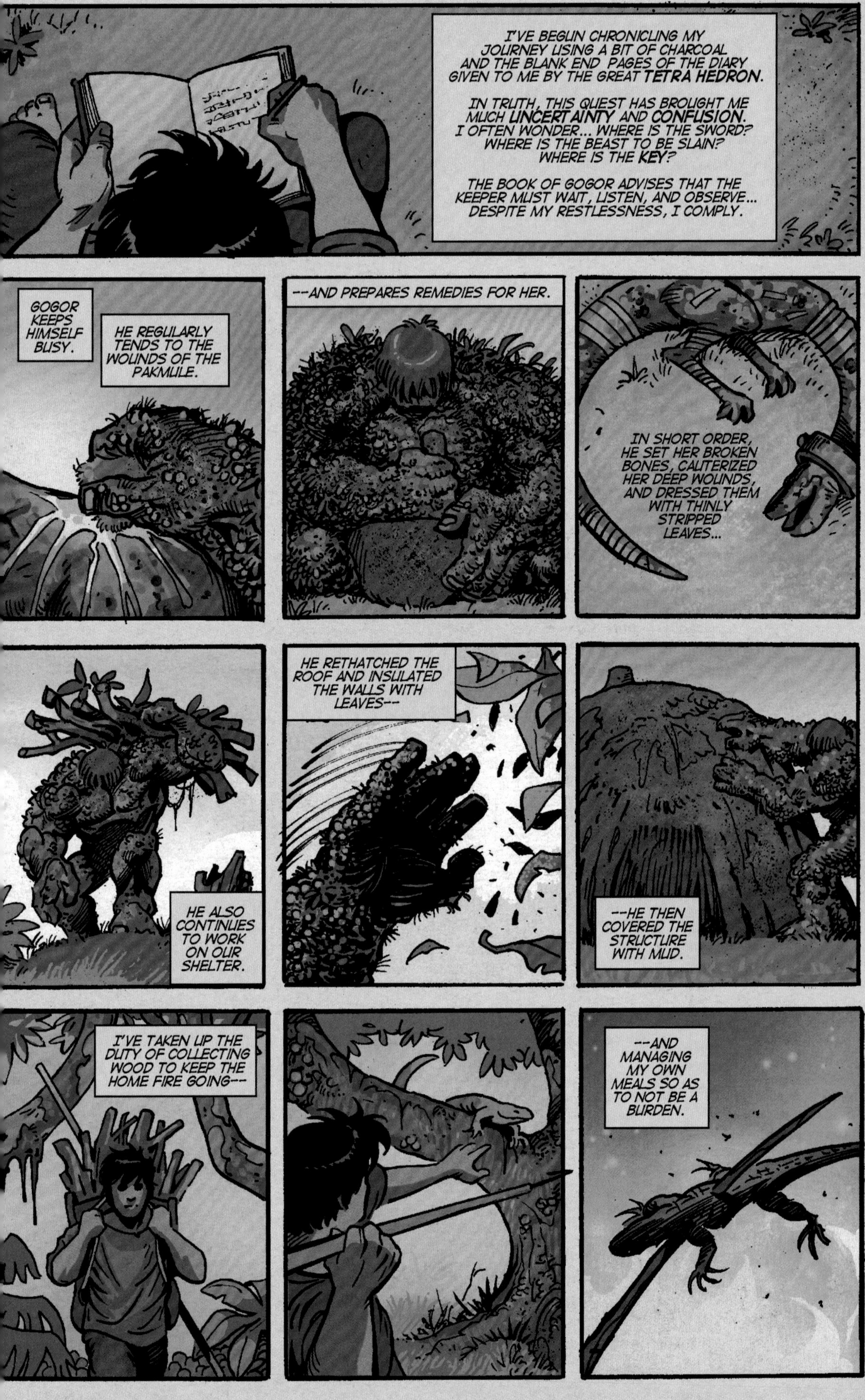
I'VE BEGUN CHRONICLING MY JOURNEY USING A BIT OF CHARCOAL AND THE BLANK END PAGES OF THE DIARY GIVEN TO ME BY THE GREAT TETRA HEDRON.
IN TRUTH, THIS QUEST HAS BROUGHT ME MUCH UNCERTAINTY AND CONFUSION. I OFTEN WONDER... WHERE IS THE SWORD? WHERE IS THE BEAST TO BE SLAIN? WHERE IS THE KEY?
THE BOOK OF GOGOR ADVISES THAT THE KEEPER MUST WAIT, LISTEN, AND OBSERVE... DESPITE MY RESTLESSNESS, I COMPLY.
GOGOR KEEPS HIMSELF BUSY.
HE REGULARLY TENDS TO THE WOUNDS OF THE PAKMULE.
--AND PREPARES REMEDIES FOR HER.
IN SHORT ORDER, HE SET HER BROKEN BONES, CAUTERIZED HER DEEP WOUNDS, AND DRESSED THEM WITH THINLY STRIPPED LEAVES...
HE ALSO CONTINUES TO WORK ON OUR SHELTER.
HE RETHATCHED THE ROOF AND INSULATED THE WALLS WITH LEAVES--
--HE THEN COVERED THE STRUCTURE WITH MUD.
I'VE TAKEN UP THE DUTY OF COLLECTING WOOD TO KEEP THE HOME FIRE GOING--
--AND MANAGING MY OWN MEALS SO AS TO NOT BE A BURDEN.

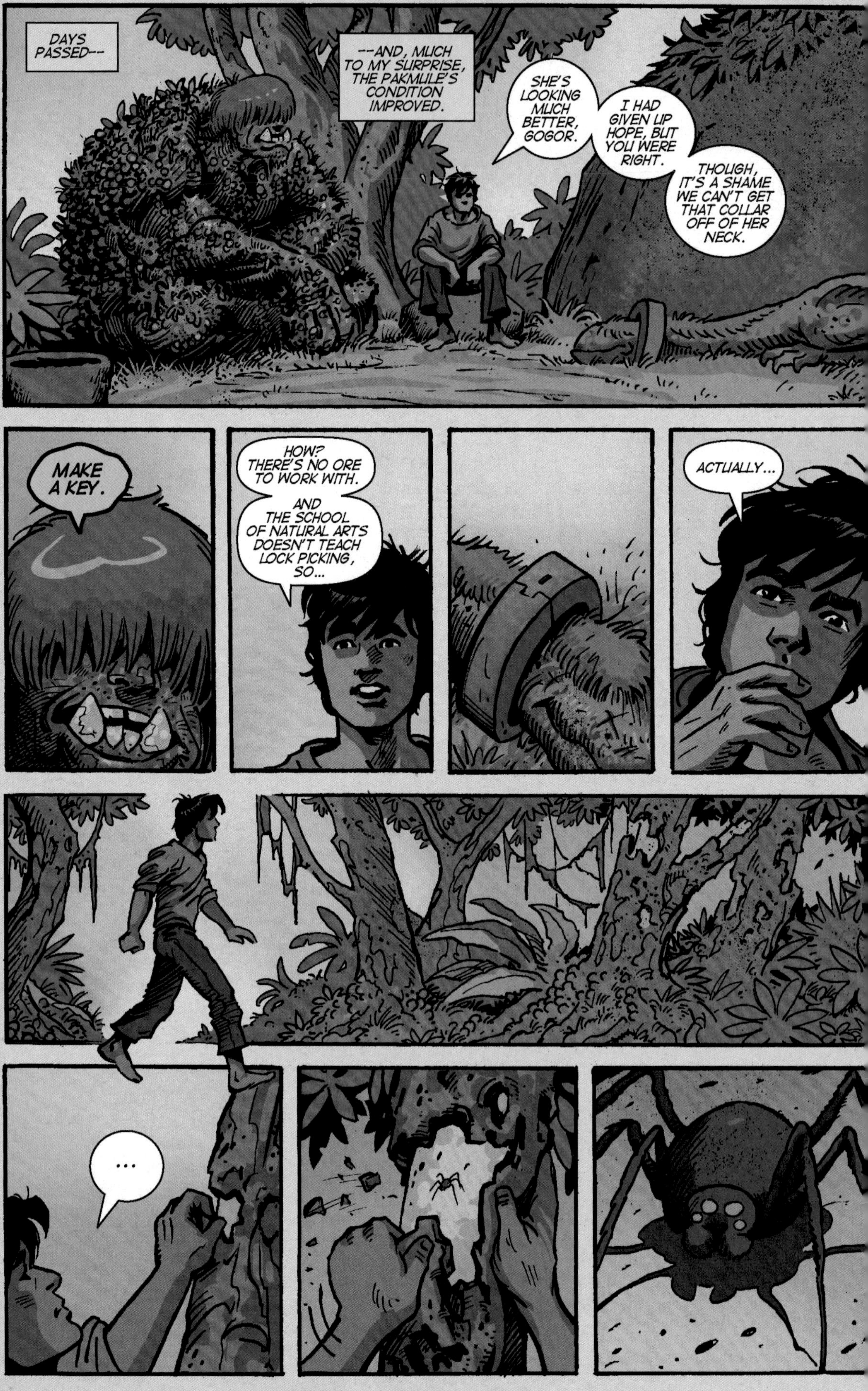
DAYS PASSED--
--AND, MUCH TO MY SURPRISE, THE PAKMULE'S CONDITION IMPROVED.
SHE'S LOOKING MUCH BETTER, GOGOR.
I HAD GIVEN UP HOPE, BUT YOU WERE RIGHT.
THOUGH, IT'S A SHAME WE CAN'T GET THAT COLLAR OFF OF HER NECK.
MAKE A KEY.
HOW? THERE'S NO ORE TO WORK WITH.
AND THE SCHOOL OF NATURAL ARTS DOESN'T TEACH LOCK PICKING, SO...
ACTUALLY...
...

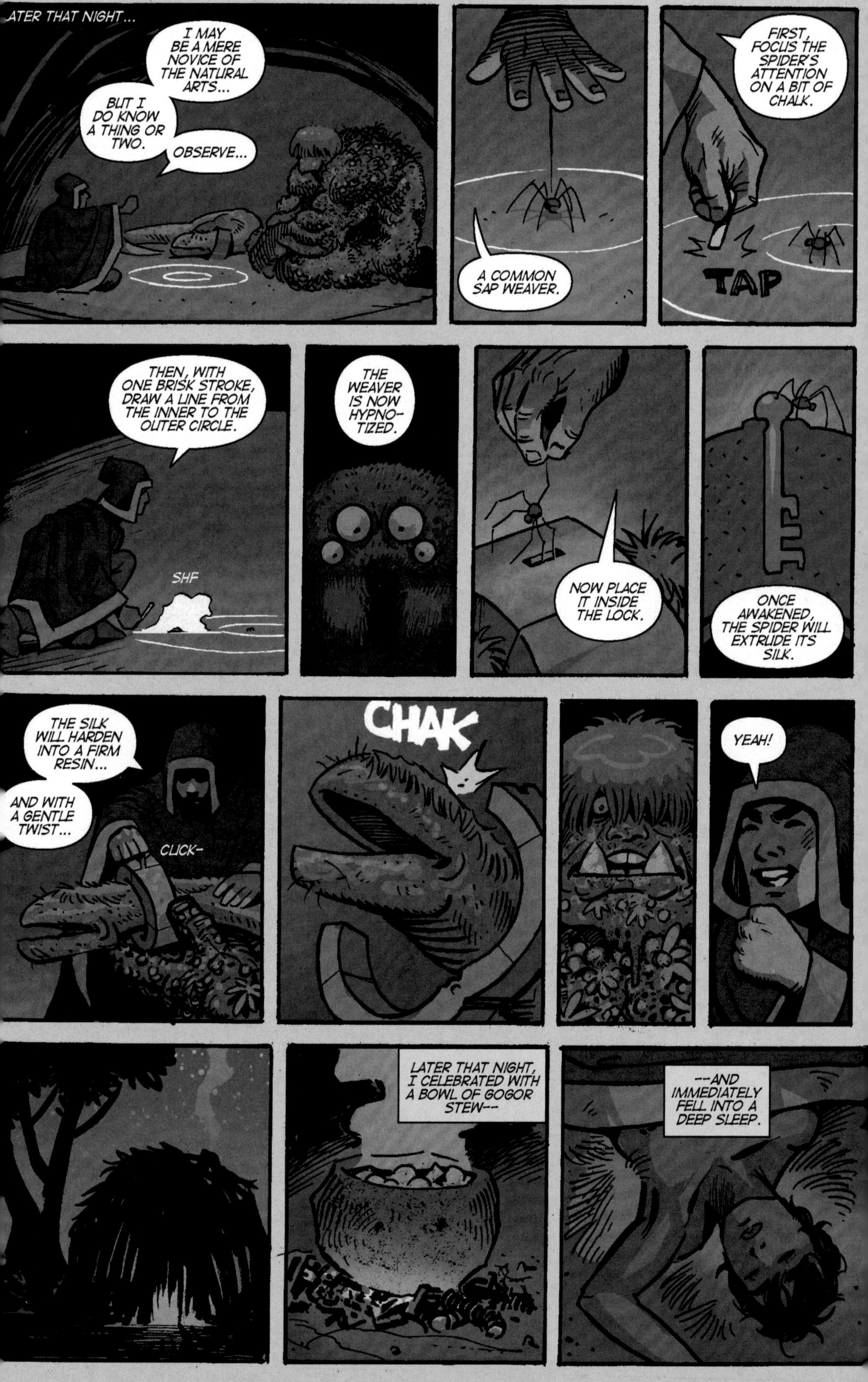
ATER THAT NIGHT...
I MAY BE A MERE NOVICE OF THE NATURAL ARTS...
BUT I DO KNOW A THING OR TWO.
OBSERVE...
A COMMON SAP WEAVER.
FIRST, FOCUS THE SPIDER'S ATTENTION ON A BIT OF CHALK.
TAP
THEN, WITH ONE BRISK STROKE, DRAW A LINE FROM THE INNER TO THE OUTER CIRCLE.
SHF
THE WEAVER IS NOW HYPNO-TIZED.
NOW PLACE IT INSIDE THE LOCK.
ONCE AWAKENED, THE SPIDER WILL EXTRUDE ITS SILK.
THE SILK WILL HARDEN INTO A FIRM RESIN...
AND WITH A GENTLE TWIST...
CLICK-
CHAK
YEAH!
LATER THAT NIGHT, I CELEBRATED WITH A BOWL OF GOGOR STEW--
--AND IMMEDIATELY FELL INTO A DEEP SLEEP.

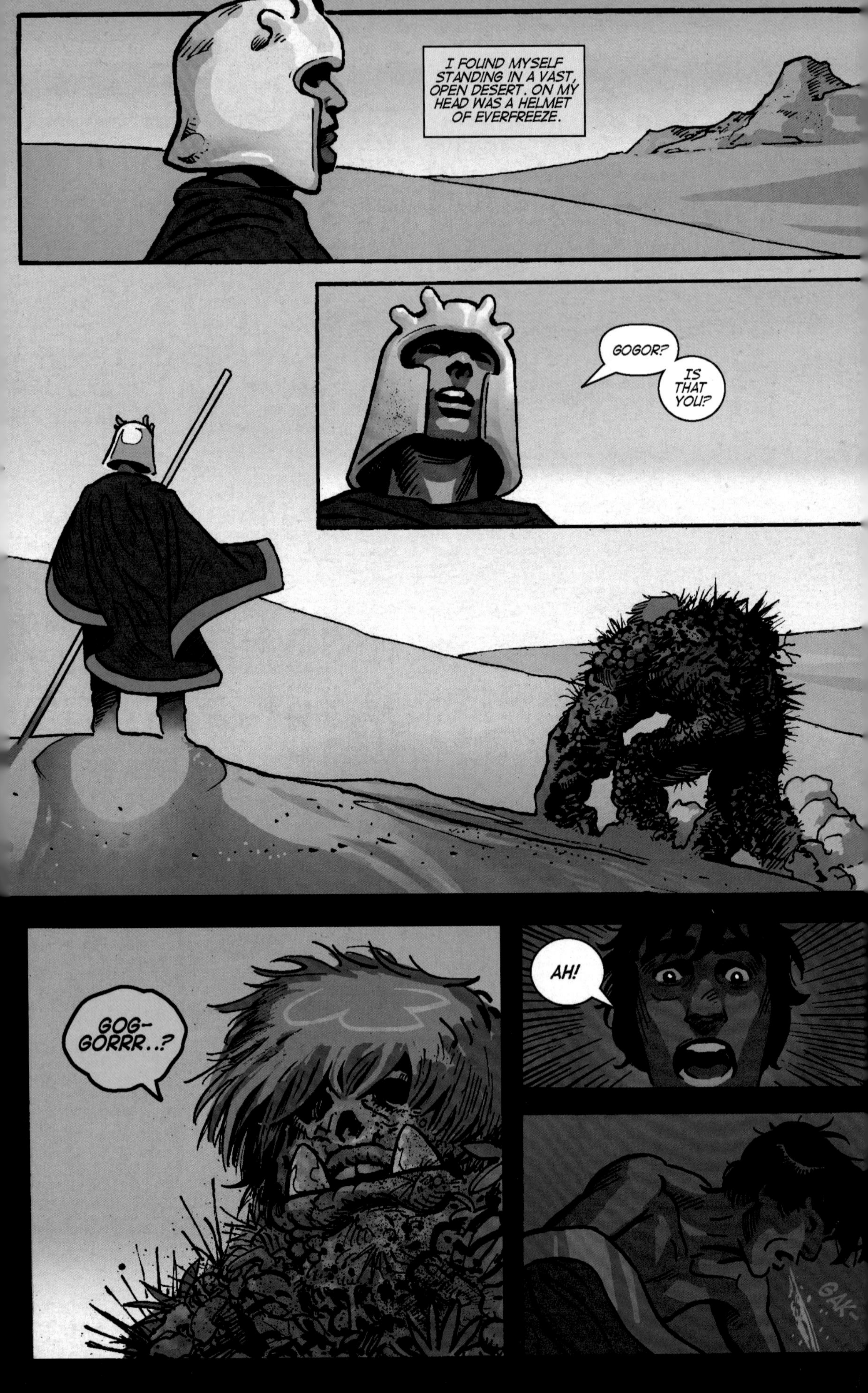

I FOUND MYSELF STANDING IN A VAST, OPEN DESERT. ON MY HEAD WAS A HELMET OF EVERFREEZE.
GOGOR?
IS THAT YOU?
GOG-GORRR..?
AH!
GAK-

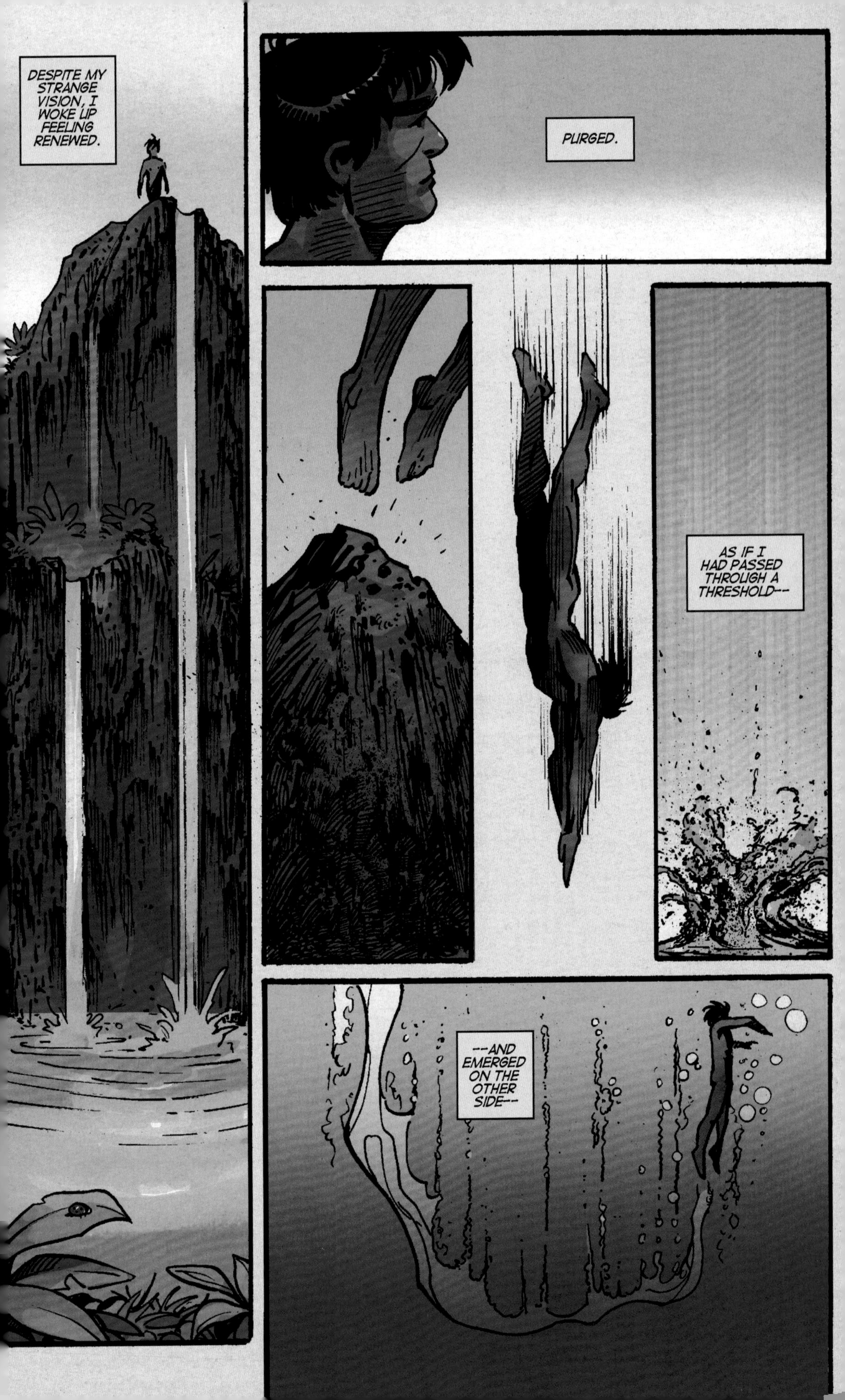
DESPITE MY STRANGE VISION, I WOKE UP FEELING RENEWED.
PURGED.
AS IF I HAD PASSED THROUGH A THRESHOLD--
--AND EMERGED ON THE OTHER SIDE--

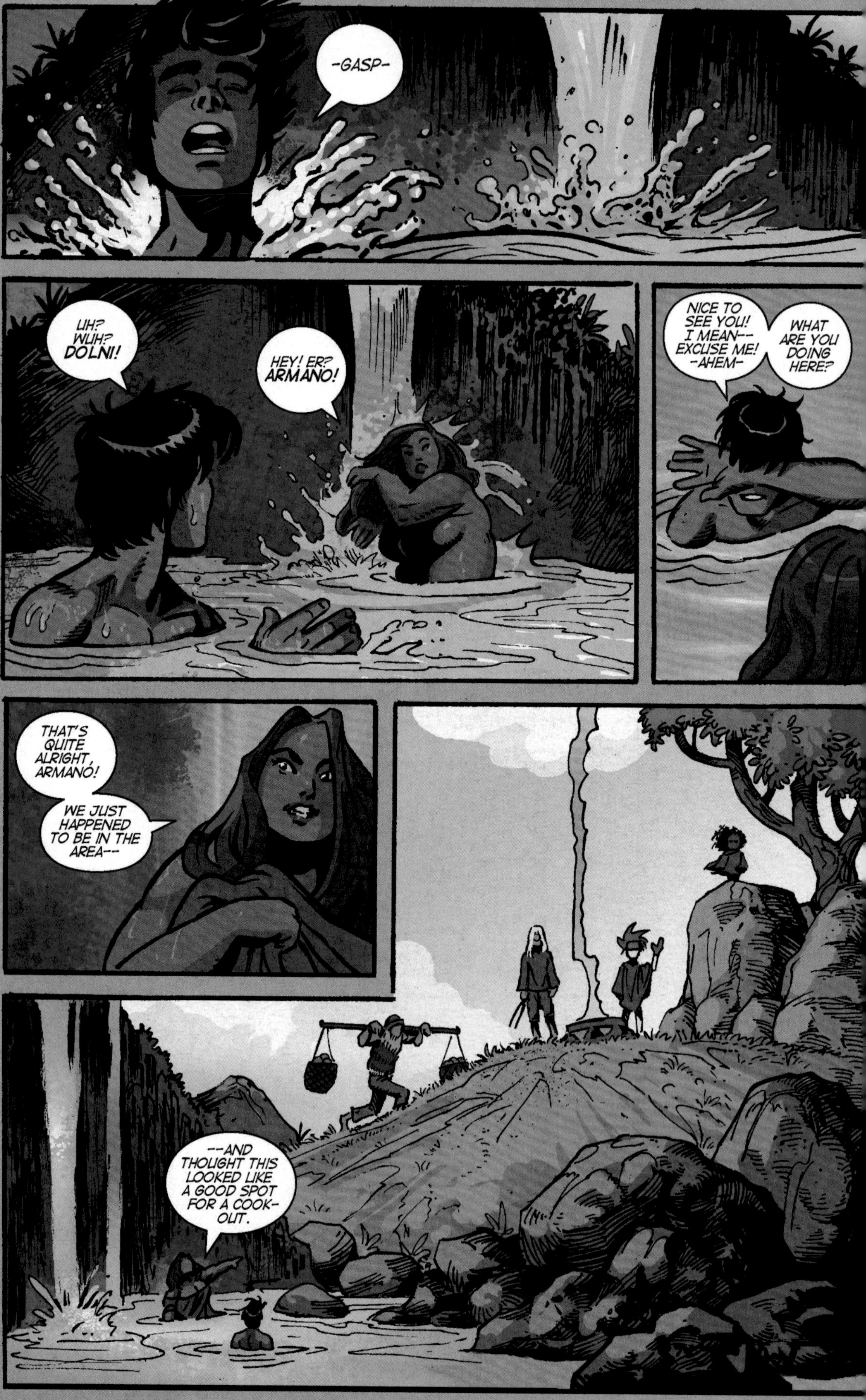
-GASP-
UH? WUH? DOLNI!
HEY! ER? ARMANO!
NICE TO SEE YOU! I MEAN-- EXCUSE ME! -AHEM-
WHAT ARE YOU DOING HERE?
THAT'S QUITE ALRIGHT, ARMANO!
WE JUST HAPPENED TO BE IN THE AREA--
--AND THOUGHT THIS LOOKED LIKE A GOOD SPOT FOR A COOK-OUT.

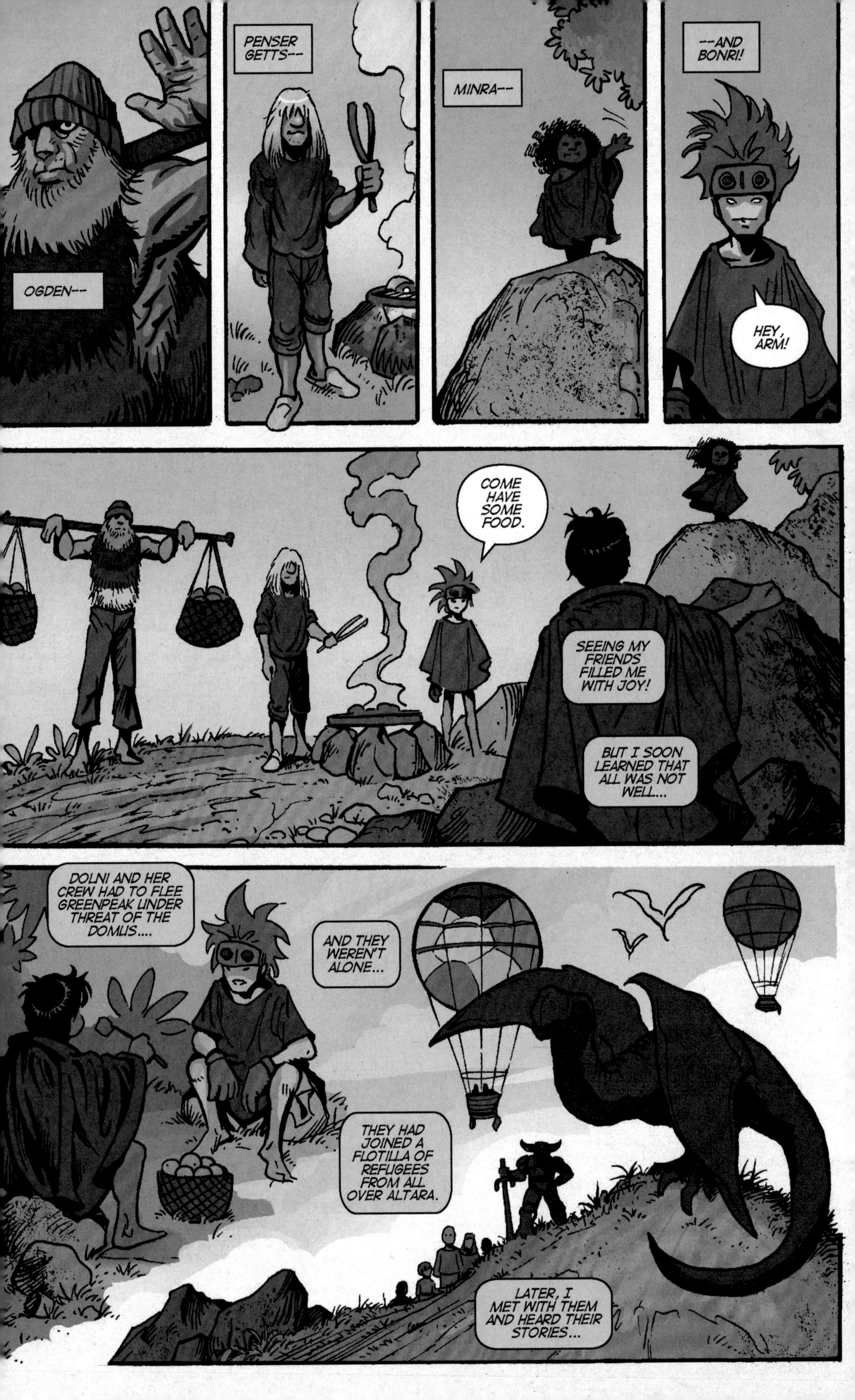
OGDEN--
PENSER GETTS--
MINRA--
--AND BONRI!
HEY, ARM!
COME HAVE SOME FOOD.
SEEING MY FRIENDS FILLED ME WITH JOY!
BUT I SOON LEARNED THAT ALL WAS NOT WELL...
DOLNI AND HER CREW HAD TO FLEE GREENPEAK UNDER THREAT OF THE DOMUS....
AND THEY WEREN'T ALONE...
THEY HAD JOINED A FLOTILLA OF REFUGEES FROM ALL OVER ALTARA.
LATER, I MET WITH THEM AND HEARD THEIR STORIES...

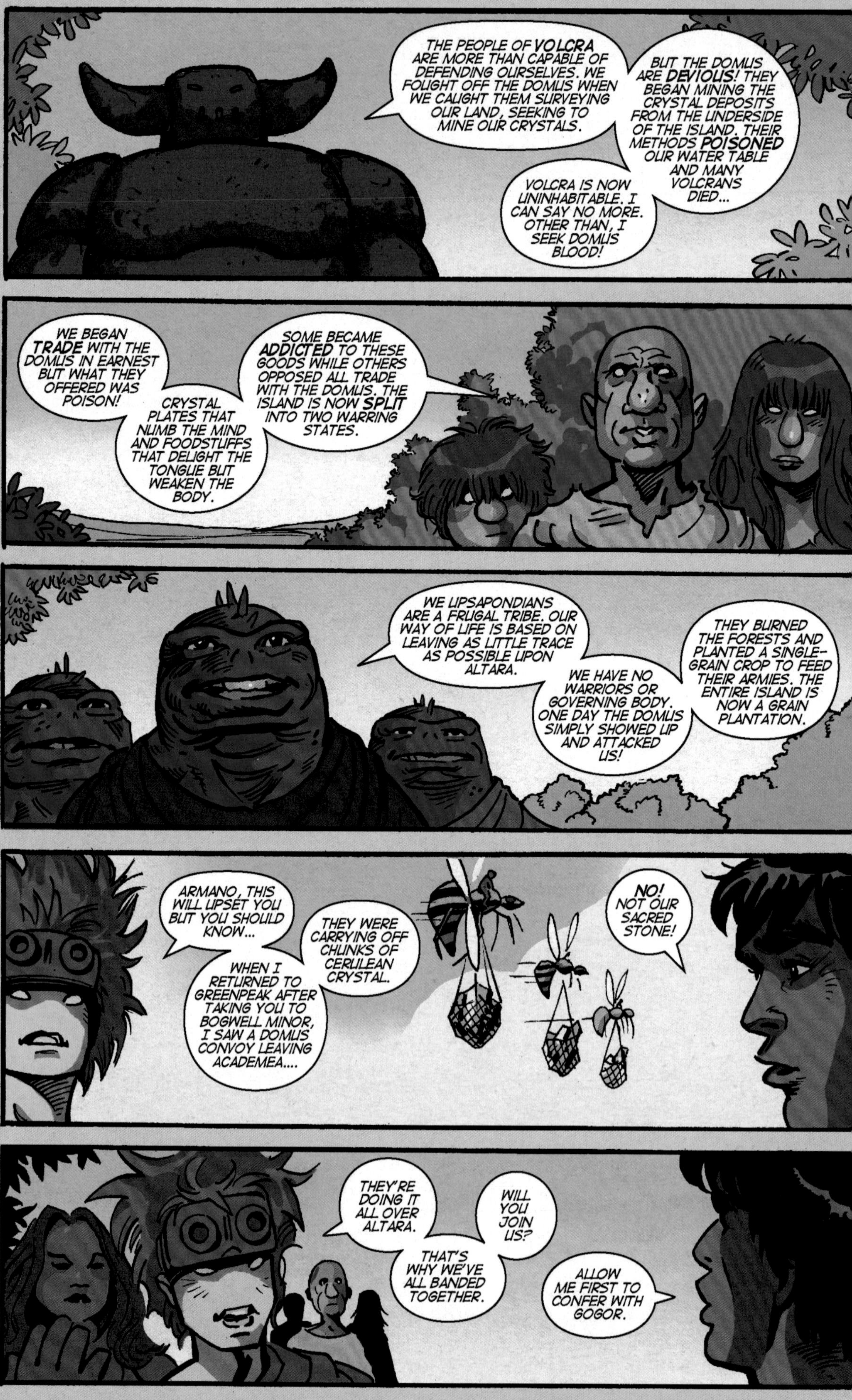
THE PEOPLE OF VOLCRA ARE MORE THAN CAPABLE OF DEFENDING OURSELVES. WE FOUGHT OFF THE DOMUS WHEN WE CAUGHT THEM SURVEYING OUR LAND, SEEKING TO MINE OUR CRYSTALS.
BUT THE DOMUS ARE DEVIOUS! THEY BEGAN MINING THE CRYSTAL DEPOSITS FROM THE UNDERSIDE OF THE ISLAND. THEIR METHODS POISONED OUR WATER TABLE AND MANY VOLCRANS DIED...
VOLCRA IS NOW UNINHABITABLE. I CAN SAY NO MORE. OTHER THAN, I SEEK DOMUS BLOOD!
WE BEGAN TRADE WITH THE DOMUS IN EARNEST BUT WHAT THEY OFFERED WAS POISON!
CRYSTAL PLATES THAT NUMB THE MIND AND FOODSTUFFS THAT DELIGHT THE TONGUE BUT WEAKEN THE BODY.
SOME BECAME ADDICTED TO THESE GOODS WHILE OTHERS OPPOSED ALL TRADE WITH THE DOMUS. THE ISLAND IS NOW SPLIT INTO TWO WARRING STATES.
WE UPSAPONDIANS ARE A FRUGAL TRIBE. OUR WAY OF LIFE IS BASED ON LEAVING AS LITTLE TRACE AS POSSIBLE UPON ALTARA.
WE HAVE NO WARRIORS OR GOVERNING BODY. ONE DAY THE DOMUS SIMPLY SHOWED UP AND ATTACKED US!
THEY BURNED THE FORESTS AND PLANTED A SINGLE-GRAIN CROP TO FEED THEIR ARMIES. THE ENTIRE ISLAND IS NOW A GRAIN PLANTATION.
ARMANO, THIS WILL UPSET YOU BUT YOU SHOULD KNOW...
WHEN I RETURNED TO GREENPEAK AFTER TAKING YOU TO BOGWELL MINOR, I SAW A DOMUS CONVOY LEAVING ACADEMEA....
THEY WERE CARRYING OFF CHUNKS OF CERULEAN CRYSTAL.
NO! NOT OUR SACRED STONE!
THEY'RE DOING IT ALL OVER ALTARA.
THAT'S WHY WE'VE ALL BANDED TOGETHER.
WILL YOU JOIN US?
ALLOW ME FIRST TO CONFER WITH GOGOR.

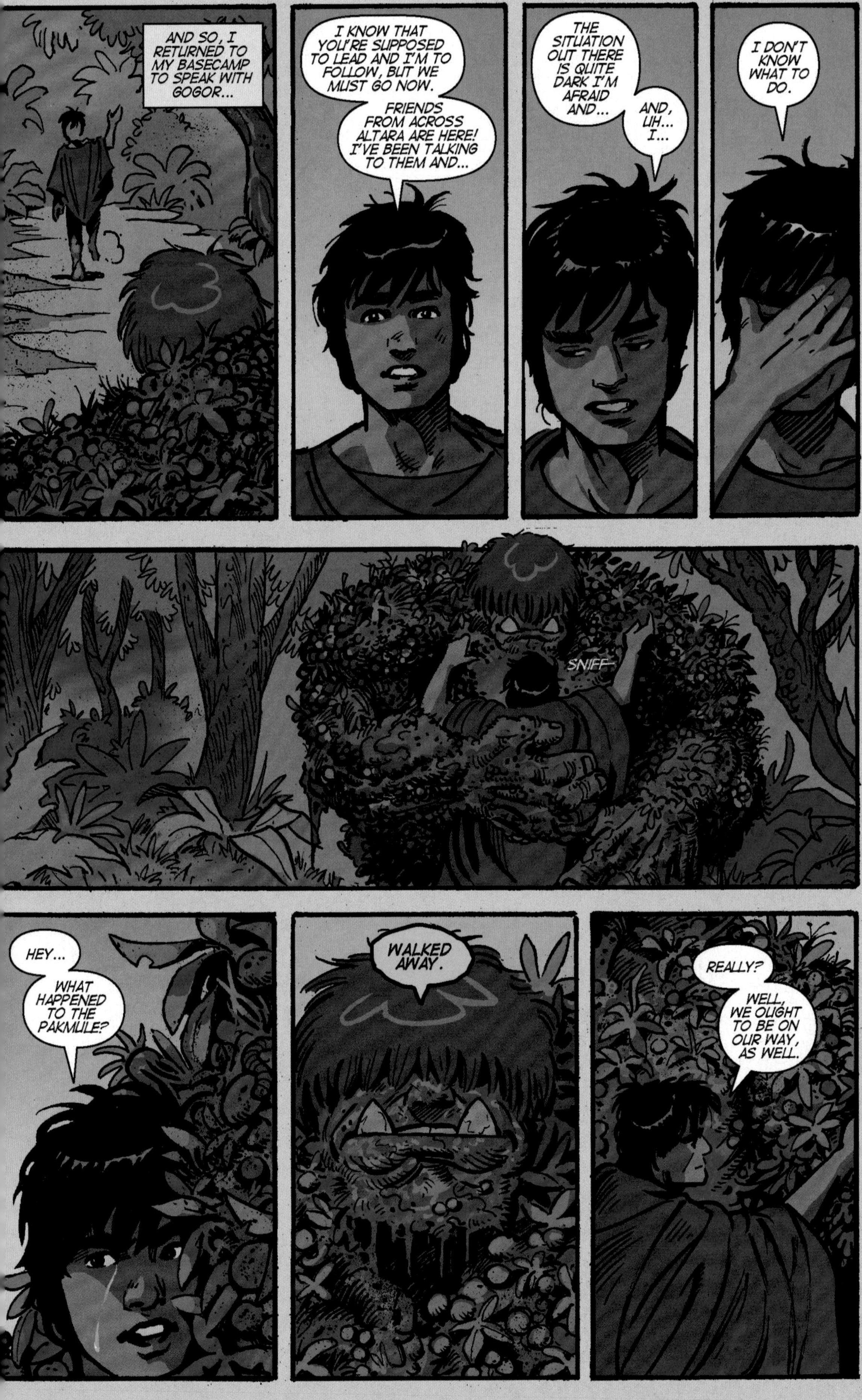
AND SO, I RETURNED TO MY BASECAMP TO SPEAK WITH GOGOR...
I KNOW THAT YOU'RE SUPPOSED TO LEAD AND I'M TO FOLLOW, BUT WE MUST GO NOW.
FRIENDS FROM ACROSS ALTARA ARE HERE! I'VE BEEN TALKING TO THEM AND...
THE SITUATION OUT THERE IS QUITE DARK I'M AFRAID AND...
AND, UH... I...
I DON'T KNOW WHAT TO DO.
SNIFF
HEY...
WHAT HAPPENED TO THE PAKMULE?
WALKED AWAY.
REALLY?
WELL, WE OUGHT TO BE ON OUR WAY, AS WELL.

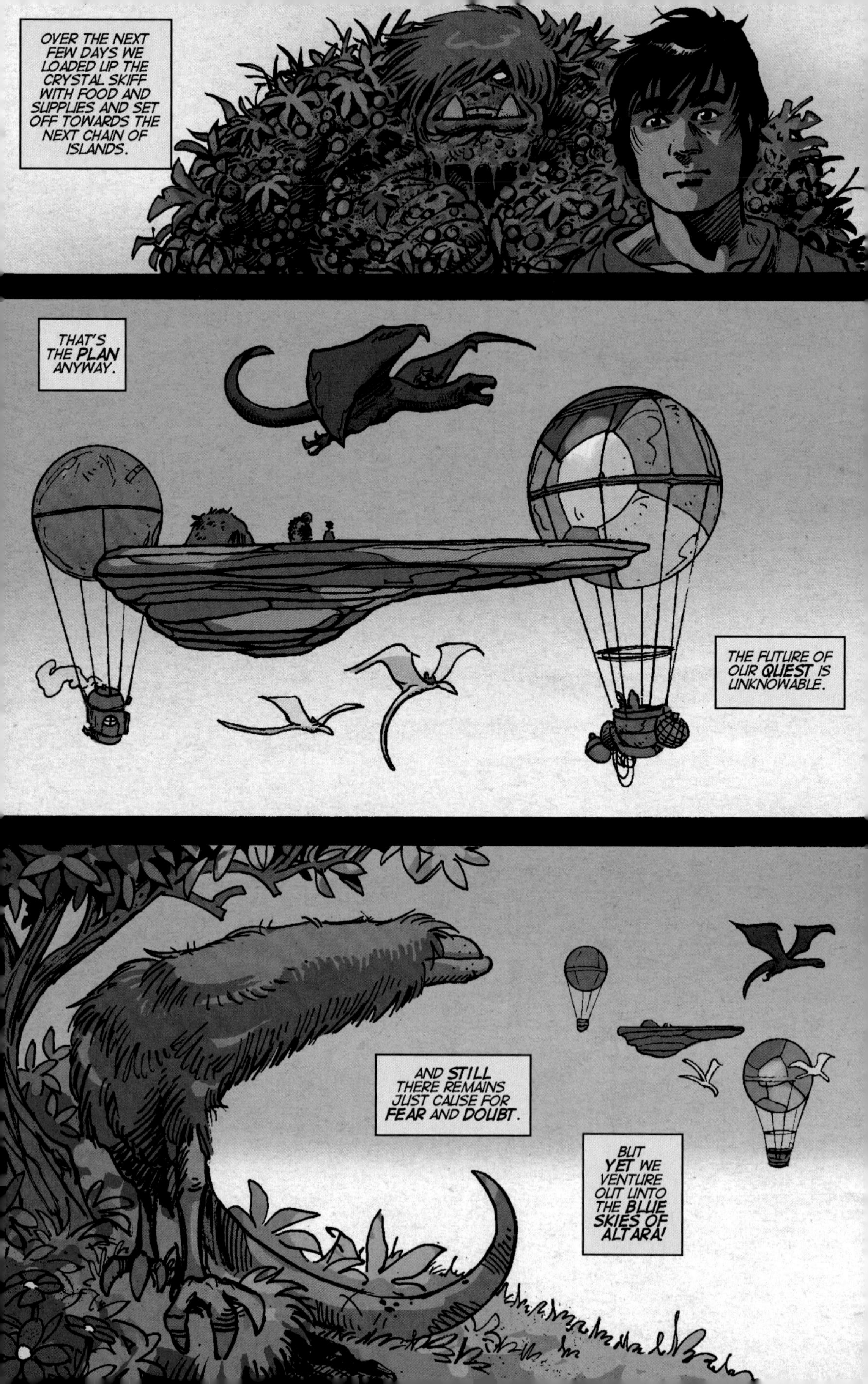
OVER THE NEXT FEW DAYS WE LOADED UP THE CRYSTAL SKIFF WITH FOOD AND SUPPLIES AND SET OFF TOWARDS THE NEXT CHAIN OF ISLANDS.
THAT'S THE PLAN ANYWAY.
THE FUTURE OF OUR QUEST IS UNKNOWABLE.
AND STILL THERE REMAINS JUST CAUSE FOR FEAR AND DOUBT.
BUT YET WE VENTURE OUT UNTO THE BLUE SKIES OF ALTARA!

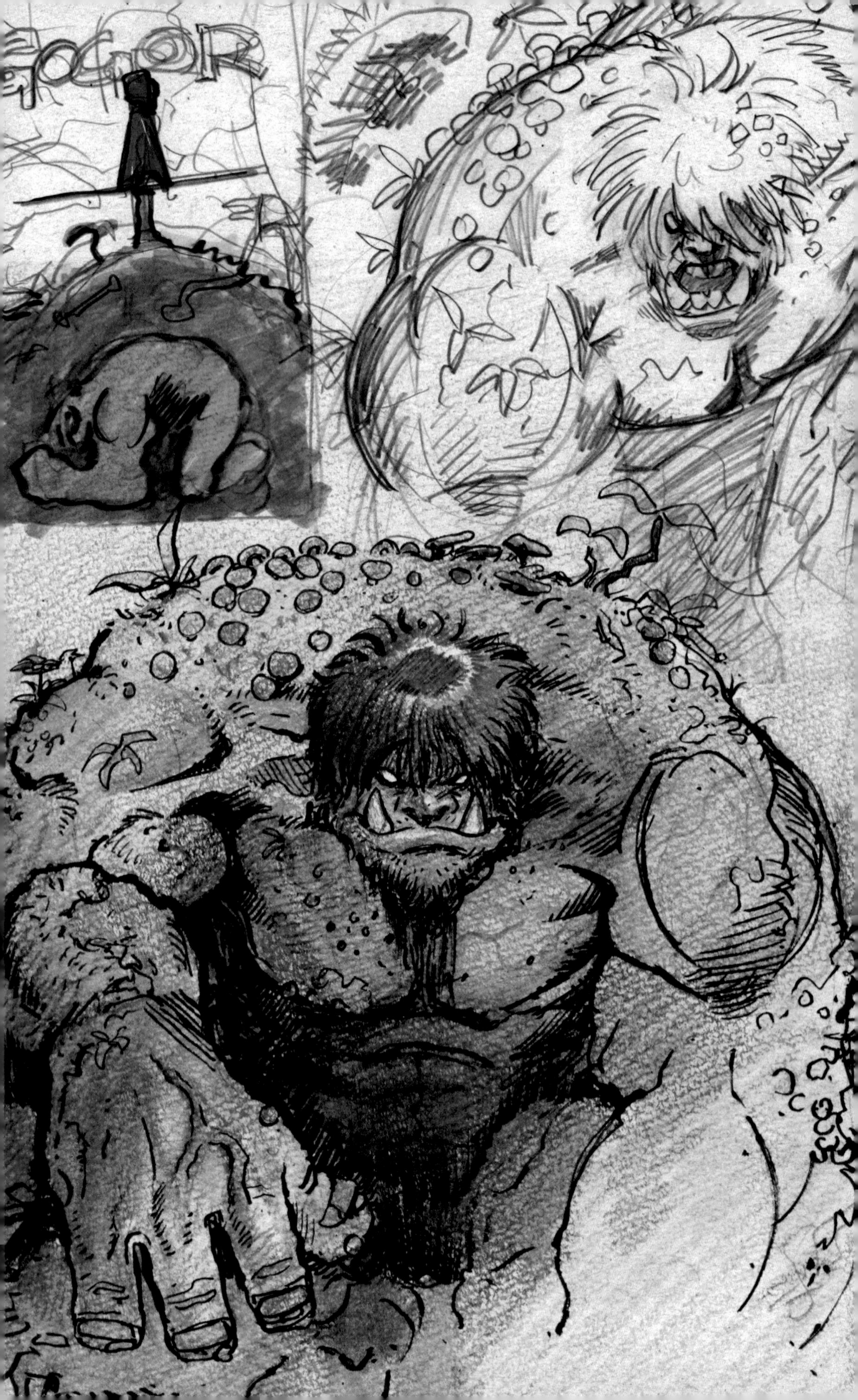

GOGOR

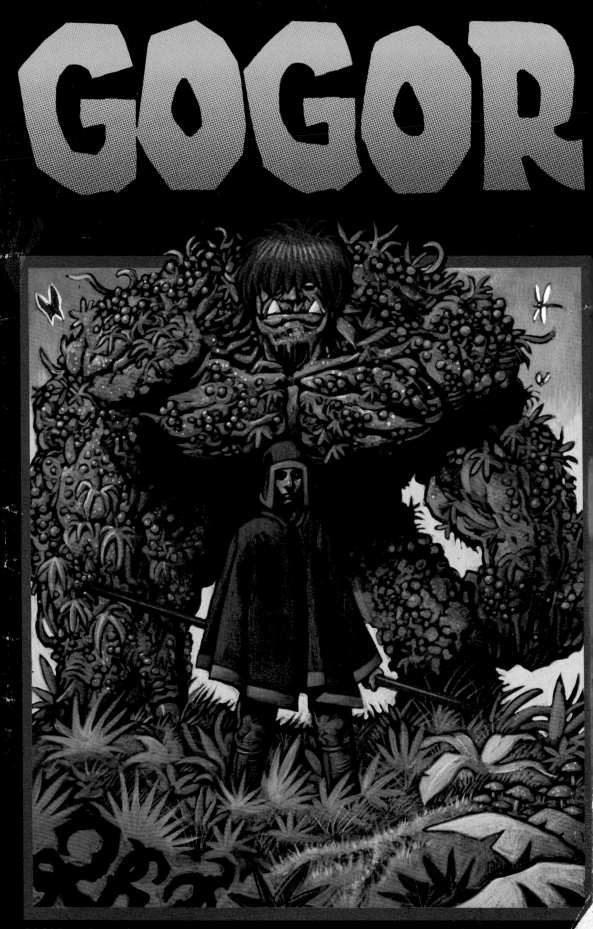

GOGOR #1 Variant Cover by Ken Garing